HOUSEWITCH

HOUSEWITCH

Katie Schickel

A TOM DOHERTY ASSOCIATES BOOK
NEW YORK

HOUSEWITCH

Copyright © 2015 by Katie Schickel

A Forge Book
Published by Tom Doherty Associates, LLC
175 Fifth Avenue
New York, NY 10010

www.tor-forge.com

Forge® is a registered trademark of Tom Doherty Associates, LLC.

The Library of Congress Cataloging-in-Publication Data is available upon request.

ISBN 978-0-7653-7730-2 (hardcover)
ISBN 978-0-7653-7731-9 (trade paperback)
ISBN 978-1-4668-5487-1 (e-book)

Forge books may be purchased for educational, business, or promotional use. For information on bulk purchases, please contact the Macmillan Corporate and Premium Sales Department at 1-800-221-7945, extension 5442, or write to specialmarkets@macmillan.com.

First Edition: February 2015

Printed in the United States of America

0 9 8 7 6 5 4 3 2 1

For Michael

ACKNOWLEDGMENTS

Two women have my deepest gratitude for making *Housewitch* a reality. My editor, Kristin Sevick, for her razor-sharp insights, and my agent, Marlene Stringer, tireless advocate and all-around goddess.

Friend and fellow author Meg Mitchell Moore was overwhelmingly generous with her time and expertise. Liz Peirce helped keep me on deadline in the early phase of writing this book when deadlines were self-imposed and easy to break. Michael Marano was an extraordinary teacher of fiction writing. Dr. Keith Ablow gave his advice and encouragement in the critical, early stage of my career. I'm blessed with the relentless support of my family—my parents, Jerry and Irene Schickel, and my brother and sister, Bob Schickel and Lise Goddard—who have believed in me from the beginning.

To my friends who have rooted for me along the way, I am sincerely thankful for your kind words and positive vibes. Inspiration came to me in the pages of a faded copy of *The Annotated Mother Goose* by William S. Baring-Gould and Ceil Baring-Gould, which I stumbled upon while wandering a thrift shop in Salem, Massachusetts, on a hunt for witchy things. I'm also grateful to the Newburyport Public Library, for providing a clean, well-lighted place.

From the bottom of my heart, I want to thank my kids, Finn and Bridget, whose enthusiasm keeps me going every day. Above all, to Michael Underwood, my first reader, my biggest champion, my husband, your grace and support have made this all possible.

HOUSEWITCH

CHAPTER 1

For every evil under the sun
There is a remedy or there is none.
If there be one, seek till you find it;
If there be none, never mind it.
—MOTHER GOOSE

Misery Shoal, Massachusetts · 1945

W here's Papa?" Aurora asked as the sisters made their way
across the mudflats and into the marsh.

"Papa's gone," Freya said, swatting at cattails, scattering their
velvety seeds into the air.

A dense fog had rolled in from the sea. It shrouded Misery
Shoal in a coat of gray, and brought with it the smell of winter.

"Where's he gone to?" Aurora asked.

"Never mind. He's just gone." Freya's red hair shined like a
flame against the brittle landscape. She was the middle child,
and the most beautiful of the sisters.

Somewhere a ship's horn belched through the stillness, and
this made the girls alert, for they were unaccustomed to the
sounds of Commoners at the shoal.

The oldest sister, Wilhemena, lifted the cauldron with both
hands, tucking her elbows into her sides for leverage. It reminded Freya of the way she'd seen her father lift the cod and
haddock to measure at the Derby Street Pier. Those fish could
weigh up to fifty pounds and stand as tall as Freya herself. Even
a strong man like her father had a hard time raising the hand
scale high enough to clear the tails off the ground. His biceps,
the tendons in his forearms, straining under the weight, his

face pinched in anticipation while the fishmonger read the scale.

"When's he coming back?" Aurora asked.

"He ain't," Freya said.

"Never?"

"Never."

"Hush now. That's just more of your nonsense," Wilhemena said.

Aurora frowned. Although Papa was often at sea, she couldn't imagine never seeing him *ever* again. She turned to Wilhemena's wisdom on the matter. "Is it true? Is Papa never comin' home?"

"Of course it isn't true," Wilhemena said. She braced the cauldron against her stomach to keep the water from spilling out. "Let's hurry on home. Before the tide turns."

Misery Shoal was a spit of land shaped like a crow's claw, formed by centuries of longshore waves dragging sand and sediment southward. At high tide the neck of the shoal slunk underwater, making it impassable. Nautical maps warned sailors of its shifting nature with a black "XXX." Only the Ellyly-dan family called it home.

Freya and Aurora skipped after Wilhemena, stopping now and then to inspect a mud crab or pry open a clam in search of pearls. Aurora had heard stories of the pearl divers in Japan and found exquisite possibilities in an unopened mollusk.

"Freya, hurry up," Wilhemena called. "Come along now, Aurora."

Freya ignored her. She had captured a pickerel frog and was teasing it with a thatch of goldenrod. She shoved the frog into the pocket of her apron and squeezed, the poor creature clambering up the thin cotton, only to be squashed by Freya's fingers each time.

Up ahead, Wilhemena slowed her pace and clucked her tongue. There was work to be done. And even though her sisters were younger and more easily distracted by childish things, she expected them to at least *try* and work as hard as she.

Wilhemena yelled to Freya, who was crouching by a rock, "Watch the baby for me. I'm going up ahead."

"She ain't a baby anymore," Freya said. "Why are you always treating her like a little baby?"

"Mind your tongue," Wilhemena snapped. "Just watch after her."

Freya rolled her eyes and went back to torturing her frog.

As Wilhemena disappeared through the reeds, Aurora, who at four really wasn't a baby anymore and felt no more like a baby than her sisters, tromped barefoot into the spongy grass to get a better look at a water beetle.

"There's snakes in there," Freya called out. "Look. There's some moving the grass."

Aurora feared nothing of earthly creatures. Hexes, yes. Enchantments, definitely. For those were real. Snakes were far too interesting to be feared. She watched the reeds part and snap back to their vertical postures. "Just a muskrat," Aurora said, to which Freya replied, "It'll eat you up with its big fangs."

Aurora stopped to consider that scenario. She wasn't sure if Freya, being a whole year older and wiser to the world, might know something about muskrats that she had yet to discover. As far as she had seen, muskrats ate marsh plants and mussels and left little girls alone.

"You sure?" Aurora asked.

"Oh yes," Freya answered. "They start with your nose and work down. A girl was eaten by a muskrat just last week. All's they found left was her skull."

Aurora decided to resolve the matter with Wilhemena, who at eight, was even wiser to the world than Freya. She started walking, but as the thought of the little-girl-eating muskrat took shape in her mind, she quickened her pace until she was running as fast as she could through the marsh. By the time she made it to the creek, her doom seemed inevitable and she didn't notice the thistle patch until she ran right through it, taking a whipping against bare legs. She cried out.

Wilhemena ran to her, scooping Aurora into her arms. "It's okay, little one. I'll fix you up." Wilhemena pulled the burrs out of Aurora's skin. She found some bright green ribwort and chewed it into a pulp, then applied the salve onto Aurora's leg. Later that night she would make a poultice of soaked burdock leaves to draw out any infection.

When Freya caught up to them, she crossed her arms, a smile on her lips.

"Can a muskrat eat me up?" Aurora asked.

"Nonsense," Wilhemena said. There was no doubt about who would put such a thought in a little girl's head. "Freya, don't be so hateful."

When Wilhemena turned around to lift the cauldron, Freya took the opportunity to pinch Aurora on the arm. Aurora screeched, thinking at first that the muskrat had bitten her, but it was only Freya. Crying, she knew, would invite more punishment.

Rather, she pulled out the heavy artillery. "I'll tell Papa on you."

"Papa will wring your neck if he hears that you're scaring your little sister," Wilhemena said.

"You needn't worry about Papa," Freya replied, a look of contempt crossing her face.

Wilhemena opened her mouth to argue but there was work to be done. "Follow me," she said and led her sisters along the creek bed to the beach where they could find firewood.

The three girls gathered driftwood, fragments of lobster traps, boards from battered ships. Tucked behind a washed-up slab of concrete they spotted a patch of wild raspberries still clinging to thorny branches, miraculously undetected by birds. They dropped their wood and feasted on the last of the season's berries. When they had picked the bush bare, Wilhemena broke off a few branches and bundled them up with the wood. Red raspberry was known to aid in digestion and to keep malevolent spirits at bay.

The whole excursion had taken close to an hour and in the fog and ebbing light, the line between sky and sea had all but disappeared.

When the girls returned to the ridge, their mother, Elizabeth, was preparing the lye. It was the waxing crescent of the hunter's moon—the time to make soap. Carefully, she poured water into an ash hopper. A thin, brown trail dripped out of the bottom of the hopper and into a bucket. This was the potash lye for the soap. You could buy lye at the general store in town, you could even buy soap, but Elizabeth said the devil made work for idle hands. She made her own lye from the ashes collected in their fires. "Just like in the Old Ways," she'd say.

The wind shifted and sent smoke in Freya's direction. She fanned it away. Freya understood the Old Ways as something tangible, not just a time and place, but a way of being that involved herbs and stories and the potions that bound the two together.

The Old Ways meant toil.

Making their own candles and spinning their own wool were part of the Old Ways. Seasons revolved around such tasks: spring for planting, summer for picking and pickling, and then there was the fall.

Fall was for slaughtering.

Fattened pigs were slaughtered, their meat cured, their fat rendered: lard from the pigs, tallow from the cattle. The purified fat was stored in barrels for cooking throughout the year, and for making soap.

Elizabeth finished the lye, and sat her girls down, youngest to oldest, on a semicircle of tree stumps. She stoked the fire with driftwood and shagbark, watching the flames rise higher and higher, changing the substance of the wood from earth to fire. Element to element.

Damp and sticky with marsh water, the girls held their hands up to the fire to warm.

Freya opened the pocket of her apron and peeked at the frog that now sat limp and lifeless.

"You've worked hard today," Elizabeth said. "We shan't go cold this winter." She opened a picnic basket she had brought from the house and laid out a dinner of rolls and jars of home-made jams and butter.

The girls ate while Elizabeth set up the tools for making soap. She hung the cauldron from a metal tripod over the flames and organized the supplies—salt, lavender, and the fat for rendering. Then she began the day's Lesson.

"Who can tell me: What's the fattest part of an animal? The belly? The buttocks? The haunches?"

Freya thought back to her father lifting the cods on the hand scales at the Derby Street Pier. She thought of the massive biceps and the sun on his skin, the sweat running down to his shirt, leaving wet marks under his armpits. "The arms," she said, certain of her answer.

Elizabeth smiled.

Wilhemena ventured a guess. "The thighs?"

"Tummy?" asked Aurora.

"Very good, my little witches," Elizabeth said. "Those are all correct. We use all the parts. Waste not, want not, my dear little witches. Waste not, want not."

Elizabeth unwrapped the fat from butcher paper smeared with grease and blood. With Papa's fillet knife, she sliced the substance into chunks and dropped a piece into the cauldron.

She handed a chunk of the substance to Freya, but Freya refused it.

"Do what must be done, Freya," Elizabeth said.

"My turn, my turn," Aurora said, grabbing for the gristle.

"No," Elizabeth said, pulling it away. "This is Freya's job."

"Why don't I ever get to do nothing?" Aurora whined.

"Because you are the youngest. And the most special,"

Elizabeth said. This didn't bother Wilhemena. She was old enough to know that little white lies were a mother's way.

Elizabeth turned her attention back to Freya, her expression shifting as severely as the north wind. "You must make the best of what you've done. The job must be finished."

Freya sneered. She crossed her arms. Then, slowly, she reached for the substance and dropped it in the cauldron. It entered the water with a plop and splattered bits of meat and oil onto Freya's apron. She brushed at her apron, her face contorted in disgust.

"All of it," Elizabeth said sternly.

Freya added the rest of the substance to the water, lump by lump.

As the water boiled, the fat melted and an oily sheen formed on the surface. Rendering was a slow process. It required heat and patience and know-how.

Eventually, Aurora grew tired. Rubbing her eyes, she crawled onto Wilhemena's lap and fell asleep.

A bitter cold settled in as the night wore on, so Wilhemena walked Aurora back down the ridge to the house and through the kitchen where bundles of drying herbs hung from the ceiling. In the pantry, jars of tonics and extractions lined the shelves: pokeweed in wine, borage in honey, great fluffy leaves of mullein in alcohol.

She tucked Aurora into her warm feather bed and went back to the kitchen to fetch a bundle of dried rosemary. Rosemary was known to the Ellylydan women to soothe the mind and stir the memory. Wilhemena swished the rosemary over her sleeping sister and sang,

"Good night,
 Sleep tight,
 Wake up bright
 In the morning light,
 To do what's right
 With all your might."

With her little sister sound asleep, Wilhemena left the house and walked back up the doe path in darkness toward the ridge. Melting fat overtook all the other smells of the shoal, the wet clay, the salt air, the coming winter.

All at once, Wilhemena stopped. She sensed something. Fear? Danger? She wasn't sure. She could feel it prickling her skin the way you feel yourself falling in a dream without being able to stop. Up ahead, Freya and Elizabeth peered into the cauldron, their faces lit up by the flames. They were whispering.

It was the clandestine way in which her mother and sister now spoke that frightened Wilhemena. As far as she knew, there were no secrets in her family. They all learned the same Lessons; they all worked together and played together, ate the same meals, practiced the same spells. She tiptoed closer to the fire until she was in hearing distance.

"All the impurities sink to the bottom. All the evil is washed away," Elizabeth said. "And we'll take that impure water and throw it back into the swamp, to settle with the cress and hawthorns. It will sink into the sludge where the gadflies lay their eggs. All we're left with is the purity. Tomorrow we'll mix in the lye and make our soap. To wash away your sins. To make you magic again. To make you whole."

"Will the soap make me pure, Mama?" Freya asked.

"The soap will hide what you don't want others to see. The soap will cast glamour over the eye. Do you know what glamour is, Freya?"

"No."

"Glamour is an enchantment. It's a way of making people see things that aren't so."

"Like a lie?"

"Not exactly a lie."

"A tall tale, then?"

"More like a deception. It's something that isn't all the way true, and it isn't all the way untrue. Just as the times in between times are neither past nor future. The *not times,* we call them. The *in-between time*. Dusk, dawn, midnight, new moon, full moon. These are the not times when doors to the other worlds are open, and when the magic is most potent. These are the times when you must become whole."

"Aren't I whole all the time, Mama?"

"We are all made up of darkness and light. Your darkness is more powerful. You are out of balance. You must transform from the dark to the light. Do you understand?"

Freya wiggled her heel into the moist ground. "I reckon so."

"Always remember this: There is no greater magic than to transform one thing into another."

"I understand," said Freya.

Elizabeth stood to gather more wood. Wilhemena got up from her hiding spot and joined Freya at the fire.

She wanted to ask what the conversation was about. Why had Mama taught Freya about glamour and not her? And why was it a secret? As her mind tackled the questions, Wilhemena noticed a bulge in the pocket of Freya's apron.

"What have you got in your pocket?"

"Nothing," Freya said.

"I can see you got something in there."

"It's none of your concern."

"Freya, you show me what you've got hiding in there right now, or I'll give you a spanking myself before Mama does."

Freya was about to argue, when Wilhemena reached into the pocket, as quick as a flash, and pulled the dead pickerel frog out.

"Hey, that's mine," Freya said.

"How long has this frog been dead?"

"It's not dead."

"Is so."

"Is not."

Wilhemena held it out by its motionless front legs to prove her point.

"You shouldn't kill innocent creatures, Freya. It's wasteful.

Now go put this frog in the icebox so we can use it for bait. Waste not, want not." She tossed the frog to her sister.

Freya thought a moment, her anger veiled behind calm eyes. Then she tossed the frog back. "*You* go put it in the icebox. You're the one wants to keep it so bad."

Wilhemena wrapped the frog in a leaf and carried it back down the doe path to the house, where she climbed the splintered steps to the porch. She lifted the top of the icebox, which was filled, as always, with packages of meat wrapped in butcher paper. She put the frog on top of a package and lowered the lid. Something caught her eye. She opened the lid again.

There was a hand poking out of a package at the bottom. She was sure it was a hand. The hand of a man. The wedding band glistening in the hazy moonlight.

CHAPTER 2

Birds of feather flock together,
And so will pigs and swine;
Rats and mice will have their choice,
And so will I have mine.

Monrovia, Massachusetts • 2015

Sophie is begging me to take her to the petting zoo to see the baby pigs. Pigs are pink and pink is absolutely, positively her most favorite color in the whole wide world. As if I need to be reminded.

I brush the black tangle of curls from her face and kiss her forehead. "In a few minutes," I lie. I could be honest and say it'll be a couple hours, but time is inconsequential to a three-year-old. There is only NOW.

"Pleeeeeeaaaassse," she whines. "Piggies."

"As soon as I'm done. I promise." For now, I've been volunteered. Everyone has to do her part, you know.

Kevin lifts Sophie onto his shoulders and grips her ankles by their pink ruffled socks. Suddenly she's the tallest person on earth and she forgets all about the pigs. "Let's meet up at the tractor rides," he says to me, and then to her, "Whaddya say, Sophe?" Right as she answers he bounces up and down, which turns her voice into a comical version of itself. This delights her. "More," she says. Kevin bounces as she sings "Twinkle, Twinkle, Little Star," her vowels tumbling in somersaults. She breaks into hysterics. So easy for dads to play the hero.

I grab the bag with the just-in-case diapers, the wipes, the sippy cups, the Band-Aids, the all-purpose marjoram-and-black-walnut lotion, the emergency stash of Goldfish (which I put in my pocket for easy access), the favorite fleece blanket with the orange bunny rabbits. I help Henry gather the entire Justice League off the minivan floor and persuade him to only bring one along. Superman wins.

I give Gillian a ten-dollar bill to spend any way she sees fit, both of us pretending it's not a bribe to endure a Sunday outing with her family. Her attitude lately is grim bordering on hostile, primarily because she's "like, the only person on earth whose cruel, awful parents haven't given her a phone yet." But I can relate. I know a thing or two about being twelve and disappointed by family.

Henry, his six-year-old legs knowing no speed other than FAST, sprints ahead, eyes turned upward on his miniature superhero who flies through the sky to battle villains and save the weaklings.

"Slow down, buddy," I yell after him, but he doesn't pay attention to me or to the bed of chrysanthemums that he tramples through, oblivious as always to his surroundings.

Petals fly. Stems are flattened. I run over to survey the damage and determine whether or not parental action is required. That's when I notice that the flowers are planted into the shape of a raven, Monrovia's school mascot. Purple mums for the feathers (flattened wing, thanks to Henry), yellow mums for the eye, orange impatiens for the beak. Flowering kale for the talons.

"They've gone all out this year," I say to my family when they catch up with me, but no one seems to hear. "Gillian, do you see the raven?"

"Lame," is all Gillian has to say about it. "I'm going to go find Breanna."

She takes off to suffer in solidarity with her BFF as the rest of us walk down the Town Green and along the waterfront, its dogwoods and giant oaks bursting with red and yellow, their vibrancy matched by the blood-red roses, still in bloom, that line the boardwalk. The colors appear even brighter against the solid canvas of gray-shingled Federalists that skirt the park. The houses are new, but made to look old thanks to Monrovia's strict zoning laws. Kevin worked on many of them, hanging Sheetrock, tiling bathrooms, helping to conceal their real ages behind wavy glass windows, period gaslight lampposts, and foundations made of antique brick.

The people milling around the Green are the opposite: old made to look young due to countless hours at the gym and thousands of dollars at the beauty salons and Dr. Yu's Botox Clinic.

At the soccer fields a small armada of white banners flap in the breeze, announcing the Harvest Festival: PROUDLY SPONSORED BY THE MONROVIA PTO, MONROVIA SCHOOLS RANKED #1 IN STATE, GO RAVENS! A gust of wind races up the field, whipping the COMMUNITY FIRST banner upside down. Erin Hastings, the town arborist, unfurls it. The wind keeps batting at the banners, and Erin runs madly between them, pulling at corners and straightening, no platitude out of place.

"See you at the tractor rides," I say as Kevin heads into the festival.

"You bet," he says. He leans down to kiss me, but the bill of his Bet Your Bass Bait & Tackle cap jabs me in the forehead. He and the kids make a beeline for the snack tent with its sugar-free candied apples, faux cotton candy, hummus wraps, and organic cider. If there's a crystal of real sugar to be found, Kevin will find it. Dad the Hero.

I turn in the direction of the games, past the bottle ring toss with giant tigers (stuffed with organic bamboo fiber) for prizes, past the duck-race pond and the dunking booth where Mrs. Honeycut, the first-grade teacher, is telling her students to take their best shot. On the makeshift stage, girls from Monrovia School of Irish Step Dance perform a jig to a row of mothers who pantomime smiles and stage directions to them.

At the end of the brick path, a dozen prams are lined up, their crisp blue canvas covers all identical except for the embroidered names. Madison. Tatum. Butterbean. Thousand-dollar prams and it's hard to tell whether they're for babies or Pomeranians.

The wind pushes one of the prams onto the grass, leaving two sharp tracks in the perfect green sod. A mother carrying her baby like a kangaroo in a chest harness emerges out of nowhere at full tilt. The baby bobbles along with her, smiling at the sudden momentum, the rush of wind in his face. She pushes the stroller back in line and snaps down the brake. Our eyes meet and she gives me an apologetic look, as though I caught her in the act of breaking the pram parking rules and defiling public property. I want to say, *I don't care if your stroller ruins the grass. It's just grass.* But of course I don't. I return her look with one all the moms give each other when we meet on the playground, or in line at the supermarket. It's a look that says, *I understand you. I know your life is an unending to-do list of field trips and registration deadlines, soccer practices, diaper changes, playdates—a domino game of a million little details.*

When I get to my station, the bobbing-for-apples barrel, I'm already late and there's a mob of kids waiting for the game to start. I herd them into single file. A kid in the back inches his way toward to the front, his belly sticking out of the bottom of his Boston Red Sox sweatshirt. When I bend down to put the apples in the bucket, he creeps ahead of a freckled-nosed kid in front.

Bryson Proctor. He's in my son's first-grade class, and I happen to know he's a little scoundrel.

There's one in every class. You can always count on Bryson to make a scene. Last year at the Christmas pageant he grabbed the Baby Jesus out of the manger, tucked it under his arm, and ran across the stage like he was making a touchdown as the whole congregation sang "Silent Night." The parents tried to pretend like nothing had happened, but you can't let a thing like that go by; this was kidnapping Baby Jesus. This was sacrilege.

Luckily, they decided to use a doll last year for the Baby Jesus instead of a real baby like they usually do. Rosie O'Shea, who is perpetually pregnant and never short of babies, is always happy to volunteer one for the role of the Divine. Part of me thinks she just does it for the night of free babysitting.

Bryson worms his way to the front of the line and looks me square in the eye. "What do I get if I win?"

"What do you mean?"

"What's the prize?"

"The prize is an apple. You get an apple. That's the whole point."

"That sucks."

"Then don't play."

He ignores me and dunks his head into the barrel. Apples scatter on the surface. After a few seconds, he comes up for air, absent of apple, water dripping from his chin. When he thinks I'm not looking, he slips a hand into the water.

"No hands," I say.

"Why not?"

"Because that's cheating."

"So?"

"So, the point of the game is to pick an apple up with your teeth."

"That's too hard."

"It's supposed to be hard. But you get three tries," I say in my saccharin-sweet-this-is-how-moms-talk-to-children voice.

"This is stupid."

"That's not very nice," I say.

"*That's not very nice,*" he mimics.

I look around for Bryson's mother, Lilith Proctor. She's manning the pie-eating table, completely unaware of what a menace her son is being. Lilith is thin. Supermodel thin. Around her it's a storm of gaiety as she jokes with other moms and passes out slices of honey-lemon custard. She's probably never eaten a slice of pie in her life.

"Do you want to try again?" I ask Bryson, trying with all my might to rise above the insidious insults of a six-year-old.

"Yeah, whatever." He dunks his head in the water and again comes up empty. He rubs his eyes dry and splatters water down his sweatshirt.

"Better luck next time," I say. I have to be nice. You're not allowed to discipline someone else's child. That's a rule, just like "No white after Labor Day" or "Be always on time; too late is a crime."

"I'm going again," he says. His head goes under, along with his hand, the little cheat.

I look at my watch. Another hour and my shift will be over and I will have filled my quota of volunteer work for the fall. I guess it beats getting stuck on cleanup crew at the Boo Bash or decoration committee for the Winter Wonderland Festival. I can endure one more hour.

My mind leaps to all the things I need to get done today: grab milk on the way home, buy supplies for Gillian's science fair project, reschedule Kevin's dentist appointment, give the dog a bath, dig Henry's winter clothes out of the attic, sew a button on Sophie's favorite coat.

I take a deep breath and close my eyes. The September sun warms my face. In the distance I hear the whirl of the cotton candy machine spinning its faux-sugar floss, the squawk of seagulls vying for scraps of gluten-free kettle corn.

And without any warning, my mother's voice roars into my head, louder than all the other thoughts and noise rambling around inside.

> *Onion's skin very thin,*
> *Mild winter coming in.*
> *Onion's skin thick and tough,*
> *Coming winter cold and rough.*

An image of an onion pops into my mind's eye. I can see its peeling outer skin, the dried patch of roots on the bottom. I can smell its sweetness. I can taste its pungent bite, and feel its weight in my hand, almost identical in size to an apple.

I open my eyes. And this time when Bryson lifts his head, he has a big yellow onion in his choppers.

At first I don't think I've seen it right. I blink hard, look again. It's still there.

The kid with the freckles sees it, too, because his eyes are like saucers and he instinctively curls his nose up at it.

Not again, I think to myself.

For a moment, Bryson is jubilant. He points to the prize in his mouth and does a little victory dance. But when the taste of the onion reaches his tongue, he spits it out. He rubs his tongue with the sleeves of his sweatshirt and spits and spits and spits. The offending onion rolls to my feet and Bryson looks at me for some sort of explanation. I just shrug.

Bryson turns beet red. His hands clench into fists and he marches off toward the pie-eating table. "Mmmooooomm-mmm!"

When Lilith Proctor sees him, she pats his head and shoves an organic cider doughnut in his hand. He keeps pointing over at me and scrunching his face into a raisin, no doubt explaining how he got bamboozled at the bobbing-for-apples station. Lilith glances at me, then at Bryson, then at me again.

And now Lilith is walking my way.

I want to run.

She's wearing tall leather boots and a pink cashmere cape, THE pink cashmere cape that announces her elite status in the ranks of Monrovia housewives. She wears a spray tan like protective coloration against the shame of being unpolished and drab. If I'd known I was going to have to face off against Lilith Proctor today, I would have at least brushed my hair.

"Allison, there seems to be a problem with the game. Can

you tell me what's going on?"—the affect in her voice honed on golf courses and yacht clubs.

"Nothing," I say.

Hands on hips, she continues, "Bryson tells me there was an onion in the apple-bobbing barrel. Isn't that right, sweetie?" Bryson scowls at me from under his mother's arm.

My cheeks are on fire. "Is he sure it was an onion?"

"Do you think he doesn't know the difference?"

"I'm sure he's very bright," I say.

"He was selected to carry the school banner at the Harvest Parade this afternoon."

"What an honor," I say.

"You can understand why I don't want anything to spoil the day for him," Lilith says.

"Of course."

"I just want to make sure everything's running smoothly for all the children," Lilith says. The wind catches her cape and it flutters behind her, like a superhero on a mission, the Amazing Hovering Mother. "Everyone has to do her part, you know."

"I know." I know. I know. I know.

"If you need an extra hand, I'm sure I can find another PTO member to help you with your shift."

"I can handle it. I'm sure there's a logical explanation for the onion. Maybe he got confused."

"I hardly think so," Lilith says.

"It was an onion. It was right there!" Bryson says and points toward my feet.

I look down at the same time as Bryson. But all that's there is a juicy red apple with a substantial bite missing. I pick it up. I hand it to Lilith.

She turns it over in her hand and sniffs (looking for evidence of onions and wrongdoing). "Well. It certainly looks like an apple. Honey, maybe you *were* confused," she says to Bryson.

"But I *swear* it was an onion!" Bryson says.

She eyes me suspiciously then says, "Perhaps you should ask

the children if they like apples before letting them take a turn. Not all children like apples, Allison."

I suppress the smile that creeps up my face. "You're right. Good luck at the parade, Bryson. Break a leg."

Bryson kicks the apple toward a group of girls doing cartwheels and then runs off to the potato sack races.

That was a close one.

I don't need anyone knowing that I can turn apples into onions.

Not here. Not in Monrovia.

I just want to fit in. I just want to be like the other moms and wives and worry about normal things like cellulite and the mortgage. I want to believe that in a place like this, I can be safe, and family can be forever. Even wrapped in the family-friendly, politically correct, health-conscious, yoga-minded, upper-middle-class bubble of Monrovia, it's still impossible for me to forget what it's like to sleep in a borrowed bed, wondering if my real family will ever come and claim me.

The next kid steps up, the sweet little boy with curly hair and freckles. He's missing his two front teeth, which is going to make it hard to bite an apple. He hesitates. " 'Scuse me, ma'am. There any more onions in there?" he asks.

"Nope, only apples," I assure him. "I promise."

My name is Allison Darling. I'm thirty-eight years old. I'm a wife, and mother of three. I live at 13 Purchase Street in Monrovia, Massachusetts. I'm a member of the PTO, an animal lover, a proficient baker of chocolate chip cookies.

I'm also a witch.

Until now, I thought my magic was gone. When I was very little, I could go to bed at night and dream about something, say, chocolate raspberry cupcakes, and when I awoke in the morning a dozen chocolate raspberry cupcakes would appear where there had only been a handful of turnips. Or, one time, when I was about Sophie's age, I lay awake listening to the cantankerous croak of the bullfrogs in the marsh, pressing my hands over my ears, willing it to stop. Later on the croaking was replaced by the musical lilt of a thousand crickets. I'm sure it was my doing. When else have crickets ever overtaken bullfrogs in the amphibious warfare of the marsh?

My mother said it was a special talent. "What you think, so it becomes," she'd say. She said I was gifted.

Then again, my mother was committed to psychiatric hospital when I was seven.

That's when I learned that I was not normal. None of the foster families found my talent as special as my mother did. Every time a thunderstorm appeared out of blue skies in the middle of my temper tantrums, eyebrows were raised, fingers were pointed, and I was pawned off on a new family.

I quickly came to understand that being different was shameful. (Seven-year-old girls are quick studies on the rules of social acceptability.) Kids in each of my new schools snickering behind their Judy Blume books at me, whispering, "Look, she doesn't even shave her legs." I remember closing my eyes in the middle of the cafeteria, alone at a table, trying to imagine myself as an ant so I could crawl away unnoticed.

But I didn't become an ant. By the time I hit middle school, I had lost my ability to make things happen just by imagining them.

Until now.

Children come and go through the line, taking their three tries. For fear of transfiguring another apple, I step back and try to keep my mind off the fruit.

After a little while Rosie O'Shea rushes up to me, a crying baby in a sling around her shoulder, a toddler walking beside her eating a caramel apple, his face and hands covered in goo.

Rosie has THE pink cashmere cape, too, but hers is smeared in baby drool.

"Sorry I'm late," Rosie huffs. "I was working the smoothie bar and we ran out of soy milk, so I had to dash to Nelson's General Store to grab some, then there was a problem with the raffle that I had to take care of."

"Don't worry about it," I say. And even though I don't want to stay, she looks so haggard, I tell her I don't mind taking another shift at the apple bobbing.

"I wouldn't dream of it. I look forward to this every year," she says cheerily. She looks around at the milling families. "Besides, how would it look if the president of the PTO shirked her duties on Apple Harvest?"

"No one has to know," I whisper.

It's almost imperceptible, but a dark cloud crosses her face.

"I need to take my shift," Rosie says at last. She turns to me and says, a little less brightly than before, "Go treat yourself to some sweet potato fritters. Or something from the organic dairy tent."

I nod.

"And Allison. Try to keep onions out of the apple-bobbing tank next time, okay?" She doesn't say it in a condescending tone the way Lilith did, but in a voice you use when admitting that your kid has lice or cavities, and that makes me even more nervous.

I force a smile. "Word travels fast in Monrovia," I say, wondering if there's something else she wants to tell me.

Kevin is waiting for me at the tractor rides. "How was the apple bobbing?" he says.

"Fine," I answer. "Are you ready to leave?" I want to get out of here as fast as possible.

"Already?" Kevin says. "Feels like we just got here."

Sophie runs toward me, arms in pick-me-up position, hay from the tractor ride poking at sharp angles out of her hair, her jacket, her pants. "We see the pigs now?"

"Oh right." I almost forgot about the pigs. I think about how quickly children lose their gift for finding delight in such simple things and I know that there's no way I'm going to disappoint her by not seeing the pigs.

"Henry wants to take another spin on the tractor. I'll stay with him, you take Sophie," Kevin says, always ready with a solution.

"And then we'll go home," I say, firmly.

"Sure," Kevin says, his mind drifting to thoughts of the Patriots game and a plate of beef chili nachos awaiting him this afternoon.

At the petting zoo, Sophie runs directly for the lambs, which are so sweet and cuddly they could even turn Kevin into a vegetarian. She nestles her face into one of them as I watch from the fence.

Just as I think about how beautiful these moments of motherhood can be, I feel a hand on my shoulder and a sharp prickling sensation up the back of my neck.

I turn around. Astrid Laveau is standing behind me, her red hair shimmering in the sun, her skin so beautiful it glows. As usual, she's perfectly decked out in pearls, Jackie-O sunglasses, designer jeans, heels, and THE pink cashmere cape. Me, in purple Crocs I got three years ago for Mother's Day.

"I've been looking for you," Astrid says, her voice like silk.

I massage my neck, which throbs. "Was I signed up for another volunteer post?" I ask.

"Just wanted to know how things were at the apple bobbing." Her eyes are unreadable behind her Jackie-Os.

Two sheep have walked over to the fence and stand in front of me. I reach into my pocket and pull out some Goldfish. I toss them over the fence, to the right so that the sheep will chase after them, but they don't budge.

"Fine. Things were fine." I shoo the sheep with a hand.

Astrid looks at the sheep, then at me. "No problems, I assume."

"None. You've really outdone yourself this year. Everything is amazing."

"I can't take all the credit. My company may have cosponsored the event, but you know what I say . . ."

"Everyone has to do her part."

"Exactly."

Two of the geese in the petting zoo waddle up to me and honk. I throw some Goldfish behind them, but they push their beaks up against my leg and honk some more. Astrid cocks her head at the sight.

"Speaking of my company, I assume you're all set for Wednesday night. For the Glamour Party," she says.

"Absolutely," I say, kicking at the geese, wishing the animals would leave me alone, wishing Astrid would leave me alone. I'm sure she's already heard about the Bryson Proctor incident.

"Excellent," Astrid says, the apples of her cheeks glowing pink. "We don't trust just anyone to host our home-shopping parties. We're highly selective. Sell enough and you might even earn one of these." She lifts the sides of her pink cape like a bat.

Sophie runs up to me holding a huge, docile rabbit against her chest, pleased as punch, her face bright red with eczema.

"I'll be sure to have Miranda bring some Honey Skin Bath Bubbler," Astrid says, noticing Sophie's inflamed skin. "It's one hundred percent natural, made with local honey. Helps children build up their immunity to allergies."

Clearly, I've forgotten about Sophie's sensitive skin, letting her pet all these animals. Feeling exposed yet again for my sloppy parenting, I dig in my bag and pull out the all-purpose marjoram-and-black-walnut lotion, made by Glamour Soap. I squeeze out a dollop and am rubbing it into Sophie's cheek when the rabbit suddenly comes to life in Sophie's arms. It jumps out of her clutch and hops up to me. The geese wander over and honk.

Astrid watches the menagerie of animals gathering around me, her smile unwavering. "Well, I must be off. I have a parade to orchestrate. Happy Apple Harvest, Allison."

"Happy Apple Harvest," I say.

Once Astrid leaves, Sophie grabs my hand and pulls me toward the pigpen. She squeezes her face in between the slats and peers in at the litter of piglets suckling at their mother's belly.

"Piggies dance?" Sophie says. Her imagination is buoyed with the tale of a dancing pig we heard this week at the Monrovia Library Story Hour. It was all about a little piglet who dreamed of becoming a great dancer and her epic journey from pigpen to Broadway. Very cute.

"Sorry, sweetie, pigs can't dance. Not for real," I tell her.

"Yes they can."

"No, honey, that was just a story."

"Please dance," she whispers to the piglets. "Please, please, please."

I close my eyes and think about the story from the book, of the dancing piglet who became a prima donna and of Sophie's favorite part of the story when the piglet performs for the first time at the opera house. When I open them, the piglets unhook themselves from their mother's nipples and stand upright on tiny hooves, teetering back and forth. They gain their balance and pair off to dance in duets, front hooves touching, balancing on hind legs.

Sophie squeals with delight.

What have I done?

I look around the pigpen in a panic. The petting zoo lady is sitting on a milk crate, nose in a Sudoku puzzle. The other kids and parents are in line for the miniature horses. No one sees. I close my eyes again and try to imagine the pigs back at their mother's belly. When I open my eyes, they return to normal pig posture and prance back to the sow, who hasn't even noticed her babies' absence.

What is happening? Why is my magic coming back now?

Sophie is laughing and clapping her hands, cheering for the piggies. I pick her up and tell her the pigs are all done and we have to go *now*.

"We watch the goats dance now?" she asks.

"We'll see," I say, trying very hard NOT to imagine dancing goats.

When I turn around, Astrid is right there, staring at me with sharp green eyes, her sunglasses pulled up on her head. Her look says it all: She knows.

I'm frozen. I can't meet her gaze.

She knows.

CHAPTER 3

It costs little Gossip her income for shoes,
To travel about and carry the news.

On the day of the Glamour Party, I spend my morning sweeping, scrubbing, dusting, and mopping, carrying out the rites of housekeeping with military precision. I make lamb puffs, baked brie, and canapés. I change the hand towels in the bathroom, chill the wine, knock down the cobwebs in the corners of the stairwell, and place honeypots throughout the house to lure away the fruit flies, something I recall doing as a child whenever the swarms invaded at the first whiff of ripening fruit. I water all the plants and prune the rosemary on the windowsill that has stretched its way to the ceiling over the summer while I wasn't paying attention.

Diving into housework is the only thing keeping me from totally freaking out. All week, my thoughts have drifted back to my mother's voice, the way it came to me as clear as if she were standing next to me. And of the magic it brought with it. I can't remember my mother's face, but her voice is another story. Sweet and lilting, it was like a song that carried the secrets of the natural world. It was the voice of magic.

I snip a sprig of rosemary and hold it to my nose, inhaling its evergreen musk. Why is my mother's voice coming back to me now, after all these years? Why has my magic suddenly reappeared? To anyone who doesn't know about these things, it may seem like the most terrific thing in the world, short of winning the lottery or waking up to find yourself transformed into Heidi Klum's body double. To someone like Henry, it may appear that being a witch is like being a superhero, and nothing on earth could beat that. But it's not like being a superhero. Magic means trouble. It means gut-wrenching loneliness and despair and heartbreak. The last time I did magic, I never saw my mother again.

Now I'm turning apples into onions and piglets into ballerinas. Oh god, the piglets! Astrid caught me red-handed. I know she knows it was me. You can't see a thing like that and just pretend it's normal. Even the most pampered, free-range, organically fed pigs on earth don't get up and boogie when they feel like it. Only a witch's dangerous imagination can do that.

I take a breath to calm down. Astrid is the only one who saw, I remind myself, and she won't be here tonight.

I pick up a dish towel with a Christmas tree on it, the one that's out all year in my house, and wipe the flour off the counter. I have a party to throw, and a pie to finish. Witchcraft or no, I need to get my head in the game.

Right now, that requires finishing a pumpkin spice pie, so I take out the rolling pin and smooth the pastry into a perfect nine-inch circle. The pages of my dog-eared copy of *Good Housekeeping* are splattered with the greasy remnants of dinner parties past. I read the recipe through once more: "The first step to creating a perfect crust is exercising patience."

I take out the ruler and measure, roll, measure, roll, measure again. I do this until my dough looks exactly like the picture in the magazine. *Exactly.* Some might call this sort of attention to detail obsessive. I call it Monrovia.

Piecrust symmetry is the kind of thing the other housewives in Monrovia notice. You can really boost your social status just by mastering these kinds of details. I once witnessed a woman get her daughter bumped off the waiting list and onto a spot on the Little Princess Equestrian Team just because she wowed everyone at a Glamour Party with her caviar-topped potato blinis. The Little Princess head coach was at the party, and must have gorged on a dozen blinis. She called them the most impressive petite bouchées she'd ever seen, and next thing you know, the woman's daughter is riding horses all the way to the state championships. I seriously doubt anyone at the party had ever even heard of a petite bouchée before then, but suddenly these little bite-size appetizers were turning up at every dinner party in town.

Such devotion to domestic perfection doesn't seem quite sane to Kevin, whose job tonight is to stay sequestered upstairs with the children, out of sight.

He walks into the kitchen in a T-shirt and ripped sweatpants. He wraps his arms around me, careful to avoid direct contact with my rolls of belly fat, those stubborn paunches that won't disappear no matter how many crunches I do, or how many spin classes I endure. He jams one of the lamb puffs into his mouth and rolls his eyes back in his head as though it's the most stupendous thing he's ever tasted. "You've got to make these more often," he says.

"They're for special company only," I say and whack him on the hand. "Do you have any idea how much work they are?"

"Why not put out some Triscuits and a cheese ball and call it a day?"

"Thanks for the tip, but I don't think that would do." I smile.

"Everyone loves Triscuits. Throw in some wings and nachos and it's a party," he says, smirking. He grabs a beer from the fridge and twists off the cap, his fingernails rimmed in black grit that can't be scrubbed clean. "You know it's a pyramid scheme, right? The person who sells to you gives a cut to the girl above her, who gives a cut to the girl above her, and Astrid gets a cut of the whole thing."

I lift the pastry into the pie plate and gently smooth down the sides. "It's not a pyramid scheme. They give all their profits to charity. It's just . . . it's important. It's expected. And it's kind of an honor to host." How can I tell him that I *need* acceptance from these women. Kevin, who grew up with five siblings in a house where they ate fish dinner together every Friday and pot roast every Sunday, cannot possibly understand my need to belong. His dad coached Little League even when he worked double shifts. His mom helped with homework and knit them all sweaters every winter. They played stickball with the neighborhood kids in the street after school and piled into their station wagon for family vacations to the shore. They all fought and made up and worked hard and played hard and grew up knowing they were loved.

He gulps down half the beer in one slug. His other hand goes to work tightening a drawer pull. "You're a great hostess. And an amazing cook. I don't want you to get stressed out about all of it."

"All of what?"

His eyes are so full of tenderness it hurts. "The pink cape crusade. They can be a little . . . well, you know."

"Ambitious?" I say. "Charitable? Stylish? Pretty?"

"Like a cult is what I was going to say. They've got their claws in everything—school board, city council, zoning board, charity balls."

"Maybe I need to get more involved in things, Kevin. It might be good for me to do something that doesn't involve potty training and playdates. Maybe it wouldn't be so bad to be around such ambitious women," I say.

"It just doesn't seem like your crowd, Allison. I don't want you to get hurt. That's all."

So my husband doesn't think I fit in with the ambitious supermoms who run every committee in Monrovia. I'm a little hurt. But he's right. The Glamour Girls are out of my league. I wouldn't mind a little of what they have, I'll admit it. Life seems to come at these women with open arms, like a sushi boat. *Take what you want, whenever it floats by, and if you miss it, don't worry, the same dish will come around again.* For me, life is more like a hot dog cart. You go in quick, grab a dog, and stand alone by the garbage can, hoping no one bumps into you.

"I can be ambitious," I say and go back to crimping the edges of the dough so it forms a perfect rope, just like in the picture.

Kevin kisses me on the neck. "I love you just the way you are. You know that."

Yes, you love me just as I am, I want to say, but what husband wouldn't want their wife to be a little more glamorous, or successful, or popular? Who wouldn't want to hug their wife without worrying about making contact with her fat rolls?

"Get upstairs to your quarters!" I command, and give him an ambitious squeeze of the cheek.

The doorbell rings, startling me from my singular concentration on arranging crackers symmetrically around a baked brie. I open the door and Miranda Greene is standing there in her pink cape. Behind her is Astrid.

I choke back my surprise.

"I brought the original Glamour Girl herself," Miranda says, all smiles, swinging her pink case full of merchandise.

"For you," Astrid says, handing me a gift basket with enough tinctures, tonics, lotions, ointments, and room fresheners to last a year. Pins and needles shoot down my neck.

I take the basket and as soon as my mouth works again I mutter, "Come in." Maybe Astrid didn't see anything at the petting zoo. Maybe I didn't really even make those pigs dance. Maybe it was all in my imagination. But why is she here?

Miranda steps inside and air kisses me on both cheeks. She marches into my living room like she's been here a thousand times. "I think I'll set up right over there," she says, pointing to the coffee table.

I fumble out some sort of response, but the only thing I'm aware of is Astrid, and her peering green eyes.

"Miranda needed some help with her presentation, so I'm here lend a hand," Astrid says as if reading my thoughts.

My head starts pounding.

Rufus, our family mutt, runs past us with a pair of dirty underwear (mine) stuffed in his mouth. I can tell they're old and straight out of the hamper; they're not even the sexy lace thongs that I'd like everyone to think I wear on a daily basis. No, these are the full-coverage granny panties with the cotton worn thin on the crotch. I try to grab him, but he dodges me and runs upstairs with my underwear.

"Maybe we should try to keep the dog upstairs during the party, don't you think?" Astrid says.

"Of course," I say. I yell up to Kevin to hold on to Rufus and he yells back "Okay," and I can tell by the look on Astrid's face that there's a lot more yelling in my house than in her nine-bedroom mansion on the other side of town.

"I need to finish up the food. I'll be in the kitchen," I say and practically run across the living room.

I'm getting a glass of water from the tap when Astrid walks in behind me.

"Can I help?" she asks, dangling her red nails over the stacks of mail on my counter.

Water flows over the glass. I put it down on the counter and rifle through a drawer for aspirin. My head is pounding now. I dig deeper in the drawer, past packs of gum, leaky pens, an old binky, until I find the aspirin.

"I've got everything. Really," I say, shaking two pills loose from the bottle.

Astrid walks over to the kitchen windowsill and picks up the rosemary plant. "Rosemary is one of my favorites. Did you know that it helps with memory?"

"I've heard that."

"Not many people are aware of the medicinal properties of herbs."

"My mother taught me when I was little," I say, surprised to hear myself mentioning my mother so casually. Normally, I never talk about her.

Astrid sets the rosemary back down. "Your mother? Is she still alive?"

My throat is like sawdust. "Yes. I mean, no."

Astrid raises both eyebrows, forming wrinkles in her perfect complexion. "Is it yes or no?"

"No. She's no longer alive," I say, averting my eyes.

"Where did you say you grew up, Allison?"

"Around here." I pop two aspirin, and chase them with water.

She leans toward me. "Your father? Is he still alive?"

My palms are sweating. I wipe them down the front of my pants. "No."

"Siblings?"

I shake my head. My face is burning.

Astrid backs away. "Well, anyway. You and Kevin have made a beautiful family of your own. In fact it was lovely seeing you all at the Apple Harvest."

I wipe the rings of water off the counter.

"I heard there was quite a ruckus over some bad apples. Lilith Proctor's poor son was quite shaken. Swears he saw an apple turn into an onion. It's impossible, though. You don't believe objects can suddenly change shape? You don't believe in magic, do you?"

I can feel her gaze go through me. "Lamb puff?" I say, lifting the tray to her.

"No thank you. Not after seeing those adorable lambs at the petting zoo. Sophie just loved them, didn't she? Not as cute as the pigs, though."

I nod, my voice seizing up again. The pigs. Why is she mentioning the pigs?

The doorbell rings. "I should get that," I say.

"Yes. You are the hostess, after all."

I'm so relieved to have an escape that I practically skip out of the kitchen. But Astrid stops me.

"You never did answer my question, though."

"Your question?"

"Do you believe in magic?"

I meet her gaze, and although my insides are spinning like a tornado, I force myself into a bubble of calm, the actor in me playing her part. "No. Of course not."

As the guests arrive, I pour wine and set out the hors d'oeuvres. Having Astrid in attendance seems to elevate everyone's mood instantly. Astrid is the queen bee of Monrovia and this is her swarm. Everyone is eager for her opinion on everything from where to get the best manicures to whether or not Connie Flanagan should consider dark lowlights in her bleached blond hair. ("Stay blond, Connie," Astrid says definitively.)

When the discussion turns to which costumes will be most prolific at Halloween (surely not Batman *again*?), I look up and catch Astrid staring right at me. I feel a pounding headache, like someone driving nails into my forehead.

"Pirates are always popular," Astrid says. "And witches."

A flush of adrenaline courses through me and my ears start ringing. Luckily Connie and my neighbor Patricia have plenty of opinions on the matter of Halloween costumes ("Can you *believe* how vampy some of these girls are allowed to dress?"), so I sit back and keep my mouth shut until Monica, a fellow Monrovia Elementary School mom, picks up a lamb puff and asks me what it is.

"Lamb puff," I say. Then I remember all the fuss I once heard her make over animal rights at a school orientation that served shortbread cookies shaped like panda bears and I add, "The lamb is from the organic farm. Would you like to try one?"

She sets it back on the plate. "Lamb. Not for me!"

"But all their lambs are free-range, I promise."

Mary-Jo, from my book group chimes in, "I'm vegan."

"Me, too," Kathy Gallagher says. "I'm doing a raw food diet."

"I've been vegan for three weeks," Tanya Buxbaum, a mom from Sophie's Montessori class, adds. "No meat. No dairy."

The lamb puff platter is next to the brie en croute, another culinary bust for the evening. Apparently, I've missed the boat on the raw food trend. It's all too much to keep track of. Last month it was cleanse diets. Before that it was Brazilian blow-outs. Vajazzling was popular last summer. The trends spread from the drop-off at Montessori through the aisles of Whole Foods until every woman in town is grazing on raw celery sticks and dehydrated soy nuts while my lamb pastries sit on the plate like little turds.

The doorbell rings again, and I spring out of my chair to answer it. Only one of my guests is missing so it's no surprise when I answer the door to find Judy standing there.

She thrusts a bottle of wine into my hands. "You owe me big time! How'd you get sucked into this anyway?"

"Shhhhh. Thanks for coming. I need some reinforcements," I say.

"Yeah, yeah. Crack open that bottle. I'm going to need to get good and drunk to handle this crowd."

"Just be nice, okay."

"No promises."

Judy is short, thirty pounds overweight, unbearably crass, and my best friend. She's the only woman I know in Monrovia (other than me) who doesn't have a nanny and a personal trainer. She doesn't do manicures, macrobiotic colon cleanses, Pilates, or recipe swaps. She couldn't give a rat's ass about Glamour Soap or home-shopping parties. She is the antithesis of domestic perfection.

Judy came into my life right after Gillian was born. Sleep-deprived and jelly-bellied, I'd spend entire days on the couch, the sun rising and setting in my brain without a coherent thought. Being a new mom is no easy thing. It forces you to tread water in an ocean even if you've never left the shallow end before. You question yourself constantly: Is my baby eating too much? Is she sleeping too little? Is she too hot? Is she getting enough stimulation? Why is she crying again? Shouldn't she be crawling already? Is her brain all right? Did I take enough folic acid when I was pregnant? How the hell do these car seats work?

I didn't know how to be a mom. So I joined a playgroup. And that made things worse.

The other moms in the playgroup baked fresh blueberry muffins and whole-grain scones on days they hosted. They filled their homes with budding hyacinths on the first day of spring. They organized toys in bright bins and read all the parenting magazines. They invested in lactation consultants and early reading programs. They were up on all the trends: baby art classes, Ferberizing versus continuum concept parenting, attachment theory and cosleeping, bottle versus breast. Their children were superior by all measures: eating, pooping, talking, crawling. I kept quiet, afraid of being exposed as a second-rate mom. I silently fantasized about Gillian standing up and walking across the room, a bipedal six-month-old to one-up them all.

Then Judy joined.

Playdates at Judy's house were chaotic. Frankie's toys were scattered throughout the living room like minefields. She served Pop-Tarts for snack.

Judy bitched about the rank smell of Diaper Genies, and her dull sex life. She wasn't afraid to show the chinks in her armor. Judy—all chink, no armor.

So I dropped out of playgroup and spent my days with Judy, navigating the world of motherhood without the pressures of Monrovia perfectionism. We drank martinis at 3:00 P.M. and didn't care if our kids made a mess.

Judy walks straight to the bar I've set up in the dining room, Boston Red Sox cap pulled tight, and pours two glasses of wine—one for her, one for me. She guzzles hers down and pours herself another.

I give her a pleading look.

"What?" she says in a deep voice.

Miranda walks over and asks if all my guests are here and I tell her yes.

"Mi-randa," Judy snaps by way of a greeting.

"Judy. I didn't see you."

"Must be the two pounds I lost," Judy says drily.

This throws Miranda for a loop. "Good for you," she says. Judy rolls her eyes at me the second Miranda steps into the living room.

"Behave," I say to Judy, even though there's little chance of that. Judy can't help herself. She needs to stoke the fire. It's like the time she brought penis-shaped cookies to Sheila Halpern's annual cookie swap, anatomically detailed in icing. She wasn't invited back after that, which was fine by her. "You ladies take your cookies way too seriously," she said as the cookie judging began, everyone pretending not to notice the plate of marzipan penises at the end of the table.

"Let's begin," Astrid says when Judy and I walk into the living room, her voice rising above the chatter.

We all take seats around the coffee table, which is laid out with Glamour products and uneaten appetizers, while Astrid stands and begins her presentation.

"I know that each and every one of you here tonight has worries," she says. "You worry about your children and whether they're getting the best education they can. You worry whether they have enough friends, good health, the right clothes. You worry about money, because, who's not worried about that." She pauses and looks around the room. All eyes are on her. "You worry about your husbands. You wonder how to regain some of the passion that you once had for him. You worry about yourselves—those extra pounds you've put on, those annoying wrinkles you didn't have last year, the gray streaks in your hair.

"But those are only symptoms. The real problem lies deeper. The real problem lies here," she taps two fingers to her temple. "The real problem lies in your perception of yourself. Raise your hand if you've ever laid in bed at night imagining a better version of yourself. One who was a little thinner, or a little prettier, or a little stronger, a little more creative."

Everyone's hand goes up, including mine.

"See," Astrid says. "You're not alone. But guess what? Today you have won the lottery."

Around the room, everyone is holding their breath, waiting for Astrid's next words. Mary-Jo, who normally can't keep her mouth shut for two seconds during our book group's discussions, is literally on the edge of her seat.

"Ladies, Glamour Soap is here for you. You might think of us as a just a bunch of soaps and hand lotions, but we are so much more! We make dreams come true." She walks over to me and puts a hand on my shoulder. Prickles go up my spine.

"Each one of you is here tonight because Allison believes in you. Allison thinks that you are special enough to be considered a friend. Why does that matter? Because female friendship is at the heart of everything we do." I look at Judy, who smirks, and I can practically hear what she would be saying right now if we were alone: *Yeah, right, you're only here because your e-mail addresses are in Allison's contacts list.*

Astrid moves away from me and back to her spot at the head of the coffee table. "Glamour Soap Company drives positive change in women's lives. We make life beautiful. And I'm not talking about this kind of beauty." She raises her hands to frame her gorgeous face. "I'm talking about this kind of beauty." Now she presses a hand to her heart.

Judy pretends to stick a finger down her throat and gag. Fortunately, no one else sees her since all their attention is directed on Astrid.

"Have any of you ever wished you could design your life exactly as you envisioned it?"

Everyone raises their hands again.

"For some of you, that means greater wealth. For some, it's spending more quality time with your family. For others, it means feeling like you're part of something bigger than yourself."

She looks at me. "And for some of you, it's accepting your natural talents and realizing them fully."

Her words make me shiver. My natural talents? Could she be alluding to the pigs? The onion? Or the witchcraft that I've tried so hard to escape from my entire life?

Astrid continues. "For me, it was all the above. When I started Glamour, Monrovia didn't have a thriving downtown, or good schools, or well-maintained homes. Through our work, we have given this town its heart and its soul. And do you know how?"

Tanya raises her hand. "With soap?" Everyone laughs and Tanya looks embarrassed.

Astrid smiles. "We enlighten, educate, and empower the women who call this place home. All our profits go back into the community, so that we can guarantee the success of our town and of our children. Of your children." She gestures grandly toward all of us. "Who makes our schools best in the state? We do. Who gives our children the solid foundation that's missing so often in this day and age? We do. Who keeps the real estate prices climbing? We do. Who instills this town with a sense of pride?"

"We do," Mary-Jo blurts out.

"Exactly," Astrid says, pointing to Mary-Jo. "We make positive changes in our community. And, together, we can make a positive change in each other's lives. Alone we're nothing, but together, we are Monrovia."

Patricia claps, quietly at first, and Tanya Buxbaum joins her. Then Connie starts clapping, followed soon by Kathy, and then everyone. It reminds me of that children's game where you go around the circle, first snapping, then patting your legs, then clapping, then stomping your feet to simulate the sound of rain rising to a crescendo.

Judy leans over to me and whispers, loudly, over the sound of the applause, "Remind me not to drink the Kool-Aid." She's swaying a little and she has a ridiculous smile plastered on her face.

I stand and cheer and lead my guests in an ovation. I cheer for my friends and for myself because the party is turning into a smashing success, and most of all, I cheer because I want to believe every word Astrid is saying.

"Thank you," Astrid says when the applause dies down. "Now, the first product I want to show you all is the Youth Rejuvenator. It does a remarkable job of lifting the fine lines and wrinkles that we all get right around here." Astrid points to her eyes, which, by the way, are absolutely wrinkle-free.

Miranda goes around the room squirting a dollop of lotion on our hands that we're supposed to rub into the skin around our eyes.

"Youth Rejuvenator gives your face a fresh glow, too. It can take ten years off in just a matter of weeks. It'll make you look and feel younger. Guaranteed!"

"Forget about looking younger," Judy blurts out. "This old broad would just be happy to sneeze without peeing my pants."

I laugh, but Miranda casts Judy a smarmy look.

Maybe it's the two glasses of chardonnay I've downed in the last thirty minutes, but now my headache comes in waves across my forehead. The aspirin should have set in by now. I rub my temples, but the pain only gets worse.

Astrid notices. "Are you okay, Allison?"

All eyes are on me. I want to excuse myself and go lie down, but that's out of the question. This is my Glamour Party and it's going so well. Everyone's having a great time. This might even go down as the greatest Glamour Party in Monrovia history. How would it look if I left? "I'm fine," I say, forcing a smile to my lips.

Astrid pulls out the next product to demonstrate.

"Cranberry-hemlock massage oil," she announces as she produces a little brown jar. "One drop rubbed into the back of your neck will wash away the entire day's stress for you."

Miranda takes the bottle and goes around the room, doling out drops of oil. When she gets to me, I hold out my hand, but

I feel so nauseous I think I might throw up. "Rub it into your neck, Allison. It relieves stress," Miranda says. When I do, the room starts spinning. I grab on to the arm of my chair.

Astrid continues explaining her products, something about the essential healing powers of agrimony and how it empowers women, but all I can focus on is my brain, which feels like it's being squeezed through the eye of a needle.

"Now I want you to try this soothing salve of bog laurel and fennel. I use it as a homeopathic treatment for migraines and PMS," Astrid says.

Perfect. Maybe it will help. Leave it to me to come down with a crippling migraine on a night as important as this. When I rub the soothing salve on my temples, the pounding in my head blinds me. I try to stand but my knees go weak, and I fall back into the chair.

Then, everything goes black.

I wake up slowly, like ripples of sun on the waves, one minute light, one minute dark. Around me I catch currents of conversation muffled in whispers.

"The doses are off. They're getting too unstable."

"You ruined that batch with too much blackthorn."

"We're out of blackthorn. That was asafetida."

"Triple the dosage on the next batch."

"She's pale. Should we call a doctor?"

"She'll be okay."

"What is that on her neck?"

"It couldn't be."

"Is it?"

"Shhh. Look. She's coming to."

I have the vague sense that they're talking about my birthmark, a purple splotch on the back of my neck shaped like a pentacle. Aunt Aurora used to call it my sacred sign, the one true mark of a real witch. I've always thought of it as a hideous deformity, an embarrassment, and I wear my hair long to hide it.

"It's beautiful."

"It's perfect."

Astrid's voice comes through the fog. "Quick. Get a clean towel," she orders. Next thing I know, someone is wiping a wet cloth over my face and eyes and then, just like that, I'm better. When I open my eyes Astrid and Miranda are staring at me, and the rest of my guests are gone.

"What happened?" I ask.

"You fainted," Astrid answers.

"Where is everyone?"

"We thought it was best to send them home," Miranda says.

"What about Judy? Did she go, too?"

"She ran upstairs to fetch Kevin."

I press up onto my elbows. "Did you sell any soap?" I ask and the second the words escape my lips I wish I could reel them back in. What a stupid thing to worry about right now.

Neither Astrid nor Miranda speaks. Their faces don't give any clue to what's going on—no roll of the eyes, no sympathetic nods. Astrid looks right through me, as though she's searching for something, as if she knows my deepest secret.

Kevin bounds down the stairs, Judy at his heels. "Are you okay? What happened?"

"I'm fine."

"You need to go to the hospital," Judy says.

"No. Really. I'm okay now. I just got dizzy."

"From what?" Kevin says.

I'm wondering the same thing. "I don't know. I might have skipped lunch today."

"Or you're allergic to all this Glamour crap," Judy says.

"We use all-natural ingredients," Miranda snaps. "I think Allison's right. She just needs to eat something."

"You're going to the hospital," Judy says. "I'm taking you myself."

While Kevin and Judy make plans to get me to the hospital, Miranda packs up the merchandise. Astrid sits on the arm of the chair next to me.

"I ruined the party. I'm sorry," I say to Astrid.

Astrid puts an arm around me and speaks so quietly I have to lean in to hear her. "It was a great success." And with that, she and Miranda leave.

I go to the bathroom and splash my face with water. In the mirror I'm horrified by the mess I see. I have raccoon eyes and my face is red and splotchy. The phone rings, but I let Kevin get it; I don't want to talk to anyone.

"It's for you," he says at the door, holding out the receiver. "Says it's urgent."

I take it.

"Hello? Allison Darling?" an old woman's voice says on the end.

"Yes."

"My name is Sister Mary Jean Francis. I'm with the Sisters of Charity of Nazareth over here at Saint Bernadette's." There's a pause. "Wilhemena Ellylydan is one of the patients in my care."

Chills run down my spine and into my extremities. Holding on to the phone is a challenge.

"Are you there, Mrs. Darling?"

"Yes."

"I'm afraid your mother is quite ill. She's asking that you come see her at once."

First her voice returns to me, now the real thing. "Are you sure?" I ask.

"Quite sure; she's at the end, I'm sorry to say," Sister Mary Jean Francis says sweetly.

"I mean, are you sure she's asking for *me*?" I say.

"Why, of course. You're her daughter," the Sister of Charity says. She sounds perplexed. "She hasn't got much time left. She's been in and out of consciousness all evening. All week, actually."

"And?"

"Mrs. Darling, she's your mother!"

The first step is exercising patience . . .

"Can I come tomorrow? I'm not feeling well," I say.

"I think you need to come at once." The nun's voice is growing more agitated.

I haven't seen her in almost thirty-one years, and *now* it's urgent. Now, when I need to see a doctor myself, when I need to be taken care of. "I'll be there soon. Thank you."

I hang up the phone and turn to Kevin. "I have to go."

"Now? Where?"

"Saint Bernadette's. It's Wilhemena."

"You mean Wilhemena—your mother?"

I nod.

"You have a mother?" Judy says. She pulls off her ball cap, smooths her hair, places it back on her head.

"I'll drive you," Kevin says.

"You need to stay with the kids," I say.

"Can't you go tomorrow?"

"She might not make it through the night." Even I can hear the lack of compassion in my voice. Judy stares at me, her mouth agape.

"Take the truck then. That's not a lit road," Kevin says.

"I'm going with you," Judy says. "And then I'm taking you to the hospital."

"Fine," I say.

I clean myself up. Judy and I get in Kevin's truck, and drive south to go say good-bye to Wilhemena Ellylydan, the woman who raised me, the witch who abandoned me, the mother whom I haven't seen in three decades. I feel a wave of anxiety and sadness and anger, and emotions that I can't even give a name to yet.

But mostly, I feel relief.

CHAPTER 4

Well, Mother Goose has written
A pretty book for you,
And filled it full of pictures fine,
And pretty verses too.

"Why didn't you ever tell me your mother was nuts?" Judy says.

I stare straight ahead, focusing on the dirt road studded with ruts the size of basketballs, some like bathtubs. "It's not exactly something to brag about."

"Still. You could have told me. Would have been a hell of a lot more interesting than swapping potty-training stories."

The truck lurches into a pothole and my stomach clenches.

"Watch out," Judy yelps.

"I can't see anything," I snap. My knuckles are white on the wheel. Muddy marsh on both sides of the narrow, unlit road makes for an unforgiving drive. I have no choice but to plow ahead.

"You sure this is the right way?"

"I'm sure," I say. You don't forget the way home, no matter how long it's been.

We travel down a long, straight road through marshland, not a tree, or a house, or a hint of human life in sight. Eventually, the road curves and lights of the granite steeple come into view, its spire piercing the dark like a needle.

"Creepy," Judy says.

"Wait 'til you see it up close."

"Why would they put a psychiatric hospital all the way out in the middle of nowhere?"

"Beats me. I grew up a short way from here. Before my mother was diagnosed with schizophrenia and locked up with the rest of the crazies."

Judy groans. "Emotionally and intellectually challenged," she corrects me.

"Sorry. I forgot you were so sensitive to the needs of the intellectually challenged."

"You don't do what I do without developing some sense of political correctness around insanity. They don't choose to be crazy. Besides, I'm quite fond of the wackos."

"So it's okay for you to call them names?"

"I say it with love."

"I see." Good old sensitive Judy. "Did you know that Saint Bernadette is the patron saint of shepherds and shepherdesses? It was named for the caretakers of the weak and helpless."

"And how do you know all this?"

I take a deep breath. "My caseworker told me."

I can feel Judy's gaze boring into me. "Caseworker? You're suddenly becoming a lot more interesting, Allison."

"Why? Because I was a social welfare case?"

"Social welfare is my life. You know that. But I never knew you had any experience with it. All these years I thought you were just a run-of-the-mill housewife like everyone else in Monrovia. Only into home-shopping parties and book group."

"Sorry to disappoint you."

"Hardly. How old were you when you went in?"

"Seven."

Judy lets out deep sigh. "Ouch."

I look out the window at the sliver of a moon directly ahead of us and something inside of me knows that it's waxing, that it will be a little brighter tomorrow.

"When did you age out?"

"Eighteen."

"Did you get transferred a lot?" Judy is speaking as gently as she possibly can.

I glance at her and say quietly, "I don't want to talk about it."

"I get it. Believe me. I understand."

We ride in silence for a while, which makes the ride seem even slower than it already is. I can sense Judy shifting in her seat, trying to respect my wishes, but at the same time dying to find out more about my mysterious past. Finally, she can't contain herself anymore. "You know, kids from foster care are more likely to commit crime. It's a sad fact. Only six percent go on to college. Half drop out of high school. And more than half of the girls end up pregnant by the age of nineteen. It's a rough life."

"Wow, Judy, is this how you inspire your patients at the halfway house? By telling them what a bunch of shitheads they are?"

She clears her throat. "What I'm saying is . . . you beat the odds. Despite all the factors working against you, you won. You went to college. You made a good life for yourself. You're giving your kids a better life than you had. Most foster kids come from abusive homes, and have had to deal with horrors I can't even imagine. So, props to you, shithead."

I have to smile. My hands relax on the wheel. "Thanks for coming tonight," I say.

"I'm here for you," she replies. I love Judy for her unconditional support, even though she has it all wrong. My home wasn't abusive. It was magical. It was filled with love, and then, one day, it was gone.

"You know, he tried to bring me out here before. Twice," I say.

"Who?"

"My caseworker. Nice guy. He thought I might benefit from a visit with my mother, once I was already in foster care."

"Did you benefit?"

"I never saw her. The first time, we got as far as the front steps when the alarm rang, and the whole hospital went into lockdown. One of the patients tried to burn the place down. Said he heard a voice telling him to do it."

"And the second time?"

"We got as far as the gate. A freak storm kicked up and flooded the road so fast we couldn't get out of the car. Had to be rescued by a tow truck."

"Talk about coincidences."

"Yup. Coincidences."

It was no coincidence, though. What I neglect to tell Judy is that my mother was responsible. Not that I ever had proof, but I knew. The patient hearing voices, the freak storm—it was all the work of my mother. She could feel I was near, and she didn't want to see me.

I wonder if she can sense my presence tonight.

Over the swamp, faint green lights rise and swirl in the air. The lights disappear as quickly as they emerge. The will-o'-the-wisps.

Hello, Mother.

Wilhemena used to say it was the spirit of the swamp. She said there was a spirit in all things in nature, if you knew how to find it. I remember coming out to the swamp at night, no more than four or five years old, my hand locked tightly in my mother's. She would sing to the marsh and the lights, her voice comforting, like warm bread.

"What do you see, Allesone?" my mother asked one night as we stood on a fen overlooking the swamp, the will-o'-the-wisps dancing before us. I told her I could see all manner of things—unicorns, elephants, fairies. "What you think, so it becomes. Transformation is the greatest magic there is," she said. Then she sat me down and told me a story of the not times, of great witches who lived with one foot in this world and one foot in the next. It began as all her stories did, "Once there was and once there wasn't . . ."

Many years later, I learned about chemical reactions. The magical lights were only photon emissions caused by the oxidation of phosphine and methane from decaying matter. Carbon dioxide mixing with sodium and minerals. *Not* unicorns or elephants or fairies from the not times.

* * *

The granite sign to Saint Bernadette's is overgrown in honey-suckle so that BERN is the only part visible. I drive past the gate and down the long driveway until the road is bisected by a swift stream where the tide has flooded a culvert. I park the truck and we get out. The current racing over the road carries clumps of straw and debris, and I wonder whether the tide is coming or going, whether Kevin's truck will be here when we get back.

"Guess they really do want to keep the crazies inside," Judy says.

"Or everyone else out." A wind whistles over cattails. I pull up the collar of my fleece.

"What now?" Judy says.

On one side of the road I notice a series of large boulders set closely together. I point. "Looks like that's how they cross at high tide."

Judy takes one look and shakes her head. "No way. You want me to cross the deathly river over a bunch of rocks?"

"We can't take the truck," I say. "We don't know how deep the stream is."

"I hope your mother appreciates this predicament she's putting us in."

"That's highly unlikely," I say.

I climb up onto the first boulder and reach a hand down to Judy. She has a hard time getting a leg up high enough to make purchase on the rock, but with a couple of tries, and some scrapes to the knees, she makes it. The boulders are spaced close enough to get across easily, but far enough apart to let the water flow between them. It's a big jump down from the last boulder onto the dry road. I make it first, but Judy lands with her foot in water. She lets out a string of expletives and shakes her foot out as we walk the rest of the way to the hospital.

In the distance I hear a horse and a pig and I remember my

caseworker explaining how animals are therapeutic to psychiatric patients, as if my mother had gone off to a yoga retreat or a spa.

When we get to the front door, it's locked. I knock, but I barely make a sound against the heavy mahogany door. There are no signs of life in this midnight hour. We walk around the back, trying every door, but they're also locked.

"Are you absolutely sure this is the right place?" Judy asks.

"This is the right place."

She stomps out the rest of the marsh water from her shoe. "Because you did black out right before you got the call."

"This is the place, Judy."

"And you were acting a little strange all night."

"I'm fine."

"And, insanity *does* run in your family."

"Are you finished?"

"Yes."

We walk around to the front, only this time, the door is wide open. We walk in. No one's at the front desk.

"Anyone here?" I say.

There are small sounds coming from every corner of the place. Moans and groans. Shrieks. Faint laughter.

Judy and I walk down a hallway lit with bare bulbs screwed into the ceiling. I hear a door open and close somewhere. I start walking faster, Judy behind me, my heart racing. At a corner I collide with a tiny woman in a nun's habit. She drops her clipboard.

"Lord almighty heaven above! Who the devil are you? How did you get in here?" she says.

"The door was open."

"Open? Never."

"It was," Judy says.

"I'll call the cops on you."

"My mother is a patient here. I was told to come. My name's Allison Darling," I say, feeling defensive.

"Allison," the nun says like we're old friends. The change in her tone is discombobulating. "Why didn't you say as such? I'm Sister Mary Jean Francis. Everyone calls me Sister Mary Jean." She extends a hand and I shake it. There is a fierceness in her eyes, and despite her tiny frame, I get the feeling she can handle anything.

"Good thing you aren't a robber. Police wouldn't have come inside. They're scared of this place, you know," Sister Mary Jean says in conspiratorial whisper. "Isn't that a thing?"

I pick up the clipboard and hand it to her. "So you know my mother, Wilhemena Ellylydan?"

The nun chuckles. "Ah, yes. The witch."

Judy raises her eyebrows. "I guess there are worse things to be called, right Allison?"

"I'll take you to her at once," Sister Mary Jean says.

I turn to Judy, who seems mildly amused by the oddity of the night. "I think I should probably go alone."

"Of course. I'll wait here," she says, then adds, "in the creepy castle full of lunatics all by myself."

I check her face for signs that she actually might be scared to wait alone, but she gives me a thumbs-up, so I follow Sister Mary Jean down a long corridor to a flight of stairs. She talks fast and walks fast, despite her age, and I have a hard time keeping pace with her. "Haven't seen you here before. Don't get around to visiting much, do you?" Sister Mary Jean says.

"No," I say, guilty as sin.

"No matter. You don't have to tell me how hard it is to watch your loved ones wither. Lose their minds a little bit more every day, they do. Not much help for them, really. All we can do is provide comfort. Both for them and their families." She stops and raises a hand as if she suddenly remembered something. "Your mum is a different story, though. Got a sharp mind, that one. Sharp as a tack. There's not much that gets past Wilhemena. To be honest, I'm not so sure they've got Wilhemena diagnosed properly. She doesn't act like a schizophrenic."

"Then what does she have?"

Sister Mary Jean stops. "Not sure she has anything."

"You don't think she's mentally ill?" I say, my voice rising.

"No. I think her mind is perfectly fine," Sister Mary Jean says.

The air is thick with the smell ammonia and blood. I halt. "Then what has she been doing here for all these years?"

"You'd have to ask her that."

"Sister, I don't mean to sound ungrateful, but why would you keep her if she's not sick?" I ask.

"I didn't say she wasn't sick. I said her mind is perfectly fine. Her heart—that's another story."

"Her heart?" My words come out like vinegar.

"There's no need for anger. God has given you a gift tonight. A chance to say good-bye to your mother."

Some gift. She gave me up when I was seven. One day everything's fine, the next I'm living with complete strangers. No warning. No explanation. Knowing my mother was crazy was the only thing that made it bearable. And now, I find out that she's perfectly fine. What the hell has she been doing for the past thirty-one years? Weaving baskets? Knitting potholders?

"When you lose someone you love, the pain can be blinding," Sister Mary Jean says.

"I didn't lose her. She left."

Sister Mary Jean pulls her glasses off and looks at me, her eyes a well of kindness. "I wasn't talking about you, dear."

With that she walks, and I follow.

"This is the infirmary," she says. "I had to move her from her room yesterday."

I pause. Everything in me resists going through.

"Just take it slowly. She's been asking for you for the past twelve hours. She's a fine lady, your mother. Talked about you almost every day. She loves you very much."

No, she doesn't, I'm about say, but I hold my tongue. "Is there anything else I should know?" I ask.

"She loved you. What else could there be?"

Answers, for one. I'm about to enter the room, when a big orange tabby cat appears at my feet, out of nowhere. It glares at me, its tail beating a rhythm in the air.

"That's Wilhemena's cat, come to say hello. We're not supposed to have pets here, strictly speaking. Made an exception for Wilhemena though. I don't suppose you'd be willing to take the creature home with you? Once your mother passes, that is? Wouldn't be fair to the other patients who want pets."

Great. One more living thing to care for. At least my kids will be excited to have a cat. Besides, how can I say no to a nun who's cared for my mother the past three decades? "Sure," I say and push open the infirmary door.

The room is dark and smells of earth, a pleasant contrast to the institutional odor in the hallway. In the last bed on the left, a bedside lamp illuminates a tangle of wild white hair.

I walk toward her, taking in the details of her little by little. Her face is creased, like a sinkhole in the earth. Her nose is longer than I remember, and more crooked. Is that my nose? Are those my cheeks, holding up the last vestige of life on her face? She looks ancient. When I get to her bed she looks at me, her eyes cloudy and pale blue, paler than any eyes I've ever seen. I can't tell whether or not she recognizes me.

I sit on the edge of the bed and take her hand, which is ice cold and feels like wax. The knuckle bones make valleys across paper-thin skin dotted with brown liver lakes. A heart monitor beeps, but there is little in the way of medical equipment in this run-down room.

My chest tightens. I should have come here sooner. She was a bad mother, a deserter, an abandoner. No doubt about that. But no one deserves to die alone, like this.

"Mother, it's me Allison," I say. "Do you know who I am?"

She speaks so softly I can barely hear her. "Mary. Mary."

"No. It's Allison."

"Mary, Mary
Quite contrary
How does your garden grow?"

"With silver bells
And cockle shells
And pretty maidens all in a row."

Aha. Now I remember why I didn't try to come again. My
mother *is* batshit crazy. Forget what the nice nun said. "Let me
get you some water. Or Jell-O." I stand up, but she grabs me by
the arm and pulls me down.

She sits up slowly. Her eyes connect with mine. "Allesone.
You've become a woman."

"Yes, Mother. That happens."

She takes my face in her hands and inspects me so fiercely
that I have to look away. Her hands move around my face, and
all I want to do is get out of there. When I look back at her, her
eyes are no longer cloudy, but clear and sparkling. "You're beautiful," she says.

I pull away from her. I feel like I'm going to cry.

She takes my hand and strokes it. "I've waited long for this
day," she says.

"You could have called," I say.

"I can leave now."

"You already left, Mother. Thirty-one years ago."

My tone is sharp but I don't care. She doesn't even seem to
notice my anger. She just studies me, her eyes sparkling.

"Allesone, did you remember your Lessons?"

"What Lessons?"

"Tell me the properties of wild ginger," she says.

"I don't know. They didn't teach things like that in school."

Her smile deepens. "Your Lessons have run away. But they'll
come back."

"I don't . . . I'm not . . ."

"Wild ginger. Classification: *Zingiber officinale*. Restores health and prevents illness. Mix with two parts comfrey and one part . . ."

"I don't remember any of that stuff."

She lays a hand against my chest right above my heart. "Worry not. It's in here. You'll see."

I grab her hand and yank it away a little more roughly than I intend to. "Whatever," I mumble, sounding more like my adolescent daughter than a grown woman should. *She has little time left,* I hear Sister Mary Jean say, and I decide I don't want to spend the last few hours of my mother's life fighting.

Now there are tears in her eyes. "I'm so sorry," she says.

I'm silent.

"I should have told you sooner, daughter."

"Told me what?" I say softly. Here it is. Here's where she's going to tell me she loves me, that abandoning me when I was so young and vulnerable was a cruel mistake. That she regrets all of it. That I deserved better.

"That you're in danger, Allesone. The enchantment dies with me."

Not exactly what I was hoping for. "I'm not in any danger," I say, my voice edged in disappointment.

"I'm so sorry, daughter. I tried to protect you. You must protect yourself now. Your Lessons will save you."

"Stop it."

"You must return to the Old Ways. They will keep you safe."

"I live in Monrovia. The only danger is getting a parking ticket."

"You are a witch of the Ellylydan Coven. Your blood is my blood. The enchantment is impermanent. It only conceals you whilst I am alive. When I die, the enchantment goes with me and you shall be revealed for who you are."

"You don't even know who I am," I say.

"Your name is Allesone Griselda Gwendyn Ellylydan Darling. You were born in the House of Saturn Rising. You have a birthmark on the back of your neck in the shape of a pentacle. You had a pet unicorn named Marshal when you were little. You fed it cranberries we picked from the bog. You are married to Kevin Darling of 13 Purchase Street in Monrovia, Massachusetts. You have three children—Gillian, Henry, and Sophie. You worry about your son more than you need to, and your daughter less than you should. You are my daughter. You have the power of transformation. You are the greatest joy of my life."

My throat closes up as I choke back my surprise.

"Everything I did, I did because I love you," she says. "But she is near. I can feel her. The Dark Witch will come for you. You will have to protect yourself from now on. And your family."

My heart skips a beat at the mention of the Dark Witch. I've always thought the Dark Witch was a figment of my imagination. My own private nightmare. The constant, unwanted companion of my youth. I've been running from her my whole life, but I've never known why. I've never known whether she was real or make-believe. And I've never spoke of her to anyone.

"Find Aurora. She will show you the Old Ways," my mother says.

Tears pool in my eyes, making everything blurry. The room closes in on itself. I need to know more about the Dark Witch, but the question that rises to my lips is more pressing. "Mother, why did you leave me?"

She grips my hand so hard I think the bones might crack. "Remember, Allesone, what you think, so it becomes."

Her eyes close and I can feel her leave the room. As if one moment she was and the next, she wasn't.

CHAPTER 5

There was an old woman
Lived under a hill;
And if she's not gone,
She lives there still.

Misery Shoal · *1949*

The salt marsh was no good for farming, but Elizabeth kept chickens, pigs, and a couple goats on a fen where the land stayed dry amidst the wet earth all around. In the early spring, they could smell the mud and algae warming in the sun at low tide, its brief moment to shine before the marsh sprouted green with grass that shaded all the life below it.

As the youngest, Freya and Aurora were tasked with feeding the animals and protecting them by casting hexes on coyotes and foxes.

"Do your Lessons while you work," Elizabeth told them as they headed to the fen one bright June day.

"Pennyroyal," Freya said, thrashing at the overgrown sedge with a stick. In her other hand she carried the apothecary kit that was required for spell casting.

"Ummm. Pennyroyal. Pennyroyal. Let me think. Latin name . . . *Mentha pennyroyalis?*"

A harrier flew low overhead before diving toward the mud and plucking out a crab.

"*Mentha pulegium,*" Freya corrected.

"*Mentha pulegium. Mentha pulegium. Mentha pulegium.*" Aurora knocked herself in the head with each repetition, hoping to pound the knowledge into her brain.

"Description?" Freya continued.

"Leaves like mint. Purple buds in first spring moon."

"Uses?"

"Cures stomach ailments, including cramps, and repels insects."

"Potion?"

"Combine with water element. Add one part pennyroyal, two parts coriander, two parts . . . meadowlark?"

Freya turned and pointed her stick sharply into Aurora's chest. "One part pennyroyal to two parts meadowlark! That would give you a deadly case of indigestion. It's one part pennyroyal, five parts coriander, eight parts belladonna. Brew for twelve minutes."

Aurora repeated the potion over and over. She stopped to watch a snail traveling seaward, a long shiny trail marking its journey in the mud.

"Try another one," Freya said, unlatching the gate to the animal pen. "Asafetida."

"I know that one!" Aurora declared. "Asafetida. Also called devil's dung. Latin name *Ferula assa-foetida*. Drives away evil forces and cleanses a confined area. Description: root of a fennel-like plant with yellow flowers."

"Potion?"

"Potion . . . um . . . let me think . . . one part asafetida to five parts . . . mugwort?"

Freya doubled over laughing. "Mugwort? Honestly, Aurora, you're going to make a pitiful witch."

Aurora bit her bottom lip. Potions were her weakness. There were infinite combinations of herbs and roots and plants that had to be memorized as well as countless methods of brewing, burning, chopping, grating, and pulverizing ingredients into just the right consistency. She was baffled by how her sisters could keep them all straight. Sometimes Aurora wished she could just go to school like the kids in town. From what she knew about the world, school seemed a thousand times easier than witchcraft. Kids got to sit at comfortable desks and paint pictures, and there seemed to be endless amounts of playtime.

Life and death weren't at stake in school. But in witchcraft, if you didn't know how to mix an arachnid antidote, you could die. If you didn't cast a protective spell on your farm animals, then they would perish at the mouths of predators. Witches were the protectors of life, the healers, the guardians of the natural order. Their craft was passed down from mother to daughter for all time. Elizabeth instilled in them the divine importance of their work. And yet Aurora felt these responsibilities to be a ferocious burden. Maybe Freya was right. Maybe she would be a pitiful witch.

Aurora preferred simple labor. Hauling water, foraging, chopping wood. At eight she was already as strong as a mule. She took excellent care of the animals, taking great joy in assisting births, or exercising care when tending to hoof rot and other ailments. At times when Aurora felt her failures as a potion maker eat away at her, Elizabeth reminded her that communicating with animals was a great skill and one that a witch could be proud of.

When they were both inside the gate, Freya latched it behind them.

"I'll do the feeding," Aurora offered.

"You can't remember the hex, can you?" Freya said.

"Would you rather do the feeding?"

"No."

"Then you cast the hex," Aurora said, sticking her lower lip out at her sister.

"They're just animals," Freya retorted. "We're going to eat them all eventually."

The chickens pranced over to Aurora as she heaved the bag of feed she'd been carrying off her back. She sprinkled it around the coop and tossed it to the chickens, who eagerly pecked at the ground. *Don't worry. You're safe today,* Aurora told them, trying to comfort them through her mind speak.

Freya opened the small apothecary kit and set it on the ground. She took out her mortar and pestle. She added a root of asafetida and five leaves of rue. The root was tough and had to be pounded and ground until it broke apart. When the plants formed a paste, she dug three large scoops of earth element and added them to the mixture. Then she walked around the perimeter of the pen spreading the potion in a protective circle.

Meanwhile Aurora gathered fresh eggs in a basket. Like a proud mother, she picked up one of the chickens and petted it.

Freya looked up from her work and saw the perfect opportunity to try out the flying ointment she'd been working on. She took a small glass vial from her pocket and opened the cork. When the vapors inside mixed with the air element, they turned bright orange, just as Freya had hoped. She blew the orange gas toward her sister. As it neared the chicken, it seeped in through the breath holes on the beak. The chicken snorted. Then, very slowly, it rose out of Aurora's arms and drifted sky ward. As it rose higher and higher, the chicken looked around, nervous about its aerial perspective. It flapped its wings and bawked.

"She's scared," Aurora hollered. "Put her down."

Freya watched intently as the chicken rose through the air. A couple of wrens dived past the chicken, lured by the yellow kernels of feed below.

"Put. Her. Down," Aurora repeated.

"Fine," Freya said, and with a swish of the stick she'd been carrying, she broke through the orange gas. The chicken descended downward and hit the ground with a thud. It got up, shook its tail feathers, and scurried back into the coop.

Freya laughed at her little trick.

"That was cruel," Aurora said. "And besides, Mother forbids it."

It was true. Elizabeth forbade her daughters from practicing witchcraft for any purpose other than protection or healing.

Aurora and Wilhemena obeyed this and all of Elizabeth's rules, but Freya's ambitions only grew under the restraints her mother placed on them. In secret, she worked on her own potions by flashlight under a blanket, after everyone else was asleep.

"You're just jealous you can't do it, too," Freya sneered.

Aurora turned sharply and moved into the goat pen. The goats were her favorite. Like puppies, they jumped on top of her and licked her face. She picked up the small one, whom she had named Edmund, and scratched his belly. "Time to eat, little one," she told him. She spread out the goat feed, and stood by to make sure that Freya didn't try any more funny business.

"I have to go muck out the pen," Aurora said to the goats, this time speaking out loud since she wasn't completely confident in her ability to communicate through mind speak. At least, not yet. She picked up a pitchfork that was leaning against the fence. "I'll be right back."

Aurora swept the pitchfork back and forth, the muscles in her shoulders working hard against the weight of the salt hay. She didn't see Edmund prance up behind her. He was looking for a treat, knowing in his goat way that her back pocket was always filled with corncobs and apples and delicious things to nibble.

It was freakish timing—the backward stroke of her pitchfork stopped short by the little goat's neck. He let out a terrible cry and fell to the ground.

"Edmund. Oh Edmund. I'm so sorry. It was an accident," Aurora wailed, cradling his head on her lap.

Red streaks seeped into Aurora's smock. The tine of the pitchfork had pierced the goat's artery, and blood was spurting in a geyser.

"Quick, Freya, it's Edmund. He's hurt," Aurora yelled. She put her hand over the wound and pressed, but blood continued to flow.

Freya came quickly. She stopped at the sight of her sister cradling the dying goat.

"Please, Freya. *Do* something," Aurora pleaded.

"What do you want me to do?"

"I don't know. Make a salve?" She was shaking.

Freya looked at her with contempt. "He's your pet. You should make the salve."

"But, but I'm not sure how," Aurora cried.

"Maybe you should work harder on your potions."

"Please," Aurora begged. "He's going to die if the bleeding doesn't stop."

Edmund's eyes were wild, his breathing labored.

"He's suffering," Freya said. "You should put him down."

Aurora could hardly see through the tears. "I know you can help him. I'll do anything, Freya, anything you ask. Just save Edmund for me." Then she saw the life drain out of Edmund's eyes and she wailed, scattering the wrens into the air.

Wilhemena heard the cries all the way to the ridge where she was tending the fire.

She ran down the ridge to the house and into the kitchen where she threw open the cabinets and rifled through boxes and jars, until she found the tin can that held the soap. The soap they had made on the harvest moon.

She sliced off a chunk of the soap and threw it in a jar with hot water. By the time she got to the fen, Edmund's eyes were closed, his body still, Aurora covered in blood and tears.

"I killed him," Aurora cried.

"We were just going to eat him anyway," Freya said.

"I'm sorry, Edmund. I'm so sorry," Aurora wailed.

Wilhemena knelt down beside her youngest sister. She shook the jar and poured the sudsy water over the wound. Then she recited the oldest spell:

"One for sorrow,
Two for luck,

Three for a wedding,
Four for a death,
Five for silver,
Six for gold,
Seven for a secret,
Never to be told."

Nothing happened at first. Aurora felt for a heartbeat but there was none. Then an ear twitched. Soon, the other. The girls looked at each other, then back to the goat. His eyes opened next. After another minute he jumped to his feet. He shook his body, and pranced back to the other goats, his neck and head streaked with blood.

All three girls were silent. They had never seen an animal die and come back to life.

Aurora threw her bloody arms around Wilhemena. "Thank you. Oh, thank you."

Freya turned to Wilhemena. Her voice was strained. "What was in that jar?"

Wilhemena looked into Freya's eyes, searching for the secret hidden deep in her soul. "You know what it was."

Freya stood defiantly, unwilling to offer up the truth.

"It was the soap from the harvest moon," Wilhemena said.

CHAPTER 6

Pussy-cat, pussy-cat, where have you been?
"I've been to London to look at the queen."
Pussy-cat, pussy-cat, what did you do there?
"I frightened a little mouse under the chair."

I wanted a cat my whole life," Sophie shrieks. She hugs the cat mightily. The cat licks syrup off Sophie's perpetually sticky flannel pajamas. "I want to call her Cleo."

"Then we'll call her Cleo," I say, even though, statistically, Cleo is the most common name for a house cat, and this is not your common house cat.

"Where'd the cat come from?" Gillian says, rubbing her eyes and yawning, as she makes her way down the stairs.

I spread peanut butter on a row of bread and jelly on the facing row, keeping the PB-to-J ratio even, then I proceed to lie to my children. "She's a stray. I found her on the front porch this morning and she looked hungry." Guilt like bubblegum in my hair. But what am I supposed to say? *You had a grandmother who died last night, who lived nearby, who I never told you about, who lived the last part of her life in an insane asylum even though she was perfectly sane. And, by the way, she was a witch. And, oh yes, while we're at it, so am I. And you probably are, too. Off to school now.*

I've had two hours of sleep, I've just lost my mother, and I'm not prepared for that conversation. For the moment, the greatest hardship in my children's lives is eating sandwiches with the crust on. I'd like to keep it that way for as long as possible.

"She's Cleo," Sophie announces.

Gillian empties the box of Cap'n Crunch into her bowl. "Mom, we're out of cereal," she says and studies her vocabulary words for a test today.

You worry too much about your son, and not enough about your daughter. What did she mean by that?

Rufus catches a whiff of Cleo. He pushes his nose into the carpet then runs wildly around the living room. When he calms down, he tries to mount her. Cleo whacks him on the muzzle, scratching her claws into his nose.

Rufus retreats in pain, comes back at her, gets walloped again on the nose. Soon Cleo tires of Rufus and his simple ways and leaps onto the fish tank. She walks around the edge of it, thrashing her tail side to side. Nemo the Seventh (Nemo the First through the Sixth have long since perished) starts swimming frantically around the castle in his tank, tracing figure eights through the water. Cleo meows, and Nemo the Seventh dives into the toy castle.

She climbs the steps and I follow. And cats are supposed to be the curious ones.

Upstairs, Fluffy the hamster and Bevis the mouse behave just as strangely in Cleo's presence, sniffing around, taking cover in their pee-stained balsa wood huts. She prances into Henry's room next. George, the tarantula, paws the glass of his terrarium when Cleo walks by. It's as though the animals are attracted to then repelled by Cleo. I wonder if they can smell the scent of crazy on her, a harbinger of the future, animals being sent to help convalesce old folks. Whatever it is, I've never seen animals behave like this.

Cleo jumps on Henry's Superman comforter and licks his ear. Henry stirs, but doesn't wake.

"Time for school," I say softly, not wanting to startle him any more than he's going to be when he sees what's on his bed.

Eyes still closed, his hands find Cleo and pet her. He opens his eyes, sits up, and continues petting this strange cat as though they were old acquaintances. It's odd for a child to react this way, to be so familiar with a cat he's just met. Then it hits me. Familiar. That's exactly what this cat is—Wilhemena's familiar, the spirit that's supposed to accompany witches throughout their lifetimes, helping them carry out their worldly deeds. They pop up in every witch tale from *Macbeth* to *Harry Potter*. But the stories always have it wrong. They paint witches as all good or all evil. Let me set the record straight: Witches are just as dysfunctional, selfish, narcissistic, neurotic, and messed up as anyone else. At least in my experience.

"This is Cleo," I say to Henry.

"Cleo," he repeats. He rubs her neck and she stretches out.

Gently, he lifts Cleo to the floor, slides into his bathrobe and heads downstairs, as if this were all normal morning routine. Cleo follows on his heels.

Downstairs, Kevin walks in the door. He's already been out for a run this morning. His shirt is covered in sweat, his cheeks flushed. He grabs a glass of water from the sink and kisses me on the cheek. He motions me into the hallway.

"You okay?" he asks.

"I'm okay."

"You sure?" He rubs my shoulders and I want to sink into him.

I nod.

"Did she . . . ?"

"Yeah. Gone."

"I'm sorry," he says and hugs me. He looks into my eyes for signs of my emotional state, but I don't feel sad. I haven't even cried yet. In fact, I don't feel much of anything right now. It doesn't seem real. The conversation with my mother is playing in a loop through my mind. *Everything I did, I did because I love you,* she said. What is it that she did, other than slip away? Abandon me? Did she really love me? Why didn't she tell me sooner? Did I even tell her that I loved her before she died?

Do I love her?

"Why are you sorry, Dad?" Gillian asks from the kitchen.

Her ability to hear and repeat a conversation verbatim from the next room while simultaneously studying for a test is astonishing.

"It's nothing," I tell her. Then to Kevin, "You'll have to pick the kids up from school today. I have an errand."

"Take as much time as you need," he says. A line of sweat runs down his neck into his collar.

Once everyone's out of the house, I search online for my aunt: Aurora Epatha Ellylydan. Last known address: the forest. No phone, no address, no place of employment, no known residence. *No results for this inquiry,* the site tells me. No kidding.

I can't even remember what she looks like.

I only have the foggiest of memories of Aunt Aurora. When I was little, I called her the Mushroom Lady because she used to take me mushrooming in the summers, and because she looked like a mushroom—short and fleshy. Kind of smelled like one, too. Aunt Aurora would show me her secret hiding spots where chanterelles and black trumpets grew in great billowing masses along the roots of conifers. The thrill of discovering a black trumpet camouflaged in leaves was on par with spotting a family of rabbits on the fen, or finding a patch of wild raspberries in summer. I can still taste sorrel tarts and chanterelle soups, maple whitecap cookies.

My mother and Aurora would argue over their medicinal properties and the best way to prepare them. "Fried. In lots of butter," Aurora contended. It was a happy time for me—my mother, Aurora, and I foraging in the woods, or on the beach, or in the marsh. They taught me about plants. Brushwood, crosswort, hawthorn, alder trees, nettles, bent grass, reed, rye, orache, flax, cress—I knew the names of plants before I knew the names of states, or presidents, or friends. I knew which ones to avoid and which ones healed.

After my mother left, Aurora never bothered to look for

me. She could have adopted me herself. For the first few months, I kept waiting and waiting for her to show up, but she vanished, too.

I know it's a long shot, but I decide to drive to the woods west of Salem where we used to forage. Where Wilhemena, Aurora, and I spent bewitching summer days under the canopy of forest, looking for mushrooms.

Greylock Woods is just like I remember it, except for the interpretive nature trail map from the parks department and complimentary dog poop composting bags installed at the trailhead. On the trail, the smell of moss and earth comes rushing back to me. The woods are beautiful, wild, and raw, and a welcome contrast to the manicured landscape of Monrovia. It starts to sprinkle but the trees shield me from most of the rain. All I can hear is the pitter-patter of drops on soft leaves.

I follow the trail all the way to Peter's Pond and then forge my own path, relying on an anemic vein of memories to guide me. For a while I walk along the edge of the pond, the rain so fine now it's like a mist that turns the surface of the water from black to silver. At the pointy end of the pond, I bushwhack my way back to the woods, wondering which direction to go, thinking, briefly, that I might be lost. Eventually I come to an old stone wall, the remnants of a long-abandoned homestead, and this gives me hope. I remember this landmark. The wall leads to a brook that bends almost 180 degrees back on itself, like water running uphill. Frogs crowd together on a rock.

I just keep walking and walking. Hours seem to pass, and I realize I've left my phone in the car. Without the sun above, I can't tell if it's morning or afternoon. I walk until my legs get tired and I have to sit down, the lack of sleep from last night creeping up on me like a bad hangover. The ground here is thick with pine needles. There's a microcosm of life on the forest floor—all these species evolving to live in the absence of sunlight. Ferns with shortened leaves, plants that feed on the bacteria from rotting leaves and bark. I find myself automatically scavenging, searching high and low for edible plants the way I did when I was a kid.

My eyes catch sight of a dark patch on the far side of a massive pine. Black trumpets—jackpot! Suddenly I am five years old, running for the fragrant, fleshy, delicate mushrooms. I pinch off a few caps and I'm about to eat one raw when a voice from behind startles me.

"Thief! Drop those black trumpets. Those are mine!" An old woman is rushing toward me out of nowhere. She's short and plump, like a mushroom.

Before I can speak, she grabs the mushroom out of my hand. She's wearing four or five ragged sweaters, mismatched wool gloves, and a man's fedora. A goat follows behind her.

A goat I've definitely seen before.

"Aunt Aurora?"

She looks up from under the brim and frowns. She eyes me up and down.

"Well I'll be damned! Little Allesone. Hell's bells. Looks like you finally grown into your face. I always told my sister, 'She's a smart girl you got Wilhemena, but boy she got the ugly gene.' Must of come from the father's side. Well, you know, your mother ain't much of a looker neither. Not like me." She laughs hysterically, even though I don't see the humor in it.

"You look . . . the same," I tell her. Aurora, too, looks ancient. Her body is even more crooked than Wilhemena's.

Aurora puts her hands on her hips and wipes her nose with the back of a glove.

"Figured you for dead by now!" Aurora says nonchalantly.

"Why would you say that?" I ask. It seems an odd statement even for Aurora.

She coughs into her hand. "Well, I never heard from ya. That's why."

"*You* never heard from *me*," I say, incredulous. "I was a

child. And you aren't easy to find. Why didn't *you* try to find *me*?"

Aurora plops her huge rucksack on the ground and opens it. It's full of leaves and berries, flowers and roots of all varieties. She takes out a knife and slices through the base of the black trumpets, sticking them in the sack. "Wasn't supposed to," she says.

"According to who?"

She looks at me like I'm the one who's out of line. "Wilhemena, of course."

"Why would she tell you not to look for me?"

"You'd have to ask her that."

I take a deep breath and try to compose myself. *Do what you're here to do. Then get out.* "Aurora, there's something I have to tell you."

She peels a piece of bark off a tree, bites off the lichens, and spits them into her rucksack. "Well, spit it out."

"Wilhemena died yesterday."

She slumps to the ground, her body a shapeless mound beneath all her layers.

I walk up to her. "I'm sorry," I say. "I know you were close once."

"But how? How can that be?" Aurora moans.

I search for the right words. "Do you know that she's been in Saint Bernadette's for the past thirty-one years? The *psychiatric* hospital."

"Was she sick?"

"Apparently not. Not in the insane way, that is. But she was ill for the past week. They said she was in and out of consciousness a lot."

"Taken in her prime like that."

"She was seventy-eight."

"So virile."

I clear my throat. "She wanted me to find you. She was talking about you right at the end."

There's a long pause. Aurora pulls a corncob out of her pocket and feeds the goat. She scratches behind its ears and kisses it on the head. When she looks up, there are tears in her eyes.

"Aunt Aurora, do you know why my mother left me? I thought she might finally give me some answers, but she was just rambling on about the Dark Witch. Do you know what she was talking about?"

"What did she say, exactly?"

"She said that the enchantment dies with her. That the Dark Witch will come. She said I had to protect myself now." Goose bumps rise on my arms. "She said I have to protect my family. Does that mean something to you?"

"No child, that means something to *you*."

"What? What does it mean? Is my family in real danger?"

"Not too bright after all, are you?" She takes some berries out of her bag and pops them in her mouth. Offers some to me.

"No. Thank you." *I don't want any of the berries from the sack that you just spit in,* I think.

"We'll have to see her out, of course. I'll have to let the others know."

"See her out?"

"It'll have to be in secret, as you can imagine. You'll have to be there, of course." There's a hint of contempt in her voice. But she's getting off subject. I need answers. I touch her shoulder.

"Aurora, who is the Dark Witch and why is she going to come after my family?"

Aurora looks at me in disbelief. "The Dark Witch is Freya, dum-dum."

"Who's Freya?"

"My other sister. Your other aunt."

Aurora gathers up her bag, cramming in bits of bark and mushrooms. She rushes off. I rush after her.

"Wait. Are my kids in danger? Should I take this seriously?"

Aurora runs like a duck and I catch her easily. I raise my voice. "Wilhemena told me to find you. That you would show me the Old Ways."

"So you come here expecting me to show you the Old Ways, like I got nothing better to do! I don't see you since you were yay high, and now I'm supposed to just drop everything and come in and rescue you?"

I throw my hands up. "Rescue me! Rescue me? You abandoned me. Just like Wilhemena. You never even tried to find me. I was seven, Aurora! And now my mother tells me that I'm in danger, that my family, my *kids,* are in danger and you just walk away again! What kind of person are you?"

Aurora stares at me, the mist collecting on the fine hairs of her face. She reaches into her rucksack and pulls out a black root, dirt stuck to it in clumps, a white flower attached on top. She jams it into my hand. "Take that with you."

"What is it?"

She rolls her eyes at me. "Angelica, of course."

I take the root and turn it over in my hands.

"You do know what it's for, don't you?" Aurora says.

I shake my head.

"By Ursula's bosom! You don't know nothing, do you? You don't even know what you are. You say Wilhemena was in and out of consciousness for her last days? Let me ask you something: Have you had any strange sensations in the last day or two? Your head feel like it was being pinched by a lobster? Anything unusual happen?"

I think of the dancing pigs and the onion incident at the Apple Harvest. I'd say that classifies as unusual. And then I got sick and fainted at the Glamour Soap party. And yes, it felt exactly like my head was being pinched by a lobster. "Yeah, I've had some strange things happen."

"Like what?"

"My magic's coming back," I say. "And I had a fainting spell at a party last night."

"Ah-h-h. That was the enchantment wearing off!" Aurora shouts. "Freya is near, that much I promise you. And Wilhemena can't protect you no more now as she's dead. You're special, Allesone. Always were. Meant the world to my sister to protect you. And now she can't protect anyone no more, rest her soul."

"What should I do? What about my kids?"

Aurora doesn't answer. After a few moments she speaks, and this time her voice is calmer. "Take that angelica root and any time as you start to feel yourself go sick, rub it three times on the back of your hand. It's the best way to ward off evil. Works against plagues, too."

She turns and walks off into the woods, the little goat prancing after her. "Come on, Edmund," she says to him.

CHAPTER 7

A gift, a friend, a foe,
A letter to come, a journey to go.

It's 10:30 P.M. when Kevin gets home from work and I'm already in bed. Finalizing his proposal for the waterfront project has required long hours bent over blueprints of ventilation schematics, elevations, and a thousand engineering details that most of us take for granted when we walk into a building.

I pretend to be asleep as he pulls off his jeans and chucks them in a corner of our room. He crawls into bed and I can smell the day of work on him, notes of ink and sawdust.

I decide to be awake. I need to be touched tonight. I need to feel secure and loved and that my family is okay, because after today, I'm not so sure.

I open my eyes to streaks of moonlight against the wall that's covered in kids' artwork. Big red hearts made of construction paper. Drawings of rainbows and flowers and houses with circles of gray crayon smoke coming from the chimney. Henry's stick figures of superheroes in capes. A Father's Day card of an oversize necktie. A Mother's Day bouquet made of tissue paper so faded it's white. Kevin wants to store these things in a drawer somewhere, or in the attic, so we can take them out years from now and remember when. I like having them out where I can see them, though.

"You awake?" Kevin asks.

"Mm-hmm."

His rough, callused hands caress my thigh. I want to tell him about my conversation with Aurora, but I can just imagine his response. *A Dark Witch is after your family? Sounds like a job for Ghostbusters.*

Aurora gave me a magical root that's supposed to help me, I'd say and he would question if insanity ran in my family.

I would finally have to come clean and tell him that I am a witch. That my mother was a witch. That I have magic, even though I can't really control it. And he'll look at me, wondering why he married a pagan, and find a divorce lawyer first thing in the morning.

No, he won't understand. He won't believe.

"How's the project?" I ask.

"It's getting there. I think it's exactly what this town needs." He sighs. It's the sigh he uses whenever he's thinking about money. "I have to win this bid, Allison. We need it."

I interlace my fingers through his to let him know I believe in him.

He pulls his hand out of mine and sweeps it under my T-shirt. I move closer to him.

He kisses the back of my neck, and I can feel the heat of his breath against the raised skin of my birthmark. I turn my head so the back of my neck presses into the pillow, away from his touch.

Suddenly, there is a cry in the dark from down the hall. It's not an "I've fallen off the bed and hurt myself" cry, but a terrified shriek. It's Sophie's nightmare.

I roll off the bed, and fly down the hall.

Sophie is sitting upright in her bed, eyes closed, face wet with tears, her arms extended for me before I even enter the room.

I pick her up and hold her on my lap. I cradle her, and rock her, and sing to her. "It's all right, I'm here."

She is still screaming, and I know this is The Dream, the recurring terror that visits her in the night.

As far as I can tell, it goes something like this: She is sitting on the ground, playing outside, when she hears a drum beating off in the distance. It grows louder as it approaches. But it's not a drum, it's a heartbeat, whether hers, or the snake's I don't know. The snake slithers up until it's right in front of her. Its head rises to meet hers, its black tongue flicking in and out, inches from her face. She tries to get up and run, but she's glued to the ground. She tries to scream, but nothing comes out. She looks around her and sees that she's surrounded by a million smaller snakes and the ground has become a slick, slithering mass.

The snake bites her, then she wakes up.

It's so real to her, that it will take hours before she can trust that it's only make-believe. I will sleep with her tonight, in her tiny toddler bed with the pink sheets and the yellow unicorns, where my feet hang over the edge. I will keep her safe. I will keep her nightmares make-believe.

Cleo lurches onto the bed and nuzzles against me. She purrs like an outboard engine. Her whiskers tickle my arm. I pet her head and scratch behind her ears. She rolls onto her back for me to scratch her belly.

"Are you real?" I whisper.

Cleo bites my hand, puncturing the skin. She licks the marks, her tongue like sandpaper. Her green eyes are directly on mine.

I'm talking to a cat. Maybe I should have my head examined. But I did turn that apple into an onion. That was real.

Once Sophie's asleep, I sneak out of her bed, down to the kitchen. There's a bowl of apples, lemons, and overripe bananas on the counter, so I pick one apple out. I close my eyes. I try to picture an onion in my mind. I envision the papery outer skin, the patch of roots on the bottom, and smell the sweet smell. I whisper the words.

> "Onion's skin very thin,
>   Mild winter coming in.
> Onion's skin thick and tough,
>   Coming winter cold and rough."

And, nothing. When I open my eyes the apple is still an apple. I try again, but nothing happens. Of course nothing happens. Apples don't turn into onions just because you say a silly old nursery rhyme.

I put the apple back in the bowl and return to Sophie's bed.

CHAPTER 8

Cackle, cackle, Madam Goose!
Have you any feathers loose?
Truly have I, little fellow,
Half enough to fill a pillow;
And here are quills, take one or ten,
And make from each pop gun or pen.

At church on Sunday, I bow my head and try to pay attention to Father Carter's closing prayer, but all I can think of is the Dark Witch. All these years my adult mind had just written her off as the stuff of my childhood imagination, the way some kids believe in the monster under their bed, or the zombie in their closet, or the snake in their nightmares.

Like Sophie's phantom snake, my Dark Witch was as real to me as my knobby knees and freckled nose. She was at least ten feet tall, dressed all in black, and very clever. She lurked in the dark corners of my room, waiting for the moment I fell asleep to snatch me up. Stop thinking about her, and that's when she'd get you, the antithesis of all imaginary friends. She was with me all the time, too. Night wasn't her only domain. She followed me home from school, hid out in every cemetery I passed, and in every empty passage of my mind.

Now, I find out that she wasn't imaginary, at least not entirely. I really did have an aunt who was a Dark Witch. How did I know about her if I can't remember ever seeing her? Why didn't my mother ever talk about her until the day she died? Why is Aurora so certain she's after me now?

Father Carter says the blessing and announces the volunteer opportunities around town—delivering welcome baskets to new families, planting bulbs along the Town Green, raking leaves off the church lawn. Perfecting. Beautifying.

My gaze wanders around the congregation, on Sandra Flanders's peacock feather earrings (a new trend I'm behind on?), Beth Walker's freshly Botoxed face, Jennifer Alberton's hair extensions.

Two pews in front of us, Bryson Proctor is hiding a video game in the weekly missal, out of view of his parents. Henry cranes his neck to get a better view. When that fails, he stands on the kneeler, and then onto the pew.

"Henry, no," I say in a church whisper.

Lilith turns around and glares at me. I give her an apologetic look and a cursory "oh what these little ones will do" shake of the head when a stab of pain pierces my neck, followed by a painful throbbing. The nausea I felt at the Glamour Party comes back and I feel dizzy. I reach into my purse and grasp on to the angelica root that Aurora gave me. My equilibrium comes back immediately. Is Lilith a witch, too?

The organ strikes up the recessional hymn and the altar servers lead the procession. My hand tightens on the angelica root.

Outside, all the parishioners visit for a few minutes, everyone commenting on the glorious weather, the inspiring sermon, on who's going to win the football game. Young kids swing from the monkey bars while teenagers cluster in groups, cool and aloof, hands jammed in pockets.

As we cross the parking lot, I notice it before anyone else. A piece of parchment stuck to the windshield of the minivan, too large to be a "Buy One Get One Free" advertisement from Monrovia House of Pizza, or a flyer for lawn-care service.

I rush ahead and grab the paper. The note is written in childlike scrawl:

Seeing Out for Wilhemena Ellylydan
Sunday at high noon

Saint Bernadette's
Remembrances requested

By the time I get to Saint Bernadette's, I'm already twenty minutes late. In the light of day, it doesn't seem as foreboding. Getting in the building is much easier this time, and once I'm inside, a nurse tells me where to find the chapel. I open the door quietly, expecting to interrupt the funeral service, but it's empty. Tall leaded windows are opened, and a breeze fills the room, flicking at the candles that have been lit to honor the dead. Could I have missed the entire service?

Sister Mary Jean enters shortly after me.

"I thought I heard someone. What a surprise to see you, Allison," she says.

"My mother's funeral is today," I say.

"Today? I shouldn't think so. No services were posted on the calendar. The hospital will organize it." Her face brightens. "We even have a patient who's a cellist. He'll play at the funeral, if you like."

I stand in the beautiful little chapel that's flooded with light, feeling silly. What did I think, that my crazy aunt would be able to pull off a funeral service by herself? Was I really expecting flowers and organ music?

A cacophony of animal noises sends both of us running to the window. By the stables, the horses and the pigs are running around in figure eights, making a ruckus. Past the stable is a cemetery and past the cemetery is a small cluster of people. *Here we go.*

The sister and I head outside, past the garden with its crops gone to seed, past the unplucked cornstalks, past the stable and cemetery to the clearing in a stand of white cedars. At first no one notices us. Aunt Aurora is arguing with an old woman holding a broomstick. Another woman is popping the heads off daisies and scattering them on the ground, and two of the tiniest men I've ever seen are sitting on the ground, rifling through an old trunk. The men are no taller than Henry. There's something familiar about them—their perfectly matching beards, their hunting caps pulled down over their ears.

"Are any of these people patients?" I ask Sister Mary Jean, on the off chance that this is a typical Sunday outing at the insane asylum.

"Certainly not." If she's freaked out by the array of characters, she doesn't let it show. "They're friends of your mother's, I suppose."

As I approach, the little men stop what they're doing and stare at me. One points. The other closes the trunk and climbs on top of it to get a better look at me. The woman with the daisies looks at me and genuflects.

"There she is."

"It's her, it's her, it's her."

"The Daughter."

"So it is."

"At last."

I look behind me, thinking they must be talking about someone else, but no one is there. I am the cause of all the commotion.

"Well, finally!" Aunt Aurora says, and grabs me by the arm. "What the hell took you so long?"

All eyes are on me. Aurora clears her throat and announces in a loud voice, "This here is Allesone. Daughter of Wilhemena. Coven of Ellylydan."

"Let's take a look at you," says an old woman, whose name I soon learn is Millie ("Short for Millicent," she says in a high-pitched voice that belies her age). Millie is holding a broomstick and wearing a straw hat, the kind you get on vacation in the Caribbean, that you simply must have until you get it home and realize how ridiculous it is set against the contents of your New England wardrobe.

Millie manhandles me, twirling me around so she can inspect all sides of me. "Yes, yes, yes. I can see the resemblance. Oh, yes, yes, yes, this is a great day. The Daughter has arrived."

The other old woman just stares at me, puffing on a cigar. Her fingers are bony, with ham hocks for knuckles. "Daughter of Wilhemena, your mother was a great friend and witch of the highest order." She blows a smoke ring in my face. "Hopefully, you're up to snuff."

I'm about to ask her what she means by that, but Aurora grabs me again and pushes me over to the others.

"Millie. Beatrice. Jonathon. Jinathon," Aurora barks by way of introduction.

One of the little men steps forward holding up a black cape for me to wear. "We thought you might need this," he says.

"You'll be more comfortable," the other man says.

"'Tis customary dress for a Seeing Out," the first man says.

"Brought you a broomstick, too," says the second man.

"Another custom," the first man adds.

Sister Mary Jean and I exchange looks as I slide the cape on.

"Do you know what this is all about?" she asks.

I shrug.

"Wilhemena deserves a proper service. With a priest. And prayer," Sister Mary Jean says.

Oh, the poor nun. When she said that Wilhemena was a witch, she probably meant a Wiccan, in the whimsical and mildly rebellious way of teenage girls.

Back in high school, there was a group of girls who dressed in black, wore crystals around their necks, and claimed they were Wiccan. They talked about worshipping the moon and the sun and Mother Earth. They drew pentagrams on their notebooks and could list all the Wiccan holidays. They petitioned the school for equal rights and one day they staged a protest, demanding to be recognized for their beliefs. Carrying signs that said WICCAN AND PROUD or I'M PAGAN AND I VOTE, they marched around the flagpole, chanting spells. They were cutting edge and trendy, and by third period, everyone in school wanted to be Wiccan. I wanted to be a Wiccan like them, and I really was a witch. But by lunchtime, when the need to eat and socialize prevailed, they moved on, leaving their religious convictions for the more important work of flirting with lacrosse players.

The only difference is that those girls were cool.

Sister Mary Jean addresses them: "Friends, our dear Wilhemena is with the Lord now. We should move the funeral into the chapel. I'll have the kitchen put out some coffee and cookies. Wilhemena would have wanted that. God bless her soul."

"Who are you?" Aurora barks.

"Sister Mary Jean Francis. Registered nurse."

Aurora plops down on the trunk next to the dwarf. She pulls the buckles tight and covers it with her coat. There's a small brass urn at the base of the trunk that Aurora tries to hide behind her boots.

"Are those dear Wilhemena's ashes? Are those her effects?" Sister Mary Jean's tone is cooling as she notices the hijacked goods.

"What's it to ya?" Aurora says.

"I'm afraid you can't just take someone's remains. There's paperwork to fill out," Sister Mary Jean says.

"My sister's ashes belong with us," Aurora says, and picks up the urn.

"There's protocol to follow. You must come inside now so we can sort this out."

Aurora shifts her eyes from the nun to the dwarf beside her. She gives him a funny little wink and he winks back. He opens the trunk, which is much larger than him, and shimmies himself over the lip so that his legs dangle a foot off the ground and his torso is completely inside.

"That's Wilhemena's trunk," Sister Mary Jean says. "He can't go through her things."

The dwarf rifles through the trunk's interior compartments,

grabs a few bottles and knickknacks, then wiggles back to his feet. "My apologies," he says sweetly.

"I insist that you all come inside," Sister Mary Jean says.

"We're fine just where we are," Aurora says.

"Aurora, Sister Mary Jean cared for my mother for thirty-one years. Let's do what she says," I say, wishing they could all just act normal.

"I ain't moving," Aurora snorts.

"I insist that you come inside at once," Sister Mary Jean repeats.

"Fine. But maybe you'll be so kind as to sign our guest book first." Then to Millie she says, "Get the guest book." Aurora winks at Millie just like she did with the dwarf.

Millie digs into the trunk and pulls out a large, leather-bound book. From under her hat she produces a feather quill. The dwarf who had been dangling in the trunk just moments earlier hands her a bottle of ink. Millie dips the nib of the quill in ink and hands it to Sister Mary Jean.

Beatrice and the dwarf circle around.

Sister Mary Jean takes the quill hesitantly and holds it up. A drizzle of ink runs down her hand. "The hospital is liable for these items. We have a protocol to follow . . ."

As Sister Mary Jean signs the book, I can hear the dwarves muttering something under their breath. I focus in on their words.

"Cackle, cackle Madam Goose!
Have you any feathers loose?
Truly have I, little fellow,
Have enough to fill a pillow."

Suddenly Sister Mary Jean stops speaking. She stops moving. Her face freezes. Her hands and arms are immobile. She looks like a statue, her eyes unblinking.

I wave my hand in front of her face. Nothing.

"What did you do?" I say to Aurora.

"She's fine. It'll wear off in an hour," Aurora says.

"*What* will wear off?"

"The old Cackle Cackle Madam Goose Elixir." Aurora takes the quill from the nun's hand and returns it to Millie, careful not to touch the ink.

"Is that poisonous?" I ask, fearing the worst.

Aurora pauses. "Not per se."

"We need to get this woman some medical attention. Something is seriously wrong here." I look back at the hospital, suddenly concerned that I might be complicit in . . . in . . . whatever this is.

"She was getting on my nerves with all that religious jibber jabber. Bunch of voodoo if you ask me," Aurora says.

"You can't go around freezing people," I say.

The dwarf slams the book shut and puts it back in the trunk. "Don't you know the Cackle Cackle Elixir, Sister Allesone?" he asks.

"NO!"

"It's the oldest trick in the book," the dwarf says, smiling, completely unfazed by the fact that he just performed witchcraft on a nun.

"We haven't got much time 'til the penguin wakes up. Everyone take a seat. Let's get the ball rolling," Aurora orders, and bangs a walking stick into the ground.

"Aurora, you can't just leave her frozen," I say.

"Don't worry. She won't remember a thing when she comes out of it. She'll probably think she was out for a stroll."

"A stroll?"

Aurora ignores me and proceeds with the Seeing Out. "First we'll have a few words of remembrance. Then we'll get to my sister's Last Wit and Wisdom. Jonathon, Jinathon, you're up," Aurora says, unceremoniously pointing a finger at the dwarves.

The dwarves walk up to the front of the group and speak in turns, rapidly.

"We will miss our dear departed Mother."

"She was a brilliant witch."

"An apt midwife."

Did he say midwife? As in, a profession? How did I miss that? My mind is racing. I'm still worried about Sister Mary Jean. I'm worried that someone from the hospital will come out and have us arrested, and I am completely confused about what this little man is saying.

"I remember the day we met her," the dwarf says.

"It was a Friday," the other dwarf says.

"Venus was in the House of Saturn."

"A good day."

"A very good day."

"We were left in a basket in the wood."

"Dear Wilhemena found us."

"She raised us as her own."

"Taught us everything we know."

"For fifty-ought years we were her sons."

"We bid her farewell."

"Sons?" I yell. "You weren't her sons. I didn't have any brothers. I think I would know if I had brothers." They look like they're about to cry and I feel awful, like I just squashed a ladybug or clubbed a baby seal.

Aurora shushes me and tells the dwarves to continue.

"But, above all," the dwarves are weeping and now they're speaking in unison, "she was a fine mother to Sister Allesone."

They each take one of my hands in theirs and kiss it.

I jerk my hands back.

"All right. Moving along. You next, Millicent," Aurora barks.

The dwarves back away from me, their heads bowed. I want this to end.

Millie walks up next. She looks about two hundred years old. There's not a straight bone in her body, and her face is carved with wrinkles. She says in her tiny, sweet voice, "I loved Wilhemena. 'Twas Wilhemena who taught me the cures of the three elements. Taught me to skin a rabbit, too. For that, I'll always be thankful.

"When the Dark Witch cast evil on our coven, Wilhemena sacrificed herself to save us and to conceal the Daughter. Those were hard times. Now we're on our own." Millie looks at me, then to everyone else. "Well, hopefully the Daughter is more powerful than she looks."

What on earth is she talking about? I look around to see if shock registers on anyone's face, but they're all nodding as though rabbit-skinning and Dark Witches were as normal as hot baths and manicures.

Millie walks over to me and squeezes my cheeks.

Beatrice gets up next. "I dunno about the Daughter. She seems kind of odd to me."

Millie pats me on the back. "Don't take it personally, honey. We all just feel a little lost without your mother right now."

Aurora pats me hard on the back. "Your turn."

"What?"

"Your turn. Say something about your mother."

"I don't really have anything to say."

"Go on," Millie cheers. "Don't be afraid."

"Um . . . Well . . ." I clear my throat. *Just say something and get out of here. Back to Normalville.* "Let's see, Wilhemena was . . ." I pause. I pause a little longer. Nothing is coming to me. The pause is beginning to feel heavy and impenetrable. I have to say something. "Wilhemena was my mother." I can see Jonathon and Jinathon on the edge of their seats waiting for what I'll say next.

Aurora butts in, "Just tell us what you remember about her."

"Okay. I remember that she smelled like moss. Not in a bad way. Just in an earthy, mossy kind of way." This is not going well. I try to cast my mind back. I close my eyes and think. Think. Think. Think.

I feel my body relax deep down in my muscles. Energy moves through me in waves that begin in the bottom of my feet and move up my legs, my spine, my neck, to the top of my scalp. I feel light inside. A window in my mind pops open. Suddenly, I can see the house I grew up in, in perfect detail— the pattern of sand-beaten shingles on the porch, the dunes spread out behind me. I can see the doe path that ran from the house up to the ridge. I can hear the song of the bullfrogs at night in the marsh. I can smell the wood fire and feel the warmth of my mother and I curled up in soft blankets as a nor'easter rages outside. The memories are coming back to me in a flood. Things I haven't thought of for years.

"Once I had a chipmunk I named Sebastian with a broken hind leg," I say. "Wilhemena wrapped its leg in bandages with goldenrod and bittersweet. I made a little bed for it out of a milk carton and a macramé blanket. We told him stories and took him for walks on the beach, Sebastian tucked in the pocket of my coat. She was very kind, my mother."

The memories pop into my head like grenades. Shrapnel from my life comes at me in rapid succession, with no sense of chronology. Details of things I once lost are right in front of me.

"I remember how injured animals would find her—a beaver, a bobcat, dozens of field mice, piping plover, a possum. A screech owl with a broken wing. Mother would tend to them with ointments and herbs. She was so good at it. She was a healer, wasn't she?"

Millie and Beatrice nod. I can see tears rolling down Millie's cheeks. I keep going, because now I can't stop the images from appearing in my mind's eye.

"She taught me Lessons. In the swamp, in the woods, on the beach. She knew every plant species by scientific name. She sang songs all the time and recited nursery rhymes. Oh my God, the nursery rhymes. She knew thousands of them. I'd completely forgotten about the nursery rhymes. She'd put me to bed every night, singing nursery rhymes."

Jonathon and Jinathon are bawling now. Millie and Beatrice have their arms intertwined.

"I miss my mother," I say. "I've missed her for a long time. She was my whole world. And then she was gone. I've been angry at her for so long, I forgot everything else."

Aurora speaks up again. "Okay, that concludes our remembrances."

Not a sentimentalist, my aunt. "Wait," I say. I want to keep talking about Wilhemena. I want to give the memories a chance to find their way back. "This is my magic, isn't it? I have the ability to see things in my mind that become. I remember now. I remember all of you. Wilhemena considered you family. That makes us family. Whatever danger you all think we're in, we can handle it together. I may not have much experience with potions and elixirs, but I'll work hard," I say. A rising sense of hope explodes in me. "All of us together can defeat one witch, right? It's like," I count everyone out on my fingers, "six against one. Those are good odds. All we have to do is work together. Like a coven. Like a family, right Aurora?"

Aurora looks at me, then down at the ground. Everyone else seems to communicate through their silence. I feel their lack of faith like a thousand fire ants on my skin.

"I'm one of you," I assure them.

Aurora finally speaks after what seems like forever. "We had to invite ya here because it was the right thing to do, for the memory of Wilhemena. But we don't want any trouble with the Dark Witch."

"Tell me what is so scary about her," I say, my voice cracking.

Aurora coughs. She spits a loogie. "It's time you found out. Was born evil, Freya. Our mother, your grandmother, done the best she could, but Freya pushed the boundaries. She did her own magic. She hurt a lot of people. Mind you, I was no match for Freya, but your mother, well, she was a strong witch. Skilled. When you come along, Freya got real scared that you were going to be powerful like Wilhemena. You showed some real promise early on, you did. Freya didn't want no competition, so when you were a little thing, she tried to off you, if you know what I mean. You nearly died. Would have died if Jonathon and Jinathon hadn't been there to save you.

"After that Wilhemena struck a bargain. She agreed to stop practicing the Craft and move away so long as Freya agreed to leave you alone. Poor Wilhemena had no choice but to disappear. She had to go into hiding and put an enchantment out to conceal you for who you were. As for the rest of us, Freya made us swear never to return to Misery Shoal, the place we grew up. 'Fine by me,' I told her. I'd seen too much heartbreak out there anyhow. 'Let it sink into the sea,' said I. 'Let it wash away with the tides.' That's what I said.

"Now that Wilhemena's dead, there's no telling whether Freya will keep up her end of the bargain."

"Doubt it," Jonathon says.

"Can't trust the Dark Witch," Jinathon adds.

I can't believe what I'm hearing. My own aunt tried to kill me? My mother went into hiding to protect me?

Sister Mary Jean's hand suddenly drops from its frozen position.

Aurora opens the trunk and digs through it until she finds a scroll of paper, which she unfurls. " 'The Last Wit and Wisdom of Wilhemena Allabaster Ellylydan,' " Aurora reads quickly.

Sister Mary Jean's other hand drops.

"We got to get to the will." She picks up the scroll again and reads: " 'I leave all my worldly possessions—my cauldron, cape, broom, lye, and ladle—to my sister Aurora, to disseminate as she sees fit. As for the contents of my apothecary kit, I leave all water elements to Beatrice. All air elements to Millicent. Earth elements to Jonathon. Fire elements to Jinathon.' "

The four witches sort through the elaborate box of jars and bottles filled with oils, liquids, dried herbs, charcoal, flowers, bugs.

"There's one more," Aurora says. Everyone stops rifling. "'To my daughter Allesone Ellylydan Darling, of 13 Purchase Street in Monrovia, I leave . . . my spirit element.'"

There is a gasp from all the witches. The cigar drops out of Beatrice's mouth. Jonathon and Jinathon shake their heads.

"What is the spirit element?" I ask.

Millie takes the urn and hands it to me. "She wanted you to have her ashes."

I take it.

"No," Jonathon says.

"We're the keepers of the spirit element," Jinathon says.

"Sister Allesone doesn't understand its power."

Beatrice speaks. "It's true, Aurora. The Daughter has much to learn."

"She wants me to have them," I say.

"I'll arm wrestle you for it," Jonathon says to me.

"She was my mother. I should have her ashes."

"But Aurora, Sister Allesone doesn't even know a simple sleeping elixir," Jonathon says.

"No offense to you, Sister Allesone," Jinathon says.

"It's true, Aurora. How can she protect the spirit element?" Millie says.

"She didn't even know about the Dark Witch," Beatrice adds.

"The spirit element is too powerful for a Commoner," Jonathon says.

"No offense," Jinathon says.

"I'm not a Commoner. I'm a witch, just like you," I say.

There's a loud crash that sounds like thunder, but there isn't a cloud in the sky. I realize the sound is coming from Aurora's walking stick, as she bangs it into the ground.

"Enough!" Aurora says. "We must trust Wilhemena's wisdom and do right by her. I can't make no sense of it either, but the spirit element goes to Allesone. Guard her well, lest she fall into the wrong hands."

Suddenly, with electric speed Jonathon jumps on top of the trunk, leaps into the air, and grabs the urn out of my hands. He lands on the ground, tucks it under his arm, and runs toward the forest.

"Run, Jonathon, run!" Jinathon hollers. Jinathon gathers up his bottles and jars and sprints in the same direction as his brother. "No offense, Sister Allesone," I hear him say as he disappears into the woods.

Aurora looks at me, her eyes softer than usual. "They mean well. You'll see."

Sister Mary Jean's shoulders move. Millie, Beatrice, and Aurora grab the trunk by the handles and carry it into the woods.

"Be careful," Aurora yells to me. "Freya'll be looking for you now."

Just as the three witches disappear into the shadows, Sister Mary Jean wakes up. She looks around. Then she looks at me. "What happened?" she asks.

"I have no idea," I say, which is the truth.

CHAPTER 9

Old Mother Goose,
When she wanted to wander,
Would ride through the air
On a very fine gander.

Mother Goose had a house,
It stood in the wood,
An owl at the door
As sentinel stood.

I t's the flying lady," Henry says, unshackling himself from his booster seat.

I look across the Bonkers Fun House parking lot, but no one's there, just the giant plaster clown face that marks the entrance.

"Who's the flying lady?" I ask.

"Her."

"You know flying ladies are make-believe, right honey?"

This is exactly the kind of thing Henry's teachers keep warning me about. They say he has a hard time separating real from imaginary, as if I didn't already know. They tell me he needs to learn how to relate to his peers. So, here we are, at Max Pearson's birthday party, for some forced socialization, some mandatory fun.

There's a tap on the door that makes me jump so hard I bang my knees into the steering wheel. Aunt Aurora is at my window.

"That's her. The flying lady," Henry says.

She taps again with a long, gloved finger, her blue eyes peering at me. She looks like a bag lady in a trench coat that is about nine sizes too big. The hem drags on the ground.

"Stay in the car, Henry," I say, and get out.

Henry watches through the window. Superman and Green Lantern are pressed against the glass so that they can get a good view, too.

"What are you doing here?" I ask.

"I got to talk to you."

"Couldn't you pick up the phone?"

She pinches her brow together at the absurdity of my suggestion.

"It can't wait," she says.

"Aurora, I'm with my son. We're late for a birthday party." I'm glad for the excuse. Having to talk to Aurora after the mockery of a funeral is low on my to-do list today.

She looks around, as if she's just realized where she is. Seeing the bright clown face whose mouth forms the front door to Bonkers causes her to do a double take. "At this dump?"

"What do you want?" I ask.

"Is the clown supposed to eat the children?"

"No . . . it's . . . one of those indoor arcade franchises." *Where a kid can be a kid.*

"Looks deranged," she says. Her too-long sleeves are rolled up into thick mounds at her wrists, a film of grime encircling them.

"Aurora, what do you want?" I ask again.

"Okay. Here's the thing, niece. After the Seeing Out, Millie, Beatrice, and I were talking. Wilhemena knew that dark times were ahead. That we have to proceed with caution. And you with your special skill, well, we thought you'd be useful."

"So now you think I am 'up to snuff'?" I say, savoring the irony.

"Exactly!" she says. "We think you might be able to help us."

Despite her abrasiveness, I have to admit it feels good that she's come to me this time. "How can I help?"

"We need to make use of your special skill."

"You mean transfiguration? I'm not very good at controlling it yet. In fact, I don't really know how it works . . ."

"Nah," she interrupts. "Not that. I'm talking about that birthmark on your neck gettin' the twitches whenever a witch is about."

"You consider that a gift?"

"We need you to find out if there's any other witches about. You said yourself you get a sick feeling around certain people. A sharp pain in your birthmark."

"That's right," I say, thinking about the nausea coming back in church when I saw Lilith and how the angelica root relieved it.

"We think Freya might be recruiting. Getting her numbers up. Strengthening her forces."

"Would she do that?"

"Maybe. Anyway, you could sniff 'em out for us."

Henry is watching me with total focus. "Let's talk about this later," I whisper. "I don't want to scare anyone."

Aurora looks at Henry with curiosity.

Another minivan pulls up and a carload of kids gets out, followed by a mother on carpool detail. The kids burst forth into the parking lot like an explosion of Pop Rocks and Coke. The mother yells for them to wait, but some of the kids have already raced into the clown's mouth. As she passes us, the woman gives Aurora a quick once-over and frowns. Potential homeless person, she's thinking. Mom radar up, she rushes the stragglers into the building.

"You don't belong here," I say to Aurora.

"And you don't understand how dangerous the Dark Witch can be. No one understands the kind of power she has, or the kinds of things she's capable of. If we sniff her out, if we know where she's at and what she's up to, we can avoid her."

Just then Henry gets out of the car and tugs on Aurora's trench coat. "Are you real?"

"Last time I checked," she answers, and winks at him.

"Are you coming to the party?" Henry asks.

"No, honey, she's not coming to the party."

Aurora raises her eyes. "It might be a good place to start."

I can just imagine my aunt Aurora walking into this party—the look of horror on the other housewives' faces. Security would be called immediately. Rumors would ensue.

"Mom, can she please come? She's my friend."

Your friend? "Henry. She can't come."

Henry takes her hand and stands next to her. "But she's the flying lady. Please?"

Aurora rubs Henry's head and smiles. "Sweet boy you got here."

The sight of my son and aunt together warms my heart.

"Okay," I say. "Just try to keep the crazy talk down to a minimum."

Aurora and Henry walk hand in hand into the clown's mouth.

Bonkers is aptly named. A gaggle of screaming kids runs past us as Henry and I are getting set up with matching paper ID bracelets—the kind you get at hospitals, or beer gardens. Security à la Chuck E. Cheese. I know the bracelets are supposed to give parents a sense of security, but they always have the opposite effect on me. If someone really wanted to steal my child, I'm sure they could elude the distracted sixteen-year-old standing guard at the exit door, who is also in charge of the novelty counter where kids redeem skee ball tickets for Tootsie Rolls and Butterfingers.

Aurora swats the attendant's hand when he tries to put a bracelet on her and I have to convince her it's the only way they'll let her in.

Before us is a mosh pit of kids. Henry stares at them with wide eyes, wondering, no doubt, how long the forced fun will last before he can go home.

I lean down and whisper in his ear, "Do you have to use the bathroom?"

He shakes his head.

"Are you sure?"

He nods.

We make our way past the massive structure of slides and suspended tunnels in primary colors, past the video arcade room and the miniature carousel, to the party room, where a group of moms are standing around talking, casting an occasional glance into the play area for their children.

Paige Pearson walks toward me open armed. She's so perfectly toned and tanned that she looks airbrushed. "Allison, darling, so glad you made it. Hello Henry."

Henry stares.

"Can you say 'hi'?"

Henry stares some more.

Paige bends down 'til she's right in his face. She says very loudly, "Do. You. Want. To. Play. With. The. Other. Boys?"

Henry looks from the plastic labyrinth, back to me, back to the labyrinth again. "Go ahead," I say. "I'll be right here."

When he gets to the jungle gym Henry sits down on the floor, ignoring the bustle of boys playing all around him, immune to their physical games. Instead, he turns inward as Superman and Green Lantern do battle with Hawkgirl and Star Sapphire. A stray dodgeball whizzes by his head, and a boy runs over and kicks it into the air. The boy says something to Henry that I can't hear. Henry shakes his head and the boy runs off.

Paige turns to me. "He's a shy boy, your Henry."

"A little," I say.

"I'm sure he'll get over it. Max was a shy baby, and look at him now. As outgoing as they come. I can't keep up with all the playdate requests."

I smile politely.

"Is Max the fat one over there with screwy hair?" Aurora says, suddenly standing beside me.

"Aurora!" I say. "I'm sorry, Paige. She didn't mean anything by that. This is my aunt Aurora."

Paige lets out a nervous laugh. "His weight is really within normal range. The doctor says Max has remarkable gross motor skills for his age."

"He is very coordinated," I say.

Paige thinks for a moment then says, "You know, my neighbor's son is the same way as Henry. Very shy. Always playing alone. Never speaks. Doesn't like to be touched. Can't stand it when anyone bothers him."

"Sounds like our little man, hey, Allesone? Finest boy here if you ask me," Aurora says.

"We always thought he was just kind of shy," Paige says. "I always felt sorry for the mother. The boy is such a handful."

I nod, praying that this conversation will end soon.

But Paige is not done. "Turns out, the boy is autistic. You know—the *good* kind of autism." Then she adds cheerily, "Like *Rain Man*."

"Oh?" I say, barely able to conceal the anger in my voice.

"What's that called again? Ozbunger's? Oh, I know— Asperger's! That's it! They're usually exceptional at math. Not at all as much trouble as the other kind."

My heart races so fast I can hear it thumping in my chest. Now *my* mom radar is up. I want to punch Paige Pearson in her perfectly exfoliated face. I want to scream that there's nothing wrong with Henry. So what if he's a little different; all great artists are different. So take that and stick it in your push-up bra. But I don't speak because if I open my mouth, I'm going to regret whatever I say.

But she keeps talking: "Is Henry doing his times tables yet? Is he good at math?"

"My son isn't autistic, Paige!" I yell.

The other moms look up, curious.

"Is that one a witch?" Aurora whispers to me.

"Yes!" I whisper. "But not the kind you're looking for."

Paige is startled. "I don't mean to offend you, Allison. I'm just trying to help. I would think it's better to have a diagnosis. That way it's easier to deal with."

It's a universal law among parents; you don't talk badly about other people's kids. It's as basic as brushing and flossing. Suggesting my son has autism is bad enough, but the fact that I've already considered that possibility about a thousand times and have had him tested, and retested and retested again, makes the accusation stab close to the heart. I'm about to speak, when I feel a hand grab my elbow. It's Tanya Buxbaum. She's just arrived with her son, Will.

"Oh look, they have a bar," Tanya says loudly, tugging me away from Paige. "Now, someone was thinking when they opened this place. Allison, I'm going to get a glass of wine, you want to come with me?"

I turn away from Paige and start walking.

"Don't listen to her," Tanya says when we're out of earshot of Paige. "She's just jealous. Henry's too smart to bother with all these simpletons. That's what it is." Just then Max and Bryson Proctor and a few of the other boys run across the room in a game of tag. Max stops short and the others slam into him like dominoes until they're piled up on the floor. "See what I mean?" Tanya says. And I laugh, because I love that my friend has my back.

We get our wine and stand by the concession area, apart from the rest of the group. Paige looks our way occasionally, exaggerated concern on her face, whispers passing between the other moms.

"What do you think they're saying right now?" I ask Tanya.

"I bet she's plotting a way to take Henry to Vegas to count cards for her."

I've almost forgotten about Aurora, until she sneaks up behind me.

"Friend of yours?" Tanya asks.

"This is my aunt Aurora."

Tanya's interest is piqued immediately. "Nice to meet you. Do you live in town? I've never seen you at any of our school fund-raisers. My poor relatives get roped into all those events. Bake sales. Montessori drumming circles. Santa's workshop. Oh, what I put them through! Count your lucky stars Allison doesn't make you suffer through all that. I'm Tanya." She extends a hand.

Aurora shakes it. "What about this one?"

"Tanya's my friend," I say, wishing that Aurora would just drop the witch stuff and let me do it my way.

"Beware of friends. Sometimes they're the worst witches of all," Aurora says.

"I know, right?" Tanya says and slaps her thigh. "That's what I've been telling Allison for years." She tugs at her faux fur–trimmed sweater. "So, how are you feeling, Allison? We were all worried about you after your Glamour Party. Was it the flu? Stomach bug? Not pneumonia, was it? I hear that's going around. Did you get my texts? I've been worried sick."

"I'm fine," I say. "Just a little embarrassed."

"Don't be! It was a brilliant party. Until you passed out. No, I'm just kidding. It happens. Nothing to fret about. But Astrid showing up like that," she raises her eyebrows, "looks like you're movin' on up in the world. Don't forget about us little people."

I cock my head at her, silent for *As if.*

"So are you going to reschedule? Throw a Glamour Party Part Two?"

"Allison's too busy for trifles," Aurora interjects. "She has important work at hand."

Tanya slams her wine down. "Oh my goodness! Will's stuck inside the fun tunnel. I'm sorry, but I have to—"

"Go. Go!" I say. *Been there, sister.*

I'm about to tell Aurora that she needs to stop talking to my friends or they're going to get suspicious. In fact, I'm about to tell her I don't want any part of her witch hunt. After all, I just walked through a whole arcade of Monrovia housewives and I didn't pick up anything strange, when suddenly Rosie O'Shea rushes past me chasing her twin toddlers, completely frazzled, and I get a wave of nausea followed by a tingling on the back of my neck.

"Rosie?" I say under my breath.

"That one, hey? You felt it, didn't you?" Aurora says.

"I felt something, but Rosie can't be an evil witch."

"Why not?"

"She's president of the PTO. She has five kids. She runs the soup kitchen every Thanksgiving. She's the volunteer crossing guard at Monrovia Elementary School, for goodness sake," I say. "Not to mention, she is one of the nicest people I know. You must be wrong about me and my ability to sniff them out. How could *she* be one of Freya's witches?"

"Anyone can," Aurora says, rubbing her chin. "Where does this Rosie live? I will have to shadow her."

Saddling Rosie with my aunt hardly seems fair. I picture Aurora showing up at her house, demanding to know where the Dark Witch is, scaring the bejeezus out of all her kids.

"Well," I stall. "She volunteers at school. You could find her there." Maybe it's unethical to send a slightly deranged old woman to a school full of children, but what harm can she do?

Aurora pats me on the back. "Well done. That's a good start. We'll continue our work tomorrow. I need to get outta here. This place gives me the creeps." A person dressed in a giant orange dinosaur costume crosses in front of us. The dinosaur is pretending to be ferocious, but a handful of children grab him by the legs and jump on his tail.

Aurora walks over to the play area and says good-bye to Henry, who hugs her.

When the cake comes, we're shuffled into a room where the kids sit at a long table. A plastic tablecloth is adorned in footballs, baseballs, and soccer balls, accepted symbols of boyhood.

I imagine the girl-party tablecloth is an equally clichéd mé-lange of princesses and ponies. Henry takes a seat all the way at the end of the table, where the younger siblings sit, away from all the boys his age.

He's fidgeting.

I'm on the other side of the room, and there are moms crammed into every spot on the wall, which makes it hard to get over to him.

I can see that he has to use the bathroom. I push across the room and whisper in his ear, "Let's go to the bathroom." I gently grab his arm, but he won't budge. He's rocking back and forth.

Lilith Proctor helps Paige light the candles on the birthday cake. The lights dim and everyone starts singing "Happy Birthday" to Max. Everyone except for Henry, who has a far-away look in his eye.

Oh God, no, no, no. Please don't wet yourself. Not here. Not now. My heart is thumping loudly in my chest, my level of anxiety rising. I kneel down to talk to him, but even in the darkness to I can see the dark stain on the front of his pants.

We have a shot of making it out of here while it's still dark. I pull Henry by the arm. "Let's go," I whisper, hoping that this is enough of a cue for him, hoping in that one phrase he'll un-derstand I am rescuing him from the inevitable pain of being a six-year-old who just wet his pants. But he's not complying, so I pull him a little harder. He stands up just as Max blows out the last candle.

Paige is standing by the door. For a split second we exchange looks. I shake my head at her, hoping she'll understand that's my way of asking her, begging her, to keep the room dark, just until we can get out of here. She seems to understand what I want.

But flicks on the light anyway.

At first, everyone is focused on the birthday boy and the cake. Max is the first to notice.

He points, the look on his face cruel amusement. Bryson Proctor sees it next, his face taking on the same awful look.

With Henry at my side, I push through the sea of moms, but when I get near Lilith, I feel a prick of pain in the back of my neck. It's so sharp it startles me. I struggle to keep moving.

Lilith is a witch, too.

I can't dwell on it. I need to get Henry out of the room. I want to pick him up the way Superman swoops in to the rescue. I want to throw my body over him to shield him. Protect him. I want to keep the world at bay and I want to soothe him the way I did when he was an infant and I would sing "Hickory Dickory Dock" a thousand times in a row to get him to fall asleep in his crib, because music seemed like the best way to communicate my feelings for him, which were something along the line of, "I love you so much it feels like the sun is rising in my heart." I want to spare him from every type of pain that I know the world will throw at him.

But it's too late.

Now other kids are looking around, even the younger siblings, and they're all wide-eyed and staring. Henry and I shuffle to the door. I can hear the whispers. "Henry peed his pants. What a baby." Some kids are laughing. I glance back and catch Paige's eye. She cocks her head, and softens her eyes at me, as if to say, *I'm sorry about your retarded son.*

Where a kid can be a kid. Give me a break.

Through the agonizing bouts of laughter, we get out of the party room, and I rush Henry to the exit.

I brush past the exit guard without even showing him our matching bracelets.

In the parking lot, I'm so angry I'm shaking. I'm angry at Max Pearson and Bryson Proctor for being such bullies. I'm angry at the moms for not stopping them. I'm angry at Paige for suggesting Henry is broken. I'm angry at Aurora for popping into my life after all these years.

But most of all, I'm angry at myself. I told Henry the party would be fun. I told him he needed to make friends. To fit in. To be normal.

But I'm not normal. My family isn't normal! How can I expect my kids to be?

In the car, Henry retreats back into his imaginary world of superheroes, uttering animated sound effects to the actions of his characters. In his lap, Flash and Hawkgirl are battling Star Sapphire for world domination. And because I know that my son's heart is an unshakable and beautiful thing, I know that today, good will triumph over evil, if only in his world of make-believe.

I think about Aurora and my mother and the witches at the funeral. I think about the other witches—Astrid, Lilith, Rosie, and Miranda. Which witches are good and which are bad? Can these perfectly adjusted Monrovia housewives really be minions of the Dark Witch? Or does Aurora have it all wrong? After all, their kids are normal and happy and perfectly capable of getting through a Bonkers birthday party without incident. And I begin to wonder if maybe being a better witch would make me be a better mom.

CHAPTER 10

> Speak of a person, and he will appear,
> Then talk of the devil, and he'll draw near.

I seriously consider keeping Henry out of school for the rest of the week. Spare him the mortification of being known as the kid who peed his pants. Maybe I can keep him home the rest of the semester. Send him back to school after Christmas bubble-wrapped in a little cocoon of self-esteem and safety, once the rumors have died down.

I know firsthand how rumors can shake you to your core, especially the true ones. I remember what it's like to sit at a lunch table while kids one-up each other with information so scandalous it can impress even the most hardened of school bullies. *Guess where babies come from? Guess what swear word my dad used?* The one with the highest shock value wins. *Guess who's an orphan?* Gasp. The biggest taboo of all. The jackpot.

Yes, I think of keeping him home today to watch cartoons and drink hot cocoa. In the end, I reason that most six-year-olds can't remember left from right, much less what happened yesterday. *Water under the bridge, buddy,* I think as I send him off to school, but not before tucking a stick of gum in his shirt pocket as an extra token of my love.

When the phone rings and I see it's Monrovia Elementary, my heart skips a beat.

"We need you to come down to the school at once," Principal Mersen tells me on the other end of the line.

I suck in all the air in the room and hold it in my chest. "Is it . . . Henry?" I say, feeling the desperate, wary word like an anvil over my head.

"Henry's fine. It's your aunt," she says.

Okay, I can breathe again. "My aunt?"

"She tried to enter the school without proper identification. She's very agitated."

"I'll be right there," I say, scrambling for my keys.

At school, Aurora is slumped in a chair in the principal's office beneath a poster of a small child holding hands with two adults, who are holding hands with two more adults in a human chain of hand-holding. The slogan reads, "It Takes a Village to Raise a Child. Be a Volunteer with Monrovia Community Outreach."

"We tried to explain that she can't just walk into school," Principal Mersen is telling me. "She became very aggressive, swearing and shouting at Mrs. Lackney at the front desk. We are very clear on the rules about visitors. They need to sign in. Keeping our children safe is top priority."

"I needed to check on your boy," Aurora barks in defense. "I don't trust you-know-who," she says to me, a hand in front of her mouth so the principal won't hear. She hears anyway.

"Who is she talking about?" Principal Mersen says.

The room stinks of garlic and I see that Aurora has a bulb of it stuck in the brim of her fedora, most likely to repel evil witches. Her broomstick is at her feet, along with her gigantic rucksack full of plants and mushrooms.

"The Irish lass. Rosie something-or-other," Aurora says.

"What problem do you have with Mrs. O'Shea?" Principal Mersen asks.

Aurora looks the principal in the eye. "She's a . . ."

"Friend," I blurt out. I give Aurora an exaggerated wide-eye look, praying she reads visual cues, wishing I hadn't suggested that she look for Rosie at school in the first place.

"I have in mind to call the police," Principal Mersen says.

"Please don't. My aunt is interested in volunteering at school and she knows that Rosie is the PTO president." I gesture toward the poster of the happy village. "She could . . . help with the Halloween decorations."

"Huh?" Aurora scoffs.

"Well," the principal hesitates. "Everyone must do her part, I guess. But she still has to follow the rules."

"We've got to ask the witch if she knows where Freya's at," Aurora says, way too loudly for the small room.

"What is all this witch talk?" Principal Mersen says, eyebrows raised.

I look at the principal, at my aunt, and then at the poster on the opposite wall that shows the food pyramid and its nutritional values.

"That's what she calls me," I say quickly. "She thinks I'm a witch because I make the kids eat granola instead of Cocoa Puffs. It's her little joke."

"There's nothing wrong with granola," the principal says.

Aurora stands, grabs her broomstick, and shakes it at the principal. "Tell me where Rosie something-or-other is at. Where does she live? My niece and I need to have a word with her."

Principal Mersen stands. She picks up the phone on her desk. "Are you threatening one of our own PTO members? Because, I have the police commissioner's number on speed dial. The commissioner's wife is on the school board."

I stand. "Please, Principal Mersen, my aunt is perfectly safe. She's really very adamant about helping out at school. Is there any volunteer work we can find for her? Maybe the bake sale?" I can just imagine Aurora procuring gluten-free brownies and sugarless Rice Krispies treats from the Monrovia mothers in between drop-off and yoga class.

Principal Mersen puts the phone down. Her expression slowly shifts from hostile to sympathetic.

"Perhaps something a little more . . . behind the scenes. There's room on the bulb planting committee," the principal says.

"That sounds good," I say brightly.

"Where's the witch?"

I sling Aurora's rucksack over my shoulder and push her to the door.

The principal knits her hands together. "Or, maybe mulching the playground. At night. After the children have gone home, of course."

"That's perfect," I say. "Thank you for your understanding."

I close the door just as Aurora presses her middle and pointer finger against her nose, a gesture I remember Wilhemena used to ward off evil spirits.

Outside, the sky is darkening and I can taste the coming rain. "You can't go around town talking about witch hunting," I say. "People don't believe in witches. They think it's make-believe. You could have been arrested. You could have been put in jail for acting like that at a school."

Aurora looks sullen. "Figured this was our best shot. We have to find Freya before she finds us. Stay one step ahead of her, and we can outrun her."

"Maybe she's not as dangerous as you think," I say, the first drops of rain hitting my face. "Maybe she's mellowed out in her old age. Maybe there's nothing to run from."

"You heard Wilhemena's warning yourself."

"I know. But Wilhemena was old, too. People get . . ." I look at Aurora, so squat and vulnerable, "less *with it* when they age. Do you want to come to my house? I can make us some tea."

Aurora spits on the ground. "Nah. We'll try again another time." She turns and walks away. I watch her pad all the way down the street, expecting her to get in her car, but she gets to the end of the street, turns, and keeps walking.

You have to love karma. Today, I saved my aunt from being arrested. My reward is in the mailbox when I get home. It's in a gold envelope, my name written in green calligraphy—an invitation to Astrid's autumnal equinox party.

Astrid's parties are the stuff of small-town legend. The

everyone-who's-anyone A-list events of Monrovia. They get talked about at the coffeehouses and Little League games, in the gym, at playgrounds, at the hardware store and the hair salon. People suck up to Astrid all year in the hopes they'll score an invitation. The brownnosing is epic. I've seen couples give up front-row seats to the Celtics as a gift to Astrid. I've heard of the local tennis pro losing a charity game to Astrid. And let's just say Astrid never has to worry about getting a seat at the Mayor's Ball every summer. Your entire social life can be made if Astrid extends an invitation. Withholding an invitation can mean social destitution.

I open the envelope and read it out loud: "Autumnal Equinox Gala. Celebrate an evening of abundance."

I drop everything and call Judy.

"How did *you* make the cut?" Judy asks.

"Maybe it's my stellar personality," I say, stepping into a red satin dress at Azure Boutique, trying not to get deodorant smudges on the sides.

"No. That can't be it."

I'm not about to tell Judy that Astrid suspects I'm a witch, or that I suspect it takes one to know one.

"Maybe I'm more popular than you think. Maybe I'm just hitting my stride in the social stratosphere."

"Doubt it."

"Are you jealous?"

"Hell, no. It's not like you cured hoof rot, Allison. It's not like you went and built an orphanage in Honduras. You just got invited to some pretentious party where everyone's going to sit around drinking gin, talking about their latest nose jobs, or boob jobs, or face-lifts, or excursions to the south of France, and kiss each other's asses. It sounds awful."

"You *are* jealous," I say.

"You couldn't drag me to that party if they were handing

out free time-shares in Aruba as party favors. Believe me, I have no interest in hanging out with the Glamour Girls."

I step out of the dressing room and twirl around for Judy. "Well?"

She purses her lips and looks me up and down. "You look like a high-class hooker."

High praise from Judy.

"You don't think the red is too much?" I ask.

"I hear red's the color of choice for social climbing," she says drily.

Judy proceeds to outline some of the rules I must follow for the evening, lest I be judged by the social arbiters of town. "For chrissake, don't show up first and don't be the first to leave. Implement a drinking plan, say, one glass in the first hour, two in the second, back to one in the third hour. You don't want to end up the asshole dancing the snake or puking into the potted ficus. You'll never be asked back."

"Good call."

I examine myself from every angle in the mirror. The dress is tighter than my comfort zone, but I look more curvy than I do lumpy. You might even say I look pretty. I sweep my hair up in my left hand, letting a few black locks dangle against my freckled shoulders. "Up or down?" I ask, turning to face Judy, slightly self-conscious about my birthmark, even though it is just Judy.

"Up," she says, a little surprised since she's never seen me with my hair up before.

"Any other words of wisdom for me before I enter Oz?"

"Yeah. You're every bit as good as those bitches. Better, if you ask me," Judy says with a reassuring nod.

"Thanks, Judy."

I tug on the sides of my dress, self-conscious about the snug fit, as Kevin and I make our way up the brick path flanked by topiaries to Astrid's house. I feel a familiar flash of white-hot dread, suddenly worried that I might be overdressed. What if everyone is in jeans? Or, worse, maybe I'm underdressed, like the time I walked into Connie Flanagan's vintage après-ski-themed party dressed in a circa-1980 men's snowmobile jump-suit because that's all I could find at the thrift store, while everyone else was glammed up as Vail ski bunnies and I wanted to die. Or what if I have the wrong venue. Or the wrong date. After all, it is incredibly short notice for a formal party.

Oh, please, please, please, tell me I read the invitation correctly. I grab Kevin's hand when we get to the front steps and formulate my plan: If I'm underdressed, then we'll just turn around and leave. Simple as that.

At the front door, two massive stone gargoyles stand guard.

"Those are interesting," I say.

"She had those brought over from some castle in Scotland. Took four guys and crane to get them in place," Kevin says.

"You didn't tell me there were gargoyles."

"I haven't been over here in years. A lot's changed," Kevin says.

Once upon a time, he knew this house inside and out. We moved to Monrovia because of this house, and because of Astrid.

We were living south of Boston at the time. Kevin did construction work around the neighborhood—porches, drywall, painting. One day, completely out of the blue, he got a call from a woman in Monrovia, up on the North Shore, a place neither of us had ever heard of. She said she had seen some of his work at her friend's house and asked if he would be interested in taking on her renovation project. It was quite large, she explained, and she needed someone who could commit. Her name was Astrid Laveau.

It started out as a tiling job of the master bathroom. That quickly turned into a kitchen renovation, then a two-thousand-square-foot addition, a greenhouse, and a pool house, all of which Kevin built. He was thrilled. He was finally doing the type of work he wanted. He found Astrid too demanding, but the pay was fantastic. And there was plenty of other work in Monrovia. Through her contacts in real estate, Astrid even found us a house—a fixer-upper on Purchase Street with great potential. Its proximity to the local cemetery scared off a lot of buyers, and she was able to negotiate a good deal. "It's an ideal place to raise children," she claimed. "People don't even lock their doors."

So we left the city, moved to Monrovia, and planted a few apple trees to block the view of the tombstones in our backyard.

"Remind me why we're here," Kevin says, both of us pausing before opening the door.

"For the free booze?" I offer.

And because I need to get to the bottom of this witch business.

Kevin pulls at his collar and rolls his neck. "You know I can't stand all these country club people. They'll probably just talk about golf."

"It might be fun. I could use some fun."

"I hate golf."

And it hits me that Kevin is just as nervous as I am. Up until now, I didn't even think about the fact that *he* might feel out of *his* league in this Glamour crowd. Kevin is the quintessential guy's guy, at ease in any pub or pickup basketball game. But a fancy cocktail party is not his forte.

We walk inside and the house seems to glow with the sparkle of a million crystals in the chandelier overhead. To the right, a violin trio plays Chopin, striking each chord in perfect, delicate tune. We have entered Oz. Immediately to the left stands a knight in full armor, his face shield and cutlass polished to a high sheen, the coat of arms of some extinct kingdom emblazoned on his chest. All I can think is how much Henry would love to see that knight.

A beautiful woman in a green uniform walks up carrying a tray of champagne and offers us a glass.

I take one and sip it right away.

"For you," she says, turning to Kevin.

"Do you have any beer?" Kevin asks.

"Certainly, sir." The server walks away to get the beer and Kevin and I step farther into the grand foyer. It's a beautifully appointed room, with silver centerpieces of fresh flowers on antique tables. There are plumes of hydrangea, lilies, orchids, and baby's breath. But there are also plenty of flowers that are out of season, like peonies, gardenias, and freesia.

"You think she just threw this party together in the last few days?" I say to Kevin, thinking back to how I could barely manage a few appetizers at my last party.

"I'm sure she has help."

"Yeah, but, where would she even get these flowers this time of year?"

"Beats me." Kevin shrugs. Flower seasons don't register with him.

When the server returns with a glass of beer for Kevin, we wander down the length of the grand foyer.

I can see people in the next room, but I don't recognize anyone and I feel jittery and awkward (though properly dressed), so I down my champagne and take another one from our lovely server. Better to make a gradual entrance, I think, as I turn my attention to the exotic mounted animals against the walls. There's a giant grizzly bear, mouth frozen in a silent growl. A full-size bald eagle is beside it. And next to that, a mounted swordfish that must be at least five feet long.

Kevin touches the lifeless body of the fish, moving his fingers down the rigid snout.

"You want one, don't you?" I observe.

"Who wouldn't want a fish on their wall?" he says. The dreamy look on his face tells me his mind is on a boat somewhere in the Atlantic, snagging a billfish of his own. "But what's up with the bear and the eagle? It's weird," Kevin says.

I step back into the center of the black marble floor and

study the arrangement of the three animals. And it clicks. "Not weird," I say. "It's the three elements. Land, air, and sea."

There's a clapping behind me and I turn to see Astrid standing there, looking radiant in a pale pink silk gown, two long strings of pearls around her neck. Peacock feathers are pinned to her hair, which is swept up in an elegant chignon.

"Very good, Allison," she says, halting her applause.

Kevin coughs into his hand.

Astrid smiles in a way that puts both Kevin and I at ease. "I'm not offended. I know that my tastes are eclectic. But there are more than three elements. Do you know the others?" she asks me.

"Fire, of course," I answer.

"And?"

I think about it for a minute and my mind wanders back to Wilhemena's funeral, and the reading of her Last Wit and Wisdom. The spirit element. Although it's not something you'll find in any science book, it's a big deal among witches, as I learned when the dwarves stole it from me.

"Spirit," I say, with trepidation. I might be revealing too much, but she already knows my deep secret. What's the point in hiding it now?

She takes both my hands in hers and smiles, her teeth as white as pearls. Her bright eyes only have the faintest touch of makeup, which lets her natural beauty stand out. The pale pink of her dress looks like something Sophie would choose, like the color of youth itself.

It dawns on me that my neck is throbbing, but only mildly now. My tingly witch sense must be weakening.

"I'm so glad you could make it," she says. "Let me introduce you to some of my guests."

She lets go of my hands and loops one arm through mine and one through Kevin's. As a threesome, we enter the grand hall, which is unlike anything I've ever seen.

The ceiling is gilded with the moon and stars rendered in crystal. Everywhere my eye turns there are marble statues and tapestries, oil paintings, and antiques, and in the center of the room a huge saltwater aquarium is lit up in aquamarine blue. If it weren't for the decadent buffet of roast meats, the raw bar brimming with oysters, crab, and lobsters, and the servers in green uniforms passing out champagne, it would look more like a museum than a home.

The people, congregated in little clusters, men here, women there, are as chic and beautiful as the setting itself. I scan the room quickly and recognize Miranda Greene and Lilith Proctor, who both glance my way and smile. Rosie O'Shea is standing by the dessert table. Others I know vaguely, like Erin Hastings, who's always pestering parents at school to volunteer for seasonal planting initiatives.

Before I know it, I've downed my second glass of champagne, and everything has taken on a sort of warm glow.

I feel like a special guest, having Astrid accompany me around the party, introducing me to all her friends. "Kevin, you know our mayor, Warren Davey, right?" Astrid says.

Warren Davey extends his hand. "Astrid's been telling me all about your plans for the waterfront development. It sounds like you've got a really strong vision for the future of Monrovia."

Kevin looks at me questioningly and I give him the same look back. I don't remember talking to Astrid about Kevin's development plans. Then again, he's talked to a lot of people around town about it. Astrid must have picked up on the details secondhand.

"Well, I sure hope city council agrees with you when it comes time to vote on the bids," Kevin says, shaking the mayor's hand.

Mayor Davey slaps a hand on Kevin's back like they're old friends, corralling him into a group of men. He introduces Kevin around, and points out that every single one of them sits on city council.

The city councillors ply Kevin with questions about his project—everything from the economic impact it will have on Monrovia to the type of roofing materials he uses. Astrid bolsters his answers with opinions of her own on why Monrovia needs a contractor like Kevin to lead a project of this scope.

I can see that Kevin is relishing all the attention. He might actually be blushing.

"You should come to the club for drinks sometime," Warren says to him. "Do you play golf?" To which Kevin replies, "I've been known to hit a few rounds."

I can't help myself, but this makes me laugh out loud. Unfortunately, it strikes me just as I take a sip of champagne, which comes out through my nostrils.

"Looks like they've really hit it off," a woman standing to my right says. "I'm Kimberly Davey. Warren's wife."

I wipe my nose with a cocktail napkin, hoping I haven't made too big an ass of myself. When I shake her hand, a prickling sensation runs down my neck, then slowly disappears.

Nice to meet you, you witch.

"I'm Allison Darling."

"Is this your first soirée at Astrid's?" Kimberly asks.

I look at her apprehensively, wondering if it's really that obvious.

"Yes," I mutter. "I can hardly believe she threw this party together so quickly."

"Oh, believe it. She can do anything she puts her mind to." Kimberly crosses her arms gracefully over her slim figure. "She believed that Warren should be mayor. And, voilà, now he's mayor. She practically ran his campaign."

Astrid Laveau. Hotshot Realtor. Socialite. Soap maker. Political adviser.

Kimberly waves across the room at someone I don't recognize, and excuses herself to go say hello.

I grab another glass of champagne. Kevin is totally engaged in conversation, leaving me on my own to navigate the party.

The room grows louder as guests circulate and drinks flow. I look for Rosie, feeling a little like a loner now in the crowd of beautiful people, like the olive pit in the martini glass, but she's nowhere to be seen. So I help myself to a plate at the raw bar.

I wander over to the aquarium next, drawn by the hypnotic motion of fish swimming in endless circles. This must be new, or Kevin certainly would have mentioned it before. It's so massive it looks like something straight out of the New England Aquarium. Fish of all sizes circle round and round, but the real showstoppers of the tank are the giant *Tridacna* clams that populate the bottom. As large as tortoises, their white, wavy shells stand in sharp contrast to the brilliant shades of purples, reds, and oranges inside. They look otherworldly. Smaller mollusks of varying sizes cling to the wooden beams that run vertically through the tank.

"What do you think?" Astrid says, appearing at my side.

Her face is illuminated by the dramatic blue lights of the tank, which makes her features look even more exquisite. "It's really incredible. You must have a marine biologist on retainer."

Astrid laughs. "No. It's just one of my hobbies."

A little bug-eyed fish with a spiky dorsal fin scurries up to us, bumps the glass, then scurries away. I can't name the species, but I know who could. "My daughter Gillian would go nuts if she saw this. She wants to be a marine biologist."

"Bring her by," Astrid says resolutely.

"No, I wouldn't want to impose."

"Seriously. Bring her. Any time."

"Well. If you really don't mind. She would love it."

I feel swept up in the beauty of the night. My necks throbs lightly, but my head is taking on that delicious carefree joy of champagne. Is this my second or third, I wonder, looking at the glass in my hand.

A man with perfect black hair and piercing eyes walks up and air kisses Astrid. "Allison," she says, turning toward me,

"I want you to meet Dr. Yu." I have to look away when he stares into my eyes because he's too gorgeous for words.

"Dr. Yu is a plastic surgeon. He has offices in Beverly Hills and Manhattan, and he just opened one of his Botox spas right here in Monrovia," Astrid says.

Of course I know all about Dr. Yu, plastic surgeon to the stars. Named five times to *People* magazine's 100 Most Beautiful People list.

"Why Monrovia?" I ask. "It's so small."

"Astrid is very convincing. She's been bugging me for years to open a clinic here," he says, and even his voice is handsome.

"And I found him the perfect location, right downtown in the old customs building," Astrid says.

"It has been nice to get away from the rat race. Monrovia is a little slice of paradise," Dr. Yu says. He looks at me again. "Do you know you have perfect bone structure?" He takes my chin in his hand and turns my face to the right and left, studying me.

I have to look away quickly, this time at the fish swimming in the circles and the giant clams, because I feel his eyes penetrating me. I want to giggle, like a sixteen-year-old with a growing infatuation. "I think my husband's looking for me," I say abruptly.

I break away from Astrid and Dr. Yu and make my way over to the other end of the ballroom where Kevin is cradling a scotch and talking to the chief of police and two other men I recognize from their campaign posters as a city councilman and city comptroller.

Kevin introduces me to them, and they immediately introduce me to their wives. Their wives—Heather, Erin, and Bethanny—each send little volts down the back of my neck when I shake hands with them.

Three more witches.

"I've heard so much about you," Bethanny says. She's a tall blonde with a perfect figure accentuated by her skintight nude-colored gown. "Your daughter is in my daughter's mommy-and-me music class. Her name is Sophie, right? My nanny says Sophie is the most adorable little thing you've ever seen."

I refrain from pointing out that mommy-and-me is supposed to be a bonding time with the mother, but then, Bethanny wouldn't be the only housewife in town to send her nanny as a stand-in for a maternal activity.

"And your son Henry is in karate with my son. He's exceptional, your Henry. Very talented," Heather says, even though I'm pretty sure she also has a nanny who shuffles kids to their after-school activities. Heather is the police chief's wife and, judging by her biceps, she spends a lot of time at the gym.

Erin asks me if I belong to the racket club.

"No. I've never played tennis."

"Well, you're invited any time you like as my guest," she says. "I'll give you my number."

I learn that all of them are Glamour Soap reps and they donate their earnings to local charities: the Monrovia Botanical Society, the Fund for the Restoration of Antique Homes, the North Shore Feline Rescue, the Boys' and Girls' Choral Club. I learn that all of the Glamour Girls volunteer on at least one municipal committee. They care about their neighbors. They're proud of Monrovia. They compliment me, they adore my kids. They sponsor charities.

A server walks by with a tray of champagne and I grab one—my fourth? So much for Judy's drinking plan. I will keep my composure. I will not end up doing the snake in front of all these fancy people.

Heather, Erin, and Bethanny chatter on excitedly about some new clothing designer whose fall collection is now available. I'm starting to feel drunk, so I step away and wander through the great room, back into the foyer, which is empty. Even the violin trio has moved into the main room where the guests are.

I walk over to the bald eagle, its wings akimbo, and stare

up at its narrow glass eyes. Its downward-curved beak looks hostile.

"What are you looking at, bird?" I say out loud.

The bird stares back at me.

"Yeah, I'm talking to you, bird. Where's your spirit element, bird? Mine was taken from me." Oh God, I am drunk.

Without any warning, my drunk haze lifts, and my mother's voice is in my head:

> *All of a row*
> *Bend the bow*
> *Shot at a pigeon*
> *And killed a crow*

This time I know what's coming. I close my eyes and rub my forehead to get any thoughts of transfiguration out of my head. But I can't control it. The vision is already imprinted on my mind. The black coat, deep and shiny like obsidian. The feathers fanning out at the tips like fingers. The sharp, black beak. When I open my eyes again, the eagle has turned into a mounted crow.

"How did you do that?" a voice behind me says.

I turn. I look. Astrid. "I don't really know," I say.

"Come with me," she says.

It's all on the table now. I've got nothing to lose. "You're a witch, too, aren't you?" I say.

She nods.

"Are you . . . the Dark Witch?" I ask.

She raises her arms and gestures at the fine furnishings, the beautiful people. "Don't be silly. Come with me. There's something I want to show you," she says.

She charges ahead into the great hall, the party now in a feverish pitch of laughter and movement. I shadow Astrid as she moves through the room, stopping for a quick hello here, a compliment there. She's all smiles and etiquette, but I can tell there's urgency about her. As we pass by the aquarium, Erin, Heather, and Bethanny step in line with us. Kimberly Davey joins in next. By the time we get to the French doors at the back of the house, Lilith, Miranda, and Rosie have all joined our little entourage.

My neck is tingling, but no longer in a painful way.

Astrid steps outside in the crisp night air. We follow her across the patio, through a break in the hedges to an English-style garden. There are plants I recognize from my childhood: evening primrose, soapwort, phlox, night gladiolus, tuberose, trumpet flower. Vines of night bloomers climb a gate that takes us to another courtyard full of rosebushes and rhododendrons.

Rosie catches my eye and gives me a slight grimace.

What am I getting myself into? I stop and look back at the house, its lights shimmering in the night, and think about turning back, but Bethanny comes up behind me and loops an arm through mine. "Don't worry. It'll be fun," she says.

"What will be fun?" I ask.

Kimberly pops up on my other side. "Allison, did I mention how much I love that dress? Red suits you."

"Thanks," I say, feeling a little dizzy.

Before I know it, we pass through another gate in Astrid's expansive backyard and arrive at a greenhouse, its windows clouded with steam. I'm the last to enter and I pause at the threshold.

"Go ahead, Allison," Astrid says, sensing my hesitation.

I look inside at an explosion of colorful flowers, leafy plants, and herbs. Now I know where the peonies and freesia came from.

"We want to talk to you," Astrid says, still holding the door. "Hear us out."

Inside, the ladies stand in the rows between the plant tables. In their designer gowns and glittering gems, they look as exotic as the flowers around them.

My hands are sweating, and the heat of the greenhouse feels suffocating.

"This is our family," Astrid says. "We are a coven."

"Yes," I say, looking around at the faces of the women. "I've already figured that out."

"Have you figured out that we are the caretakers of our town? We are what makes Monrovia beautiful, safe, and prosperous. Our schools are top tier. Our businesses are thriving. Home values keep climbing. Nothing is left to chance. We take care of the higher good for everyone. The planning board, the chamber of commerce, the PTO, city council—it's all at our command."

Kimberly Davey gives me a reassuring nod.

"Even the town arborist," Astrid says.

"That's me," Erin chirps.

I feel their eyes burrowing into me.

Astrid steps toward me. "Our family takes care of its own. We trust each other. We support each other. We can give you whatever your heart desires. Riches. Beauty. Prestige. A better life for your children."

"Better sex," Bethanny blurts out and the women laugh.

"And love," Astrid adds.

I look at her with a fierceness now, wanting whatever drug she's pawning. A blur of faces closes in around me, faces of the most beautiful, charitable women in town. Faces of wives. Of mothers.

This is not the kind of magic I know. My mother's magic was wasted on healing chipmunks and squirrels when she could have been building a great life. Aurora, Beatrice, Millie, Jonathon, and Jinathon don't know this kind of magic either. Witchcraft, for them, is hidden in woods.

"How?" I ask. "How does it work?"

"Potions," Astrid says simply. "We make potions."

"No pointy hats, or broomsticks? Animal sacrifices?"

"Forget everything you think you know about magic. Times have changed," Astrid says.

"I don't know," I say, my mind flicking back to Aurora and my mother.

"I know you're special, Allison. I've seen what you can do," Astrid says.

I rub my neck. Surely, these are not the minions of a Dark Witch. These women raise money for charities and keep the flower boxes full. What could be so wrong with that? What could be so wrong with making a few potions to help my kids? What could be wrong with love?

Miranda steps forward with a garment box and Astrid opens it. She pulls out a pink cashmere cape. THE pink cashmere cape. She wraps it around me. It's the softest, most luxurious thing I've ever worn.

"What do you say, Allison?"

I close my eyes and strain to hear my mother's voice. Her final words come back to me: *Your blood is my blood. You are a witch of the Ellylydan Coven.* Is it treason to join another? Maybe I can do both. I can be a part of my mother's old coven and still be a Glamour Girl. Then again, Aurora didn't exactly welcome me into her coven the way Astrid has. She never promised me anything. Certainly nothing to help my family.

"I don't know," I repeat, expelling the words from my lungs.

"Think about it for a day or two," Astrid says. She hands me her business card, which is gilded with green calligraphy. Her face darkens in the smoldering heat of the greenhouse. "But, I only ask once."

CHAPTER 11

Three blind mice, three blind mice,
See how they run, see how they run,
They all ran after the farmer's wife,
Who cut off their tails with a carving knife,
Did you ever see such a thing in your life,
As three blind mice?

Boston, Massachusetts · 1955

Despite the heat of the August day, Elizabeth buttoned her cape to her neck, shielding herself against the filth of the city. Leading the way, she marched down the cobblestone street of Haymarket, past fruit and vegetable vendors, Wilhemena, Freya, and Aurora following close behind. They each lugged yellowed cardboard boxes through the maze of merchants setting up shop, craning their necks every which way to take it all in. Having never been to Boston before they were dazzled by the bustle of people and commerce.

"Quickly. Make haste," Elizabeth said, cutting a path through the dense cluster of people. A car horn honked, which startled Aurora. She tripped over a crate of oranges, sending them rolling in all directions. An old man in a crisp apron shook his fist and bellowed at her in a language she didn't recognize. Aurora hurried away.

Boston was an assault of new sounds and smells, alien from those of the mudflats and marsh waters. There was the sugary aroma of the NECCO candy factory in the distance, grease from the fish-and-chip stands, the odor of sewage and rotting fruit that ran in a dark stream along the length of the market.

They continued on past the fishmonger, to a spot at the fringe of the cobblestones where the morning drunks leaned on crates, cradling amber-colored bottles.

"Why can't we sell our wares over there?" Freya asked. "With the others."

"We don't belong there. Here, we are free to do as we like," Elizabeth said.

"Why must we come here at all?" Freya persisted, kicking at a rat that crossed in front of her to gnaw a smashed tomato.

"To live in this world requires money, Freya. With your father gone, it falls to us."

Freya, wishing to avoid any talk of Papa, dropped her line of questioning.

Helping their mother, the girls lined up homemade bars of soap, tinctures and salves, dried herbs, and infused oils on a stack of boxes covered with bright tapestries. Elizabeth set out a display of brooms they had made in the Old Way, birch twigs bound to ash rods with willow rope.

A little girl with hair the color of corn silk wandered near them while her mother perused the selection of whole bass and trout perched on beds of crushed ice at the fishmonger. The girl stared from face to face, sucking on her bottom lip and twirling the straps of her sundress in her fingers. She inched closer until she was right in front of them. Her attention was quickly snatched up by the unusual soaps, cast in every color of the rainbow. She picked up a bar of lime-green soap flecked with bits of lavender flower.

"For magical dreams," Elizabeth told her.

The girl held the soap like a treasure in both hands and sniffed. A smile snuck out from her chubby cheeks and she sniffed some more.

Freya, who had no experience with other children, watched the girl the way she might watch a coyote, or a black bear, or any other kind of predator. She trusted no one. But the child looked innocent and so delighted by the soap that Freya smiled at the girl and the girl smiled back.

"She likes it," Freya said.

The girl's mother appeared, a waxed bag of fish in her hand. She was well dressed and Freya noticed that her hair looked as though it, too, had once been the color of corn silk, but had darkened on the stalk. She yanked the soap from her daughter's hand and placed it back on the boxes. Roughly, she grabbed her girl's hand.

"Come away from there, Betty Ann. They're street people." The mother whisked the girl away. The little girl turned and pouted.

Freya narrowed her eyes and concentrated her attention on the back of the mother as she hurried down the street. Freya's face hardened and she began to murmur.

Elizabeth stepped in front of Freya and lifted her cape to break Freya's intense gaze.

"You do not understand their ways, nor do they understand ours," Elizabeth said in a stern voice.

Freya crossed her arms over her chest.

"Do you hear me, Freya?" Elizabeth said.

Freya grunted a sour assent. "Yes, Mother."

"Magic used for ill intentions only leads to trouble," Elizabeth said.

As the morning wore on, more and more people passed through the market. None of the girls had ever seen such a pageantry of people—white, black, Asian, Indian. People from all walks of life, as they were called. They saw beggars wandering by with vacant eyes and college students wearing the colors of their tribe like badges—crimson, blue and gold, gold and red, green and black.

As Elizabeth sold a few odds and ends to the market's more adventurous visitors, Wilhemena helped stock the merchandise by tying bouquets of dried flowers and cloves into bundles. At eighteen she already understood that to live meant to toil. Her hands were callused. Her body wizened. A stranger could easily have put her at twice her age. Wilhemena studied hard and knew all of Elizabeth's elemental potions by heart. "Hands to work, hearts to the goddess," she was fond of quoting, especially to Freya, who eschewed work at every possible chance.

Freya had matured into a striking beauty as perfect (and as poisonous) as the lily of the valley that blanketed the woodlands in spring. At fifteen she was beginning to understand the power that beauty had over people. She saw it on their occasional trips to the Salem grocer—the way the butcher smiled at pretty women and offered up the best cuts of lamb, the most marbled roasts; the way he brushed aside the homely ones, wrapping up their meat without a lot of idle chat. She studied people as well as potions, the nuances of body language, the styles of clothing.

And then there was the youngest. Unlike her sisters, Aurora grew outward instead of upward, sprouting into adolescence like a fungus, short, plump, and pungent. Aurora was the easiest going of her siblings, and the simplest. She was adept at foraging and fishing, but the finer points of spells and enchantments still eluded her.

"As different as the tides," Elizabeth would say of her three girls.

While Wilhemena and Aurora worked alongside their mother through the morning, Freya leaned against a lamppost, watching the parade of people come and go. It was, according to Elizabeth, "a sea of filth and devil-doers, a place to keep distant the dangers of man." But Freya felt entranced by it, by the buildings that stretched up to the sky, glittering in the sun, by all the glamour and filth the city had to offer. The darkness as well as the light.

By midday the sun was brutal. Elizabeth pulled a dollar bill out of a pouch on her belt. "Run along and buy yourselves some frozen bananas. There's a cart just down yonder."

"I don't want a banana," Freya said.

"It will nourish you," Elizabeth said.

"I want ice cream."

"Have a banana. It's just down the way," Elizabeth said. She added, "You mustn't wander off. Stay in the marketplace."

Freya slouched.

"Thanks, Mother," Wilhemena said, taking the money. "We'll be back soon."

Elizabeth smiled and fanned her cape against the torpid heat.

The girls walked down Haymarket through the pushcart vendors until they came to the frozen banana cart.

"Three bananas please," Wilhemena said.

The banana vendor nodded. Frosty air billowed out of the cart when the man opened the lid.

"They look like turds," Freya said.

"Freya, hush," Wilhemena scolded.

"He probably picked them out of the street," Freya said loudly for the man to hear.

The banana vendor scrunched his face up under his hat.

"Shut up," Aurora said.

"I'm not eating those," Freya continued. "They're ugly and rotten. Just like his face."

"Freya!"

"She didn't mean nothing by that, sir," Aurora said.

Wilhemena pulled the dollar bill out of her pocket to give to the banana man, but Freya snatched it and ran away, down the street, away from the market, the dollar bill wadded up in her hand.

"Where are you going?" Aurora yelled.

"Ice cream shop," Freya yelled back.

"Mama says we're not to leave the square."

"Stay here then. I'm going to get some pistachio ice cream."

Wilhemena and Aurora had no choice. They knew the trouble that Freya would create run amok in Boston by herself, and

138 · Katie Schickel

so with one decisive shrug, they turned a heel and gave chase. Freya ran like the deer in the forest. She crossed Congress Street to Faneuil Hall, narrowly missing an oncoming cable car on State Street.

Wilhemena caught up to Freya when she stopped to look at a shiny display of gold chains in the window of a jewelry store.

Aurora lagged behind. She was slow and heavy and covered in perspiration when she finally reached them. "Slow down, will ya?" she panted, running up to her sisters. "I'm coming with you."

Together, they walked up Faneuil Hall, mesmerized by the stores and restaurants. At a place called Durgin Park, Aurora stopped to read the menu, her mouth watering at the mention of meatloaf sandwiches, french fries, onion rings, and steak. The city may be a treacherous place, she thought, but it certainly ate well.

At the end of Faneuil Hall, they walked together down Tremont. The sun beat down hot and relentless.

"Where's the ice cream store?" Wilhemena asked. She felt growing concern over the distance they had put between their mother and themselves in their brief, rebellious journey.

"How should I know?" Freya said.

"I reckon they have more than one in a city like this," Aurora added, suddenly keen on the tempting prospect of a cold scoop.

Halfway down the block they passed by a movie theater. A line of patrons, mostly teenagers, were waiting in line at the ticket counter. Freya stopped, eyeing an opportunity to escape the heat.

"We're seeing a movie," Freya said.

"A movie? Are you crazy?" Aurora said.

"Mama says movies are the devil's work," Wilhemena added.

"You're chicken."

"Am not."

"Are, too."

"Am not. Mama needs us back at the market." Wilhemena crossed her arms.

"I don't care about some stupid market," Freya said.

Wilhemena looked around the alcove at the posters of seductive movie stars with rouged lips and bleached hair. Even the titles of the movies suggested sin: *To Hell and Back, Rebel Without a Cause, Guys and Dolls.*

"Come on. It'll be fun. Haven't you always wanted to see a picture?" Freya said.

"What would Mama do if she found out?"

"She'll never know about it."

Aurora waited for Wilhemena's thoughts on the matter. As the youngest, she always deferred to Wilhemena's wisdom.

"All right," Wilhemena said. "It'll be our secret."

"Our secret. I swear," Freya said and crossed her chest in a five-point star, invoking the sign of the pentagram. Secrets were her specialty.

They got in line behind a group of teenagers—three girls and a boy who was holding the hand of the prettiest one. The girlfriend wore a pale pink skirt that fell just below her knee and looked like it was made of fine gabardine. It matched the ribbon tied around her ponytail, Freya noticed.

The teenagers knew a lot about movie stars, and summer jobs, and high school football games, and things of equal importance; things that were as foreign to Freya as Africa.

As they carried on, the boy turned around, and for a moment his eyes fell on Freya.

Freya met his gaze, his smoky brown eyes framed by dark lashes. The curves of his body suggested hours spent on an athletic field, his skin tan and smooth like juniper berries just before they ripen. She smiled at him.

He smiled back.

In that moment, Freya felt a current of something new rush through her. She felt electrified. A magnetic force was pulling her to him. It was euphoric and blissful and out of her control.

Up until that moment, Freya had never felt that anything was beyond her control.

The euphoria ended when the girlfriend in the pink skirt turned around. "Matthew," she said sharply. She glanced over at Freya, Wilhemena, and Aurora in their ragged cotton skirts and scraggly tangles of hair. "Matthew, I said, who do *you* like better—Jane Russell or Marilyn Monroe?"

Matthew cleared his throat. He turned his back to Freya. The girlfriend looped her arm around the boy's and leaned against him, the perfect curl of her ponytail bobbing against his neck. She glanced back at Freya, her lips in a smug smile.

The group of teenagers purchased their tickets and stood in an alcove for a cigarette before the show. Freya heard the snap of their Zippos, and saw the deep purple aura that surrounded these beautiful creatures. She watched them take drags and blow smoke expertly out of the sides of their mouths. She heard whispering, then giggling.

Freya steeled her emotions, and moved up to the ticket counter.

Wilhemena slid the dollar bill across the top. "Three tickets please."

"It's a dollar fifty," the man at the ticket counter said.

"But I thought it was only a quarter per ticket."

"Fifty cents for adults, a quarter for kids twelve and under."

"Rats," Wilhemena muttered. She turned to her sisters. "I guess we should just head back to Mama."

Freya quickly stepped up the counter. "I am twelve. So is my sister," she said, pulling the too-short hem of her shirt down her waist.

"You're not twelve, Freya. That's a lie," Wilhemena said.

The man looked down his crooked nose at them.

Freya kicked Wilhemena under the counter.

"Ouch!"

"I am twelve," Freya said. "You can only charge me a quarter."

"Freya! You're fifteen."

The man at the ticket booth was indifferent. "Either you give me another fifty cents or let the next customer through."

"We haven't got another fifty cents," Wilhemena said.

"Next!" the man said, looking past them.

Wilhemena, Aurora, and Freya stepped aside. "Forget about it. Let's just go to the ice cream store," Aurora said.

"It's all your fault," Freya said to Wilhemena.

Wilhemena took on an air of authority. "You can't lie to get into a movie. It's wrong."

Suddenly the girl in the pink skirt yelled over to them. "What's wrong? Can't afford a matinee?"

The other girls laughed.

Freya snarled at them.

"Nice aprons by the way. Where'd you get them? The soup kitchen?" the girl in the pink skirt taunted.

"Yeah, that's where they live," another girl said.

"Shut your mouth!" Freya snapped.

"They look like gypsies," the girl in the pink skirt said. This sent the others into fits of laughter. Matthew laughed, too, and this, more than anything, sent waves of anger through Freya's body.

"They're the weird sisters," another one of the girls said.

"The older one looks like she has fleas," said another.

"Like a dog."

"Woof, woof," the boy howled.

Wilhemena spoke. "You must stop that at once."

"*You must stop that at once,*" the girl in the pink skirt mimicked.

Now the girls were roaring with laughter. A look of fear crossed Wilhemena's face. Aurora felt the fear, too. "Please stop!" Aurora yelled. "At once!"

"Can't you afford a comb, doggie?"

"Look at the fat one. She hasn't taken a bath in a month."

"She belongs in a pigsty. Oink. Oink."

Freya's face turned fire red, the anger heating up inside of her, tectonic shifts beneath a calm sea. All the hate inside her narrowing in on the face of her tormentors.

"Don't worry about them," Aurora said. "I don't care about them."

"Woof, woof."

"Oink. Oink."

Wilhemena gently squeezed Freya by the arm. "It's okay, Freya. Let's go get that ice cream."

"That's right, go back to your doghouse," the girl with the pink skirt mocked.

"Forget about them," Wilhemena whispered. "Leave them to their cruel destruction."

But it was too late. The anger welled inside Freya, rising through her veins, continents shifting inside her, pushing to the surface. Hatred burrowed deep down was unleashed in one complete and perfect wave. Aurora and Wilhemena felt the heat emitting from Freya's body. They braced themselves.

Silently, Freya reached into her pocket and let the grains of salt slip between her fingers.

"Little pig, little pig, let me come in," Freya said, her voice cool and steady.

"What a freak!" the girl said.

"Woof, woof."

"Oink. Oink."

"No, no, no," she grabbed a handful of enchanted salt and pulled it out of her pocket. "Not by hair on my chinny chin chin." With those words she threw the salt at the girl with the pink skirt. When the salt collided with her face, it was like pellets of buckshot. The girl stumbled backward. She felt around her face with her hands. She could feel something was wrong before she could see it. A coarse, black ruff of hair sprang from her chin. Down her neck it went, growing thicker and longer.

A loud shrill from the girl sent the others into a nervous silence. At first no one quite understood what had happened, or how it had happened, but soon the reality hit them. In a matter of seconds, the girl in the pretty pink skirt had grown a long, black beard.

Matthew pointed at Freya. "What did you do to her? What are you?"

Now it was Freya who was laughing, a mean cackle of a laugh grotesque in its bitterness.

"Make it stop," Matthew said, but his voice had lost its confidence.

"Come on, Freya, we need to get out of here," Wilhemena said, pulling on the back of her apron.

"So, you don't want to see your girlfriend so ugly and deformed?" Freya laughed.

Aurora tried next to rein her sister in, pulling and pleading and distracting her with promises of a thousand flavors of ice cream, to no avail.

"You're some kind of witch," Matthew said, a look of disgust on his face.

Freya was already gathering the next handful of magic salt. "Three blind mice, three blind mice. See how they run, see how they run," she said. She threw the salt at the boy. It sailed through the air, hitting him squarely in the eyes.

Matthew staggered backward, reeling from the sting. He clutched his face, blinking hard to get the bits of salt out. And when he opened his eyes, he could no longer see the mirth on Freya's face at having outwitted her enemies, nor the pale pink ribbon that matched his girlfriend's perfect skirt.

All was dark for him.

CHAPTER 12

> Specks on the fingers,
> Fortune lingers;
> Specks on the thumbs,
> Fortune surely comes.

I n the backseat of the minivan, Sophie is counting scarecrows in the front yards of homes along Route 1, the first hint of Halloween.

"We make a scarecrow?" Sophie asks.

"We'll carve pumpkins soon," I tell her, my head a little foggy from all the champagne last night at Astrid's house.

"Today?"

"Not today. It's not even October yet. They'll rot. You don't want a rotten jack-o'-lantern for Halloween, do you Sophe?"

"Do scarecrows rot?"

"No."

"We make a scarecrow today?" she says, undaunted.

In the rearview mirror I see the gleam in her eye, the wheels spinning in that little head. In the space of a couple minutes, she has already declared that she wants her scarecrow to be the biggest one in the world, that it's going to wear a pink dress and a have long blond hair, that she'll bring it to school for show-and-tell, and that she is going to make a girl scarecrow instead of a boy one, and the way she says "girl" like "gwirl" as in "squirrel" kills me every time, and I know that I will succumb even though making a scarecrow is the last thing I want to do. All that running around to multiple stores to get the materials, the terrific mess of straw to clean up afterward. I'll be sweeping bits of straw out of porch floorboards along with pine needles from the Christmas tree until next summer. A total waste of time. But, truthfully, who can say no to Sophie?

As she continues on with her fantastical plans for accessorizing her scarecrow (tiaras, capes, fairy wands, tutus), I run through the conversation I'm going to have with Aurora in my mind. I'll tell her that I've discovered a secret clique of potion makers in Monrovia and she will be so proud of me. "You've done a fine job, niece," she'll say. I will tell her that together we will sniff out Freya, and we will, once and for all, put an end to whatever evil dominion she holds over us.

Deep down, I also hope that Aurora will take one look at Sophie, at those big, brilliant eyes and that head of curls, and melt. She's already bonded with Henry. Maybe seeing her grandniece will remind her of all that she's missed out on over the years, of what she turned her back on, and of what I was like as a kid. Maybe seeing a child as beautiful as Sophie will make Aurora come to her senses and ask me—no, beg me—to take her into my life, so we could be one big, happy family again, like we were, once upon a time, so long ago that I sometimes wonder if it was ever real.

I hope that bringing Sophie isn't a mistake. If Aurora happens to be skinning a rabbit or dancing naked around a balefire, the poor girl could be scarred for life. But I have no choice. Montessori school has canceled classes today so everyone can take part in the bake sale fund-raiser for children in Haiti. Or is it Guatemala? One or the other. I was signed up to bring brownies, but I'm skipping it this time. There will be plenty more do-good bake sales for children in far-off lands in which to enlist. Today, my charity work is closer to home.

When we get to the trailhead at Greylock Woods, Cleo lurches out of the back of the minivan, over my headrest and out the door. It happens so fast, Sophie and I both shriek as she prances down the trail.

"Did you let Cleo in the car?" I ask.

"Nooooooo."

"Looks like we have a stowaway."

Cleo stops and sits on her haunches, tail beating the air, cat for *Follow me, you slackers.*

Sophie charges ahead of me down the path, chasing after Cleo. I wrestle the stroller out of the back of the minivan, snap it into position, and follow.

The trail is covered with brittle leaves, the smell of fall in the air. Sophie scoots ahead, then crouches down to get a better look at a fern that's covered with tiny black egg sacs. A snake slithers across the path, inches from her. I scream. Sophie looks at me. She is afraid because I am afraid, even though she didn't see the snake.

"Why don't you get in the stroller now," I say, trying to keep a cool demeanor. Sophie obliges. I tuck her into a fleece blanket and recline the back of the stroller. I give her a sippy cup and push forward, keeping a careful eye on anything rustling under the leaves.

By the time we get to Peter's Pond, the path is pocked with roots and rocks, and navigating the stroller gets challenging. Something scampers into the brush next to us.

Cleo leads the way along the old stone wall and up a small hill.

"What's that?" Sophie says, yawning.

"Staghorn sumac," I say, and pick one of the fluffy red buds for her.

"Pretty."

Something inside of me remembers a Lesson from my childhood. "We can make a tea out of it. Mix it with two parts cayenne pepper to cure whooping cough." *And summon the spirits of the dead on Mabon.*

"What's that?"

I follow her gaze. "Horsetail grass. Mix with honey to get shiny hair." *And to break hexes cast by jealous witches.*

I once read in a parenting magazine that exposing children to nature helps them grow into adults who cope better with stress and relationships. Blah, blah, blah. If that were true, I'd be the most stress-free adult on earth.

Sophie is nodding off now, tucked into her blanket.

"There," I say, pointing across the brook to a sunken swath of land covered in moss and peat. "That's a bog."

A bog. A special place. A place that is neither land nor sea. An in-between place. Where the will-o'-the-wisps live. Where magic dwells. My mother and I would go to the bog to pick wild cranberries to string on twine for the Feast of Gratitude, or what nonwitch folk call Thanksgiving. But ours wasn't the fourth Thursday of November. The Feast of Gratitude fell on the ninth full moon, between Samhain and the vernal equinox.

I learned about Thanksgiving my first year in foster care. The family I was assigned to had legions of kids staying with them for the holidays, plucked from the system like trout from the stream. I had the job of setting the table, which I didn't know how to do. The mother of the house yelled at me when I poured salt on the floor around the table in a banishing circle. The other kids laughed at me.

When the father of the house took his seat and said, "Let's pray," I watched my hands fold together like everyone else's, and my head bow. I watched the girl I was pretending to be say thanks for the food. Nothing felt real. I was acting in a play about a family at Thanksgiving, and I was cast in the role of Child Number Seven. Watching myself play the part had a powerful effect I me. At night, when the loneliness crept in, I would pretend I was still in that play. "Playing the part tonight of the orphaned child, Allison Ellylydan."

Even my name was no longer my own. A clerical mistake while I was being processed by the Department of Social Services changed me from Allesone to Allison.

As I look over the bog and listen to the croak of the frogs and the cry of the wood thrush, I realize I've been in this bog my whole life, the world of the in-between.

Cleo leads me farther past the bog and into a wooded area where the trees crowd together and grow thick with moss and lichen. The smell of earth is so strong I can feel it in my lungs. I look up, the sky cloaked behind a canopy of trees, and a white owl peers down on me from a branch of hemlock. I point the owl out to Sophie, but she's sound asleep.

When we get to a massive tangle of vines, Cleo lies down. Concord grapes wrap around the edge of the tangle. I step back and notice a chimney poking through the top of the brush, a stream of smoke rising above.

"This must be it," I say out loud. Cleo beats her tail on the soft ground.

I push aside leaves and reach a hand through the tangle of vines until I feel something solid. I pull aside more vines, knocking down clusters of bright green grapes, not yet ripe. There's stone and mortar underneath.

I feel my way around the leaves until I come to a door. I open it. Aurora, Beatrice, and Millie are seated at a rustic table, the glow of candles lighting their faces. The low ceiling is covered with bundles of dried herbs and a fire burns in a wide fieldstone hearth at the end of the room.

"How in the name of Mother Shipton did you find us?" Aurora says.

Cleo runs between my legs and hops up on the round table. Aurora pets her. "So you brought her here, hey?" Cleo purrs under her hand.

Millie walks over to me and grabs my hand in both of hers. "Come in, Allesone. We were just talking about you."

I pause, taking in the details—a shelf of dusty leather-bound books, a cauldron over the fire, an old cast-iron stove propped up on stones. "One minute," I say, gesturing toward the door. I push my way back through the curtain of vines and wheel in the stroller.

"Isn't she darling?" Millie says.

"Her name's Sophie." The fire and candlelight cast a warm tint on Sophie's pink cheeks, giving her an angelic glow.

Beatrice walks over and peers into the stroller. "Yup, it's a kid," she says, scowling.

I turn to Aurora, smiling.

Aurora sits back down and goes to work rolling sheets of beeswax into candles. Honey drips from the table onto the pine floorboards.

"This is Sophie," I say to Aurora, wondering if she missed the introduction the first time around, or if she's being intentionally aloof. "I have another daughter, Gillian. And you've already met my son, Henry."

"I know how many kids you got, niece."

"Do you think Sophie looks like me?" I say, a wisp of desperation in my voice. "Everyone says she takes after Kevin, but I can see some Ellylydan in her. What do you think, Aurora?"

But Aurora doesn't even look at Sophie. She doesn't notice the sweetness in her face that is only magnified when she's sleeping. She puts her head down and rolls her wax.

I take a seat next to her. "What's wrong? Are you angry with me?"

"You shouldn't be here," Aurora says.

Millie and Beatrice exchange a nervous glance. "Now that the enchantment's worn off, well . . . ," Millie begins.

"You're putting us all in danger," Beatrice snarls.

The conversation I had so carefully rehearsed in my head disappears and all I can sputter out are a few childish words: "But . . . I did good." I take a deep breath and continue. "I found a coven in Monrovia. They revealed themselves to me last night. They want me to join them. Their leader, Astrid, is very powerful."

Aurora picks up a ceramic pitcher on the table and pours from it. Bright red liquid gurgles into the brown mug. She passes it to me.

"Was Freya there? Did you see her?" Aurora asks. Millie and Beatrice look at me, as intense as a cat watching its prey.

"No." I take a sip and it makes my mouth pucker. It's cranberry wine, tart and sweet, just like I remember. "But I thought you should know about them. They want me in their coven. I thought about it, and, well, I realized my real family is right here."

"How did you know they were real witches? Did you see their magic with your own eyes? Did they make anything levitate? Anything transform?" Aurora asks.

I pause and take another sip of wine.

"No."

"Did they possess all the five elements?"

"No," I say.

All three of them exhale loudly.

I steel myself and continue. "But I *felt* it. I felt my neck twitch every time I was around one of them. Just like you said it would."

Aurora rolls her eyes. "But you didn't see my sister? You weren't witness to her power?"

"Maybe, well, I don't know, maybe Astrid works for her. You said yourself that Freya might be recruiting help. Astrid runs the entire town. From the PTO to the city council. You see, they make soap and they throw these home-shopping parties, and it's really a big deal to get invited to one. This coven, they're behind every party, every trend, every business, every school activity, every charity, everything in town. No one puts up a flowerpot without their approval."

"What does she look like? How old is she?" Aurora says.

I want to be right so badly, but now it all seems ridiculous. "She's about my age. Rich beyond belief. Beautiful. And powerful. You should have seen this party she threw together last minute. No one can do that without magic. There was a champagne fountain. There were posh people. Besides, why would Astrid claim to be a witch if she's not?"

Aurora laughs so loudly the table shakes. Millie and Beatrice laugh, too. I want to curl up in a ball and die.

Aurora slugs back some wine. "They ain't real witches. You found nothing but a bunch of imitators. Being a witch is all the rage nowadays. Everyone wants to run around joining a coven. It's very . . . chichi."

Beatrice snorts. "They all come out on Halloween, dressed up in black. It's a sorry sight."

"Allesone, sweetie, we know you did your best," Millie says, her eyes apologetic. "But you'd know if you ran across the Dark Witch. Dark forces surround her."

I look to Aurora for some hint of acceptance, but find none. "But these are real witches," I protest. Anxiety gathers in my stomach like a hollow pit.

"Freya can command the sea, niece. You see any of these lady friends of yours commanding the sea? Summoning the devil?"

"Astrid *knows* about me. She *knows* I'm a witch. A *real* witch. An Ellylydan," I say, my voice cracking.

Beatrice grunts something about the Dark Witch not futzing with champagne and parties.

"Allesone, your skills are a little rusty around the pipes," Millie adds. "Maybe you just need to brush up on some of your Lessons."

"But I am one of you," I yell. "I'm a real witch. I can transform things just by thinking about them. What do you want to do, dunk me in water to see if I drown?" I notice Sophie stirring in her stroller, her eyelids flutter. I lower my voice. "I can help you. I can help you find the Dark Witch, and we can talk to her and put an end to all this."

Beatrice walks to the fire and stokes it. "Dark times lie ahead, Aurora. You know that. Having Allesone in the coven will hinder us."

Aurora looks at me then lowers her eyes. "Beatrice is right. Having you here puts us at risk. You'll lead Freya right to us."

My heart sinks. I feel myself drifting into nothingness. I might faint. "But I'm one of you."

"You must leave now," Aurora says.

I turn slowly, grab Sophie's stroller and leave. Not one of them looks at me as I push my way back through the vines. And I remind myself that I've been here before. Untethered from family. Alone in the world. Abandoned by my own mother. Rejected by my aunt.

Cleo slinks ahead of me and leads the way home.

As I make my way back out of Greylock Woods, through the smell of raw earth and bog, I feel like I've been punched in the chest.

When I get back to the car, I pull out my phone and the card Astrid gave me last night and I compose my text:

I'm in.

CHAPTER 13

This knot I knit,
To know the thing I know not yet,
That I may see
The man that shall my husband be.

I am expecting something more macabre. Animal sacrifice. Oaths in blood. Broomsticks and brimstone. At the very least some sort of ritual dancing or sage burning.

Not a limo ride and a day of pampering at the most exclusive spa in Boston.

Right now, I'm buried up to my neck in a silky mud bath. I have to take Bethanny's word for it that this part of my Glamour initiation is, "like, totally normal and not as gross as it looks." Besides, this isn't just any mud. It's a mixture of volcanic ash imported from Hawaii, Canadian peat, and clay flown in from the Dead Sea. This is fancy mud. It smells like citrus and cinnamon. It feels divine. My freshly polished toes stick out at the end of the tub like bright pink Chiclets.

Miranda and Kimberly are tucked into mud baths on either side of me, while Erin, Heather, and Bethanny lie on chaises, wrapped in Egyptian cotton towels, with cucumber slices over their eyes.

The ladies act like this level of luxury is perfectly normal, so I've followed their lead all day. When Miranda requested a bee venom peel, I did the same. When Erin ordered an extra shot of wheatgrass in her beet-and-kale breakfast smoothie, I asked them to make mine a double.

Finally, I can't contain my astonishment anymore.

"This is heaven," I say.

"No," Heather says, "this is the Phoenix Club."

"Is this what everyone gets when they join Glamour?" I ask.

"We were all like you," Miranda says, sipping a mint tea. "I had never even been out of Massachusetts when I joined. What a hillbilly, right?"

"I was a size twenty and had a husband with a gambling problem," Erin says without a hint of shame.

So the sushi boat crowd wasn't always such. Privilege isn't part of their DNA, not like the children they're raising, who know nothing of consumer moderation or bargain hunting at the sales racks of T.J.Maxx.

"Don't misunderstand. Glamour's hard work, too," Kimberly says. "Lilith and Rosie had to miss your initiation to work at the factory today. Production's always hanging over our heads. It takes lots of man hours to make all that soap. I'm in charge of the factory. These guys do greenhouse, marketing, and distribution."

"Distribution? You mean the home-shopping parties?" I ask.

"For starters. There's also the welcome baskets, retail outlets, donations of Glamour Soap to charities. Everyone in Monrovia gets some Glamour, whether they know it or not," Miranda says.

"Astrid expects a lot from each of us," Erin says.

"Don't be such a downer," Bethanny says. "Trust me, Allison, the benefits outweigh the work, by, like, a gazillion."

Heather rolls her eyes.

Heather is sitting next to Erin who is nibbling on a chocolate truffle. I've come to think of them as HeathErin since they're always together. They were the ones who picked me up in the limo and arranged my entire day, including coverage for child and pet care so I could enjoy my initiation without distraction. They even covered husband care, in the form of an invitation from their husbands (the city councillors) to have drinks and discuss waterfront plans and football.

"Wait until you try the hot stone massage," Erin says.

I envision myself lying naked on a table while a stranger covers me in scalding rocks. It makes me a little uneasy, both the rocks and the nudity. Even in the mud bath, I keep my underwear on.

As if reading my mind Erin says, "Use some of this and you won't care who sees your stuff." She pulls a spray bottle out of her purse and sets it on the empty chair next to her. "Works like magic."

"What is it?"

"Courage in a bottle," she says.

"Is that the elderberry and primrose relaxer oil?" Miranda asks.

Erin nods.

"From the new batch?"

Erin nods again.

"Better give yourself three sprays then," Miranda says.

"Seems like you've been having a lot of problems with consistency lately," Heather says.

"It's not my fault," Miranda says, sounding rather defensive. "*You're* the potion master."

"Well we're out of some important ingredients," Miranda snaps back.

Kimberly pantomimes a zipper over her lips and I wonder what they are talking about, but I'm still feeling my way around these new friends, trying to find the boundaries. For now, I figure it's better to talk less and observe more. At least the twitchiness in my neck is gone now when I'm around them. Either the enchantment has worn off, or I'm immune to it the way people with tinnitus get used to the constant ringing in their ears.

"Let's not spoil Allison's initiation," Kimberly says. "How are you feeling, Allison?"

I slide deeper into the mud. "I haven't felt this good in a long time," I say.

"You always remember your first time," Kimberly says, eyes

closed, semicomatose, in her mud bath. "I had never even had a manicure when I was initiated. Sure as hell didn't know the difference between oysters Moscow and oysters Florentine. Take it from me, Allison, you'll learn about the good things fast."

"My first time . . . I didn't even know what foie gras was," Erin says. "I was a quick study though." She pops another truffle in her mouth.

Bethanny stands up from her chaise lounge. She peels the cucumbers off her eyes and lets her towel drop to the floor. Her body is a perfect hourglass, her skin flawless and radiant. For an awkward moment I look around at the other women to see what they'll do, but no one is paying any attention to her. She aims her dark eyes at me. "I'm going in for a sauna. Anyone want to join?"

I look down at the greenish brown sluice of mud that is simultaneously moisturizing, detoxifying, nourishing, and cleansing me.

There are no takers.

"See you at the shopping session, then," she says and walks away, swinging her hips. She puts her hands on her backside and gives herself a seductive caress. She turns around and when she sees I'm looking at her, gives me a wink.

I look away—at the chandeliers, the tiles, my toes—embarrassed.

"She does that all the time. If you ask me, she's drunk a little too much of the love potion," Heather says.

"We all have our vices," Erin says, popping another truffle.

Love potion? Vices? I have so many questions. What kind of magic do they do? How does the magic work? How did Astrid get her powers? How did Astrid find them? If you're not born a witch like me, can you have real powers? Or are they all imitators like Aurora says? Do they know about me and my skills? What do they think of me joining them?

Since these aren't exactly the typical getting-to-know-you questions, I pick the easiest one and throw it out there.

"How did you all become Glamour Girls?"

Kimberly laughs. "We've been wondering how long it would take you to start asking."

"We've all been the new girl at one point," Heather says. "We know it's a lot to get used to."

"I'll tell you how it happened to me," Miranda says. "I used to be a townie, believe it or not. I grew up across the river. You should have seen me back then, Allison. Breaking into abandoned mills with my friends, warm six-pack in one hand, boom box in the other. Piercings everywhere. I was grunge before grunge was a thing.

"And it was a tough town. Cars propped on cinder blocks on my street. People shooting up in the middle of the day, since they had nothing else to do. At night the fights that broke out after last call when everyone was wasted." She shakes her head. "It wasn't working class; it was no class.

"And stupid me, it was like I had 'victim' tattooed on my forehead. I drew in every shitbag loser in the county. Junkies, cheaters." A dark expression crosses her face. "One was a hitter." She closes her eyes for a moment, then continues.

"A few years ago, I was with this one guy Reggie and thought things were going great. We moved in together in a crappy apartment with slanted floors and crumbling Sheetrock, but I was in love, and it didn't matter. He treated me well. His only flaw was that he was a pot dealer."

"Sounds like a real catch," Kimberly says.

"I wanted to marry him. I was dying to get married. All the girls I went to school with were already married and divorced by then. Anyway, Reggie decides to start growing weed in our apartment, you know, become his own supplier. Have you ever smelled a marijuana plant?"

I shake my head no.

"There's a reason they call it skunk weed," Miranda continues. "It gets in your skin, in your mouth. It's awful. Reggie knows nothing about horticulture, so he lets those stalks grow and grow, right up to the ceiling. One even starts poking through a crack and goes right into the floorboards above us. He didn't know how to pollinate them, or harvest them. He'd just pull off the leaves, and sell them along with his regular stuff. Some of his customers stopped by to demand their money back."

Miranda's accent has changed during the telling of her story. Gone is the polished inflection she uses while demonstrating Glamour products to housewives, and in its place is the rough cadence of her townie voice, the words slightly clipped at the ends.

"And then, you know what he does? He leaves. Runs off with some girl whose father owns a laundromat. And I got all these dirtbags pounding on my door in the middle of the night demanding to see Reggie.

"I was scared. I didn't have a job, or any family to help me, but I found a few seeds, and I get this idea to start growing my own. Only I was smart about it. I read about hydroponics and gene mutations. I experimented with pollination techniques. I had a talent for it. My first crop of bud was better than that shit Reggie grew."

She tilts her head and tightens her expression.

"I was so good at it, I expanded my operation. I got a bit of a reputation in town as a high-quality grower. I was making money, too. I could even afford two apartments—one to live in and one to grow my crops.

"Then one day, the cops knock on my door. More blues than I'd ever seen anywhere. Wondered where the hell they'd been when the windows of my Datsun were getting smashed in, or when my apartment was getting robbed for the third time. They cuffed me and took me away. Turns out, they'd been tracking Reggie for months, when they discovered my little operation and started tracking me instead. And since the apartment was within three hundred feet of a school, my crime carried a mandatory sentence. I was sitting there in jail that night, crying 'til I was dry inside. My parents were gone. I had no one."

Miranda pushes herself up to her elbows out of the mud. Kimberly, Heather, Erin, and I are all listening intently. "And Astrid shows up and makes my bail. I'd never seen her before. She tells me that she's a Realtor from Monrovia and that she has a greenhouse and is looking for a gardener. She hired a lawyer for me, and somehow got my trial moved to Monrovia. Who the hell knows what kind of strings she pulled. Once the trial was held in Monrovia, she had no problem getting me exonerated."

"Why you?" I ask, thinking back to how Astrid plucked Kevin from south of Boston to hire him as her contractor.

"I was good with hydroponics. I set up her lab. She had me grow all kinds of shit I'd never heard of—asafetida, night crawler, witch hazel—but nothing illegal. I couldn't figure her out, then she started showing me how to grind and mix plants with other crazy ingredients like oyster shells and clay."

"She was showing you how to make potions," I say.

"Exactly. I was the first employee at Glamour Soap."

"So, what do the potions do?" I ask. "Can she levitate? Can she transform objects?" I pause. "Can she command the sea?"

They all laugh. "You've read way too many fantasy novels," Erin says. Knowing Astrid can't command the sea is actually a great relief, though I'm still confused about what powers she really does possess, if any. My mind wanders to Henry and his world of make-believe. I wonder if this is how he feels when I tell him his heroes and villains aren't real.

"You'll see. She makes your wishes come true," Miranda says.

"What kind of wishes?"

She wipes the mud off her shoulders, the skin underneath streaked in pink from the heat of the bath. "She gives me a potion that lets me see people for who they are."

"How?"

"When I meet a guy, I take this special potion she gives me, and I sprinkle it on a string. Once I get to know him a little better, I tie the string around something he owns—like a shirt, or car keys, or a picture, or something. If the knot comes undone, he's trouble. If it stays tied, he's worth pursuing. So far, it's been foolproof."

"So you've met someone?" I ask.

"No. The knot's come untied every time." She pouts. "But it's saved me from making any more bad choices."

I look at her closely and she meets my look and we both crack up. All the nervousness I've ever felt around the Glamour Girls vanishes. There is no judgment. Suddenly I feel very close to these women, the way I've always imagined it would feel to have sisters.

After the mud baths and massages (which turns out to be relaxing thanks to Erin's magic spray), I'm taken through a beauty regimen that includes being pumiced, scrubbed, exfoliated, hydrated, peeled, waxed, polished, and infused with lotions.

Everywhere I go, one of the ladies is waiting for me with advice on everything from the best eyebrow shapers in Monrovia to the best way to run an effective committee meeting.

"Always throw on lip gloss before you leave your house, even if you're just going Nelson's General Store for a pint of milk," Bethanny tells me as we're getting our cellulite blasted by lasers.

"When you get your committee to pass one of your initiatives, let someone else take credit for it," Miranda informs me as we're getting lash extensions.

"Never wear last year's shoes," Kimberly says as we sip champagne. "Shoes are the heart of any new trend."

This makes me laugh. "I've never thought of myself as a trendsetter."

"You're one of us now." Kimberly lifts her glass and we clink crystal. "You are a leader whether you like it or not. Women will look up to you."

It occurs to me that the old Allison would want to vomit over such vanity. But there's someone else inside of me—a new Allison—who's having a really great time with these women. I like the attention. I like having a day that's all about me. I like feeling important.

No one here knows the girl I was, sick with shame in my secondhand corduroy pants so thin I could feel the rough skin of my knee through the spiderweb fibers as I sat alone in the school library. The too-small rugby shirts I bought from Salvation Army, the polo shirts, always with a hole or a stain put there by the original owner. Showing up for my first dance in sixth grade without the right clothes because I didn't have a mother to show me how to dress, hiding in the lavatory the whole time, sitting on the toilet, my Hush Puppies pulled up off the floor, out of sight, as the pretty patent-leather Mary Janes gathered at the mirror. Swearing to God and myself that if I ever had girls I would make sure my girls had the right clothes for the right occasions.

Erin, who's had at least a bottle of champagne, checks her watch. "It's time," she says and stumbles out of her chair.

"This is my favorite part! Allison, you have no idea how totally lucky you are. I wish I was you right now." Bethanny is hopped up on shopping adrenaline and pink champagne, which we're all drinking from long fluted crystal. "You're like the bride and we're all, like, the bridesmaids. Isn't it great!"

"Chill out," Heather snaps.

Kimberly loops her arm around mine. "Just enjoy it. And don't be intimidated by Sissy Star. She comes on strong, but she's hired to make you look your best."

"Sissy who?"

Sissy Star, Kimberly tells me, is a New York stylist whose regular appearances on the red carpet have made her something of a celebrity in her own right. When in Boston, she's hired to dress the wealthy daughters of bankers and plastic surgeons, girls who spend their summers on Martha's Vineyard and their winter holidays in Aspen. That is to say her clientele is a group for whom style and beauty are as fundamental to the human form as a spinal column.

She also happens to be a personal friend of Astrid's.

Sissy is about five feet tall with blisteringly blond spiky hair. She wears black palazzo pants and a fur vest, and oversize sunglasses. "Let's get started," she says. She claps her hands and two assistants roll out racks of clothes.

She lowers her glasses and eyes me up and down. "Five seven. A hundred and forty-two pounds?"

"Yes," I say, impressed by her accuracy.

She pushes her glasses back on. "You'll lose a couple pounds once you start wearing couture. For now . . . wear Spanx."

I look back at all the ladies. Erin gives me a huge smile of encouragement. She lifts her shirt slightly to show me the corset-like Spanx she has on.

Sissy starts pulling clothes off the rack and hands them to her assistants, who soon are weighed down with skirts and tops and coats. "What's your shoe size?"

"Nine and a half."

Sissy looks appalled. "I'm calling in a favor to Christian. I'll have a special pair of Louboutins ordered for you. Snakeskin and crystal. Very on trend."

Bethanny jumps off the couch. "Louboutins! Oh, Allison!" For some reason, I find Bethanny's overly developed superficiality endearing.

In the changing room, outfits are laid out for me to try on. I flip over the price tag on a funky pink and orange tunic. My jaw drops. It costs more than my first car. Erin sees my sticker shock. "Don't worry about it. Astrid's picking up the tab. She does this for everyone at their initiation."

My phone vibrates. I check. It's a text message from Judy. I was supposed to meet her for a walk after her work so I could debrief her on the equinox party in glorious detail. I turn the phone to silent and slip it back into my purse. There's no way I can talk to her about the party right now, much less Sissy Star, bee venom peels, and secret covens. Her head would explode.

I slip on the first outfit, the pink and orange tunic over black leggings and over-the-knee leather boots with a tall heel. I look in the mirror. My jaw drops again. I look like one of them. One of the beautiful people. I twirl around and look some more.

I'm taking way too long to come out and model the clothes. Sissy calls for me. "Just a minute," I say. I look at myself again. Is this me? These clothes? These women?

I don't know how much time goes by, but I'm panicking.

"Knock, knock." Erin's voice.

She pushes open the door a crack and slips in.

"What's taking so long?"

I can't answer because I'm worried my voice will break.

"They're all waiting for you. You look gorgeous. Come out and show everyone."

"I can't."

"What's wrong?"

"I don't know if this is me."

"What do you mean? Of course it's you."

"I mean all of this." I hold up the pile of designer labels. "What have I done to deserve all this?"

Erin slurs her words a little, buzzed on champagne. "Honey, we need you just as much as you need us."

"What do you mean?"

Erin smiles nervously. "Nothing. I didn't say anything. I'll wait for you with the others. You look perfect."

I straighten my tunic and head back into the parlor to show off my new look as a diva witch, wondering, just a bit, if the coven is trying to sell me as much as I'm trying to sell them.

CHAPTER 14

Star light, star bright,
First star I see tonight,
I wish I may, I wish I might,
Have the wish I wish tonight.

I awake to the sound of a car engine. A door opens, slams shut. The car pulls away. 5:45 A.M. on the clock. Dark outside.

I look to see if Kevin's heard it, too. I nudge him, gently first, then harder, then sharply, in the ribs. He rolls over and pulls the covers over his head.

I get out of bed, sling my new pink cape over my newly exfoliated shoulders and head downstairs. Cleo is going crazy at the front door. When I open it, she runs out and pounces on top of the wicker basket that's just been delivered. A green van spews exhaust as it pulls out of my driveway and heads down the street.

Cleo has knocked over the basket and spilled its contents on the porch. She's batting at a bundle of herbs like it's a ball of yarn. "Easy girl." I pick up the mess, grab the basket and go inside to the kitchen.

The basket has a sundry assortment of items. There's a jar of green Salem clay, a bottle of witch hazel, a bottle of some sort of oil, a roll of beeswax, a mortar and pestle, a sieve, a miniature hourglass, and a bundle of dried herbs, of which I only recognize rosemary.

On top is a note, written in green calligraphy:

Dear Allison,
We welcome you with open arms. What every woman
needs is to put herself first. No waiting, rushing, or

hurrying today. Wear this masque and show your true
face to the world. Say the words "me first" and the world
will wait for you.

Deepest affection,
Astrid

Another gift from Astrid. Something to go along with the
bags of designer clothes wrapped in scented tissue paper that
are stashed in my closet from yesterday. I look at the clock
again. No one in my house is going to be awake for another
hour. So, alone in my kitchen, I lay out the ingredients and
start making my very first magical potion.

Step one, it says, is to grind the dried herbs in the mortar
with the beeswax and three drops of witch hazel. It's messy at
first, but once the beeswax begins to break down, it forms a
paste that's easy to work with. Soon a wonderful fragrance
spreads through the room. Step two: When the paste is done,
I set up a double boiler and add the green clay, oil, and paste.
Step three: From here the directions get very specific. I'm to
stir the concoction clockwise for one whole turn of the mini-
hourglass, then tip the hourglass over and stir counterclockwise for another cycle, and repeat this pattern three times. I
watch the sand slip through the neck of the glass as I stir.

Cleo jumps up onto the counter and watches, her head circling right, left, right, along with the spoon. She snarls and
hisses at the concoction, then jumps down. After the goop is
cooked I follow step four and pour it through a sieve into a
glass jar.

Another three turns of the hourglass, and the masque is
cool enough to handle. The final step is simple: Apply to face. I
dip a finger in the jar and spread the warm, slick mixture onto
my face. It's immediately soothing. I spread it over my eyelids,
down my cheekbones, over my lips, along my chin. Soon my
whole face is covered and it feels fabulous.

Rufus runs into the room, tail wagging, excited for an

early-morning companion. But when he sees me, he barks and runs out again, tail tucked between his legs.

Quietly, I go upstairs into the bathroom, flick on the light, and . . . oh my God, my face is green!

I rub my face with tissue, but it doesn't come off. I run the water and splash it all over my face, making a mess of the vanity, but when I look in the mirror, I'm still green. I scrub and scrub with the hand towel. I wash with soap. I exfoliate, but nothing works. My skin has completely absorbed the green clay. What have I done to myself?

Outside the door I hear footsteps, and by their slow, labored pace I can tell that it's Kevin carrying a child. I look in the mirror again. I lock the door.

Kevin tries to open it. "Allison, why is the door locked?"

"Mommy?" Sophie says, in a groggy voice.

"I just need some privacy," I say, my horrid green face staring back at me in the mirror.

"Are you going to be long?"

"Just use the bathroom downstairs!"

He heads downstairs with Sophie and I search the cabinets for something that will remove the masque. Rubbing alcohol, witch hazel, loofah.

Kevin yells up from the kitchen, "Allison, where's the apple juice?"

Sophie is yelling for me, too. "Mom-my. Mom-my! I want cinnamon toast."

I ignore them, hoping they'll get along without me. But Kevin yells for me again. "Allison! Are we out of butter?"

"I'm in the bathroom," I yell back.

Gillian and Henry are up now. Footsteps come and go between bedrooms as kids get ready for school.

"Mom, where are my red shoes?" Gillian yells.

"In the mudroom," I yell through door.

"Allison, Henry wants Honey Snaps," Kevin yells.

"In the pantry, behind the Bisquick," I yell back.

"Allison, can you come down here?" Kevin yells.

I look in the mirror. I'm hideous. How am I going to explain this to my family? What kind of magic did Astrid send me?

"I don't feel good," I yell.

I hear Kevin's footsteps bounding up the stairs. He knocks on the bathroom door. "Are you going to be much longer?" There's agitation in his voice.

"I feel sick. Can you handle getting the kids to school without me?"

He's silent for a moment, the magnitude of the task before him sinking in.

"Do you need to go to the doctor?"

"No."

"Too much champagne yesterday?" he asks, alluding to my extravagant day at the Phoenix Club, the details of which I've selectively shared with him.

"Yeah. Something like that."

There's a pause. Kevin is not great at multitasking, and getting three kids out the door in the morning is an exercise in multitasking.

"All right," he finally grunts and returns to the trenches.

I stay quarantined in the bathroom through the entire morning ritual, yelling out directions when needed. Kevin can't find Sophie's lucky barrette. Gillian needs a note that she's going home with Breanna. Henry's lost a Jedi lightsaber in the laundry. Sophie needs something for show-and-tell. There are field trip permission forms that need to be filled out, there are lunches that have to be made, there are mismatched socks, and missing homework folders, and coffee that's not made, and a coat with a stain that needs to go to the dry cleaners today, and a loose tooth that needs addressing. "I need, I need, I need," is all I hear.

In the shuffle I'm pretty sure that Kevin has forgotten to

make the kids brush their teeth and wash their faces and brush their hair, but I'm green and I can't exactly intervene right now.

I look down at the card in my hand again.

Desperately I read it over again. Either Astrid is playing a trick on me and hazing the new girl, or I made a mistake. But I've done everything exactly as it's written. Then I read the letter again. "Say the words 'me first' and the world shall wait for you."

I take a deep breath. "Me first."

And, just like that, there is silence.

I press my ear to the door. I can hear the shuffle of feet up and down the stairs. I can hear the front door open and close and the truck door open and close and I can hear Kevin's truck puttering away, full of kids and purpose.

I step outside the bathroom to an empty house. Downstairs, there is a mess from breakfast bowls and cups, and a pile of hats and shoes, but the lunch boxes and the kids are off to school.

It worked! The Me-First Masque worked! My family survived a morning without me! I feel like dancing for joy, then I catch a glimpse of myself and my green face in the glass of the door, and decide I'm not completely in the clear yet.

In my makeup drawer, which suffers from gross neglect, I pull out a tube of concealer and a foundation palette. They do the job well. When I'm done, my face is skin-colored, which is an improvement. And since I'm already delving into new territory, I decide to go all the way—eye shadow, mascara, lipstick.

I pick up the phone and start to schedule some doctors' appointments. "Me first," I say as I dial the numbers. The impossible-to-get time slots for the pediatrician and dentist open up as the receptionists bend over backward to accommodate me.

At nine o'clock I get in the car to meet Judy at Starbucks,

where we always meet on Tuesday after drop-off. "Me first," I say as I approach the Starbucks on Front Street. There's no parking in front, as usual, but just as I reach the shop, a car pulls out of the prime spot and I pull in.

Judy's already there, holding a table for us. The line is out the door.

"You look good," Judy says, a little too much surprise in her voice.

"Lipstick," I say.

"Oh."

"What's with the line this morning?"

Judy looks over the row of athletic-looking women in color-coordinated spandex, yoga mats tucked under one arm, baby strollers in the other, hair pulled into ponytails. Visions of perfect health and happiness. "New Pilates studio opened up next door. Class must have just gotten out. They're all waiting to get their nonfat, no-foam, no-calorie, no-taste cappuccinos."

"You save the table," I say, "I'll grab the coffee."

"Get me a chocolate chip muffin, too," says Judy.

A pair of the Pilates moms look over at her in surprise. "That's right. It's called a carb. You should try one sometime," she says.

The women look away, and I can't help but laugh.

The Monrovia Starbucks has to be the slowest Starbucks in the country. The baristas are overly chatty. Normally I can measure the time it takes in line by the number of random thoughts that go through my mind. But not today.

"Me first," I whisper as I walk toward the line.

Suddenly, the line melts away. People step aside to use their cell phones, or wave me ahead so they can contemplate the drink menu. Some just walk out of the store completely. Without any waiting, I'm in the front of the line ordering two lattes and muffins.

"That was fast," Judy says when I set down our coffees on the table.

"Yeah, I guess so." I try to act like it's no big deal.

Judy dives into her muffin, dropping streusel down her shirt. "So, give me the dish. How was Astrid's party? Have you gone over to the dark side?"

"The dark side?" I feel cagey. For a second, I wonder if my green face is visible through my foundation.

"You know—the pretentious Glamour bitches. The look-at-me-and-my-perfect-life crowd."

"Oh. They were fine. Pretty nice, actually."

"Hmmm," Judy says. She seems disappointed. "Did they bore you to death with all their charity bullshit? What did you talk about?"

I'm very vague about the whole thing. I describe the champagne fountain, the raw bar, the giant aquarium, the violinists, the mounted grizzly bear, the amazing floral arrangements, but I leave out the most important details, like the part about discovering the witches of Monrovia and being initiated into their coven.

"That's it?" Judy says. "Nothing about who got the latest boob job?"

My voice goes up an octave as I lie to her. "I didn't really notice any of that."

She blows into her latte. I can see in her eyes that she's disappointed. Postparty gossip is one of our favorite pastimes.

"What about Astrid? Did she try to recruit you into her home-shopping pyramid scheme? Tell me you're not going to be wearing one of those pink capes."

I keep my eyes on the table.

"I mean, all the posturing. All that pseudo do-goodness," Judy continues. "They act like planting a rose bush is on par with donating a kidney. I don't know how you could stand it. Just promise me you won't turn into one of them."

I wish Judy would drop it. For the first time in my life, I'm in the in crowd. Why can't she just be happy for me? Why does she have to judge me for it? All these years I've been struggling to hide who I really am. It would be nice show my true identity for once.

I'm a witch. I always have been. Why should I run from my magic? What if Aurora used her magic instead of hibernating in the woods? What if my mother had used her witchcraft out in the open? It couldn't have been worse than ending up in a psych hospital for the rest of her life, hiding from the world. Hiding from me.

Astrid gets it. *Wear this masque and show your true face to the world.* This is my true face.

Judy is still going on with her list of grievances against the Glamour Girls.

I whisper, "Me first," and the talking stops.

CHAPTER 15

Old Mother Hubbard
Went to the cupboard
To get her poor Dog a bone;
But when she came there
The cupboard was bare,
And so the poor Dog had none.

I won't be home for dinner," Kevin says. He's dressed in khakis, an oxford shirt, and a tie, a bold departure from jeans and a tool belt.

"Is it just you and Mayor Davey tonight?" I ask.

He crouches down to look at himself in the kid-height mirror over the kid-height coatrack in the front hallway. "Half of city council, too."

"Do you have the blueprints?"

"Yup."

"Budget proposal? Schematics?"

"Check and check."

"You'll do great," I say.

He gathers his wallet and keys off the counter, and flips through his waterfront proposal plan for the hundredth time. "This is going to be big for us, Allison. No more scratching by. We'll be able to go on a real vacation finally. We'll get you a new car, too. Maybe some new jewelry."

"I don't need jewelry." Besides, I have a feeling I could just put in an order with the coven and jewelry would appear.

"I want to get you something special." There's a brightness in his voice.

I smile, thinking about how quickly things can change when you have Astrid on your side.

"Go ahead and say it," he says.

"What?"

" 'I told you so.' "

"I would never say that." I pause. "But I did tell you they weren't so bad."

"I should send Astrid a fruit basket or something. I really misjudged her. When she gets behind something she makes things happen."

"Or someone." The Glamour Girls in action. Taking care of our own.

Kevin kisses me and looks into my eyes for a long, delicious moment, like he did when we first met. His eyes are filled with love and gratitude.

"You're welcome," I say.

After Kevin leaves, Sophie and I hunker down for a game of Candy Land. She's advancing to the Gumdrop Mountains when the doorbell rings.

"Door!" she hollers, sliding her game piece. "Who's it, Mommy?"

I'm not expecting anyone. I haven't even managed to put a bra on yet. I tell Sophie to take another turn while I get the door.

A maid from Domestic Glamour, Astrid's housecleaning service, is at my door with a delivery. "Sign, please," the maid in the green uniform says.

There are herbs, leaves, and flowers, and a recipe card in the basket. A handwritten note says,

Dear Allison,
  We cherish you as one of our own. You deserve a life of ease and glamour, beyond the drudgery of household duty. Accept this potion as token of our new friendship.
                                      Sincerely,
                                      Astrid

The gifts just keep coming.

The Well-Bred Pet

INGREDIENTS:
  Pinch of sugar
  2 leaves crow's foot
  1 bunch catnip
  4 stalks hound's tongue
  ½ cup swine's snout
  1 daddy longlegs spider (alive)

Bring 4 cups water to a boil. Add sugar and stir counterclockwise until dissolved. Reduce heat to simmer. Add the next four ingredients to pot. Lift spider by one leg and dangle over pot as you repeat three times: "If you wish to live and thrive, let the spider walk alive." Release spider outdoors. Steep herbs for thirteen minutes. Strain. Add two drops to water bowl and watch as your pet becomes a model of domesticated perfection.

I plop Sophie in front of a cartoon so I can get to work.

In the kitchen I add crow's foot, catnip, hound's tongue, and swine's snout to the pot. But I'm in need of a daddy longlegs, so I descend into the dark, cluttered basement. I trip over a cracked sled and make my way through an obstacle course of camping equipment, dried-up cans of paint, dusty bottles of wine, cases of beer, old gardening projects, and abandoned toy sets.

Spiderwebs crisscross the low beams like nets of spun wool. I have to duck to avoid them. Most of the webs are empty, abandoned by their architects long ago. In a dark corner near the toboggan, I capture a spider in a shoebox and come back upstairs.

Touching the daddy longlegs gives me the creeps, but as strange as they seem, I've already learned that Astrid's potions pack a punch. They help make things better. It's as though she can see into my boring little life and knows exactly what I need.

I trust her.

So I lift the spider by one of its legs, hold it over the pot, and say the words, "If you wish to live and thrive, let the spider walk alive." When I'm done, I release it outside.

I suspect the magical potion is intended for dogs and cats, but after steeping and straining, I go through the house serving it to all the Darling pets. Two drops in Rufus's water bowl, which he laps up. A drop for Cleo in a bowl of milk, but she just twitches her whiskers at me and walks away. Upstairs, I add a squirt into the mouse and hamster bottles. George the tarantula hardly ever drinks, so I open the lid of his terrarium and splash a couple drops on top of his hairy back.

I don't know what, exactly, I'm expecting to happen. He just stands on his woodchips, contained in his tiny glass world. A leg flinches, the other seven remain still.

I go back into Gillian's room to check on the hamster. She's on her squeaky exercise wheel, as usual. But when I get closer, I can't believe what I see. Fluffy the hamster has a little wad of newspaper clutched in her teeny paw, and she's wiping down the wheel. Work is slow; she wipes one section at a time. She puts the soiled newspaper in a pile in the corner then runs into her hut to get a fresh piece. When she returns she starts scrubbing right where she left off. The bane of all household chores is being done by a rodent.

Back downstairs, Sophie is upside down on the couch, rolling around on the laundry. Candy Land cards are strewn across the floor.

"Do you have to go to the potty?" I ask.

She thinks about it for a minute. Using the bathroom is still a production, and it takes time away from other important things like playing.

"Come on," I encourage. "Go potty, then I'll make you a snack."

This gets her attention.

I lift her up and carry her to the bathroom. I push open the door and nearly drop Sophie when I see what's inside. Rufus is sitting on the toilet. He's panting with concentration.

"Rufus. My turn," Sophie says, unfazed by the peculiar sight.

Rufus finishes his business, flushes the toilet, and jumps off. He scoots past me and out of the bathroom, as though it was the most normal thing that ever could have happened.

I stare after him in disbelief. If this is what witchcraft is all about, then sign me up!

Sophie takes her turn next, then we go to the kitchen for her snack of Goldfish and apple slices. I'm filling up a sippy cup when Sophie screams.

George the tarantula is crawling across the floor. My first instinct is to squash him, but I resist for Henry's sake. As I'm fumbling around the closet for the broom, George pushes his way out the doggy door.

"We have to find him!" Sophie says.

"You're right."

I open the door and in walks George, with a cricket writhing in his jaws. We stand there, Sophie and I, and watch him devour his prey.

"What's he doing?" Sophie asks.

"He's feeding himself, if you can believe that."

"Good spider."

When the last of the cricket disappears into the tarantula's mouth, he walks back into the house. We follow.

He makes his way across the kitchen, the living room, to the stairway. He climbs his way laboriously up the bannister, across the hall, and back into Henry's room. I keep a safe distance behind him. He climbs onto the bed, onto the nightstand, and up a pile of superheroes to the shelf just above his terrarium. From there he lowers himself down onto the rim of the glass, all eight legs working in tandem. Slowly he lowers himself down into the terrarium.

"Amazing," I say.

"What?"

"Our pets can feed, clean, and walk themselves. I don't have to take care of them at all, Sophie. I don't have to clean the stinky hamster cage, or order live crickets online, or follow Rufus around with the pooper-scooper. It's like magic."

Sophie is not as impressed.

"More juice?" she says, shaking her sippy cup.

CHAPTER 16

If you love me as I love you,
No knife shall cut our love in two.

Bethanny has invited me over for breakfast and a lesson on how to make love potions, which she insists everyone can use.

So I'm buying gluten-free coconut oil croissants at Nelson's General Store to bring over. I grab two kombuchas, too, just in case Bethanny is on the probiotic obsession du jour. I contemplate throwing some red goji berry trail mix and raw cashew butter in my basket to go with the croissants, but decide against them. For all I know, nuts and berries could already be passé.

At the register, Mr. Nelson rings me up, his cloudy blue eyes fixed on me. "That going to be all?" he says and winks.

I pull out a couple twenties and give him a wry smile, "That should do it."

A voice behind me shrills, "What in name of Cerridwen's son is this pig swill?" I turn around and see Aurora with her nose in the drink cooler.

"Can I help you, ma'am?" Mr. Nelson says.

Aurora walks over and slams a small bottle of green juice on the counter. "What is it?"

Mr. Nelson picks up the bottle and reads the label through bifocals. "Says here it contains kelp extract and water."

"And people pay you for that? I can find that for free," Aurora balks.

Mr. Nelson shrugs.

I take the bottle from him and return it to the cooler. "It's supposed to be a natural appetite suppressant. At least that's what I heard at Bunco."

"Ah, yes," Mr. Nelson says, more than happy to sell ten-dollar-a-bottle kelp extract to housewives who are convinced they need it. The trend in expensive, exotic food has been a boon for his business, even if he doesn't personally imbibe.

"What are you doing here?" I ask Aurora.

She leans up to me, her head down. "Got to feeling pretty bad about how you left last time. Maybe I didn't explain things so well about . . . ," she gives Mr. Nelson a sideway glance, "you-know-who."

I gather my groceries and head outside, Aurora right behind.

Once we're out of earshot of any passersby I stop. "So you feel bad?" I say, feeling a shimmer of hope.

"I think you might have taken what I said the wrong way," Aurora says.

"You told me I was putting you at risk. You told me to leave."

"Yeah, well, what you got to understand is that I might not be the great and powerful witch you think I am."

I cock my head at her and raise my eyebrows.

She continues. "I'm no match for the Dark Witch. Never was. I'm more like a C-minus, D-plus sort of witch. Freya, now she's an A-plus. I don't want you to coming to me expecting protection. That's what I meant to say the other day."

Even though it's not the best apology I've ever heard, I appreciate her effort. "I understand," I say.

"Maybe you can come over for dinner on Samhain if you want. Bring your kids. I'll teach you how to make a poultice of ribwort. Cures everything from poison ivy to jaundice."

The sky is streaked in ripples of cumulus clouds. Mackerel sky, as Wilhemena used to call it. *Never long wet, and not long dry,* she'd intone. I think how nice it would be to learn the Lessons of the natural world where my mother left off. Returning to the Old Ways is what she wanted for me when she died.

Then I look over at Aurora who is dressed today in what appears to be a horse blanket. The wool is frayed and pilled in the spot where she's cut holes for her arms. Her rucksack is slung on her back beneath the blanket, giving her a hunchback.

"Thank you for the invitation," I say warmly.

"Haven't met your oldest one yet. It's a girl, right? Gillian? What's that, some sort of yuppie name?"

I can just imagine Gillian traipsing through the woods to go to her aunt's vine-covered cabin. I mean, Gillian experiences total mortification just getting into the minivan at Christmastime when I put the reindeer nose on the front. Being an adolescent is hard enough without throwing a witch aunt into the mix.

Besides, Astrid's coven holds a big Samhain party. Only they call it Halloween, like normal people.

"Let me check my calendar and get back to you," I say, wondering if she'll take the hint.

She gives me a crooked smile and walks away.

I'm two flagstones up the path to Bethanny's front door, croissants in hand, when it swings open. Bethanny and a man in a pinstriped suit, entwined in an embrace, pour out onto the porch, unaware of my presence. They make out like teenagers, tongues deep in each other's mouths, bodies moving over each other like a pair of mating snakes. Bethanny leans into him as he gropes her.

I freeze. Should I leave? Should I say hello? Did I just catch her having an affair? Why wouldn't she be more discreet?

The couple breaks apart after what seems like the entire opening sequence of a porn flick, and only then do they notice me. I'm pretending to study the Venus de Milo sculpture on the front lawn.

When I finally look up Bethanny giggles. The man giggles. I don't giggle.

Bethanny's tone is unapologetic as she speaks to the man: "This is Allison. The new girl." She smiles. "Allison, this is my husband, Chad."

"Husband?"

"But he has to go to work now," Bethanny says, curling her lower lip into a hyperbolic pout.

Chad kisses her puckered lips and strides toward me, hand extended, cufflinks sparkling. "I need to be off. Nice to meet you, Allison." He casts a smile at his wife and winks. The dimples pop on his handsome face.

"Good . . . day . . . to meet you," I sputter, still in awe of their marital bliss.

Bethanny giggles again. "Sorry about the public display."

Chad pulls away in his sporty red convertible and Bethanny motions me inside.

Despite the chill of the fall day, the house is warm and humid, and has a welcoming smell of yeasty bread. I hand her the croissants and kombucha.

"Let me give you a tour," Bethanny says, and her hips sway as she walks, her jeans snug, accentuating her flared hips and hourglass waist. "This is, like, the entrance, obviously."

She leads me up a grand curved staircase, whose walls are sheathed in glossy black-and-white photos in gilded frames. There's a family portrait on a snowy mountain, everyone in ski gear. There's the family standing before an elaborate fountain in some European city I can't place. Farther up the stairs is Bethanny, nude and pregnant, her belly a shiny balloon. There's another of her, breastfeeding a newborn, skin on skin, her body toned and flawless.

She points to that one. "Believe me, I had some help getting my figure back so quickly after giving birth. Dr. Yu is a miracle worker," she says.

The mention of Dr. Yu's name makes me self-conscious. I think about gorgeous Dr. Yu holding my face, admiring my bone structure, and the embarrassing number of times I've savored that delicious moment in the past week. "Plastic surgery?" I ask, hoping my voice won't reveal my lascivious thoughts.

"No surgery, just a few lasers in the right places. Have you been to see Dr. Yu yet?"

I stretch the skin of my crow's-feet out. "Do you think I should?"

"Definitely. I noticed he took quite a liking to you at the party," Bethanny says with a smile.

"He did?" I say, unable to contain my delight. "But, he knows I'm married, right?"

"It never hurts to read the menu, as long as you eat at home," she says. She breaks out into a long, seductive laugh, and I marvel at how even her laugh is brimming with sexuality.

As we enter the hall to the master bedroom the photos become increasingly provocative: Bethanny, nude and not pregnant, reclining on a red chaise lounge; Bethanny and Chad, Chad shirtless and buff, Bethanny in a satin corset and thigh-high stockings; Bethanny, nude, her eyes closed in ecstasy, Chad, nude, kissing her neck. Something out of a Calvin Klein underwear ad.

The photos scream out: *Look at us! We are in love! We are beautiful. We have lots of sex!*

And I think by contrast of the message that the photos at the Darling domicile must convey: the kids on the deck of the *Mayflower* replica squinting in the sun, the stiffly posed wedding photo of me and Kevin in the church basement, the kids in their Halloween costumes from last year carrying plastic orange pumpkins, Henry's little body padded with fake muscle under the Superman suit. All signs that our life is boring and safe.

"And this is where the magic happens," she says.

The bedroom is decorated in silks, satins, and furs. A collection of erotic nude sculptures, cast in stone, brass, glass, pewter, iron, and one pieced together with bullet casings, stand in every corner of the room. A pair of overstuffed chairs, their pillows pink and plush, practically beg to be lounged upon.

"I love the furniture," I say.

"Chad does all the decorating," she says wistfully. "Pretty good eye for a lawyer, right?"

The main feature of the master suite are his-and-her's closets, each of which is larger than my first apartment. The her's side has a wall of shoes filled with pumps and sandals in every color and every exquisite material imaginable. In fact, the only place I've ever seen more shoes is in the his wing of the closet. He has more shoes, more crisp, pressed shirts (of every color and material imaginable), more slacks, belts, ties, and suits than seems possible for one person to wear in the course of a year.

But then, this seems to be the House of Abundance (and Sex).

We continue downstairs, to more framed photos of glossy-eyed Chad and his nubile bride, more erotic sculptures and collections, African fertility masks on the wall, an assortment of giant clamshells on the baby grand piano, and more silk furnishings, to the kitchen, which is clad in white marble and pearl chandeliers.

On the counter is a glass fruit bowl swelling with ripe melons and mangoes, grapes, and kumquats. Bethanny picks up the grapes and rearranges them so they cascade over the edges. A perfect, bountiful still life.

I sit at the counter and push aside a plate of uneaten eggs.

"Sorry about the mess. Chad didn't have time to finish breakfast," Bethanny says and clears the plate.

She sets the croissants out. "Fresh from Nelson's," I say.

Bethanny is succumbed to a giggle fit. "Chad and I never have time for breakfast. I don't even know why I bother making eggs."

"Oh?"

"We have to have our morning sex first!" The words practically explode out of her. "Do you and Kevin like morning sex? Chad and I are, like, crazy about it."

My cheeks are burning. No! We don't have morning sex. We have children and jobs and bills to pay. I can literally count on one hand the number of times I've had morning sex in my entire life. Sex, in my limited experience, is exclusive to the darkened domain of night.

"Sometimes," I lie.

"You've *got* to try it," she shrieks. "It's the best way to start your day. Better than a cappuccino."

A cappuccino would be nice. A cup of coffee and some normal, nonsex conversation, I think.

But Bethanny's going on: "Nothing motivates us to get the kids up and out of the house like a morning session. Chad used to always want to do it with the lights off. But then one day I was like, 'Honey, we should celebrate our bodies, not hide them.' And he was like, 'Okay, I'll try it.' And ever since then it's been, like, amazing sex every single day. Practice makes perfect you know."

"How long have you two been married?" I ask.

"Ten years this July," she chirps.

Married ten years. Still having daily sex. Still unable to keep their hands off each other. Either she's lying, or there's something seriously wrong with me and my marriage. I can't even remember the last time Kevin and I kissed with tongue.

My feeling of inadequacy must register on my face because she laughs again and says, "I know what you're thinking, but it's true. We still do it every day. Chad and I think that sex is, like, totally important for a marriage."

"It's just hard with the kids and work and . . . it's just hard to find time," I say, feeling grim.

"That's why you're here. Follow me."

We walk out through the sunroom, to an expansive patio, a pool, an outdoor fireplace, a glass-and-marble fire pit overlooking the sweeping yard down to the river. Every inch of yard is landscaped with hydrangea and roses, lilies and dogwoods. "Chad does all the landscape design, too," Bethanny says.

The river is mirror-calm and shrouded in fog. At the end of the dock we board a center-console Boston Whaler.

We idle past the stately river homes, past the low marshes, through Monrovia Harbor and pull onto a silty beach on a desolate strip of shore that smells of sulfur and wet clay.

This was not at all what I envisioned when I received Bethanny's text yesterday inviting me to coffee. I had planned on chatting a bit, and finding out more about the Glamour Girls. "What are we doing here?" I ask.

"Clamming," she says and shoves a trowel and bucket in my hands.

In her designer jeans and French manicure, Bethanny trudges knee-deep through the mud. "There," she says, pointing to a spot where putrid bubbles break the slick brown surface.

She plunges her trowel into the mud, wiggling it around. From the muck, a cherrystone clam emerges. She lifts it skyward and smiles. "Five more is all we need!"

"Need for what?"

"The potion, of course."

"What potion?" I ask.

"I'm going to teach you how to make an Adoring Husband Potion. It's, like, totally foolproof."

"The *potion* is what makes Chad so crazy about you?"

Bethanny drops the clam in her bucket. "Don't get all self-righteous. You have to understand how the magic works. You can't just make something out of nothing. It's not like I could make a complete stranger fall in love with me. The magic works on what's already there. It enhances. That's what Astrid always says. It makes people see what you want them to see. Chad was crazy about me once. The magic just brings that old feeling up to the surface."

A light sprinkle falls from the mackerel sky. *Never long wet, and not long dry.* Bethanny frowns, though I can't tell if it's from the rain or our conversation.

"It's not a trick, Allison," she says, a hard edge in her voice.

"Think of the moment you knew you were in love with Kevin. Imagine if you could relive that moment every day. It's the most powerful feeling in the world." She pauses. "Unless, of course, you never were in love in the first place. Then, you're out of luck."

This makes me defensive. "We were in love. *Are* in love," I correct myself.

"Good. When? When did you first know?"

I was in my second year at community college. People like me were called "mature" students because of our advanced age, although I lacked the wisdom or experience the term implies.

I didn't fit in. My fellow classmates moved effortlessly through their schoolwork and spent exorbitant amounts of time talking about boys and even more time gossiping about girls. I struggled to keep up with my schoolwork, and spent most of my Saturday nights in the library.

Kevin and I had just started dating when I asked him to join me for a lecture from a visiting professor that my medieval literature teacher recommended to the class, even though it was on a Saturday night. Attending meant extra credit, so I jumped at it. Kevin obligingly said it sounded like fun.

The night was a disaster. Not only were we two of only five people in attendance, but the visiting professor gave most of his lecture in Middle English, and insisted that the question-and-answer period be conducted in Middle English. I didn't understand a word. When I turned to Kevin at one point, he looked at me, cross-eyed, with a finger up his nose. I spit my soda through my nose I laughed so hard. He laughed, too. We were shushed, but we couldn't stop laughing and eventually we were asked to leave the lecture hall. I knew I was in love with him then. Two immature "mature" misfits. Trying to fit in.

"You need to think about that moment when you say the spell," Bethanny says.

"I don't know. It feels like cheating."

"How can love be dishonest?"

I shrug and grab another clam out of the muck.

"Can I tell you something? You're, like, totally going to die. I mean, it's unbelievable."

"Sure," I say, firing with curiosity.

"Chad, my husband, is gay. *Gay!* Can you believe that?"

The shoes and the desperate show of marital bliss permeating their house, everything so perfect that it seems like fiction. Yes, I can believe it.

"I make this potion every week to keep our lives together. He wanted to ruin our marriage, our entire life, by coming out of the closet. What would that look like to all our friends? People would think there was something wrong with me. I was so furious."

"People change," I say. "It's no one's fault."

Bethanny's face turns hard. "It was *his* fault! He loved me once. He took a vow when he married me. He had children with me. He was going to ruin my life and my children's lives because of his own selfishness."

"I don't think being gay is a matter of selfishness."

"You can say what you want, but we're happy now. Astrid's potion saved us. We love each other, just like we used to. Did it look like I was forcing anything on him this morning?"

I feel Bethanny's desperation and decide to let it drop. "From what I saw, it seemed like you two were very much in love."

This seems to quell her. "Trust me, you'll be happier with your marriage, too," she says. "The potion is foolproof."

"Now what?" I ask, as we get back in the Whaler.

Bethanny dips her hands and feet over the gunwale to rinse off the mud. All the clamming has made her a surefooted seaman. "Now we boil these slimy suckers with some milk and honey, toss in some belladonna and kiss of Aphrodite. Let it harden into soap. Slip it in the morning shower for him to wash with and, voilà, instant morning sex."

188 · *Katie Schickel*

* * *

I'm skeptical. A love potion seems like such a cliché. After all, I saw what Bethanny put into this soap, and there was nothing sexy about it.

At five I take a shower and wash with the soap. It smells earthy and salty and sweet. It suds up very quickly, and I lather myself all over. The smell permeates the steamy shower. It gets in my lungs and brain. It wriggles something loose inside of me, like a soda that's been shaken and opened.

All I can think of is sex. I imagine every scene of every fantasy I've ever had—the pirate one, the doctor one, the police officer. Desire sweeps me away. I want to be kissed passionately. I want to relive the real magic of being sixteen and feeling totally annihilated by love. Obsessed with it. I want to be a silly girl who is so single-minded with HIM that she writes his name in the margins of her notebook during history class, and gets butterflies in her stomach when he smiles at her in the bleachers. I want that exhilaration of being able to turn him on with a simple touch.

But first, I have to make dinner.

I'm on autopilot peeling carrots and chopping celery, because my mind is focused only on sex.

When Kevin comes home, he flings his keys on the counter and kisses the kids, then me.

It takes every ounce of self-control I've ever had to keep my hands off him while the kids are around. Gillian's doing homework at the counter and keeps looking up at me, aware that something is different.

"Go take a shower," I say to Kevin.

He laughs. He sniffs his armpits. "Do I smell that bad?"

I don't care about hurting his feelings right now. My need to get him alone is too strong. "Yes."

"Can't it wait 'til after dinner?"

"No."

"After a beer?"

"No."

"Okay. I sweated more than I thought today." He heads upstairs.

"And Kevin . . . ," I say. He turns to face me. "Use the black soap I just bought. You'll love it."

I'm a zombie mom. I pound chicken and bread it. I mix salad. I try to conceal what I'm really feeling.

Soon Kevin comes into the kitchen in his bathrobe. He pulls my hair aside and sniffs my neck. His eyes gloss over. He caresses my shoulders and I can feel every inch of my skin respond under his touch. Electricity, raw and exciting, runs between us.

I turn off the stove and quickly order a pizza. I grab a wad of cash from my purse, hand it to Gillian, and tell her to pay for the pizza when it comes.

"What about the chicken?" she says.

"Dad and I have to discuss something very important," I say.

"What?"

"Gillian, it's . . . it's none of your business. You kids can have a pizza party. Put a movie on."

She mumbles something about how weird her parents are.

Kevin and I run upstairs, lock the bedroom door, and proceed to maul each other. I can't get enough of him, his smell, his flesh. I want to devour him.

Then, we fuck. There's no other way to put it. It's not sweet, gentle lovemaking. It's pure, exquisite passion. Desire. Lust. We fuck like there's nothing that can stop us. We fuck like people who don't have a worry in the world.

He's not Kevin my husband; he's Kevin, the boy who asked me out on a date for the first time when we weren't sure of each other, when kissing at the front door at the end of the night felt risky and daring. When the stakes were high. When rejection or acceptance were the only possible outcomes, and we didn't know which it would be.

We are both complete strangers and intimate friends who know every detail about each other. There's nothing safe and practical in it, whatever this is.

It is pure euphoria.

I don't know how long it lasts. I'm oblivious to time. All I know is that slowly the passion dissipates, the magnet drawing us together weakens.

I throw my clothes back on, smooth my hair, which has turned into a rat's nest.

Back downstairs, all three kids are in the living room, watching a movie. The pizza hasn't even arrived yet. I glance at the clock, amazed that only ten minutes have passed. Gillian looks up, her expression so interrogating I feel she might bore a hole into my forehead. "Is it about my phone?"

"What?" I ask.

"Is that what you and Dad were talking about? Because I'm totally ready for one."

I let out a sigh of relief, which she could easily misinterpret as impatience. "No, sweetie, we weren't talking about your phone. Keep an eye out for the pizza guy, will you?" I say and head to the kitchen.

I finish frying the chicken and dressing the salad for Kevin and me.

It's the first meal I made for Kevin when we started dating. Back when I dreamed about being married to him, so unaware that marriage is the end of passion. That marriage is like passion's older, wiser sister. It is practical, safe, and unwavering. It has no room for euphoria.

Unless you have a little magic on your side.

CHAPTER 17

Wear you a hat or wear you a crown,
All that goes up must surely come down.

Being a Glamour Girl is the bomb. In the past week, I've become the envy of all my friends, I haven't waited in a single line, my pets have become self-sufficient, and I've discovered the amazing, astonishing world of morning sex. I feel closer than ever to Kevin.

There's no end to the invitations. Heather came over once to show me how to infuse oil. We had tea and she told me about her first potion that involved slicing apart spider sacs to extract eggs. She almost quit right then and there, she said. Didn't think she had the stomach for it. But, Astrid really helped her turn her life around. "I owe her everything," Heather told me.

Erin came over to show me how to grind herbs for a Temporary Weight Loss Potion. It takes off five pounds for five days then you're back to normal.

If the magic can make our dreams come true in so many ways, I figure it can do wonders for the people we love. So I texted Astrid yesterday and asked her for a potion that could help Henry. I explained how he has a hard time fitting in with other kids and how I worry about him spending so much time in his own make-believe world.

The Domestic Glamour van was at my door one hour later. The basket contained a whole chicken, a recipe for Sweet and Sticky Chicken Thighs, a larger-than-usual delivery of roots and herbs and spices, Red Sox tickets, and a note:

Dear Allison,
  Your family is our family. When we suffer one, we suffer all. Give this potion to your darling son, that his life, too, may be rich with Glamour.

Sincerely,
Astrid

Now I'm in the kitchen brewing a special potion and reading Astrid's instructions with a fair amount of skepticism. Simmer two cups of honey with the petals of bluet flower. Stir clockwise three times, then counterclockwise six. I have to wonder if she's messing with me, just a little. Then I'm to repeat the rhyme:

> Boys and girls, come out to play,
> The moon does shine as bright as day,
> Leave your supper, and leave your sleep,
> And meet your playfellows in the street;
> Come with a whoop, and come with a call,
> And come with a good will, or not at all.

The phone rings. "Want to walk together, or meet there?" Judy says on the other end.

Friday. Lunch date with Judy. I completely forgot.

"I can't, Judy. I have other plans today." If I hadn't been so focused on the recipe, I would have screened my calls and let it ring. I feel guilty blowing Judy off. And even guiltier that I'm ditching an old friend for a new one.

"Standing me up for lunch? What's going on?"

I consider lying, but the truth comes out. "I'm going to Boston. To see the Red Sox."

"You're fucking with me," she laughs.

"No, I'm not."

"I know you're fucking with me. You hate baseball."

Judy, on the other hands, *loves* baseball. Her Red Sox baseball cap is a permanent fixture on her head. She was married at Fenway.

"I don't hate baseball," I say. "I just never gave it much thought before. I'm taking Henry as a special treat."

Judy chuckles. "Honey, you don't just walk into Fenway on the last game of the playoffs and buy tickets. It's sold out."

"I already have tickets," I say, my palms sweating around the phone.

"No you don't," she says confidently.

I don't answer. I wish there was some kind of spell to prevent best friends from going apeshit when they learn you have the one thing they want most and aren't sharing it with them.

"Okay, then, check your tickets and tell me who they're playing?" she says, breaking the silence.

I scan the tickets on my counter and reply: "The Yankees."

"Oh my God. You really are going. How did Kevin get tickets?" she says.

"Kevin's not going. I'm just taking Henry."

"You're taking Henry and not your best friend? You know I love your kids, Allison, but that's like playing Mozart to a deaf person. He cares about baseball less than you."

I laugh. Sort of. She knows I've never been to Fenway, which is paramount to treason in her book. I'm just hoping she'll drop it. That she won't press me for more information, more evidence of betrayal.

There's a ridiculously long pause.

"Judy?" I say. "Are you there?"

"How the hell did you get tickets? Today's the last game of the regular season. Against the Yankees, no less."

I clear my throat and try to sound casual. "Astrid invited me."

There's another long pause and I imagine Judy's brain spinning in circles trying to figure out at what point her best friend traded her in for a newer model. "It's not a big deal," I add.

Judy raises her voice. "It is so a big deal! It's a fucking big deal. This is the playoffs. How can you say it's not a big deal?

It's the last stop before the World Series. Don't say it's not a big deal. Don't disrespect the game like that, dammit. You don't know anything at all about baseball."

"I'm sorry, Judy. Astrid invited me. I couldn't say no."

"Yeah, you can't so no to anyone lately. At least not to any of the Glamour Girls. Are you wearing one of those stupid pink capes yet?"

"Why are you so upset?" I ask.

"How come you haven't returned any of my calls this week? Tell me that," Judy says.

"I've been busy," I say, knowing exactly how feeble that sounds.

"Busy. Yeah, right."

"Why don't I see if Astrid has any more tickets for the game. She might . . ."

"No thanks. I'm busy, too," Judy says.

"Let's get together next week," I say, stirring the honey.

"Sure. Next week. Have fun at the game. Make sure you cheer for the right team," she says, and hangs up, her words as sour as curdled milk.

I feel the guilt like a punch to my stomach. I'll make it up to her, I tell myself. I'll get a special magical experience just for Judy, I promise. Maybe I can ask Astrid for tickets to the World Series. Then again, why can't she just be happy for me? Why do I need her approval for my new friends? My new, extremely generous, kind, and charitable friends.

Besides, today isn't about me and my needs. It's about Henry. He could use it after the disastrous birthday party.

I try to get Henry excited for the game while I cook.

"You know we're going to a baseball game today, right?" I say, chopping bluet flowers and stevia leaves, while Henry sits at the counter.

I pluck the feathers from the freshly slaughtered chicken. "Do you know what Boston's team name is?" He's silent. I answer the question for him. "The Red Sox. The Boston Red Sox. They're playing against the Yankees."

"Do they fight each other?"

"No. They play. It's a game."

"Does anyone have superpowers?"

"No."

"Samurai powers?"

"No."

"Ninja powers? Jedi powers?"

"No. They play baseball."

He returns to his Star Wars figures, choreographing their battle.

"There's going to be lots of other boys there. Maybe we can even get a baseball glove for you. Start playing catch. If you want to, that is." I glance up to see if he's paying attention, but he's already tuned out.

When the chicken is ready he eyes me suspiciously before he takes a bite. "It's kind of good."

By Henry standards, a rave review.

By the time we get to Fenway, Lilith, Rosie, Erin, and Heather are already there. I haven't spent any time with Lilith yet and it feels a bit like a girlfriend blind date orchestrated by Astrid.

I want to make a good impression so I've dressed in skinny jeans and my pink cape.

When we walk from the bustling lower level of food vendors and beer lines, up the ramp to the sunlit expanse of the stadium, it takes my breath away. Fenway doesn't just welcome you in, it grabs you by the throat. It's a dance for the senses—the aroma of popcorn, the crack of bats on balls, the songs of the hawkers who learned their trade from a bygone era, and the current of energy running from Sox fan to Sox fan, unbroken except by the sporadic out-of-towner. And everywhere it's green.

Forest green of the stands, light lime green of the grass, a giant field of clover against a cerulean sky.

Even Henry can't turn away.

When we find our seats, I'm hit with another dose of veneration. Astrid got us seats on the Green Monster, the famous left-field wall with a single row of seats and an unobstructed view of the field.

And a sheer forty-foot drop down to the outfield.

I'm suddenly thankful I don't have Sophie with me. Which is why I'm surprised to see that the other women have brought all their kids, including all five of Rosie's children as well as three toddlers and two babies tucked into car seats.

"These seats are amazing," I say, as we enter the box.

Rosie, Erin, and Heather give us a big welcome. Lilith barely acknowledges me.

"You already know the O'Shea kids: Norah, Maeve, Thomas, Finlay, and Nolan. And this is Harleigh, Bryson, Addison, Carson, Emerson, Keagon, Porter, Parker, Tucker, and Treyton," Erin says. There is no way I'll remember all those stylish names.

Henry sits down in an empty seat, but quickly tunes them out to play with his action figures. Adrift in his own world of make-believe, he doesn't pay attention to the game or kids. He doesn't notice when the crowd does the wave, or chants, "Let's go Red Sox" *clap clap clap-clap-clap.* He's oblivious to the giant foam fingers and pennants waving around, or the Hood blimp circling above, or the forty-thousand wild fans. Whatever magic Astrid put in that chicken thigh rub had better be strong.

As we settle in to watch the game, Rosie, Erin, and Heather fill me in on upcoming parties and committee duties, but Lilith remains cool toward me. I have a hard time focusing on anything other than the young kids sitting so perilously close to a cliff out of arm's reach. It would take Sophie all of ten seconds to discover the game of seeing how far she could lean over the Green Monster or dangle a limb off the edge.

"Should we split up so we can keep a better eye on the kids?" I ask.

"They'll be fine," says Lilith, with a wave of her hand.

"I don't mind," I say, envisioning a child plummeting through the air.

"But then we won't be able to talk to each other," Erin says.

"Aren't you worried about them falling?" I ask.

"No," says Rosie. "They won't fall."

It's the mom instinct in me—I can't stop hovering or anticipating a disaster. The young children are so close to the edge, and it's a long drop down. My nerves are rattled.

"Allison, calm down. The kids are fine. We made sure of it," Heather says.

"How do you know they're not going to fall?"

"They all had a big helping of Stay-Put Stew this morning," Erin says with a smile.

"What's in it?" I ask.

"Nothing bad. In fact, it's full of vegetables. Very nutritious," Heather explains.

I must look doubtful because Rosie reassures me. "They're having a great time. Look at them all."

They are, in fact, deliriously happy. They don't whine or cry. They don't ask for juice every five minutes. They don't fidget or fight with each other. They are absolutely perfect. Absolutely, unbelievably, freakishly, spookily perfect.

Who am I to judge if my friends use a little magic on their kids? Didn't I ask Astrid to grant Henry a magical experience today? Is it any different from feeding him a Stay-Put Stew?

When the hot dog vendor comes around we all buy Fenway Franks for our kids, except for Rosie, who gives her children homemade sandwiches. "Eight dollars a dog. It adds up," she says, and I smile in return.

Finally I'm able to sit back and relax. And I notice that Erin is eating a hot dog very fast. She finishes it and starts on a second one. Then a third. Then a fourth. She is completely pigging

out. Next to her, Heather is gorging herself with sweets. Swed-
ish Fish, Skittles, Twizzlers (the jumbo stadium size, not the
wimpy six-pack ones in the checkout lane at the grocery store).

I watch them gorge. Heather has a blob of mustard on her
chin that Erin wipes off for her.

They both laugh.

"Wondering how we stay so thin?" Erin says.

"I think I can figure it out."

"Ask, and Astrid will answer," Heather says.

"So is that what you mostly wish for—to be skinny?"

"Doesn't everyone?" Heather says.

I look at Henry who is kneeling on the ground, with his back
to the baseball game, playing with his action figures on the seat,
not playing with the other kids, not aware of himself in the
world.

No. Being skinny is not what everyone wishes for.

"What else do you use magic for?" I ask.

"Gray hair."

"Wrinkles."

"In-laws," Lilith says. "You have no idea how a visit can im-
prove with a little Mother-in-Law Migraine Tonic."

"So how did you guys meet Astrid?" I ask, curious if they,
too, were lured away from another city like me and Miranda.

Erin answers. "I was a top sale rep for a pharmaceutical company in Boston. I was making good money, too. My sister-in-
law invited me to a Glamour Soap shopping party and Astrid
was there. I don't know how, but she knew I was in sales, and
she offered me a job as sales rep. At first I was like, no way, I'm
doing fine where I am. But my husband wasn't doing so well.
He was an addict." She whispers in my ear, "Gambling." Then
she sits back and continues her story. "Our marriage was falling
apart. He was draining our savings with his habit. Then Astrid
showed us a house in Monrovia that was so much nicer than
anything we could afford in the city. She helped Daniel with
his problem. She gave me a potion that took off thirty pounds.

I was hooked. When she offered me a full-time job at Glamour, I jumped at it."

"What about you, Rosie? Why did you join?" I ask. Of all the women, Rosie is the one I've known longest and I can't imagine that she needed Astrid's help the way Erin did.

After all, Rosie is a rock. She's been president of the PTO for the past seven years. Homeroom mother, soccer league coordinator, school librarian, crossing guard organizer—she's the role model mom. She plays Mrs. Claus at every Winter Wonderland Festival. She chaperones all field trips from apple picking in the fall to the maple sugar shack walk in the spring. She sends out e-mails reminding the rest of us when it's time to register for Girl Scouts or get flu vaccines. She knows every sports schedule, play practice, band rehearsal, homework assignment, every allergy of every kid in town, and she can disseminate information faster than Facebook. Rosie is who you turn to when your household is in Sickville and you can't make it to the store for a pint of milk. She's the go-to of all emergency contact friends.

She rubs her arm mindlessly. "Do you know what psoriasis is?"

"It's a skin condition," I say.

"It's not just a condition. It's a torment. In the worst cases, it leaves red scales all over your body. And it itches like crazy. There's medication for it, but I can't take the medication, because I have a liver condition. So, whenever I had flare-ups, I'd cover every inch of myself head-to-toe, or simply stay home. It got so bad, I spent an entire summer indoors. I worried myself sick about my kids inheriting it. It's bad enough for me, but I'd die if my kids had to go through adolescence with that plague."

There's a faraway look in her eye.

She continues. "Astrid approached me one day and handed me a bottle of tonic. It cleared up my skin within the hour. You can't imagine what it's like to be cured. Every day, you're covered like a crocodile in red scales, and then, in a single moment, your skin is clear and radiant."

"What a relief it must have been," I say.

She chokes back a tear. "That's when I started to believe in magic. When I ran out of tonic, Astrid invited me to work at Glamour. She said I would have all the tonic I ever needed. All I had to do was hand out Glamour welcome baskets to new families in Monrovia and add a few things to the PTO agenda."

Rosie looks out over the field, the sun casting an apricot glow over her skin. She forces a smile to her lips. "As long as I keep doing what's required of me, I'll keep getting that tonic. And, believe me, I'll do anything she asks for it."

Heather munches on a bag of M&M's, brushing candy crumbs off her shirt. "Every single one of us will do whatever Astrid says."

"Astrid depends on us, too," Lilith says haughtily. "We do all the work."

"You'll get your job soon enough, Allison," Erin says.

Lilith looks right at me. "The thing I don't understand, Allison, is why you get a free pass. You've never set foot inside the factory. You've never worked the greenhouse or volunteered on a committee in your life. Do you have any idea how hard the rest of us had to work to be a part of the Glamour team? I spent three years volunteering my time in production, mixing lye, burning my hands, sweating over soap. I have the scars to prove it." She pulls back her sleeve to reveal a burn the length of her forearm.

"Leave her alone, Lilith," Erin says.

"What have you got to offer?" Lilith demands.

I think about this for a minute. What can I tell her? That, unlike them, I'm a real witch? I can transform objects with my thoughts, even though I don't have any control over it.

Lilith is about to speak, but we're distracted by the roar of the crowd. The player up at bat has the crowd going wild. Since I'm not a true fan, as Judy would say, I don't know what the big deal is, but I gather from all the cheering that it's got something to do with a home run record. The kids seem to know all about it, because they're screaming their heads off. Even the little one (Porter? Tucker? Harleigh?) who can't be more than two years old is screaming his head off, just like he's supposed to.

The first pitch comes in wide. The ump calls a strike and the crowd revolts with boos and hisses. The second pitch is fast and inside and he swings and misses. Strike two. Everyone stands.

Henry is completely oblivious to the action. I lean over to get his attention. "Honey, why don't you stand up and watch the game. This is the best player on the team," I say.

Henry stands, but his eyes are still on his toys.

At home plate the pitch comes in fast, the bat makes contact, and the ball sails over second base, rising like a rocket. The stadium is in an uproar. The ball is flying over center field, soaring over the earth. Fans are screaming like their lives depend on that ball, like that single fantastic trajectory is the most important thing that's ever happened.

Suddenly, defying the laws of both physics and gravity, the ball swerves and sails over left field toward the Green Monster. It makes a sharp curve from the sky toward us, slowing down as it descends. And against all odds, it lands softly in Henry's free hand, the one not clutching an action figure.

All the kids are cheering for Henry. Everyone in the whole stadium, all forty-thousand people are cheering for Henry. On the giant screen, they've zoomed in on Henry holding the ball. They keep running the loop of him in that stupendous moment. Older kids are high-fiving him. Everyone is chanting his name, "Henry, Henry, Henry."

Heather and Erin cheer and give me a secret wink. I catch Lilith scowling.

Henry's face is frozen in a smile and I think I might just have a heart attack from joy.

"Look," he says to me, holding up the ball. "I used the Force."

Not only am I the best mom in the world, but the best mom on the Planet Krypton, and in the Galaxy, and that is a great feeling.

That night I'm putting Henry to bed, tucking him into his *Star Wars* sheets.

"Did you have a great time at the game today?" I ask.

He makes animated sound effects as Green Lantern blasts off into the air.

"Catching that ball was pretty special, wasn't it?" I continue.

He shrugs. "What ball?"

"The home run ball. When everyone was cheering for you." I expect him to light up recalling the day's events, but his eyes are blank.

"Henry, don't you remember catching the ball?" I plead.

He looks down at the sheets, then at me, searching for the right answer. But I can see it in his sad eyes: He doesn't remember a thing. Worse yet, he looks disappointed in himself for not remembering. "Yeah, I guess so. Everyone cheered, right?"

It's a stake through my heart.

"That's right, honey, everyone cheered."

"Was I good at it—at catching the ball?"

"You were excellent."

He returns to the world of Green Lantern.

I kiss him, and turn off his light. The magic chicken got me what I wanted, not what Henry wanted. Henry doesn't care what people think about him. He doesn't care if he's the star of the day, the kid whose name is chanted by all of Fenway. He's happy the way he is. And I wonder whether I have any idea how to be a witch, or a mom.

CHAPTER 18

> I'll sing you a song:
> The days are long,
> The woodcock and the sparrow:
> The little dog he has burnt his tail,
> And he must be hanged tomorrow.

Salem, Massachusetts • *1957*

Elizabeth had grown weary of Freya's defiance. If Elizabeth told Freya to feed the chickens, Freya would cast an obedience spell to make Aurora do the chore for her. Instead of gathering wood for fires as she was told, Freya made elemental fire potions that kept one log burning all day. It was, in Elizabeth's opinion, a selfish sort of magic.

As a mother, Elizabeth didn't want to imagine what sort of tricks Freya was using in town, in full view of the Commoners, without any thought of consequences. Twice, Elizabeth had been visited by Salem police officers. There was no evidence directly incriminating Freya, but there were suspicions and coincidences, and complaints. Many complaints. That a girl in town was struck with paralysis the same day that Freya had been seen arguing with her did not go unnoticed. Neither did the vandalism—lewd drawings above the second-story window—at a haberdashery on King Street. The shop owner reported "something peculiar when the girl from Misery Shoal entered the store." Police dropped by to investigate.

And if there was anything Elizabeth couldn't abide, it was strangers dropping by. Privacy was essential. History had taught them that. She took extreme measures to guard their isolation.

After all, they lived on land no one else dared settle, with only one tidal road going in and out. As far as Elizabeth was concerned, Freya was jeopardizing their sacred safety with her shenanigans.

She had a good mind to turn the girl into a donkey.

That summer, Freya managed to get hold of a bicycle. When the weather was good, while the three sisters studied their Lessons, Freya disappeared under the pretense of gathering herbs or seaweed, only to be seen by her sisters riding down the wet road toward Salem, all alone.

At night, Aurora often awoke to find Freya's bed empty. There was no doubt where she was, or how she got there. Under concealment of night, she was sure Freya was flying by broomstick into town to mix with Commoners.

"What do you do when you go into town, anyhow?" Aurora asked one day as they were walking the beach collecting sand dollars to practice a Good Fortune Spell their mother was teaching them.

"Stuff," Freya answered.

"What kind of stuff?"

"You wouldn't understand."

Aurora pinched her eyebrows together. She had learned to say as little as possible around Freya to avoid traps. "I might."

"Well," Freya smiled devilishly, "do you know what French kissing is?"

"Yeah."

"You do not."

"I do, too."

"What is it then?"

Aurora looked around, wondering how she'd managed to let Freya put her on the spot like that, again. "It's a type of kissing they do in France," Aurora answered, content.

Freya rolled her eyes. "It's kissing with your tongue."

"Kissing *what* with your tongue?"

"Boys, dummy." Freya laughed her mean laugh.

"Oh."

"You should see how crazy it makes them. It's like casting a spell without using magic."

Aurora thought she might like to try French kissing boys, too. She was really no good at magic anyway. Casting spells without potions seemed like a very promising enterprise. "Can I come with you sometime?"

"You? Hah! You'd scare away all the boys."

"Please, Freya. Bring me with you."

Freya mulled this over and decided that having a coconspirator could serve her well. Mama was on her back all the time. Why not let her little sister take some of the heat?

"Fine, but you have to do exactly what I say," Freya said.

"I will."

"And you can't tell anyone about it. Not even Wilhemena."

"I promise."

That night they lay in bed waiting for their mother to fall asleep. When the rumble of her snoring fell over the house, Freya and Aurora got out of bed, dressed, and crept down the hallway, past their mother's room to the bathroom.

Freya attempted to make Aurora look pretty. She applied blush to her cheeks, sprayed her with perfume that smelled like lily of the valley, and untied the braid down her back. She slicked Aurora's hair down with scented oil and used her fingers to style it loosely.

Wilhemena stood in the door of the bathroom, hands on her hips. "What are you two doing?"

"We're going French kissing," Aurora said proudly. "It's what you do with boys," she added, quite happy to have some valuable knowledge that her oldest sister might not possess.

"Don't be ridiculous," Wilhemena said.

"Never mind her. She doesn't know how to have any fun," Freya said, turning her attention on Aurora's unruly eyebrows.

"Sneaking around at night isn't fun," Wilhemena said.

"What do you know?" Freya whispered. "You think wading through wet clay, looking for crawfish is fun."

In fact, Wilhemena did think crawfishing was fun, but she was twenty now, and was beginning to wonder if the world had more to offer.

"I'm coming, too," Wilhemena said.

"Fine. But try to make yourself look presentable," Freya said, throwing her a comb.

Under Freya's reckless leadership, the three girls snuck outside, jumped astride their broomsticks, chanted the flying incantation (which even Aurora was good at), and took off into the sky. Clouds shrouded the stars and moon, concealing them in darkness as they passed over marsh and farmland, over the growing suburbs, to the center of town.

For the first time in a great long while, Wilhemena was having fun. She looked over her shoulder at Aurora and Freya and saw that they, too, wore expressions of pure exhilaration.

They alit on the Salem Green where centuries earlier a dozen witches had been hanged.

"This way," Freya commanded. She led her sisters to a pavilion on the Green where they stashed their broomsticks. Then she marched them down Hawthorne Boulevard to Derby Street and on farther to the honky-tonk section of town. Here, the street was lined with taverns and pawnshops, the smell of city gutters, and the hum of streetlights reminding them how far from home they were. On the corner, a laundromat's flickering neon sign cast an eerie light on a group of tough-looking men who leaned against cars smoking butts. The men gawked at the young girls with salacious smiles. Aurora looked down at the cracked sidewalk and ran ahead. In front of a bar called O'Neill's two men spilled out of the door, punching and gouging each other. Wilhemena gasped as one man knelt on top of the other throwing punches until the other man was unconscious and bleeding from his head.

The fight drew a crowd of onlookers, men and women who found entertainment in the violence. Freya enjoyed it, too.

When a police car came, the crowd dispersed. Freya grabbed her sisters by the hands and ran with them through a back alley to a dimly lit street away from the blue police lights.

"How do you know your way around so well?" Wilhemena asked Freya. "How many times have you been here?"

"Just try not to embarrass me, okay?" Freya said, stopping at a bar called the Rusty Nail.

Wilhemena swallowed hard, wishing she never agreed to come along in the first place.

Inside the Rusty Nail, heads turned as Freya made her way across the dark room, past the booths of burgundy vinyl and tables scarred with graffiti, to the long oak bar. Patrons were perched on their stools as still and lifeless as egrets in the salt pans.

"That's Mike," Freya announced to her sisters, pointing to a man with a mustache and greased-back hair. "He's my boyfriend." The phrase was uttered so nonchalantly that Wilhemena and Aurora were both dumbstruck. How did their sister come to have a boyfriend? What sort of secret life had she been living amongst the Commoners?

Seated beside Mike was a woman of approximately the same age as him. She had brassy blond hair and blue eye shadow. Her legs were crossed and her body leaned in his direction. Even to Wilhemena and Aurora, whose understanding of mating rituals came strictly from their knowledge of animal husbandry, it was clear that these two were together.

"How old is he?" Wilhemena gulped.

"Thirty-five, I think. Who cares?"

Freya walked toward Mike, her sisters tagging behind like timid mice. The bar was crowded, but one by one, patrons moved aside for Freya to pass. This seventeen-year-old girl with the slight build and thick red hair held authority over the hardened clientele of the Rusty Nail.

The color drained from Mike's face when he saw Freya. He looked away, but Freya took Mike's neck in her hands and kissed him hard on the mouth. His body went rigid.

If that was a French kiss, Aurora thought, then she changed her mind about wanting to French kiss some boys tonight.

"Get away from him, you little slut," the woman said.

Freya laughed and kissed the man again.

The woman with the brassy hair threw a punch at Freya, but Mike blocked it with his bear paw of a hand. "Lisa, don't. It's nothing. Let's get out of here."

"Who is this little tramp?" Lisa screeched.

Mike whispered something to Lisa; he seemed to be pleading with her to leave, but Freya pulled him away. "Tell her. Tell her you're my boyfriend. Or I'll make you."

The bartender pounded a fist on the bar. He was a big man with tattoos covering his beefy arms. "Take it somewhere else. I warned you already, Mike, none of that shit in here."

For reasons Wilhemena and Aurora couldn't understand, this made Freya laugh wildly. "Shut up, Donny. And get me a drink." She turned back to Mike and planted another wet kiss on his mouth.

Donny pounded the bar again, this time with a baseball bat. "I don't want any trouble. You need to leave now."

Mike looked nervously at Freya. "We're leaving."

"I want a drink," she said, slapping the bar.

Donny held the bat with both hands. Sweat ran down his collar. "I don't want any trouble. There's no need for any of your . . . magic," he said, his voice cracking.

Freya rolled her eyes and cackled. "Are you afraid of me, *Donny?*"

Donny's eyes fluttered around his bar. Wilhemena wondered what sort of magic he had witnessed at the hands of her sister. What terrible spells and potions had caused him such fear? And how had Freya strayed so far from the ways their mother taught?

Lisa didn't have the benefit of knowing what Freya was, or

what she could do. She grabbed Freya by the arm. "Leave my husband alone."

Freya had had enough. She dug into her pocket. "Hey diddle diddle, the cat and the fiddle, the cow jumped over the moon." She pulled out a handful of enchanted salt. She threw it at the woman's stunned face.

The woman froze. Her eyes glassed over. She couldn't speak. She couldn't yell. All she could do was moo.

Outside, a police siren wailed. Wilhemena and Aurora turned and ran, and this time, Freya followed her sisters.

The mob was already at the house when the girls got there. Two pickup trucks were parked in front, headlights shining on blackened windows, men piled in back, a shotgun over someone's shoulder.

The girls landed their broomsticks on the beach and ran up the dunes to the house where their mother slept all alone. They got to the front just as the porch light flicked on. All they could hear were the chants and taunts that rose in fits over the blackness. "Witches. Burn in hell." Chills rippled down Wilhemena's spine.

She ran to the house. Elizabeth stood on the front porch, groggy with sleep, wrapped in a quilt, confused. Wilhemena got to the porch just as a rock landed against her mother's left temple. Elizabeth fell to the ground; blood oozed from the gash. Wilhemena cried out. She looked at her mother's face, the gash bright with blood that trickled into her eyes. As she tried to curb the bleeding, her mother's face turned blurry through her tears, as did the faces of the men.

Strangers yelled intolerable words "Witches, die!," the anger in the voices building with every passing second.

Wilhemena tried to focus on her mother. She cradled her head and shielded her with her body. Slowly, her mother's eyes closed and she lost consciousness. Wilhemena looked around at the mob of invaders, then to her mother's bloody face and felt the mad, wild fear of a trapped animal.

A man in army fatigues held a bottle with a long rag hanging out of the opening. He lit the rag and hurled the Molotov cocktail at the house. It bounced off the roof and into the scrub brush in front of the porch. The dry brush lit up. Flames lapped at the sun-bleached shingles until it caught hold and fire crept up the side of the house.

With great effort, Wilhemena dragged Elizabeth by the arms into the house as flames tore at the side. The crunch of falling wood and plaster jarred her.

Aurora ran up the porch and into the house. Together, they dragged Elizabeth's body into the kitchen. Wilhemena held her from her shoulders, Aurora from the legs, struggling with her weight until they managed to gain purchase and lift her limp body off the floor.

"What should we do?" Wilhemena said, her voice weak with desperation. Smoke billowed into the living room, and seeped into the kitchen, covering the herbs that hung from the rafters.

They looked around, but there was nowhere to hide from the smoke. "Where's Freya?" Aurora coughed. "This is all her fault!"

Wilhemena tucked her face into her shoulder to breathe. "Let's get Mama to the back porch," she said.

The back porch abutted the dunes and was buried in sand. The encroaching drifts had blocked the back door, rendering it useless for many years. They pried a window open and passed their mother through it onto the soft sand. Then they pulled her up the dune, as the heat from the flames strengthened.

Aurora and Wilhemena held their mother across their laps, coaxing her to wake up. They could see the men, the fire illuminating the monstrous look on their faces.

"We have to run," Aurora said. "We have to get Mama away from here."

Wilhemena looked around. There was nowhere to flee. On

one side was ocean, on the other, a murderous mob. Suddenly a great wind whirled, sending cyclones of sand spinning in the air. "What is that?" Wilhemena cried.

The last thing they saw was Freya standing on the dune high above them, her arms raised to the sky, a swirl of wind and sand encircling her. She was summoning a wave from the ocean. She bid the wave over the beach, and sent it crashing down on the little shack to douse the flames. A surge of water then barreled down on the pickup trucks, sweeping men off their feet and into the mire.

Freya, the Dark Witch, was commanding the sea.

CHAPTER 19

My little Pink,
I suppose you think,
I cannot do without you,
I'll let you know
Before I go,
How little I care about you.

I'm lying flat on my back in a room that's 105 degrees and smells like dirty feet. *People die in heat like this,* I think. Sweat is seeping down every crevice of my body, and the workout hasn't even started yet.

"I don't think I can do this," I whisper to Kimberly, who insisted I join her.

"Yes you can," she says, striking a pose of divine harmony.

"I can't breathe." I sit up feeling so light-headed I might tip over.

"You'll get used to it," Bethanny adds. She's seated next to me in the lotus position.

I look around the room at the most athletic, glistening people I've ever seen, their calves toned, their shoulder blades perfectly pointy.

Kimberly claims that this torture will somehow free my mind and purify my body. All I can think about is how I'm going to faint at any minute. Then again, fainting could be my ticket out of this room, and that wouldn't be so bad. Now that I'm a Glamour Girl, there's no end to the invitations and duties, the trends and demands. Leading the life of a Glamour Girl turns out to be a full-time job. My social life is on overdrive. In the past week I've gone to Zumba with Miranda, I've done a group cleanse at the Monrovia Wellness Center led by Heather, I attended a PTO meeting with Rosie which was all about replacing the lavatory soaps with an all-natural tea tree oil soap that the Glamour Soap Company would happily donate, and I helped Heather pass out gift baskets from our new Manly Man product line to the entire Monrovia police department.

It's all starting to feel a little claustrophobic.

In front of us, a woman is stretching in a forward split wearing the skimpiest workout clothes I've ever seen. Her top ties in a halter, leaving her entire back bare. When the woman sits up, I see that it's Paige Pearson.

Paige catches me looking at her in the mirror. She gives me a smug smile as she spritzes herself with a bottle of cucumber spray.

Just the sight of her makes me boil with anger. Even though the Bonkers party was a couple weeks ago, the wounds are still fresh. Suggesting that Henry was autistic, the way she turned the lights on when he wet himself, the way she spoke down to him. Memories of that awful day sear forward. I wipe the sweat off my face, only to have it immediately replenish, and try to focus on the peaceful face of the Indian yogi painted on the wall—anything other than my hatred for Paige Pearson. But I guess I don't hide my emotions very well because Kimberly leans over and asks what's wrong.

"Nothing," I whisper.

"Are you sure?"

The door opens, a wave of relief washes over me. Then sweltering heat again.

Kimberly leans toward me. "What is it? I can tell you're upset."

"Her." I gesture with my chin.

"Paige Pearson. One-eleven Jefferson Court. Three children, ages nine, seven, and six. Regular buyer of comfrey and sage facial wash. Good customer."

"She picked on my son."

Kimberly narrows her eyes, looking very perturbed on my behalf.

Sean, the yoga instructor, walks in, and everyone stands up on their mats. "Namaste. Let's begin," he says. Sean is slim and built like a Greek god. He's also dressed like a Greek god in nothing but a tiny loin cloth of yoga shorts. Within minutes he's slicked with sweat, which just makes him look even more Adonis-like.

"We begin with our breathing," Sean says.

The class mirrors his moves, interlocking our fingers into tight fists under chins, pulling our elbows up toward the ceiling while simultaneously filling our lungs with air then exhaling and leaning backward, in what has to be the most uncomfortable range of motion I've ever experienced. After a few breaths like this, my neck is sore and I'm sweating like no human being should.

"What did she do?" Kimberly whispers between breaths.

"She told me Henry was autistic, for one."

A look of indignation crosses her face. Of course *my* feelings were hurt by Paige, but the fact that my friend is so rankled makes me feel like a righteous victim. Allison, good. Paige, bad.

"And she turned the lights on after Henry wet his pants so that all the kids could see," I say, piling on the evidence to my already biased juror.

Now Kimberly looks riled, as if she has been personally attacked.

Sean cues the side bend next. We are to stand with our feet six inches apart, arms straight overhead, inner arms glued to the sides of our heads, fingers interlocked, forefingers pressed together pointing up, backs bent, reaching for the sky and then leaning as far as possible to the right side, while kicking hips to the left. The pose is difficult and I feel like I might fall over.

"Watch this," Kimberly whispers.

In the mirror I can see her lips move as she repeats a silent spell, gaze fixed on Paige.

"Lean, lean, lean. Stretch, stretch, stretch. More, more, more," Sean instructs. "And . . . switch."

Everyone automatically changes directions and leans to the left, except for Paige whose body remains forty-five degrees to the right.

"Switch," Sean repeats, but Paige doesn't move.

Her face twists in pain as she bends her knees and tries to straighten her body. Her hands are glued together over her head, her torso is cocked to the side. She falls to her mat. "Help," she says, pain in her voice.

Sean comes to her aid and tries to help her out of the stretch, but her body won't budge. He holds her waist. He pushes and pulls, but no matter what he does, she's stuck in position.

Class is cut short. An ambulance comes for Paige, the EMTs struggle to get her on the gurney with her body shaped in a V. The class disperses for the showers while Kimberly, Bethanny, and I head to the juice bar

"That was creative," Bethanny says in admiration.

Kimberly laughs. "The permanent side bend. She deserves it. She picked on Allison's son."

Bethanny gasps as if it's the worst thing she's ever heard.

"She made the poor boy wet his pants in front of everyone," Kimberly says.

"What a cow!" Bethanny exclaims.

"Well, she didn't exactly make him wet his pants. She just didn't help me cover it up when it happened." Suddenly I'm feeling guilty. I'm not sure the punishment fit the crime. "Will she be okay?" I ask sheepishly.

Bethanny ignores my question. "We cannot sit by and let that sort of stuff go unpunished. Women like that need to learn a lesson."

"Besides, Astrid would have approved," Kimberly says weakly.

"Totally," Bethanny says.

Kimberly seems to notice my skepticism. "It's altruism, Allison."

"That means putting the good of the group before the individual," Bethanny explains.

"I'm sure she knows what altruism is," Kimberly says. "Still, we're not supposed to use magic without approval. It would be best if you didn't mention this to Astrid."

"We just want you to know that we have your back. We stick together," Bethanny says, looking directly at me. "You have to know who you can trust."

"And who you can't," Kimberly adds.

I picture Paige at the hospital with a team of doctors unfamiliar with magical contortion, trying to unbend her. *She deserved it,* I tell myself. I hold my cool smoothie up to my forehead. She did deserve it, right?

"Do we have your word, Allison?" Kimberly says after a long pause, her fingers tapping the table. Her eyes dart over to Bethanny.

"My word on what?" I ask, confused by the sudden serious shift in her tone.

"That you won't report this to Astrid," Bethanny says.

"We might get in trouble," Kimberly says, her anxiety palpable.

"I won't say anything."

"Good. Besides, it was the right thing to do," Kimberly adds.

"Is she seriously injured?" I ask.

"It'll only last a week."

"And you're sure she's going to be all right?" A hollow pit is gathering in my stomach.

"I'll stop by her house with bottle of Glamour muscle-soothing salve," Kimberly says. This makes Bethanny laugh.

"How did you do it anyway?" I ask.

"It was easy. She was covered in our cucumber spritzer. I just used a basic spell: 'Piping hot, smoking hot, what I've got, you know knot.'"

"You've figured out how it works, right Allison?" Kimberly says.

"Not exactly." In fact, I've been trying to figure it out. The witchcraft of my mother involved potions and words, too, but it only healed that which was broken or sick. I don't remember magic that could injure people or inflict permanent side bends.

"All Glamour Soap products are enchanted," Bethanny says cheerily. "The soaps, oils, lotions, sprays, and tonics are what spread spells. If it weren't for the Glamour products, the magic wouldn't have anything to latch on to."

"That's why we spend so much time on distribution," Kimberly says, and takes a long slug of her banana-mango protein blaster.

Behind the counter of the juice bar there's an assortment of Glamour Soap spritzers and body oils for sale alongside the coconut water and herbal teas. Between the welcome baskets, the home-shopping parties, the gifts, and the retail outlets, every woman in Monrovia must have dozens of enchanted Glamour products in her house. Every time they rub some all-purpose marjoram-and-black-walnut lotion on their hands, or wash with lavender soap, they're priming themselves for magic to be done on them. How many times has magic been done to *me* in this way? Is that how Astrid got me to agree to host a Glamour Party in the first place? Is that why all of us are always chasing trends and volunteering for every charity event in town? How long has Astrid been using magic on us? And where does the enchantment come from?

"What's in the soap?" I ask.

Bethanny shrugs.

"We don't know," Kimberly says. "Only Astrid knows that."

"It's all-natural and it works. That's all we need to know," Bethanny says.

I want to know more about the soap and how it's made, and how it makes the magic work, but Kimberly changes the subject. "Allison, do you want to come with me to city council tomorrow night? Warren's holding a budget meeting. It might be good for you to get to know all the city councillors. It might help with Kevin's proposal."

"I'll go. If you think it will help."

"I'm in charge of cookies and refreshments. Putting my Harvard MBA to good use as always," Kimberly says.

I must look awestruck.

"Are you surprised?" she says, fanning herself with a smoothie menu.

I wipe my arms with a napkin, amazed that I'm still sweating. "A little. Do you . . . work?" I ask, the question slipping out.

She rolls her eyes.

It's the most dreaded question amongst the legions of stay-at-home moms. Three decades of feminist angst is in it. It's the question with no good answer. Either you're riddled with guilt for surrendering to stereotypical "female" roles or you're consumed with guilt for being a bad mom who puts her career before her kids. I quickly amend it: "I mean, obviously, you work for Glamour. What did you do before?"

She smirks. "I was the chief political strategist during the last presidential campaign," she says.

"Of the United States?" I say, my jaw dropping.

She nods. "I was working seventy hours a week. On the road forty-five weeks a year. I was never home. I never slept. I never exercised. My blood pressure was through the roof." She crosses her arms, accentuating the sharp lines of her biceps. "I loved it."

"Then why did you quit?"

She pauses. "I was in Iowa when my daughter performed her solo in *Swan Lake*. When my son broke his leg, my nanny was the one who took him to the hospital and stayed with him overnight."

I scan the juice bar to see if anyone is listening. A woman holding a coconut water in one hand and texting with the other passes our table and out the door. "And let me guess, Astrid invited you to work at Glamour, and your life has been better ever since."

"Something like that. I would have missed out on seeing my children grow up. It was Astrid's idea to make Warren the mayor. She said I would be able to put my political background to use for a higher cause, and I could stay home with my kids."

"Why didn't she just make you mayor? You're the one with all the experience," I say, taking a slug of smoothie.

A cold look crosses Kimberly's face. "It's better this way."

"Why?"

"It's what Astrid wants."

A few women emerge from the locker room, clean and dressed.

Bethanny whispers, "Astrid saved us all in some way."

Kimberly nods and suddenly I realize that Astrid could ruin their lives just as easily. Bethanny's husband would come out of the closet. Rosie would be riddled with psoriasis. Miranda would be in jail.

I feel light-headed again, but this time it's not from the heat. There's a rising question in my chest, a feeling of darkness. I wonder if Astrid is as benevolent as she seems. What kind of witch is she? After all, she controls an entire town by spreading her potions on unwitting customers, making them susceptible to her spells. What are her intentions?

Who is Astrid Laveau?

CHAPTER 20

A woman, a spaniel, and a walnut tree
The more you beat them, the better they be.

After that, I decide it might be a good idea to get rid of all the Glamour Soap in my house.

I start in the bathrooms and work my way down to the laundry and under the sink. A storm is rolling in and Rufus, my brave protector, has crawled behind the couch, panting and shaking. I try to calm him down with a slice of salami, but he's too scared to eat, so I tuck a blanket into his nook and run outside to find his favorite chewed-up dinosaur toy. In the backyard, the wind whips at the apple trees, stripping them of their fall coats, exposing the steely tombstones in the cemetery behind them.

When I return to Rufus, Cleo is cuddled up beside him, which seems to give him comfort. "Good cat," I say and continue de-Glamourizing the rest of the house. It's staggering how much product I actually have—Glamour dish detergent, Glamour doggy shampoo, Glamour hand soaps, Glamour air freshener.

There are even little packages of Glamour bath salts still tied in pretty ribbons, left over from the welcome basket the Monrovia Greeting Committee brought over when we first moved to town.

The magic needs something to latch on to.

In the pantry, tucked behind boxes of quinoa and flaxseed (items that will never find their way into a Darling family meal), I retrieve the jar of Me-First Masque. There's at least one more application's worth. I know I should dispose of it, but I can't.

Just for emergencies, I tell myself, though I can't rationally justify how being first in line at Starbucks constitutes an emergency.

I tuck it back in its hiding place and continue my sweep of Glamour hand sanitizers, floor polish, and skin moisturizer. By the end of my rounds, I have a garbage bag full of soap products. I step outside to dispose of it just as the Domestic Glamour van pulls into my driveway.

"Sign here," the maid in green says, wind batting at her perfect coif. I look up and see the black thunder clouds rising like an anvil in the sky. Somewhere, a siren rings out.

It's just a letter today—no basket full of herbs and oils, no recipe for a potion. The letter is terse and businesslike:

> *Allison:*
> *Report to my house tonight at 7:00 P.M. sharp.*
> *Attendance required.*
>
> *Astrid*

I guess the honeymoon's over. Never mind the nor'easter that's blowing sheets of icy rain across town. Never mind that there are kids who need baths, and homework that needs to be checked, and shutters that need to be closed, and lawn furniture that needs to be stowed in the shed, and dinner dishes that aren't going to clean themselves.

I have to lie to Kevin. I tell him it's Bunco night at Judy's house and off I go.

The driveway is already packed when I get to Astrid's house. Spikes of sideways rain pelt my jacket, flattening my hair. I run up the walk as the wind tears at the topiaries on either side of me.

The door is unlocked, so I step inside, the wind rattling the suit of armor in the foyer. Rain drips from my slicker into a puddle on the floor.

I peek through the foyer at the darkened house. It looks

unfamiliar tonight, dark and unwelcoming, the doors to all the rooms shut tight.

Led by the sound of voices at the far wing of the house, I head down the long corridor, when something catches my eye. A sliver of light escapes underneath a set of double doors. I press an ear against the door, but no one's inside.

I turn the glass knob, and I'm in the kitchen.

A single pendant casts a circle of light on the counter. Putrid smells cut through the cold room. Piles of herbs and seeds spill over the counter and onto the floor. There are buckets of beeswax, leaves of mullein, garlic, thorny branches of raspberry, mushrooms with clumps of soil on their stems, roots and flowers, a basket of what I'm fairly certain is poison ivy. A butcher block holds a wasp's nest. Sterling silver vases hold marsh grass and cattails.

The sink is full of mussels, their shells cracked open, the animals inside dead and rotten.

It's hardly the kitchen of a domestic diva like Astrid.

Alone in the dark, I listen for anyone who might be near, but it's silent. I hold my breath, and tiptoe across the room.

A calendar on the wall shows every committee and board meeting in Monrovia for the month, along with the names of which coven members will attend.

Well-organized stacks of folders and maps line a desk near the refrigerator. This is Command Central. I open a folder with real estate listings tucked inside, each house accompanied by a list of names, alongside their occupations, salaries, and phone numbers. Potential buyers? It seems invasive and unethical, but then again, she is the most successful Realtor in town.

In another folder, I find agendas for every Monrovia committee, each annotated in the margins. "Introduce new parking restrictions on Front Street." "Motion to expel Cindy Adams from school board." "Offer Glamour gift baskets as prizes for Home Garden Tour." There's a folder for the city bylaws, one for its penal codes, one for its budgets. I dig a little deeper and find a folder labeled "Glamour Clients." It lists the names of every woman in Monrovia, along with which Glamour products they've purchased and when.

I look for something that might give me more insight into her personal life—photos of family or friends, tax documents, letters, grocery lists—but there's nothing. No kids' artwork taped to the wall from a niece or nephew, no corny birthday cards, no chipped souvenirs from vacations, no stacks of bills, or stray sneakers left on doormats.

Who are you Astrid Laveau?

It dawns on me that I don't even know how old she is. Older than me? Forty? Fifty? She can't possibly be older than fifty, even with an unlimited supply of Glamour Youth Rejuvenator Serum and Dr. Yu's Botox Clinic.

The door swings open and Lilith glares at me.

"What are you doing?"

"Uh. I was looking for the bathroom."

"You shouldn't be in here."

I follow her down the hall to the study, where the whole coven is convened.

Astrid glowers at me when I walk in. "You're late."

"Sorry."

"If you can't make it on time, I'll arrange to have one of the other ladies pick you up." She enunciates every word.

"I'm sorry," I repeat.

"Sit down."

But I can't sit. I need to get near her. To see into her eyes. Ageless Astrid. With an unknown past.

Astrid's eyes flare in my direction. "Sit. Down. Now."

Freya would be in her late seventies. Is it even possible?

The room crackles with lightning. Wind and rain slash at the windows. I take a seat between Heather and Erin.

Astrid moves her eyes from me to the rest of the coven. "Now, then, let this meeting commence. Before we get to assignments, are there any Special Appeals?" Astrid is standing at an oak podium, in full command of the room. Branches beat against the outside of the tall, leaded window.

Bethanny raises her hand. "I have a Special Appeal," she says.

"What?" Astrid says, unable to conceal the edge in her voice.

Bethanny inhales deeply, exhales to gather her nerve. "I am absolutely dying for the new Christian Louboutins. They're covered in crystals—Swarovski, of course—stiletto heels and one-of-a-kind emerald charms placed by the designer himself. They're special order, as you can image. Geoffrey's Emporium downtown has tried to order them for me, but there's some kind of waiting list."

Astrid rolls her eyes. "State your case."

"Okay. Here goes. Chad's been invited to this party at the governor's mansion next month and I need to show up in some Louboutins."

"The governor's mansion?" Astrid's leans into the podium.

Bethanny twirls her hair. "Chad's firm does some work, for, like, a lobbyist, or something like that. Chad's always saying that's where the money is. It's something to do with tax laws or banking laws or, something like that. Boring, boring, boring."

"And the shoes?" Astrid's voice sends a chill up my spine. Bethanny lowers her head and speaks.

"Last time I noticed that the wife of this top lobby lawyer wore Prada to the party. Prada's fine, *obviously,* but all the young celebrities are wearing Louboutins now. It's much hipper. Not that any of those stuffy old lawyers would notice, but the governor's wife is, like, a major fashion diva. Total trophy wife. She was in *People* magazine last month having lunch with Angelina Jolie for some charity thing. So, believe me, *she* will notice the Louboutins. And I thought if we had something in common, then I could strike up a conversation with her and I could bring her a Glamour Soap basket as a hostess gift, and if she likes it, maybe she'll use it, and that means the governor himself might use it and then we'd have the ear of the governor."

There is total silence in the room as everyone waits for Astrid to speak.

Astrid pounds a gavel on the podium. "*This* is the kind of strategic thinking I'm looking for. I will grant you a Special-Order Spell," Astrid says.

Bethanny squeals with delight and accepts congratulations from the other women who seem to agree that crystal-studded shoes and hostess baskets are the key to success.

Erin and Heather get into an animated discussion on the genius of Christian Louboutin, in which I am neither capable nor interested in participating.

"Anyone else?" Astrid says. The room gets quiet again.

Lilith raises her hand. "I'd like my oldest son, Carson, to win his tennis match against Mike Abbot on Friday to secure the top seed at the high school." Lilith sounds like she's giving a business proposal. "This would serve two purposes. First of all, Carson is at a very impressionable age. He wants to spend all his time futzing around with music, and isn't putting enough effort into tennis practice. If his interest in tennis continues to wane, I'm concerned that he's going to start hanging out at the skate park playing guitar. And since we're moving to reform that part of town, I don't want him getting involved."

Everyone nods in understanding, except for me. Is she talking about the skate park where I take Henry and Sophie to watch kids on the half-pipe, where I secretly go to escape the judging eyes of the playground moms? Is there something that needs to be reformed there?

"Secondly," Lilith continues, "Mike Abbot's mother is Susan Abbot, who just opened up a Pilates studio downtown. She has a large number of devoted followers. I think she is positioned to influence a lot of new moms and would benefit the coven as a Glamour Soap home sales rep. If our sons have a healthy rivalry on the tennis court, I think I can segue into a conversation about Glamour Soap."

Lilith sits back and bites her nails. Despite the chill in the room, there's sweat on her nose and forehead. She takes out a handkerchief and wipes her face.

Finally, Astrid speaks. "I'll mix up an Ace-Serve Serum for you to give to Carson on Friday. I also want to make you the head of Glamour Soap recruiting."

Applause breaks out across the room. Lilith beams with pride, and, if I'm not mistaken, relief.

"Any more Special Appeals before we get to Work Assignments?" Astrid asks.

I'm about to speak up. If these women can ask for frivolous things such as shoes and stacked tennis matches, then surely I can request Kevin win the bid for his waterfront project.

But Rosie beats me to it. Her hand shoots up. I hadn't even noticed her sitting in the corner until now.

Astrid motions for her to stand.

Rosie stands and speaks in a subdued voice. "I request that Steve get a promotion at work. The market's been down lately, and he hasn't closed any sales in months, even though he's been working weekends and nights to try to get something going. He works strictly on commission. There hasn't been a paycheck in months. We need the money. I know it's a lot to ask, but we're behind in our mortgage payments and I'm worried that we're going to lose the house."

The room is silent. No one is breathing. I look at Rosie, who looks more ragged than the last few times I've seen her. Her eyes are puffy and her skin sallow.

Astrid's eyes are cool and steady.

"No," Astrid says. "Appeal denied."

"We're desperate," Rosie blurts out. "I know it's a lot to ask, but we need this."

"Denied," Astrid says.

"I don't know where else to turn. We're so in debt. I can't even make the minimum payments on our credit cards."

Astrid sighs. "Magic is a tool for serving the coven and the coven only." A flash of lightning illuminates her face. For the first time, I notice wrinkles around her eyes. "It is *not* a vehicle for personal gain. Everyone must do her part."

Rosie sniffs back a tear. Her hand goes in her mouth to silence her sobs. Everyone stares straight ahead, ignoring Rosie. I want to go console her, help her, talk to her, give her a hug and some tissues, tell it's going to be okay, be a friend to her, but instead I just sit there with the rest of them. Astrid has spoken. The rest of us have listened.

"If there's no more personal issues, we'll move on to jobs. Heather, let's start with you."

Heather tenses up in her chair.

"Since we made your husband the new police commissioner, he's done a decent job," Astrid say.

"Thank you," Heather says, breathing deeply.

"But we have a problem in town. There was a homeless man spotted sleeping under the Route 1 Bridge this week. Monrovia has no tolerance for vagrancy. I want the police to patrol the bridge on every shift and if they spot any vagrants, I want them removed from the city at once."

"Yes, Astrid," Heather says.

"And," Astrid continues, "I'd like to increase the police presence on the Town Green. I want them cracking down on dog owners who violate the leash law, and on young punks who trample the grass with their bicycles and skateboards."

I gulp so hard it hurts. I can't believe what I'm hearing. She's a total control freak.

"Miranda."

"Yes?"

"On the planning board this week, I want you to suggest a measure that would require all shop owners and homeowners in the city limits to sign a maintenance contract. Homes should be kept up to certain standards. Once everyone signs off on this policy, you'll need to get Mr. Nelson to paint his store immediately. It's an eyesore, and it's one of the first businesses you see when driving into Monrovia. We need to keep our city beautiful."

I raise my hand.

"What is it, Allison?" Astrid says, her eyes fixed on her podium.

"I'm pretty sure under the city bylaws, business owners can only be compelled to make improvements in situations where the building is causing a hazard to public safety. I've been involved in Kevin's contracting business for a long time. I file a lot of his paperwork with the city and I'm pretty up on the laws."

Astrid laughs a deep belly laugh. "Allison, it's up to us to keep Monrovia beautiful, safe, and prosperous. We do *whatever* we have to in order to achieve this goal. Do you want to live in a town of vagrants and derelict buildings?"

I can feel her eyes boring into me. Outside, the storm has picked up. Wind echoes in the fireplace.

"Kimberly, I want you to talk to the mayor this week. It's come to my attention that the liquor store has been carrying pornographic magazines. This is in direct violation of our community standard. I want the mayor to fine the liquor store. We need to send a message that this sort of indecency is not acceptable here."

Oh my God. My head is spinning as it all sinks in. Maybe Aunt Aurora was right all along.

As if she can read my thoughts Astrid looks directly at me. "You see, Allison, it's my business to know everyone's business."

How much of my business does she really know? How much of my aunt and my mother's business does she know?

"On to work duties," Astrid says. "Bethanny, Kimberly, and Erin, you three are on factory duty this week. We're low on hand soaps and bath salts. I'll expect you at the Glamour facility first thing tomorrow." Bethanny and Erin groan in unison.

"Heather and Miranda, I want you working the greenhouse. Take extra care with the Venus flytraps. Lilith, you will work on home-shopping party recruitments." I look around and all the women are taking notes.

Astrid continues. "I will visit Mrs. Honeycut the first-grade teacher in the hospital this week as a show of PTO support. I'm told she's recovering from the scurvy just fine."

"Scurvy?" I whisper to Erin.

Erin whispers back, "Mrs. Honeycut wasn't willing to bend on math grades. Kimberly made a Special Appeal for a substitute teacher last month."

"So we poisoned the teacher?"

Erin shrugs noncommittally.

Astrid clears her throat. "Rosie, I want you to clean all the iron pots with lye and a steel brush."

I peek over at Rosie who looks like she's just been handed a prison sentence. It's safe to say that she drew the short straw in this week's chore pool.

With jobs issued, Special Appeals granted (and denied), and everyone put in her place, Astrid bangs the gavel again. "Meeting adjourned."

We file out of the study, through the dark corridor and into the foyer. The wind rattles the mahogany door, and the light flickers. The maid appears with our coats draped over her arms. I'm waiting to get my coat when Astrid pulls me aside. "I'd like a word with you," she says.

I stand rigid as stone beside her and we wait for all the ladies to leave.

"I have a special job for you," Astrid says, her voice echoing in the cavernous room.

Poison another teacher? I think. Infiltrate Beacon Hill?

I look down at the polished marble floor with its mosaic of crystals and minerals.

"There's a problem with the group home over on Howard Street. I believe you know the place," Astrid says.

"Sunrise House?" I say. It's Judy's baby. The house for learning-disabled adults.

"So you know it?"

"What's the problem?"

"It's not a good fit for Monrovia. It's driving house prices down in that neighborhood. And, really, who wants that type of person as a neighbor?" Astrid says.

"They're perfectly harmless," I say. "They actually do good work for the community."

Astrid stands very still. I can feel heat rising off her body. Heat in this very cold house. "I don't want a bunch of retarded people running around town. Those people leer at the children. They scream at all hours of the day. They are no use to society."

I'm aghast at what I'm hearing. "They're not retarded. It's not like that. My friend Judy works there."

"As a matter of fact, your friend is doing such good work that she's starting to open up residency to indigents from other towns. They're applying to the state for a license to expand their services." She takes a step toward me. "I want you to make sure they don't get that license."

"What?"

"I'll give you a little potion. All you have to do is get in there and release it. Just so they don't expand. Consider it your job for the week." Suddenly the room has gotten so hot that I'm sweating under my raincoat.

"But the house gives them a place to live a normal life."

"Sunrise House doesn't exactly fit in with Monrovian values."

"I can't do it, Astrid."

Astrid puts a hand on my shoulder. "Tell me, do you like using magic? Do you get much out of those potions I send you? Has your life improved since you joined Glamour?"

I don't answer.

"Everyone must do her part," she says.

"But . . ."

"It's just a few cockroaches. That's all." Her smile is infectious. Gone is the terrifying Astrid from the meeting. She's been replaced by Astrid, the charismatic company president. "There's a meeting on Friday at the house. HUD will be there along with their entire board of directors. Use your friendship with Judy to get in."

"I don't know . . ."

"All we're doing is stopping them from expanding. Would you want a place like that next door to you? Next door to your kids?"

I shake my head, feeling terribly two-faced.

"We're not monsters. It's not like we're getting rid of them. We just want to keep the numbers manageable," Astrid says. She laughs her silky laugh. "You get what you give. Isn't that fair?"

"I guess so," I say meekly.

She hands me a potion bottle from the credenza in the hallway. "This should help you."

CHAPTER 21

Ladybird, Ladybird
Fly away home,
Your house is on fire,
Your children will burn.

Sunrise House is an old Victorian painted clementine orange in an attempt to be cheery.

When I arrive, Judy is standing on the front porch giving one of the residents a hard time about his necktie.

"Where in the hell did you find that thing?" she says.

"Salvation Army store. Three-oh-five Main Street, Haverhill, Massachusetts," the man says.

"Well, it looks like something my father would have worn, which isn't saying much," Judy says. She tightens the knot at his neck and the man tilts back his head in compliance.

She doesn't notice me standing beside her. "Hi, Judy," I say.

"What do you think of Leonard's tie?"

Leonard is a middle-aged man with an enormous grin and a suit that's too small.

"It's nice," I say.

"She's lying," Judy says to Leonard. "She thinks it's hideous."

This makes Leonard chortle. "Miss Judy, it's a nice tie. I bought it for one dollar and fifteen cents. I gave the salesman two dollars and he gave me eighty-five cents back."

"Well, it's a good thing you didn't break the bank," Judy says.

Only Judy could treat the mentally challenged like she treats everyone else and actually get away with it.

She turns to me. "Allison, meet Leonard. He's one of our long-term residents of the house and he's a master craftsman. Leonard, Allison is my best friend and she promised to help out in the kitchen tonight."

I put my hand out, and Leonard shakes it. He pulls a notebook out of his back pocket and a pen from behind his ear. "When's your birthday?"

"May seventeenth. Why?" I say.

"What year?"

"1977."

Judy says, "Leonard keeps track of everyone's birthdays. When's mine?"

"March twelfth, 1975. Eight fifteen A.M. in the morning. Boston, Massachusetts," Leonard says. He doesn't look in his book for the answer.

"He's a freak when it comes to numbers."

He writes in his book.

"Don't quote me, Leonard. That's all I need is someone writing me up for calling you a freak," Judy says.

Leonard smiles so wide that the corners of his mouth disappear in his cheeks. "You're the freak, Miss Judy."

"I consider that a compliment, Leonard."

Sunrise House doesn't exactly fit in with Monrovian values, I hear Astrid say. I feel sick knowing what I have to do. Knowing that I lied to Judy about wanting to help make her dinner a smashing success tonight.

"I'm going to show Allison around the house. You're on door duty. When the board members walk up, greet them, and show them to the dining hall. When the people from HUD show up, lay on the charm. All right?"

"How will I know they're from HUD?"

"Because they work for the government and they'll probably have on neckties as ugly as yours."

"Ooooh. They have good taste." Leonard fans himself with his tie. "I'll tell them to give us lots of money for the house."

"That's the spirit," Judy says.

Inside, a basset hound flopped on a braided wool runner opens his eyes, blinks, then goes back to sleep. "You haven't been here in a while," Judy says. "Let me give you a tour." She takes me through the living room. "Communal zone, technically." There are vinyl records stacked beneath an old record player. Glass figurines of frogs and knickknacks garnered from flea markets are lined up in a curio cabinet. The baseboard heaters hiss. Books with ragged bindings are stacked neatly in a bookshelf, in alphabetical order, I notice.

A chore chart in Judy's aggressive handwriting is tacked to a wall, with categories in Dusting, Clean Bathrooms, Feed Dog. I notice a gold star for someone named Marcus in the Meal Planning column. On a table that functions as a desk, coupons are clipped and stacked in order. There's a collage of photos pinned to a corkboard; residents in a game of checkers, flipping pancakes, planting a tree, a group photo in front of a sparsely decorated Christmas tree, everyone in red and green sweaters imprinted with reindeer and snowflakes.

"What do you think?" Judy says as we walk from the living room to the kitchen. "Not bad for a shoestring budget, huh?"

"It's depressing as hell," I say.

"It's better than being institutionalized," she snaps.

"I'm sorry. I didn't mean anything. The residents are great and you've done an amazing job. It's just that . . . it reminds me of foster homes I grew up in."

"How so?"

"They were called homes, buy they were never really *my* homes. The things in them weren't mine. The people weren't family. It's a home without feeling homey. That's what I meant."

Judy fluffs up one of the pillows on the couch and puts it neatly in place. "Then you'll feel right at home in our less-than-homey kitchen," she says with a smile.

We walk into the kitchen, which is a flurry of activity. Judy introduces me to Michael and Matt, the resident cooks, as well as David and Pete whose jobs are to serve the food tonight. "Allison is here to help you, so put her to work, okay?"

David hands me a tray of glasses. "You can fill these with water. Please and thank you. And remember to use your manners so Miss Judy can butter her butt and call you a Bisquick."

"Biscuit." Judy smiles and David smiles at the inside joke that passes between them.

Just a few roaches. That's all I'll do. Just enough to keep Astrid off my back, but nothing to ruin this night for them.

"Thanks for helping out tonight. This dinner has to go well," Judy says.

"I know. You need approval to expand the house," I say.

"I wish," Judy sighs. "We actually need to pass this inspection, or they can shut us down permanently. We're still in our probation period. If we don't pass, HUD can cut off the crappy little bit of funding we get now."

I hold my purse tightly to my side, a bright green jar of Roach Infestation Potion sloshing around inside.

"I thought you just needed to get permission to expand," I say.

"There's nothing to expand if we don't pass probation," Judy says. "But I'm not worried. These guys have worked so hard. The house is spotless. We've met all our requirements. Unless someone finds a hair in their goulash, we'll pass no problem."

Astrid lied.

She doesn't want to block Sunrise House from expanding its services. She wants to shut them down completely. Sunrise House, with its gaudy orange façade and less-than-perfect residents doesn't fit in with her vision of a perfect Monrovia.

She doesn't care that even a house as dreary as this is better than an iron bed in a cinderblock room.

Leonard pops his head in the kitchen and tells us that the

people from HUD are here and that everyone's in the dining room.

"All right, people, let's get dinner on the table," Judy says. "Look sharp."

She starts to leave when Leonard comes back in the kitchen with Lilith. "She says Allison invited her," Leonard says.

Lilith walks right up to Judy and me. "I hope you don't mind me dropping in like this. Allison thought it would help to have the president of the chamber of commerce at your dinner tonight to show the HUD folks that you have community support."

Judy coughs, unable to hide her surprise.

I choke back my objection. That is definitely not what she's here for.

"Thank you, Lilith. We actually could use your support. Let me introduce you to the board members," Judy says.

"May I use your bathroom first?" Lilith says. She looks right at me.

"Down the hall. Leonard can show you."

"No," I say abruptly. "I'll show her the way."

When we're alone, I grab her arm. "Lilith, listen. Sunrise House will be shut down if they don't get approval tonight."

"Astrid was right. She knew you wouldn't be able to go through with it. That's why I'm here, if you haven't guessed."

Lilith unzips her purse and retrieves a jar of powder.

"Wait," I plead. "Astrid is wrong about this place. They're good people. Spend some time talking to them. You'll see."

"You were given an order," Lilith says.

"But she lied. She said we would just stop them from expanding." My stomach drops. Lilith is going to sabotage this dinner and I have to stop her. It will ruin these people. It will crush Judy.

"Astrid tells people what they need to hear."

I can feel the back of my neck pulsating.

With catlike speed, Lilith tosses the powder into the air.

"There was a rat,
   For want of stairs,
   Went down a rope
   To say his prayers."

As the powder floats to the floor, it spreads into a fog. A little pink nose pokes out of the fog and then the whole rat emerges. Another one follows. Then another, until dozens of rats emerge from the fog and scatter in every direction.

"STOP!" I yell.

Rats scamper down the hallway to the kitchen. "Don't do this, Lilith," I say.

"Astrid is going to be very disappointed in you when I tell her how you failed a simple task." She pulls out another potion jar and unscrews the cap. I reach for the jar, but she jerks her hand back, and accidentally I knock the jar to the floor. A thick yellow substance like honey oozes out of the cracked jar.

"Very disappointed," Lilith says again. Then she recites:

"A swarm of bees in May
   Is worth a load of hay;
   A swarm of bees in June
   Is worth a silver spoon;
   A swarm of bees in July
   Is not worth a fly."

The honey starts to bubble and boil and then the bubbles float into the air and as they rise, the bubbles turn into bees. At first there are only a couple of bees, but soon there are hundreds. I swat at the air in front of me. Just as the first scream of "Rat!" comes from the kitchen, the bees swarm together and fly down the hallway.

I run after the swarm.

I get to the kitchen moments after the bees. Michael and Matt have dropped platters of food and are batting at the bees.

Brown blobs of beef goulash are splattered across the floor. Matt slips on the mashed potatoes trying to run away. Michael grabs my hand and leads me out the door, but I pull away. I need to stop this ambush.

"Go," I yell. "I'll open the windows."

From the dining hall I can hear shrieks of terrified guests, the scuffle of chairs.

The swarm flies through the dining room, back into the kitchen, and out through the opened windows.

The bats come next.

Then, the cockroaches.

Finally, the fire. Plumes of smoke waft through the rooms of the house, and although I can't see flames, the smoke sets off the sprinkler system, drenching everything.

By the time I get outside, the board of directors and all the people from HUD are standing on the sidewalk. Sirens wail in the distance. Judy is trying to calm down the residents, some of whom have become hysterical. I see Leonard walking in circles, cradling his notebook in his arms.

Lilith walks out of the house, calm as can be. "Very disappointing" she says to me before she walks down the sidewalk, and out of sight.

I feel like the ground beneath me has dropped away. I grab on to a bike rack to steady myself. How can anyone do such an evil thing? And worse, how could I have been a part of it?

A thought drifts in front of me, so solid I can almost reach out and touch it. It's been there right along, first when Wilhemena spoke of it, then Aurora, and then again when Astrid noticed my birthmark that first night at my house. What if Astrid *is* Freya? My mother's sister. My aunt. The Dark Witch.

I pull out my phone and text Astrid the simplest message I can:

I QUIT.

CHAPTER 22

> See a pin and pick it up,
> All the day you'll have good luck.
> See a pin and let it lay,
> Bad luck you'll have all the day.

My landline is dead the next morning.

The TV doesn't work either, the lights won't go on, the coffeemaker has shut off on its own. Next door I can see Patricia's TV is on, tuned into the soft news of late morning, the hour of housewife programming, where peppy reporters cover topics like leftover turkey recipes or the versatility of the pashmina.

Across the street, a garage door opens and a minivan pulls out.

Apparently, I'm the only one on the block who's lost power. I guess this is Astrid's way to telling me she got my text last night.

Luckily, my cell still has a charge. I take a deep breath and call Judy.

"Want to go for a walk?" I ask.

"Not really," Judy says, the events of last night hanging in the air.

"It might do you some good. Come on."

"Can't. Too busy contemplating how to kill myself," she says and the knot in my stomach tightens.

"I need to talk to you," I say.

There's silence on the other end and I wonder, just briefly, if she really would hurt herself.

Then her voice comes across the line, riddled with defeat.

"Leonard came unhinged. They carted him off to Saint Berna-dette's. How's he going to survive there? He needs a home, not a cell block."

"Let's talk," I say. "Meet me downtown."

I don't need to tell Judy where, exactly, we are going to meet. She knows I mean the fountain in the Town Green with the massive iron raven perched in the center. It's our point of origin, our debarkation point for countless days as stay-at-home moms with hours to fill.

Judy's waiting for me when I get there.

"Sorry I'm late. No parking in front of Starbucks." I hand her a double espresso.

We walk down the cobblestone path, past a gardener trimming the edges of sod in a sharp line. Every summer flower has been snipped and filled with a hardy fall replacement. Every Federalist house has three miniature pumpkins lined up in a row on the cornice above the door, and a bleached starfish in every window. Posters for the Boo Bash, sponsored by the Monrovia PTO, are taped to light posts. "Volunteers Needed," they say. The Town Green that used to look so pretty to me, now seems anesthetized and ugly in its graffiti-free conformity.

Judy's silence is unnerving. I reach for the right words, but nothing good surfaces. "I got a parking ticket," I say, finally. "For being three inches over the line. Can you believe that?"

"Fucking tragedy," Judy says, the sarcasm dripping from her lips. She sips her coffee and burns her tongue and lets rip a storm of *fucks* and *shits* and *goddamn motherfuckers*.

We pass an elderly woman on a bench, who looks up at Judy with wide eyes. She's feeding cookies to a dog as small as a rat nestled in her lap. A police officer approaches her and we watch as he writes her a ticket for having a dog without a leash.

"Monrovia's finest. Cracking down on our violent crimi-nals," Judy says.

I'd laugh, but the truth behind it is too sick to joke about.

Astrid's evil hand is behind that poor old lady getting a ticket. Just like it's behind Sunrise House.

Farther down the Green, a baby-and-me yoga class is spread out, forming a sea of moms in black yoga pants and bright pink designer sweatshirts with babies in matching yoga pants.

"What's this shit?" Judy says.

A woman who's trying to get her infant into downward-dog position overhears us and says, "Outdoor yoga gives babies the opportunity to explore movement. It increases confidence and body awareness in infants as young as six months." The kid falls to his belly and scoots away to chase a moth.

"Bullshit," Judy barks, more ornery than usual.

I notice a bottle of Glamour Soap cucumber spritzer in the cup holder of the woman's stroller, right next to the expensive French bottled water. I want to tell Judy everything. Knowing the truth could ease her guilt. And mine.

"Well, that's what I read on the Web site," the yoga mom says defensively. There's a hint of doubt in her voice, as though she is the one who wants to yell "Bullshit," but the pressure to be on trend is too strong.

"These women are seriously deranged," Judy scoffs as we make our way to the river's edge.

"It's not their fault," I say. "They're under a lot of pressure."

"Pressure? Pressure? What, like making sure their yoga pants aren't on backwards before they walk out the door?" Judy looks at me with sharp eyes. "You know what's stressful? Knowing that you are responsible for ruining the lives of people who counted on you. Knowing that the people in your care were sent away to institutions where they will suffer in loneliness."

I picture Leonard in his new tie, wandering the halls of Saint Bernadette's. "You can't blame yourself for what happened," I say.

"Why not? It's completely my fault. What was I thinking having the residents host a dinner? They have too much pressure in their lives already without having to deal with bureaucratic bullshit. I'll tell you what I was thinking, Allison." Tears fill her eyes. "I was so sure of myself, of the bang-up job I was doing as director of Sunrise House, that I thought the people from HUD would be blown away. It's my ego that brought us down."

I look out over river. Only a few boats remained moored, their owners too optimistic about New England weather to admit boating season is over.

"It's not your fault," I say.

"It's definitely my fucking fault."

"No," I say. I look her in the eye. "It's not."

I proceed to tell Judy everything from the onion at the Apple Harvest to my mother's crazy funeral, to the witchcraft I grew up with, to the night of the equinox party and my induction into Glamour Soap. I tell her about the magical spells, the enchanted soaps, the home run ball at Fenway, the thrill I felt when I was part of it. I tell her about the magical control Astrid holds over Monrovia, the committees, the trends, the needs.

She listens, quietly sipping her espresso.

I tell her about my orders to release cockroaches at Sunrise House and how Lilith brought the rats, bees, bats, and fire with her. I tell her that I quit the coven last night after what happened, after I realized that Astrid was using me to get into the house.

Judy doesn't speak for a very long time. Then she turns to me.

"I always knew there was something fucked up about this town," she says.

I let out a sigh of relief. It feels like a hundred-pound barbell's been lifted off my shoulders. "So you believe me?"

"You're a pagan. I guess that explains a lot."

I laugh, but cautiously. "I've wanted to tell you, but . . ."

She interrupts me. "Here's what I don't understand though.

Why did you do it? Why did you join them if you knew they were trying to turn us all into a bunch of brainwashed Martha-fucking-Stewart, baby-and-me yoga idiots?"

On the river, a cormorant dives underwater, breaking the glassy surface.

"I guess . . . I wanted to be like them. They're all so beautiful and smart and successful. They have the best parties and the right clothes. Their kids get all the advantages. I wanted to stop feeling bad about my sloppy house and my kids' troubles. I liked being first in line. Life's easy for them. I wanted all of it. Who doesn't?"

"I don't," Judy says. "And I wouldn't throw my best friend under the bus to have it."

"I'm sorry," I say, dragging out the words, wishing my apology was enough. Knowing it's not. "I know it was wrong. I just got swept up in it. I liked belonging to something for once. I liked thinking that all the crazy witch stuff I grew up believing in wasn't so crazy after all. Astrid treated me like family. She gave me all the love and acceptance I didn't have growing up."

Judy turns toward me, and I can see the fight in her eyes. "You know who you are, Allison? You're the skinny girl in high school who sits with the fat girls at lunch because you know we have the best snacks, but then one day when the cheerleaders invite you to their table, you forget all about your fat friends. Until you realize that the cheerleaders aren't you."

Two women pass in front of us, their babies tucked safely into the strollers they push like appendages. They walk slowly, savoring this brief social encounter that breaks up the morning between breakfast and nap time. Without even hearing them, I know the pattern of their conversations. They talk about their husbands, their children, their homes, their diets, what books they're reading, what shows they're watching on television. They express horror over their child's new obsession with biting other kids, as well as their husbands' inexplicable bathroom habits. They reveal brutally honest details of their sex lives that will make the other one laugh. They share anecdotes of their past lives when they were younger and wilder. They will encourage each other no matter what the day brings; they will validate each other's choices. They are me and Judy.

When they return home, they will spend most of their afternoon sitting on the floor with their child, watching his every move with sheer wonder, while slowly, unbeknownst to them, their own identities will slip away, until they become known as so-and-so's mom.

And, while this is the life they fought for, the life they were privileged enough to get, they will want more. They will want to feel . . .

"Astrid made me feel special," I say.

Judy stares at me, her face riddled with disgust. "Because she invited you to her fancy party? Because she gave you some potions to make your pets poop in the toilet? Because she fed you some line about how you were all going to be one big happy family? I hope it was worth it." Judy stands up to leave but I grab her hand.

"It's more than that. I grew up ashamed of being a witch. She ennobled the whole idea of it. I wanted to believe that being a witch wasn't shameful. That the words and potions we put out in the world have meaning. I wanted to believe that I was part of something greater than myself."

Judy sits back down.

"Did I ever tell you about the will-o'-the-wisps?" I ask.

Judy shakes her head.

"There are these green lights that flicker over the marsh at night sometimes. My mother, who was a great witch, told me they were spirits from the in-between, and when I was little, I could see a whole other world in them. I could straddle this world and that world. But when my mother went away, everyone told me that magic wasn't real, and I stopped being able to see the will-o'-the-wisps as anything other than a chemical reaction."

I catch my breath and continue. "Being in Astrid's coven let me believe again."

"Until you realized what a complete bitch she is. And what a complete bitch she turned you into," Judy says.

"I'm sorry, Judy. I don't know what else to say."

"How about 'good-bye'?"

The walk home is lonely. People have already started decorating for Halloween, which is usually my favorite time of year, but I've lost my best friend and everything is tainted. Not even the family of jack-o'-lanterns carved like the Three Stooges cheers me up.

Geoffrey from Geoffrey's Emporium rings on my cell and informs me that my custom-order Louboutins are in and that I can come and pick them up at my earliest convenience. "I'm afraid we still need to receive payment for them. Ms. Laveau has withdrawn her credit card. She said you were paying for them since they *are* under your name."

"Uh, how much do they cost?" I ask, bracing myself.

"Six thousand five hundred dollars," Geoffrey says. He adds quickly, "They're simply stunning."

I choke on my own saliva. "I didn't realize they were that much."

"Obviously, I can't return them since they are special order. Sissy Star has an amazing eye, doesn't she? I have no doubt you'll love them. So, I'll expect you down at the store this week to pick them up," he says. He adds, "And pay for them."

What am I going to do with shoes that I can't possibly afford? Astrid sure is having fun sticking it to me.

When I get home, Rufus is barking in the front yard. A car peels away, kicking up smoke and leaving black marks on the asphalt. I look and see that it's Miranda's Land Rover, her "Give Bees a Chance" bumper sticker cruising down Purchase Street.

Rufus is frantic. He runs at me, then around me like a spastic pinball, then down the street, still barking. *Follow me,* Lassie-style.

I chase after him. When he reaches a brown lump in the sidewalk he stops.

My heart skips a beat when I catch him. It's Cleo. Her eyes are wide open, her legs extended. Her tail points in a straight line; it's not limp and saggy like a dead cat's tail should be. I reach down and roll her onto her back. Claws are distended.

This is not a hit-and-run or sudden heart attack; she looks like she's seen a ghost.

Or a witch.

Sophie and Henry are distraught with the news.

I tell Henry he can stay home from school the next day, but he's sullen. Sophie is inconsolable. I promise a trip to the toy store, knowing full well that a new Polly Pockets is no substitute for a favorite pet. However, it eases her suffering for a while until she remembers why she was sad in the first place and then the emotions come surging forward and backward, leaping between sorrow and joy, depending on what she's doing moment to moment. Gillian is torn up over Cleo, too, but she directs her energy to helping her younger siblings, treating them to a rare invitation into her room to play with her hamster.

We manage to get through the rest of day with lots of cartoons and pudding. Salve for a broken heart.

We bury Cleo in the afternoon and say a few words about the cat we didn't know for very long. The kids ache and I ache for them. A child's first brush with death is no small matter. But I feel Cleo's demise the deepest. She wasn't just a cat, she was the last connection I had to my mother. And to make matters worse, her death is my fault, a casualty of my insubordination.

While the kids watch TV, I pour a glass of wine. Then another. Another.

Vaguely, I notice that the cartoons have ended and the innocuous preteen sitcoms have taken over the evening programming, and I realize that it's late and my kids haven't eaten, and

Kevin hasn't come home from work yet. I look in the fridge for something to call dinner. Settle on half a bag of frozen fish sticks. I keep wondering where Kevin is. I don't have any messages from him, and he's not answering his phone. What is holding him up tonight? I don't remember him telling me about any late meetings. I feel a sickness in the pit of my stomach.

As soon as he walks in the front door, I know. Disappointment in his eyes. Jim Beam on his breath.

He just shakes his head. "I was underbid." His words are slurred, the veins on his forehead pulse.

"How?" But as soon as the word comes out, I know the reason. Mayor Davey was just listening to his wife, Kimberly, who was just listening to Astrid.

She knows how much this one will sting. Winter's coming. There are no big construction projects in Monrovia in winter. Kevin was counting on the city approving his bid for the waterfront project, which would carry him for the next three years. Now he'll have to find little jobs: painting, tiling, refinishing basements, handyman-type stuff.

I'm seized with a familiar dread. Destitution. Poverty.

This is what happens when you cross Astrid.

CHAPTER 23

A pullet in the pen
Is worth a hundred in the fen!

Monrovia, Massachusetts • 1960

After the night the mob torched their home and nearly killed their mother, the Ellylydan girls ran away. They went underground, hiding their magic, silencing their spells, and suspending Lessons.

They wandered the small hamlets and townships from Cape Ann to Cape Cod, happening upon places like Beverly and Ipswich, where everyone paid taxes, and where no one was a stranger. Had it not been for the fact that Freya had saved her sisters and mother by dousing the fire and driving away the mob, Wilhemena and Aurora would have had no tolerance for Freya's constant complaints. In each new town, it was always Freya who eventually drew attention to them, arguing with a shopkeeper here or getting too involved in the goings-on of local teenagers there. Once she became involved, she became a curiosity, and once she became a curiosity, questions were asked, and once people started asking questions, it was time to pack up again. So they kept moving on, seeking refuge, searching for a place where they could fit in.

They found it in a neglected mill town on the shores of the Merrimack River where they could slip by unnoticed; where everyone was too drunk or despondent or idle to take heed of newcomers.

Monrovia, it was called.

Most of the buildings were abandoned, overtaken by weeds

or boarded up with water-stained plywood. Streets were rutted and decayed. The river itself ran brown and toxic from the vacant textile mills that still oozed industrial waste. There was no industry here anymore. Even the Boston railroad stopped two towns to the south.

Elizabeth and her girls rented a three-bedroom house on a corner in town with a patch of dirt that passed for a yard, where Edmund could graze. At night the town drunks urinated over the chain-link fence into Edmund's pen and Aurora would have to clean his hair with a solution of chamomile and tea tree oil. Next door, there lived a family with a seemingly endless brood of children whose parents fought every night by an open window.

Elizabeth had suffered a stroke shortly after the night the mob came, the night that Freya commanded the sea. Her speech was impaired now. She limped. It was as though she had aged twenty years overnight. Her daughters fed her, bathed her, and tried to keep her spirits up.

Between the drunks and the neighbors, and the foghorns on the river, there was no quiet. They wished to return to the stillness of the marsh. They yearned for the smell of clay and sea.

They no longer made soap from scratch or raised chickens. Wilhemena and Aurora worked odd jobs cleaning and cooking to bring in a little bit of money for rent and groceries.

"Soon. We move. My w-w-witches," Elizabeth would say from the couch, the left side of her mouth turned downward in a slack V, while Wilhemena and Aurora cooked beans and rice in the small, grease-coated kitchen. But they all knew it was a lie. They would never be able to return to the marsh. This was their new destiny.

The state of their lives rankled Freya the deepest. She wanted to squeeze the throats of the men who had set their home on fire and forced her family into these squalid conditions. She wanted revenge. Her thirst for blood only grew with every day that passed.

Worst of all, Elizabeth forbade any practice of witchcraft. The world was changing, she said, and so must they. Like an athlete whose career is cut short by a broken leg or a ripped tendon, Freya felt robbed of a promising future in magic.

During the long, aimless days, Freya scavenged. She looked beneath the Route 1 Bridge, amidst the cardboard shanties. Tattered clothing, old tires, a chair missing a leg—these were the types of treasures she retrieved either to use or sell. In the boarded-up mills she recovered oil drums and bolts of mouse-chewed fabric. She took her chances, breaking into the crumbling warehouses through their plaster shaken loose whenever a large truck rumbled by.

She didn't mix with the Commoners anymore. She *was* a Commoner.

Wilhemena and Aurora tried to keep up some of the Old Ways. They still made their own brooms and candles. They dried their own herbs from the ceiling.

"Why don't you just buy those at the store?" Freya barked one night as Wilhemena wrapped beeswax into long, thin tapers.

"This is what I know. This is the way Mama taught us."

"What good did it do?" Freya said. "What good did any of the Old Ways do?"

"We wouldn't be here if you had respected the Old Ways," Wilhemena snapped. "But instead of feeling sorry, all you do is complain. You're a selfish, ungrateful daughter. And you're a wicked sister."

Freya opened her mouth to object, but Wilhemena threw up her hand and cast a Silencing Spell, breaking her mother's rule just that one time. Freya's words disappeared into the air.

One gloomy afternoon, Freya rode her bike to the wharf where the lobster boats docked. She had good luck finding treasures here—zinc cartridges, yards of nautical rope, lobster traps washed ashore. Some of the lobstermen liked Freya. She was a stunning beauty and there was something beguiling about her. They gave her free lobsters.

Down the wharf at the end of the boatyard, she leaned her bike against a beached dory and walked along the muddy riverbank. It was a filthy place where the river currents pooled and sent ashore all manner of debris.

A family of sand crabs flitted across the beach in front of her. Their pale shells blended into the sand, camouflaging them from seagulls. How lucky for them, Freya thought, to blend so easily. To walk safely amongst their predators.

She followed a trail through the saw grass to a campfire pit strewn with broken beer bottles. Sitting on a stump, she poked at the charcoal, lost in thought. An ant crawled up the stick she was holding. She shook it off. Soon there were two more ants and she shook the stick again, but they clung on. Ants marched over her shoes, an endless army of miniature invaders. She stomped them into the ground.

More came.

Freya found herself mesmerized by the persistent, single-minded purpose of the ants. She followed them to an anthill and watched them work. She noticed how one would climb out of the mound, make contact with an ant coming from the opposite direction, and continue marching until it reached the next ant. Then those ants would stop and repeat the encounter identically to the one before. When the next ant came, both would stop and make contact, and on and on. They communicated through scent. And they obeyed their orders. A perfect, orderly community of slaves.

And deep within the colony lay the queen, ruling with absolute sovereignty.

Queens lived ten times longer than worker ants. Elizabeth had taught her that in Lessons long ago. Back when they had Lessons, Elizabeth forbade the killing of queen ants for potions. Queens were leaders in the natural world and were to be respected.

Freya wished to be like the queen, ruling over a colony.

An idea began to form in her head. A wonderful, terrible idea. She could turn Monrovia into her anthill. It was begging for a leader, eager to follow anyone who could lift it from its filth and despair, and elevate it to prosperity.

She stomped on the anthill and walked back down the muddy riverbank.

CHAPTER 24

When the wind is in the east,
'Tis neither good for man or beast;
When the wind is in the north,
The skillful fisher goes not forth;
When the wind is in the south,
It blows the bait in fishes' mouth;
When the wind is in the west,
Then 'tis at the very best.

For the rest of the week, I keep a low profile. Other than essential trips to the grocery store, school, and soccer practice, I stay home, for fear of accidentally bumping into a witch.

But Thursday is the science fair and I have to go. Gillian's worked too hard to stay home and hide.

Luckily, the coast is clear when we get to the school. Kevin, who has adopted a sort of dejected slump in his walk since losing the city's bid, takes Henry and Sophie to play in the bleachers while I help Gillian put the final touches on her display.

"Do you really think I'm going to win?" Gillian says, threading gumdrops and marshmallows onto the ends of toothpicks.

I glance over at Bobby Bower's display of fossils on the next table. He's got a couple pictures he printed off Wikipedia glued to cardboard and trilobites that he's squished out of Play-Doh. Gillian has 3-D helix models and an interactive game that compares genome graphs of different marine animals from largest (the marbled lungfish) to smallest (a plant-parasitic nematode).

"I think you're going to win," I whisper. "Just remember what we practiced: The red licorice represents strands of deoxyribose sugars."

"And black is for the phosphate groups," she says. "We've been through this, like, a thousand times."

"Do you have your index cards?"

She holds them up, neatly bound with a rubber band.

"You're going to do great," I say. It feels good to be focused on something other than covens and adult worries.

Breanna, Gillian's BFF, marches up and stands in front of the display. "This whole science fair is, like, so lame," Breanna says, snapping bubble gum.

"First prize is a membership to the New England Aquarium. That's kind of cool," Gillian says.

Breanna blows a bubble and it pops. "Science is so boring."

Gillian lines up her candy helix models. "I don't know, I think it's fun."

"Cute," Breanna says, picking up a red gumdrop and plopping it in her mouth with the gum.

"Thanks."

"Kind of babyish, though. It reminds me of those macaroni necklaces we used to make in Scamper Camp."

Gillian shrugs sadly, no doubt wondering when her best friend moved on to cooler things, leaving her in dust. "How did your weather display turn out?"

Unlike Gillian who started working on her project weeks ago, Breanna hadn't even chosen a topic last week when she came over so they could "motivate each other." In fact, Gillian worked while Breanna watched TV and ate sandwiches.

"Good, I guess. I don't really care about it. I mean, what's the big deal? If you win all you get is a membership at the aquarium. Like, what kind of loser still goes to the aquarium?" Breanna says.

I can't believe what I'm hearing. I don't want to be a meddling mom, but I have to say something. "What do you mean? The two of you have been talking about becoming marine biologists since kindergarten. You both always said you were going to move to California and train dolphins."

"Whatever. I'm over that. Anyway, good luck, Gill," Breanna says and walks away.

I can see in her eyes that Gillian is crushed and confused.

"It's just sour grapes," I tell her, even though I have a sick feeling that the coven is behind Breanna's sudden shift in priorities. After all, if you really want to hurt someone where it counts, go after their kids.

Inside the beige-tiled auditorium, parents wander through rows of science projects while students demonstrate their knowledge of beach erosion, photosynthesis, how steam engines work, solar ovens, thermodynamics, the earth's crust. Kevin, Henry, Sophie, and I walk through the auditorium scoping out the competition. I feel increasingly confident that Gillian has this in the bag.

We get to Gillian's aisle moments before the judges do. "Here they come," Kevin says and gives Gillian a wink.

Clipboards in hand, Mr. Hamm the science teacher, Mrs. Mersen the principal, and this year's special guest judge, the chief biologist from the New England Aquarium, walk up to Gillian's display.

And behind them is Astrid, clipboard in her hand.

"What are you doing here?" I say.

Principal Mersen looks shocked by my rudeness. "Since Ms. Laveau's real estate agency is sponsoring the fair we asked her on as a guest judge."

"Isn't that a conflict of interest?" I blurt out.

Astrid's eyes pierce me. My birthmark twitches.

"No. She doesn't have any children at the school," Principal Mersen says.

"Well, don't you think it's strange that someone with no children is so involved in the school?" My throat is dry.

"Mom!" Gillian says.

Kevin touches my arm. "Allison, it's okay."

Principal Mersen says, "Ms. Laveau has volunteered her precious time to take part in our school. It's because of volunteers like her that we can operate. Everyone must do her part."

Mr. Hamm changes the subject. "Why don't you tell us about your project, Gillian."

Gillian begins. "Have you ever wondered which animals have the largest genome? I have. DNA is the building block for all of life. It's the glue that holds all families together." She looks up from her index cards and makes eye contact, just like we practiced.

I watch Astrid like a hawk, ready to pounce if she pulls out a potion or chants a spell.

"In Greek, the word *genome* means, 'I become. I am born,' which is probably why the founder of the genome, Hans Winkler coined the term . . ."

Astrid shifts her eyes from Gillian to me. Then from me to Henry, who is in an imaginary lightsaber battle with an imaginary villain. Her gaze moves to Kevin, then to Sophie.

Panic rises in my chest. Why is she zoning in on my family? What awful spell is she going to cast on them? I've seen what she's capable of. I know what she does to witches who betray her.

Astrid picks up one of Gillian's DNA helix models and pretends to inspect it, but her eyes are trained on me.

Gillian flips to her next index card. She pauses. She flips to the next card and the next, but doesn't read out loud. She shuffles through the cards for a long, awkward pause. "Sorry, just a sec. I lost my place."

"It's okay," Mrs. Mersen says. "Do your best."

"Yes, Gillian, it's okay," Astrid says, all smiles.

"What are you doing?" I say to Astrid.

Unfortunately, everyone hears me, and it makes Gillian flustered. She picks out a card and reads, "In Greek the word *genome* means . . . wait. Wrong card. Sorry."

Astrid sets the helix model back on the table.

"Leave her alone," I snap.

Gillian looks up from her cards and stares at me. Mrs. Mersen, Mr. Hamm, and the aquarium biologist look bewildered.

"Is there a problem?" Mr. Hamm says.

"Mom, what's *wrong* with you?" Gillian says.

"It's her," I say, pointing to Astrid. "She's a witch."

Principal Mersen sighs. "Mrs. Darling, not this again. I think you should take a minute to compose yourself."

Astrid grins. Her voice is coated in faux concern. "These moms are so overworked in this day and age. The poor thing is probably exhausted," she says to the other judges, who shake their heads in concern.

"Mom, what are you doing?" Gillian says.

"I'm sorry. I just . . . I thought . . . ," I say. I turn red with embarrassment. This is not the way to handle a vengeful witch. "I'm sorry," I say. "Never mind me."

I turn and push through the crowd to the exit. When I get to the door, there's a thundering crash from the last aisle. Everyone runs to see what the commotion is. I join the crowd and soon realize that the deafening noise is coming from Breanna's exhibit.

Breanna is standing in front of her display table, demonstrating how hurricanes work. Behind her, a vortex of fog is spinning in a whirlwind, picking up bits of debris in the air. As she speaks, the vortex crosses to the table where she's built a scale-size model city with a mini ocean, papier-mâché mountains, Popsicle-stick trees, and Lego buildings. The vortex spins over the ocean, spraying water everywhere.

She points to the Doppler radar, showing pixilated blobs of green and blue sputtered over landmass. Blips of red appear in the middle of the green mass like a cherry tomato in the eye of the hurricane salad.

"The red means three things," Breanna narrates. "Barometric pressure is dropping, convection is increasing, and outflow is improving. In other words, a hurricane is forming."

On her table, the vortex moves across the ocean to the miniature coastal city.

"Hurricanes emerge over the Atlantic and grow in strength and size as they pass over thousands of miles of ocean. In a closed circulation, rain bands form and tropical storm force winds begin to emerge."

Now there is rain. Yes, actual water droplets accompanying the spinning vortex as it moves toward the landmass.

"By the time a hurricane makes landfall on the coast, its strength is so powerful that it leaves a path of destruction in populated areas," Breanna says. Behind her, the spinning vortex tears through the city. Popsicle sticks and Legos fly through the air.

I search her display for the powerful fan that must be making the hurricane, but I don't see one. Shy of both vacuum and fan, there is no logical explanation for this display, other than magic. Everyone else is so enraptured by the display they don't notice Heather, who standing off to the side mumbling.

And then, as suddenly as it began, it's over. The hurricane is gone and Breanna's coastal city lies in ruins.

The auditorium breaks out in applause.

I feel sick. My head is spinning. I push my way to the gymnasium door. The last thing I see is the chief biologist of the New England Aquarium shaking Breanna's hand.

When I went up Sandy-Hill
I met a sandy-boy;
I cut his throat, I sucked his blood,
And left his skin a-hanging-o.

Gillian's second-place ribbon for the science fair is stuck to the fridge with a big smiley-face magnet. To make matters worse, Kevin is hunched over the help-wanted ads at the kitchen table. He circles an ad for a handyman, black ink bleeding into the newsprint.

"Why don't you call some of your old clients? See if they have any work?" I suggest.

He goes to the fridge, pulls out a beer. "Like who? Astrid? I don't think she's ever going to talk to any of us after the way you attacked her yesterday." He sits back down, snaps the paper open, and scans the long column of classifieds.

Okay, I deserve that, I think. I lost his biggest client for him. I decide to keep quiet rather than try to explain what I really believe to be true: that Astrid is Freya, the Dark Witch.

I chop a salad in silence.

Kevin is adept at the silent game, too. He doesn't speak to me at all while I make the spaghetti. When I set the table, he simply lifts the newspaper into the air, so I can set down a fork and napkin in his spot.

When he does finally speak, the words crackle with tension. "By the way, you're on snack duty for Sophie's class tomorrow. The teacher said it should be cut-up fruit," he says.

I stare at him in disbelief. He stares at the paper. "You're just telling me this now?" I say.

260 • *Katie Schickel*

"I just remembered."

"Why couldn't you have told me earlier when I was on my way to the store, when I had plenty of time to get this together?"

He shrugs. "What's the big deal? We have a bunch of apples. Just cut some up in the morning."

"They brown too fast."

"They'll be fine."

"No, they won't," I snap. "You can only bring grapes or oranges for snack. Now I have to go to the store tomorrow morning."

"Relax," Kevin says.

"Don't tell me to relax. I'm the one who has to deal with this."

"It's not exactly an international crisis. You're making a big deal out of nothing."

"You should have told me sooner," I say, feeling my family coming unglued.

By bedtime, we're still not speaking.

In my mind I go through all the things I need to say: that our fight wasn't about apples browning too fast, but about so much more. Him. Me. Our marriage. Our lives together. The extreme sacrifice of making playdates and potty training more important than paychecks and promotions. The need for something more. The need for magic.

I'M A WITCH! I want to scream. I want to come clean. I want to tell him the truth: that I've been tormented over my mother abandoning me. That when Astrid came along and offered me the family I was denied growing up, I took it. And as much as I want to blame this whole situation on a few potions and spells, I know I'm the one to blame. I'm the reason Kevin lost the waterfront project. I'm the reason Gillian lost the science fair. I'm the reason Cleo died. But the words disappear.

That's when it hits me.

Maybe I'm not the only member of the coven who's pissed

off Astrid before. Maybe some of the other ladies have been at the blunt end of Astrid's wrath. Rosie was. What about Kimberly? What did she sacrifice to enter the ranks of Monrovia's elite? What skeletons are hiding in her closet?

I decide I'll pay Kimberly a visit first thing in the morning. For the early class.

The windows of the hot yoga studio are fogged over, obscuring the view inside. Kimberly's Porsche is in the parking lot, along with Bethanny's silver Mercedes. Conspicuously absent is Paige Pearson's minivan with the "Proud Parent of a Monrovia Yacht Club Junior Sailor" bumper sticker. With a twinge of guilt, I wonder if her back has healed yet.

It's a sauna inside. Sweat soaks into every surface of this place, and I worry for a second that evil is transmittable, like the flu, or herpes. The door to the yoga room is open and the room is empty, so I go into the juice bar where shiny, sweaty women bask in the post-yoga glow with shots of wheatgrass. Kimberly is at a table, texting.

I approach her tentatively. "Can we talk?"

She looks up, annoyed, as though it's too debasing for her to acknowledge my presence. "I'm not really supposed to associate with you."

"Just for a minute? Please."

She puts down her phone and scoots over to make a place for me.

The heat is oppressive. I take off my jacket and sit down. "I know you got Warren to vote against Kevin's waterfront project."

She is cool and composed. "Yeah. I heard about that. I guess Kevin's proposal wasn't as super special as you thought. He's not the only contractor in town, you know."

"Cut the bullshit. Astrid ordered you to get Kevin's proposal squashed, didn't she?"

262 · *Katie Schickel*

She looks down at her phone, texts something, then looks back at me. "What do you want, Allison?"

"I want you to talk to Warren. Ask him to reconsider Kevin's project. I'm not asking for special consideration, I just want a fair fight. I want the city council to vote for what they think is best, without any magic or potions or anything."

"You know I can't do that."

"Kimberly, I know you resent the fact that you have to sit on the sidelines while your husband gets to be in charge."

"How do you know that?"

"It's obvious. You're the ambitious one. You're the one with the political background and the Harvard MBA. You should be the mayor. You're more than qualified."

"It was best if a man took the role. It's less suspicious," she says, looking down.

"You don't believe that."

She wipes her forehead. "I basically am the mayor."

"But you're not. You're just a housewife who brings cookies to city council meetings."

I can see this gets her. Her nostrils flare, and there's a dangerous anger hidden in her eyes. "What do you suggest I do? Quit? How did that work out for you?"

"She doesn't control you. You can live your own life." The heat is getting to me. Sweat forms on my forehead. I wipe it away with my sleeve.

"You made your choice, Allison. Now let me make mine," Kimberly says.

"But it's wrong, and you know it."

Bethanny is suddenly standing beside me with two large Styrofoam cups from the juice bar. "Problem?" she chirps.

"There's no problem," Kimberly says. "Allison's just trying to stage a mutiny, that's all."

Bethanny sits down. "You look hot, Allison. Have a smoothie."

"I don't want a goddamn smoothie. I want you both to start being honest." The air is stifling.

"Calm down and let's talk about it," Bethanny says, her button nose curled up.

"You don't need Astrid. You can live without her magic," I say, feeling faint. Bethanny notices and places the smoothie in my hand. I take a long swig, which is cool and refreshing and absolutely the most delicious thing I've ever tasted. The cold goes right to my chest and I sip some more. It soothes my whole body from my brain to my fingertips.

Feeling replenished, I continue. "What about you, Bethanny? Your whole life is a lie. Don't you want a husband who loves you without potions? Chad can't be happy pretending to be something he's not. Don't you want to live honestly?"

Bethanny is calm. "Sweetie. I don't know what you're talking about. We're the happiest couple in town. Everyone says so."

"Any woman would kill to be in our position," Kimberly says.

Just then Dr. Yu walks up to the table, looking showered and painfully handsome. He and Bethanny air kiss on both cheeks. I haven't seen him since the equinox party when he told me I had perfect bone structure.

"Great class, wasn't it?" he says, white teeth gleaming.

Bethanny smiles. "You have amazing balance. Your warrior series is very strong."

"Thanks," he says and his eyes sparkle.

"Well, I was going to grab a coconut water, but that line is so long," he says.

Bethanny grabs his arm. "Wait. Here. I have an extra smoothie. I ordered Raspberry Razzle Dazzle but they gave me passion fruit. Do you want mine?"

A thought flickers across my mind. It's strange that Bethanny ordered two smoothies and didn't drink either one. I take another sip of my delicious smoothie.

Dr. Yu accepts the drink and sips it. His eyes light up.

Then the strangest thing happens. We look at each other, taking our sips of smoothies, and I feel a bolt of electricity run through my body. At first I think it's brain freeze, but it doesn't hurt. In fact, it feels warm and wonderful.

I don't know how I got here.

I'm not sure whether I'm asleep or awake. This I know: I'm no longer at the yoga studio. I'm in a car. Not my car. And I'm kissing someone. Not Kevin.

The sensations come back one at a time. I taste passion fruit, a tingling sensation all over my body, something bordering euphoria, a man's tongue. I smell leather, a new-car smell. I feel the soft cotton toe pads of my socks. Every nerve ending comes alive with sensation. I can feel my skin against the fleece on my arms. I can feel my hands moving over shoulders, through hair. I see a tree outside the window. A willow tree like the one in our front yard. I hear a dog barking.

I know that dog. That is my dog. That is Rufus.

The next few seconds are like coming out of a deep sleep, a dream that's so good you never want to wake up. My mind is fighting to make heads or tails of where I am. I want to stay here forever and ever, but I know I can't. The dream is fading.

Now Rufus is jumping on the door of the car, scratching at it. He wants me.

Then I see Kevin walking down the sidewalk toward me, his eyes pinched, his head cocked, looking as confused as I feel.

I look down and see that I'm sitting on top of a man. I'm on top of Dr. Yu.

How the hell did I get here? I wiggle off Dr. Yu, open the driver's door, and fall onto the sidewalk.

Kevin keeps coming toward me. He's been out for a walk and his cheeks are flushed and his breath turns the cold air white.

I scramble to my feet.

In a flash, the whole scene fits together like the last piece of a puzzle. The smoothies. Bethanny gave one to me and one to

Dr. Yu. It must have been a love potion, and I've been in a total trance for the last twenty or thirty minutes.

Dr. Yu is just coming out of the trance now. He looks all around, trying to figure out where he is. He looks as perplexed as me. He opens his mouth to speak, but he sees the look on Kevin's face, and he sees me fumbling with my shirt, and without a word, Dr. Yu drives away.

Kevin's head is covered in a tight wool cap, little wisps of hair sticking out from underneath.

"Allison," he says. My name on his lips is both a question and an accusation. "Allison?"

I let out a deep breath. Maybe I'm still dreaming. Maybe the potion is still making me experience things that aren't real. But I look into his eyes and I know that hurt is very real. "It's not what it looks like."

What can I say? My witch friends put a love spell on me? "Kevin, please listen to me," I plead.

But he doesn't. He turns and walks up to the house. He drops the grocery bags he's carrying and a dozen oranges roll out of the bag and onto the sidewalk.

CHAPTER 26

Spit, cat, spit,
Your tongue shall be slit,
And all the dogs
In our town,
Shall have a bit.

Kevin went to stay with his parents. Said he needed time to think.

He told the kids he had to go away for work. This was something new and fascinating for them. They wanted details. Where are you going? How are you getting there? Does the hotel have a pool? Do you get to order room service? Will you bring us back a souvenir? They were, no doubt, picturing a vacation like our trip to Cape Cod where they played the game of jumping between hotel beds, pretending the carpet was hot lava, and they ate grilled cheese sandwiches with french fries from room service while watching movies on pay-per-view as Kevin and I drank beer from the minibar and played rummy. And even though it rained almost every day that trip, we all remember it as the best vacation ever.

"How long do you think you'll be gone?" I had asked as we stood shivering on the front porch out of earshot of the kids. I had tried to explain about the witchcraft and the coven, but it was too late. He didn't hear past his anger and pain.

"Don't know."

"More than a week?"

He shrugged.

"It was just a kiss, Kevin. Just that one time. Nothing more.

I haven't been sneaking around on you. I was under a spell. So was he."

"A love spell? Is that how it goes?" he said.

"Say you believe me."

His eyes were puffy and cold. "I know you lied about being at Judy's house for Bunco that one night."

"I was at Astrid's."

"The leader of the coven?"

"Yes. And she's a really powerful . . . witch," I said, the word so hollow it echoed between us.

"Why couldn't you just tell me how unhappy you were?"

"That's not what it is. I'm telling the truth. Say you believe me?"

He couldn't answer.

I cradle a cup of coffee in my empty kitchen as my life falls apart around me. Three pumpkins sit on the patio. Kevin left before he carved them with the kids, one of our Darling Halloween traditions left unfinished.

There's only one person who can help me and that's Aurora. Like it or not, she's the only family I have. Normally this would mean another trip to Greylock Woods, but I look at the calendar. October 28. Four days before Halloween.

I know exactly where to find her.

I get in the minivan and race down the interstate to Salem, which is mobbed with tourists this time of year. Streets are packed and I drive around forever, looking for parking. Damn these tourists. When a woman dressed in ruby red slippers and absurd striped stockings gets into her car and pulls away, I take her spot.

I run to the Salem Green where throngs of people stand in line for tickets to the Witch Museum, the Wax Museum of Witches, the Witch Dungeon Museum, the Haunted

Cemetery Tour. It's a Mardi Gras for wannabe witches. There's a witch on every corner, dressed in black hat and cape, clutching a broomstick. There are witch hats for sale, witch's brew in the bars, witchy potions, and witch rocks, and witch candy. And there, in the midst of the mayhem at the pumpkin patch, I spot the only real witches in the whole city, Aurora and Millie.

Once a year, before Samhain, my mother and Aurora would get drunk on cranberry wine, and steal pumpkins from the Salem Green, although, as a child I never realized it was stealing. "Reparations," they called it, payback for all the hangings, the burnings, the drownings, and the pressings-to-death of witches past.

"Astrid is Freya," I yell, stumbling over a pile of gourds.

Aurora looks up, ready to take flight.

"I found Freya," I say again as I run up to them.

Aurora ducks behind a straw bail. "Where's she at?"

"She's not here," I say, crouching down beside her. "She's posing as a woman in my town. The one I told you about. I'm sure it's her."

Aurora pushes a finger against her nose. "Aphrodite almighty!"

I can smell cranberry wine on her breath.

Millie comes up and hugs me. "Darling Allesone. Have you come to help with the Samhain preparations? How lovely."

"No," I say. "I'm here because I've found Freya."

"Tell us what you've learned," Aurora says.

"Freya lives in Monrovia. She's the woman I told you about who throws the parties."

"Still in Monrovia after all these years, hey?"

"She threatened my kids. She drove Kevin away. She killed Cleo. I'm sure it's her."

"Who's Cleo?"

"The cat. That's what we named Wilhemena's familiar."

Aurora stands. She looks like she's about to cry. "Well, good work finding Freya anyway, niece." She pats me hardily on the back.

"You have to help me, Aurora," I say.

A child runs around Aurora, hiding from his playmate in Aurora's horse blanket cape.

"Scram," she says to him, lifting up her blanket, exposing his hiding spot. The child looks terrified and runs away.

"So you'll help me?" I say.

"Of course," Aurora says. She scratches her chin, thinking. "There's an abandoned chicken coop in the woods next to mine. Must have been part of the old homestead. We can move you in there. We'll get Jonathon and Jinathon to put some concealment magic on it."

"No," I stammer. "I don't want you to hide me. My family's in danger. You have to help me. Show me some spells. Give me some potions. You know magic, Aurora, I know you do."

"Hah!" she says. "You're not thinking of going back there! If Freya's in Monrovia, you have to stay out."

"I can't just run away!" I say, incredulous. "My kids are in school. We own a house. I have a life there."

Millie rolls a pumpkin over to Aurora, who picks it up and slides it under her cape.

"It's no use. Freya doesn't respect our ways, Allesone," Millie says.

"But my family is in danger."

Aurora glares at me. "Run away. That's all that can be done."

"I'm not going to leave my home. My kids don't deserve that."

Aurora takes my shoulders in her hands and looks me in the eye. "I know how it is for you. I know what it's like to have your home taken from you. I've had mine taken from me. Wilhemena done her best to prevent this from happening again. But you must listen to me. Run. It's the only way."

"But you know magic. You can help me. Aurora, think of my kids."

Aurora stands back, the stolen pumpkin conspicuously tucked into her cape. She looks pregnant. Like a seventy-year-old homeless pregnant woman. "Come with us. We'll find you a place in the woods. We'll teach the kids mushrooming."

I look into her eyes and see fear. There's no chance she's going to help me.

Only one person can help me.

Freya, herself.

I turn and walk away, feeling like I've just been kicked to the curb. Again.

I text Rosie for directions to the Glamour Soap factory since she's the only one who will still talk to me. I have to check my phone over and over to make sure I've got it right. Rosie's directions send me down a long beach road with wide roaming dunes to the right. There's a vast salt marsh visible behind a rocky ridge. I park the minivan at the base of the ridge and walk. Sand gets in my sneakers. Horsetail grass slices at my jeans.

Glamour headquarters is a shingled hut with a wraparound porch nestled between the dunes and the ridge.

I stare at it in amazement, repressing every urge to run up the path, fling open the door and yell, *I'm home!*

This is the house I grew up in. Suddenly it's so obvious Freya would use it as her headquarters that I feel regret in every pore. This whole time, she's been right under my nose, but I wanted to believe in her and her ideas about coven as family so badly I couldn't see her for what she was. The realization that this place, the home of my only happy memories, has been stolen for such sick, dark magic shakes me to the core.

Even the creak of the loose floorboards is a memory. Here is the spot where my mother spent Friday afternoons tying bundles of birch twigs into brooms to sell at the market. Over there is where I made a cardboard bed for a seagull with a broken wing. Below the ridge to the right is a raspberry bush that keeps its berries until early fall. Without stepping inside the house, I can smell the rosemary and dill hanging from the ceiling.

The front window is covered in soot. I try the door, but it's locked, its hinges rusty.

I walk around to the back of the house, where shingles bleached with age hang at sharp angles. Briny air blows in from the sea. Sand drifts press against the siding. As I get closer, I hear voices inside and see Lilith and Erin in the kitchen, or at least, what used to be the kitchen.

Erin carries a tray of metal molds as I watch through the squiggly panes of glass. She sets the tray on a worktable and turns the molds upside down. When she taps on the bottom, long slabs of soap fall out. With a machete, Lilith slices the slabs into smaller bars. She arranges them on pink paper, wraps each bar, and sticks a frilly Glamour Soap label on each one.

"What do you want?" Erin says, pushing open the door.

"I need to talk to Astrid," I say, regaining my composure.

"She's rendering. Go away," Erin says with a chill and I can't believe this is the same woman who offered her friendship so easily just a few short weeks ago.

Inside, the shack is dark and somber. There are shelves stocked with metal molds, labels, barrels of lye, jars of oils, an old icebox refrigerator. On the far end, in the room my mother had once painted dandelion yellow, a pegboard holds dozens of knives of all sizes and shapes.

Lilith appears at the door. "Back to work," she snaps at Erin, who cowers like an obedient dog.

"Where is Astrid?" I ask.

"Down by the brook," Lilith says. She points to a footpath through the marsh grass. "That way."

"I know which way."

I walk down the winding doe path that cuts through the dunes to the mudflats. The past comes to me in snapshots: the slant of the afternoon sunlight, the sloggy bed of mud beneath my feet, the song of the bullfrogs, patches of rust-colored water, rainclouds above. The deep odor of sulfur.

I have a sudden urge to plunge my hand into the mud and dig for clams, the way my mother showed me. But I keep walking. I need to make a deal with Astrid: *Leave my family alone, and I'll rejoin your sordid ranks. I will sell you my soul. I will do whatever awful, sinful, wretched thing you ask of me, as long as my family is safe.* I practice this speech in my head as I walk, trying to sound assertive, every bit of me scared shitless.

At the end of the flats I go deeper into the marsh, the little shack disappearing into the dunes behind me. An owl hoots in the distance.

When the path forks in two directions I go left. It leads to the brook, which I follow along the edge, heaps of dead grass floating by on the current. Farther in, the water turns red, and the smell of sulfur is overpowered by the stench of rotting flesh.

Ahead I can see smoke from a fire in a clearing of trodden grass. A figure in a black hooded cape crouches near the fire. My eyes are on the person ahead and I don't see the dead, mangled woodchuck until I step on it. Or it could be an otter. Whatever it is, it's disgusting. I wipe my bloody sneaker in the grass and walk slowly toward the fire.

Animal carcasses are strewn along the path. Skunks, possums, squirrels, raccoons, foxes, the head of a deer. Their dismembered bodies are hacked open, mounds of guts and bone and bowels tossed in every direction. The horsetail grass is soaked in pools of blood, so thick it looks black. Flies buzz around. I look down and see what looks like a rabbit, its decaying corpse wriggling with maggots.

As I inch my way toward her, the bodies only get thicker. I lean over the brook and retch my guts out. I wipe my mouth and cover my nose with a sleeve.

Run, everything in me screams. But I need to stay. I need to strike a deal. I need to make sure my family is safe.

"What do you want?" the person by the fire says, not turning around.

"Freya?" I ask, unable to train the fear out of my voice.

She turns to face me and lowers her hood. Her hair is wild and white. Her eyes are cloudy and set deeply against a fan of wrinkles. Her skin is mottled with brown spots, not a bit of makeup concealing anything. Her mouth and forehead are etched with deep creases. Her teeth are yellow.

Her hands are drenched in blood. Fur and blood and mud stiffen her clothes.

"The one and only," she says. With a long knife she cuts into a raccoon's chest, pulls back its ribs with her hands and tears its heart out of its body.

Hotshot Realtor, company president, socialite. Dark Witch.

"What are you . . . doing?" I stammer.

"Making soap." Even her voice has aged.

I walk closer. Piles of charred bone and ash litter the clearing.

"Out of animals?"

"You have to render the fat from somewhere. Where the hell do you think it comes from?"

"Flowers?" Definitely *not* dead raccoons.

"Yes. That's what everyone assumes. They think soap is pure and pretty. A pretty bar of soap to wash away the dirt and grease. Well, dirt and grease is what it starts out as. Ash and oil. That's all soap is. Isn't it interesting they anoint babies with oil to wash away their original sin. To wash away their impurities. Oil to purify. Dust to dust. Ashes to ashes."

Vultures circle overhead. The knife in her hand drips blood.

"You're . . . the Dark Witch," I say. I can feel myself trembling.

"Guilty," she chortles.

"You and I are . . ."

"Blood," she says, holding up a slick, red hand.

I stagger backward. "But how did you make yourself look so young?"

"I save the best tinctures and tonics for myself." She traces a finger around the wrinkles of her eyes. "The ones with real magic in them."

"Are you going to kill me? Is that your plan? You tried once."

"Tried. Failed."

She wipes her knife clean against her skirt.

I think about Aurora's advice. *Run away,* she'd said. But I can't just leave Monrovia. I can't just sell my house and uproot my kids and tuck my tail between my legs. It won't do any good. Freya will find me wherever I go. Of this, I'm certain. She has a plan and I'm part of it, and she won't give up until she sees it through. "I've never done anything to you. My mother can't do anything to you. She's dead now."

"So she is."

I stare at her, looking for compassion, for a sign of goodness. I find none.

"Allesone, do you know what glamour really is?"

I shake my head.

"Glamour is an enchantment. It's a way of making people see things that aren't so. You see a beautiful woman and you think she is all good and you want to be like her, but we're all made up of darkness and light. Glamour is the *in-between*— something that isn't all the way true, and isn't all the way untrue. It hides. It conceals."

"I want to make peace with you."

"I want. I want. I want," Freya snaps. "You women always want something."

"I'm not asking for shoes. I want my kids safe. I want my husband back."

She laughs wickedly. "Yes, I heard you got caught with the handsome Dr. Yu. You naughty vixen, you."

The fire glows behind her. She grabs a long wooden ladle off the ground and stirs the iron cauldron that hangs on a tripod over the fire, steam rising above it. Little chunks of fat float on the top.

"What do you want from me, Freya? Do you want me back in your coven? Is that it? Because I'll do it. I'll join you."

"I want your mother's ashes."

"Why?" I ask, my mind flicking back to Wilhemena's funeral, to the reading of her Last Wit and Wisdom.

Freya takes my chin in her bloody hand. In the glow of the fire, I get a good look at her face. It's gray and covered in liver spots, but there's something familiar in it. She looks right into my eyes. "You really don't know anything, do you?"

"What should I know?"

She releases me from her clutch.

"Your mother had two dwarves in her coven. Identical twins, which is rare in wizards."

"Jonathan and Jinathon," I say.

"They're holding on to your mother's ashes. I want you to steal your mother's ashes from them, and bring the ashes to me."

"What are you going to do with them?"

"They're for the soap. Dirt and grease. Ashes and oil. You get out what you put in. That's something you seem to have forgotten when you decided to take the easy road and let magic do your work for you. You women are so simple. You want shiny hair and flat bellies, designer shoes, expensive cars. You don't even wonder where your magic comes from. You think I just go down to *the mall* to pick it up? To Crabtree & *Evelyn*? Magic potions need magic ingredients, like the ashes of a dead witch. And I have a very special potion I'm working on."

"Why don't you use your magic to get it from them?" I ask.

"Wizards are very skilled in concealment magic. I need someone they trust to go in and find it. They'll trust you. They'll reveal it to you. And then, you'll steal it. Do you think you can do that?"

"If I refuse?"

"Then I hope Kevin has better luck at his next zoning board meeting. And I hope that nasty girl stops bullying Gillian at school. And I hope Henry gets over all his problems. And that adorable little Sophie of yours. I haven't even thought about her yet. Get me those ashes and I'll leave you alone."

I'm seeing red. I want to kill her. And while I'm at it, I want to kill Aurora, too. Leaving me to fend for myself is what got me here in the first place. Anger rises like bile in my throat. I lunge forward and grab Freya by the neck.

Her lips turn upward in a cunning smile. She throws something in my face that feels like grains of salt. My hands automatically release her and I fall to the ground, my body weak and depleted. She's the one who has *me* by the throat.

"Too bad your mother didn't teach you some of *her* magic," she says with a laugh.

I'm sitting on the ground in a pool of blood. I feel completely hopeless, completely at her mercy. "Fine, I'll do it," I say.

"Good. Get them to me by the harvest moon. This Friday. When the magic for making soap is most potent."

"But it's Tuesday."

"Then you better hurry."

CHAPTER 27

Rowan-tree and red thread
Gar the witches, tyne their speed.

Monrovia, Massachusetts · 1963

"Pancakes are ready," Aurora said, poking her head into her mother's bedroom.

"Still warm," she added. She carried the breakfast tray into the room and sat down on the edge of Elizabeth's bed. Balancing the tray on her blubbery knees, she straightened the fork and stared at the pancakes, her mouth salivating. "I heated the maple syrup, too." Now twenty-two years old, Aurora had taken on most of the cooking, cleaning, and brewing of remedies with herbs from her garden. She even sold her balms for sore joints to fishermen at the pier.

Elizabeth lay motionless beneath the coarse wool bedspread. Probably exhausted from the constant bickering between her sisters in recent weeks, Aurora thought.

"Aren't you hungry, Mama?" Aurora tugged at a piece of pancake and crammed it in her mouth. "Would you like oats instead? Or barley? Buckwheat? Millet?" Aurora ran through a list of breakfast grains, then moved onto dried beans before she realized that her mother had not moved since she'd entered the room.

She touched her mother's shoulder and found it cold as ice. "Wilhemena, Freya, come quick. It's Mama," she yelled.

Wilhemena and Freya burst into the room. Gently, Wilhemena rolled Elizabeth onto her back. One eye was opened and one closed. The open eye sparkled sharp and blue. Wilhemena checked for a pulse. When she found no life left in the veins, she closed the open eye, then bowed her head.

"She's gone to the in-between," Wilhemena said, choking back a cry.

Aurora sobbed. "Oh, Mama. Don't leave."

Freya sighed.

Aurora grabbed Freya by the arm. "Can't you do something? What about the soap? The soap from the harvest moon? Ain't there any magic that can bring back Mama?" She was thinking of Edmund who, at nineteen years of age, had already exceeded the natural life expectancy of any goat she knew.

"We're not supposed to do magic anymore," Freya said. The contempt in her voice was chilling. Years of hiding her extraordinary gifts had turned Freya even more spiteful than she had been as a child. She had lost her youthful radiance; her mouth was fixed in a permanent frown. All she had ever wanted was to perform the magic that was her birthright, but Elizabeth had forbidden it. Now, with her mother gone, Freya smiled for the first time in as long as she could remember.

Aurora wailed, snot and tears flying. "What will we do without Mama?"

Wilhemena wiped away her tears. "We will send her off the way she deserves."

A dull rain drizzled outside the windows of the dining room. Elizabeth lay on the table wrapped in white cotton, her face and hair exposed. The table, with its spindly legs and warped surface creaked under the weight of the body. Wilhemena lit candles around the room and combed her mother's hair until it was pin-straight before plaiting it.

Freya stood at the sink, pulverizing salt and bark of rowan tree with a pestle. She mixed in the delicate purple buds of vervain and a fragrant stalk of dill. Long ago, her mother had taught her how to make the Seeing Out Potion for precisely when this day came. She was to spread the potion like a mask onto Elizabeth's face in order to help her exit to the in-between. Freya found its color hideous and hated the idea of sending her mother out of this world in such an ugly state. Surely it was better to enter the spirit world looking young and beautiful than caked in bitter green paste.

Outside Aurora knelt in the muddy patch of yard of their dismal house, cutting sprigs of rosemary from the garden. Edmund stood faithfully by her, his coarse hair tousled with mud and rain. Aurora spoke between sobs: "Rosemary. Latin name: *Rosmarinus officinalis.* Good for stirring up old memories. Helps with headaches, too. Brew in a tea, or burn alone to awaken the spirits of those before us."

Edmund brayed. Aurora patted his head and gave him a branch of rosemary to nibble.

Inside the house, Wilhemena burned sage around the body.

Freya walked into the dining room with the mortar full of green potion.

"Put it on her," Wilhemena said.

"It's disgusting," Freya said, holding the pestle limply over the mortar.

"She needs it for the Seeing Out."

"Says who?"

Wilhemena looked at her sternly. "Put it on her."

"No." Freya had begun to think of her older sister in the same way she thought of the derelicts who loitered under the Route 1 Bridge with their unwashed hair and idle days.

"Give it here, then," Wilhemena said, reaching for it.

Freya held the mortar out of reach. When Wilhemena got close, Freya turned it upside down, dumping its contents in a slimy plop on the floor.

Wilhemena knelt down, scooping the potion into her apron. "You have no respect!"

"For what?" Freya barked. "The Old Ways? What good did they do any of us?"

Wilhemena looked at her with wild rage. "We must See her Out and deliver her to the marsh." She glared at her sister. Her voice took on a sinister tone. "To settle with the cress and hawthorns. To make us magic again. To make us whole. Or don't you remember?"

Freya sneered. "You don't know what you're talking about."

"Where'd we get the fat for the soap that night of the harvest moon, Freya?"

"Shut up."

"Tell me what happened."

"Ain't none of your business," Freya said.

"Where did Papa disappear to? What'd you do to him?"

Freya raised a hand to silence her sister with a spell, but Wilhemena blocked it with an oven mitt and a counterspell of her own.

Wilhemena hurled herself at Freya, striking her cheek with closed fist. Freya heaved forward from the blow, half with shock, half with pain. She made a fist and swung for Wilhemena's nose, but missed.

Just as Freya was about to throw another punch, Aurora burst through the back door, her thick wool sweater dripping with rainwater.

"Stop it at once," Aurora yelled.

Both Wilhemena and Freya stood, breathing heavily.

"We need to stick together now that Mama's gone. What's to become of us?" Aurora said.

Just then the doorbell rang. None of the Ellylydan girls had ever heard the doorbell ring in their house since no one had ever visited them before. They froze. Each feared that the ghostly chime was their mother, reaching out to them from the spirit world, slapping their little hands with a stick, like she did when she caught them stealing an extra dessert, or lying about completing Lessons. Aurora turned pale. Freya's eyes searched the room.

Wilhemena cocked her head in a peculiar way then followed

the ringing noise down the hallway to the front door. She opened it.

A woman with dirty blond hair stood beneath a red umbrella. She looked like someone who had been around the block a few times, and was trying very hard to be pretty. "Avon calling," the woman said.

"What?"

"Avon calling," the woman repeated.

Wilhemena said, "No one by that name here."

The woman's mouth slid from a smile to a quizzical circle, like the dot of a question mark. "I'm Avon. That is, I represent Avon." She held up a little plastic suitcase to clarify her point.

"I'm sorry, ma'am, but we're busy right now," Wilhemena said.

The woman squared her shoulders and took a deep breath. "I'm your neighbor. From right over there. Don't you recognize me? I've started selling Avon, and, well, I thought you and your sisters would want some of the products."

"Products?"

"Makeup. You know, lipstick, foundation, eye shadow, perfume. I can do a demonstration for you right here in your home. I've gotten good at layering shadows for different moods. You'd use pinks and whites if you were going out to the movies, for example, and browns or grays for a more serious occasion, like the office. If you had an office job, that is."

Wilhemena stared at the woman, studying the layers of pink and more pink on her face, trying to decipher their meaning.

"I just started with Avon," the woman said. "Thought I might pick up a little income while Dennis is laid off. It would sure help me out if I could give you a demonstration." There was a sad earnestness about her.

"It's a bad time," Wilhemena said.

Freya had come into the hallway now and was listening intently to the exchange.

"All right then. If you change your mind just knock on my

door any time," the woman said. She turned back into the dreary road.

"Wait," Freya called. "Aren't you that lady from next door with all them little kids? The ones always screaming their heads off?" In fact they had been neighbors for almost five years, though this was the first time they had ever spoken. A vision of this woman surrounded by loud, loathsome children, yelling at her drunken husband through the screen door on hot summer nights was emblazoned on Freya's mind. This woman and her wretched children and her beastly husband represented all that Freya had come to despise about her magicless existence. The ordinariness of people like that, people who couldn't command the sea, or make a chicken levitate. As she watched this woman, Freya was struck by the profound transformation before her eyes. This woman was the lowest sort of Commoner, yet here she was dressed in a clean red skirt suit, her face a pleasing shade of pink, her eyes bright, asking to present the secrets of her metamorphosis to complete strangers.

The woman was unfazed by Freya's insult. "My oldest son has a paper route now. Has a hard time collecting though. Imagine folks skipping out on their paper boy."

"You look different," Freya said, more as an observation than a compliment. "Your face is . . . pinker. Your hair's pretty. Not like it used to be."

This lifted the woman's spirits.

"It's the products," the woman said brightly, holding up her little suitcase with the Avon sticker to her chin.

Freya slid in front of Wilhemena and opened the door wider. "Show me."

"Freya, this is not a good time," Wilhemena said.

"It won't take long," the woman said. "We'll have you done in a jiffy."

"There's still the Last Wit and Wisdom to be done," Wilhemena whispered. Although the Ellylydan girls were not familiar with the penal code of Massachusetts, they were quite certain that a dead person in your home (even your own mother) was something to be reported to the proper authorities. Commoners were persnickety about such things.

"It won't take long," Freya said, repeating the woman's promise.

The woman shook out her umbrella and stepped inside. Her low-heeled shoes were sopping wet and water seeped up her nylons. "You won't be disappointed," she said. She spoke rapidly and with determination. "Avon has changed my life. It's a wonderful way for women to earn money. You don't even need a car. You can walk door to door."

"You knock on doors and people let you in?" Freya asked, stupefied by such a pedestrian concept.

"Of course. Avon is recognized worldwide as the brand women can trust for all their fragrance and cosmetics needs. All it takes is a little perseverance. And I've been assured that the money will start flowing in once I'm established."

The woman followed Freya down the hallway and into the living room. She sat on the grungy green sofa and opened her suitcase. She pulled out a number of fragrance samples as well as a makeup kit with a rainbow of colors. "You could sell Avon, too, you know," the woman said to Freya. "You have a beautiful face all right. A little foundation and mascara, and you could be a real knockout. I could teach you how. All you need are a few faithful clients. You could do it."

"If you can do it, I'm sure I can," Freya said.

The dim-witted woman smiled. "That's the spirit. Women have more opportunities today than ever before. It's not our lot to sit home all day, waiting for our husbands to find work." For a moment, the smile disappeared. "Tomorrow starts today, that's what I always say. Now who should I do first?"

Freya pointed to the dining room table.

At first the Avon lady was invigorated at the prospect of discovering so many female clients in one house. Confidently, she marched into the dining room, her red suitcase swinging. Then she saw Elizabeth and screamed.

"Why, she's dead."

Aurora spoke through tears, "It's our mama. She passed to the not time this morning."

"I'm terribly sorry."

"Do you think you can put some of that makeup on her? Make her look pretty for the spirit world?" Freya said.

"No," Wilhemena snapped.

The Avon lady was about to object, too, but stopped herself. The fact was, she hadn't actually managed to secure any new clients since purchasing the Avon starter kit two months ago, and it was beginning to weigh heavily on her. "When opportunity knocks, we need to answer," she said, chin up.

Freya smiled. She gave Wilhemena a condescending look, and then all three girls watched with fascination as the Avon lady applied foundation and blush to their mother's cheeks. She ran a dark brown swipe of eyeliner at the tip of her eyelids (since death certainly qualified for the more serious hues of brown and gray). Freya was riveted by how the woman filled in the eyebrows with pencils and streaked layers of color on her lips. When she was done, the Avon lady stood back from her work.

"She's beautiful," Freya whispered.

"We need to See her Out now," Wilhemena said sternly.

Later that night, the three Ellylydan girls carried their mother to the marsh and set her on a funeral pyre on a fen above the creek where they had played as little girls. As the flames rose and fell, they were each struck with the uncertainty life held for them now.

Aurora sobbed, wiping her nose with the back of her hand until her nostrils were raw. Without her mother, she would have to rely on the wisdom of Wilhemena to guide her. She realized with sorrow that she would never again taste her mother's homemade jams, or savor the warmth of a fresh loaf of bread her mother had made. All she felt was loss.

Wilhemena watched the flames, thinking back to the ancestors, who had carried on the same rites for generations. She worried that she wouldn't have the chance to pass along the knowledge and gifts that had been passed to her. She was no longer a carefree young woman. She was the family's new matriarch. And she felt the burden of responsibility squarely on her shoulders.

Freya felt something else entirely: freedom. There was no one to forbid her from going to the movies or wearing makeup. She could finally experiment with new potions and spells without looking over her shoulder. She felt the possibilities were as large as the world itself. Yet the one image that raced through her mind were those tiny palettes of eye shadow, lip gloss, and nail polish, and all the legions of women sitting in their homes waiting to buy them. As her mother's body turned to ash, Freya's mind turned to the Avon lady with the red umbrella.

CHAPTER 28

Six little mice sat down to spin;
Pussy passed by and she peeped in.
What are you doing, my little men?
Weaving coats for gentlemen.
Shall I come and cut off your threads?
No, no, Mistress Pussy, you'd bite off our heads.
Oh, no, I'll not, I'll help you to spin.
That may be so, but you can't come in.
Says Puss: You look so wondrous wise,
I like your whiskers and bright black eyes;
Your house is the nicest house I see,
I think there is room for you and for me.
The mice were so pleased that they opened the door,
And Pussy soon had them all dead on the floor.

I check the address again: 42 King Street, Lowell. Working under the assumption that Jonathon and Jinathon were adopted by my mother, like they said at the funeral, I did a search using my myriad surnames—Griselda, Gwendyn, Ellylydan. One result popped up: J. and J. Gwendyn in Lowell.

My directions take me past the old textile mills downtown, through a run-down neighborhood of tattered homes to an asbestos-shingled building that tilts to one side. On the corner, a man urinates on a fire hydrant. Half a Budweiser sign flashes in a window, casting a red pall on the sidewalk strewn with trash.

You'd think a pair of magical wizards would live in a cottage in the woods, or a hollowed-out tree stump. Not a tenement in Lowell.

I walk up the rickety stairs and ring the bell. In the front window, the blinds part and two sets of eyes stare out at me. The blinds close. There are murmurs, a crash of objects inside. The door swings open, and a dwarf in a red nightshirt and nightcap like a miniature Santa leaps at me with open arms. "I knew it, I knew it, I knew it."

The other dwarf appears in the door in a matching nightshirt and joins the hug. "She's back. She's back. She's back." I pat them on the head since they only come up to my belly button.

"Jonathon and Jinathon. Hello," I say.

"Jonathon," one says and pats his belly. Then he touches his brother on the head. "Jinathon."

"Jinathon," the other says pointing to himself. "Jonathon," pointing to his brother.

I study them to find some distinguishing feature I can use to tell them apart, but they are absolutely identical right down to the trim of their full, black beards. They both have bright green eyes that wrinkle outward in the exact same web. Their faces, their hair, their builds, their voices, are all perfectly matched.

They both talk fast.

"Come in."

"Come on."

"Pardon our appearance."

"We were sleeping."

"Must sleep during the day."

"Work all night."

Very fast.

"Like owls we are."

"Or hedgehogs."

"Nocturnal, that is."

This makes them both laugh.

"We're the foremen at the wastewater treatment plant," one says proudly.

"Dirty job."

"Someone's got to do it."

They both laugh again. The laughing stops as abruptly as it started.

"We're sorry for all that nasty business at the funeral," one says.

"It was no offense to you."

"Not personally of course."

"Nearly tore us apart to hurt you like that."

"Had to be done, though."

"Wilhemena's spirit element is powerful indeed."

"Only we can keep it safe."

"It is our mission."

I look around the room for the urn. There's no fireplace or mantel on which to display it. There's no cabinet or display cases, and hardly any furniture at all, other than two oversized La-Z-Boy rockers and a small television stuck on top of a milk crate.

"Is it here?" I ask.

Their smiles dissolve. They exchange a quick look of concern.

"Coffee?"

"Tea?"

"Coffee sounds good," I say.

They run into the galley kitchen and get to work. One pulls up a stool. The other climbs the stool and reaches into the cupboard for the coffee tin. One gets down on his knee in front of the sink. The other uses the bent knee as a step to reach the faucet. One swings the stool over to the counter. They both climb on top of it. One pours the water. The other grinds the coffee. One climbs onto the counter and grabs a box of filters, tosses one in the air. The other catches it and puts it in the coffee maker. They are a well-oiled machine.

"Sit."

"Sit. Sit."

As the coffee brews, the dwarves squish together on a La-Z-Boy and I take a seat on the La-Z-Boy across from them.

"Daughter of Wilhemena."

"Sister Allesone."

"Here in our home."

"It's a great honor."

"A great honor indeed."

They stare at me, waiting for me to speak.

Their affection for me is unconditional. *You're here for a job,* I tell myself. *You have no choice. Get the ashes. Save your family from Freya.* I look up at them and their smiles grow so wide and so deep they look like they'll split in two.

"So," I say, easing into conversation, trying not to be too obvious about my motives. "I was wondering if you could tell me more about Wilhemena? At the funeral you said she was like a mother to you."

They howl.

"Not *like* a mother."

"She *was* our mother," they speak through fits of laughter.

Jonathon gasps for breath. Jinathon motions him to stop. He crosses his hands and legs and peers at me. "Don't you know?"

"I was raised in foster homes. I didn't get to spend as much time with her as you did." *Tone it down,* I tell myself. *You have to earn their trust.* I cradle my purse in my lap.

Jonathon makes a pitying *tsk* and shakes his head. "We met Wilhemena the day we were born," he says.

"Babes in the woods we were," Jinathon answers.

"Left by our own mother and father beneath a hemlock."

They look at each other, then they take turns telling me the story.

"We never met our own parents."

"It's sad for us to think of."

"Sad indeed."

Jinathon holds his pinkie finger out and Jonathon crosses his pinkie over it. "That we might some day know them." They do their pinkie swear and turn back to me.

"But it wasn't meant to be."

"So they left us to the forest."

"Dear Wilhemena found us wrapped in blankets."

"She carried us to her home in the dunes."

"Raised us from that day on."

"Her sons," I say, forcing a smile to my face. I search their faces for some sort of filial connection. "I'm sorry I didn't realize you were my brothers at the funeral. You must have moved away before I was even born."

They jump out of their chair and hug me again. I hug them back. Jinathon brings us all coffee, while Jonathon stares at me adoringly.

"Auntie Aurora was there, too," Jonathon says. They climb back onto their chair.

"It was Aurora's idea to feed us goat's milk the day we were born."

"Yum, yum."

"Mmmm. Mmmm."

"Jonathon didn't take it at first."

"But once I saw my brother drink it, I was okay."

I have to interject. "You can't possibly remember the day you were born. Wilhemena must have told you these things. Infants don't remember."

"Oh, but they do, Sister Allesone."

"We remember everything!"

"Everything."

"It's one of our skills."

"Concealment is our other."

"Remembering . . ."

"And hiding . . ."

"Wilhemena taught us concealment magic before we could even speak."

"Taught us hexes, enchantments, concealments."

"Entrusted us with her most precious possession."

"You mean her ashes?" I ask.

"No," Jinathon giggles.

"You," Jonathon says.

"Me?"

" 'Twas my brother and I who put the enchantment on you to conceal you from the Dark Witch all these years."

"Mother saw to it that you were safe from the Dark Witch."

"She made us take an oath to protect you from her."

"Rather we'd die than break that oath." They raise their hands to their hearts and bow deeply.

"So we created an unbreakable enchantment."

"Unbreakable only whilst Mother was alive," Jonathon says, raising his finger.

" 'Twas a fine spell."

"Our best work."

"But alas, the Dark Witch kept looking for you."

"Mother Wilhemena feared she could never protect you, so long as she was near you."

"The Dark Witch would see the child with the mother and know."

"So she left you."

"She left you to save you."

I swirl the coffee in my cup, watching it rise up the sides, just below the rim. My hand holding the cup is trembling.

The dwarves sip their coffee, their eyes never leaving me. I tense up under their gaze.

"What's the matter?" Jinathon asks, noticing my strained posture.

"You remember everything from the day you were born. But I barely remember anything. I don't really remember you. I only remember my mother in bits and pieces. I can't even remember how to do magic. I remember my mother talking about my special gift, but I can't actually remember how to do it. I have no control over it."

Jonathon stands beside me and takes my hand. "Memories make us who we are. They never leave us completely."

"Sometimes memories run away," Jinathon says.

"And the enchantment we put upon you gave them a place to go."

"A perfect hiding spot."

"But they'll come back to you someday."

"You'll see."

Their faces brighten.

Maybe I can tell Jonathon and Jinathon the whole story and see if they can put a protective enchantment on my family the way they put one on me all those years ago. Maybe I don't have to steal the spirit element. Maybe I can fight magic with magic.

I look around at the peeling linoleum of the kitchen floor, the walls cracked and grimy, the dusty blinds. Who am I kidding? As far as I can tell their most valuable possessions are two La-Z-Boys. They work the night shift at the wastewater plant, for god's sake. They are no match for Freya. Neither is Aurora. Neither am I. The only thing to do is give Freya what she wants.

"Sister Allesone. We are so happy today."

"If you ever need anything, just ask Jonathon and Jinathon."

"Anything at all."

"Actually," I say, "I'd love to see my mother. To say goodbye."

The look of concern comes back to both of them.

"After all, she did want me to have the ashes in the first place."

I'm wearing an orange hard hat and a hazmat suit, walking through a shit factory.

Jonathon and Jinathon take turns explaining the intricate workings of the plant. Jonathon is the foreman, they inform me, and Jinathon is Employee of the Month for twenty-eight consecutive months. Their pride is palpable.

"Sister Allesone, look at this," Jinathon says, pointing to a grinder pump.

"Ninety percent of all solids will be removed here," Jonathon says when we get to the aeration tank.

The factory smells of chlorine, which is not altogether unpleasant.

"Do you really like working here?" I ask.

"Don't be silly."

"What a prankster you are, Sister Allesone."

"We love it," they say in unison.

They tell me they've chosen to conceal my mother's ashes here since no one would ever think about looking for a spirit element in a wastewater treatment facility. I'm learning quite a lot about magic (and wastewater management) from Jonathon and Jinathon. They tell me that powerful witches are just as potent in death as they are in life. When a witch dies, her spirit continues to live on both in her potions and in her remains.

Wilhemena was smart in dividing up her potions to the remaining members of her coven, they tell me. Fire, earth, water, air, and spirit. That way, no one will command all of her powers at once.

Finally we come to the end of the tour. They take me into the employee locker room where we strip out of our hazmat suits.

My stomach turns at the thought of what I have to do. "Where's the bathroom?" I ask.

They point the way.

"We'll wait for you right down there," Jonathon says.

"In the break room," Jinathon says.

"Do you like blueberry doughnuts?" Jonathon asks.

"Yes," I say.

"We'll save you one," says Jinathon.

I grab my purse, step into the bathroom, and take out my jar with the last remnants of the Me-First Masque. *For emergencies only,* I had told myself. In the mirror, I smear the green clay into my skin, watching myself transform into a green traitor.

294 · Katie Schickel

After the clay sets, I pull out my foundation, my brushes, my powders. When I'm done, the green pallor is gone.

In the break room, Jonathon is holding the urn with Wilhemena's ashes. Jinathon, a blueberry doughnut.

I take the doughnut.

"May I have a moment to myself with my mother?" I ask.

They both hesitate.

"Oh, we mustn't leave her."

" 'Tis our duty to protect the spirit element."

"Me first," I whisper.

Slowly, I can see the Me-First magic working on them. Their eyes glass over. They hand me the urn and I walk away.

CHAPTER 29

Tinker,
Tailor,
Soldier,
Sailor,
Gentleman,
Apothecary,
Ploughboy,
Thief.

I tuck the urn into my side and walk up the brick pathway,
slick with dew. With every step, I feel more like a traitor and
a fool. She played me all along. She lured me to Monrovia. She
seduced me into her coven with her little magic tricks. She told
me I was special. She knew how badly I needed to be accepted,
and she played on my insecurities. I fell for the whole thing,
and all the while she was just using me to get to my mother.

"Set it down there," her voice cuts through the mist.

She's standing in the middle of the path, the topiaries rising
like giants on both sides of her. It's dark and she's draped in a
large cape and I can't see her eyes beneath her hood. I can't tell
if she's Astrid, the young and beautiful, or Freya, the old and
wretched.

Either way, she's a horrid sight.

"You'll leave my family alone now?" I ask, my fingers cold
against the metal of the urn. The sycamores lining the street
moan.

"Put the urn down."

"Promise me first," I say, bracing for whatever potions she's
planning on throwing at me.

"Very well. You have my word."

I set the urn down on the spot her long white finger points to. I wrap my fleece tightly around myself, feeling the chill of the night. I rub my hands together for warmth.

My mother's remains, her spirit, look small and meager. This is all I have left of her. This is the only thing she left me, and I'm handing it over to the Dark Witch herself. And for what? So she can make a potion to hide her wrinkles and gray hair? So she can look younger than the rest of the housewives in town?

I bolster my courage and speak. "What are you going to do with her?"

"I have special plans."

"What? More hand soaps for welcome baskets? More facial lotion for unsuspecting housewives?"

She laughs wickedly. "Hah. I wouldn't waste my sister on a bunch of Commoners. No. I'm making something special just for me."

My heart races. "You have everything. Money. Power. Control. What more do you need?"

"Time," she snorts.

"What do mean, time?" I say, my voice shaking from the chill.

"I want more time."

I breathe heavily. I want to be home with my kids. I turn to walk away, but she stops me.

"One more thing, Allesone. Your mother believed you had the gift of transfiguration. She believed you were special. Show me."

"She was wrong."

"I disagree. I saw your transformative powers right here at my house the night of the equinox party. You turned an eagle into a crow. Remember?"

"I was drunk."

"And I saw it when you were a little girl, too. Don't you

remember? Imagine my surprise to find such powers in a child so young." She takes a step toward me. "Surely, you haven't forgotten your Lessons completely. Now show me what you can do."

I think back to what Jonathon and Jinathon told me right before I stole from them. "I guess the memories ran away and hid," I say.

"Show me how you transform." Her voice is deep and threatening. "Turn that gargoyle into something else. A fish, perhaps."

The stone statue behind her looms in the mist.

"I don't know how."

"Do it," she orders. My stomach lurches.

I look at the statue and try to imagine it becoming a fish. I close my eyes and concentrate. I pull up a picture of a goldfish in my mind's eye. Orange tail. Big black eyes. Fins fluttering out like geisha fans. I hear the sycamores moan. My toes are freezing. I shut my eyes tighter. I try to concentrate. Orange tail. Big black eyes. Gillian sulking in her bedroom. Sophie and Henry sitting on the couch watching cartoons while the sitter talks on the phone. I'll have to talk to her about television before bedtime when I get home. Concentrate. Orange tail. Big black eyes.

I open my eyes. The gargoyle sits unmoving in the mist, its stone eyes and snarling snout lifeless.

Her laughter rumbles in my chest. Astrid. Freya. The Dark Witch. She picks up the urn, turns and walks inside. Just before the door closes, I hear her singing to herself, "Long live the witch on Samhain high."

CHAPTER 30

Beware of that man,
Be he friend or brother,
Whose hair is one color
And moustache another.

W hat the fuck is in that soap?"

"Hi Judy," I say, answering my mobile.

"Frankie is wearing Izod shirts, Allison. Izod! With the collar up. He's tucking them in! I found a belt with little whales around it. Penny loafers, too. Penny loafers, Allison! He asked me for homemade sushi in a bento box for lunch. He even brought home samples of Glamour Soap from school and hands them out to people on the street. Obviously he's under some fucked-up spell. Your witch friends are behind this, aren't they?"

"They're not my friends anymore."

"The worst part is he thinks he *likes* it! My son actually *enjoys* acting like a douchebag. It's like his brains have been sucked out of him. That's how it works, right? They give you the soap and you do whatever they say. They make you run around like a trained seal? Isn't that it?"

"Something like that," I say dismally.

"I don't even know what the fuck a bento box is." Her voice is raspy.

"Calm down, Judy."

"How do I break the spell? You have to tell me. How do I reprogram him?"

I'm late for pickup. I push open the door to the cubby room at Montessori, the NO CELL PHONES PLEASE! sign directly in front of me. "I have to go. Frankie will be fine. The spell will wear off. I promise. Just get rid of all your Glamour products. I'll call you later." I turn off my phone as Judy berates me with a litany of colorful adjectives.

Sophie comes out of her classroom and into the cubby room. Her mop of curls flies around as she searches the crowd of moms for me. I wave and she jumps into my arms. "Let's get your shoes on," I tell her. She plops on the floor to take off her slippers, tucks them into their spot, and replaces them with the shoes from her cubby, a task that takes infinitely longer than it should.

There's a ruckus at the doorway as Aurora barges into the tiny room, pushing aside the other moms in their yoga pants. Her fedora is slung over her scraggly hair. "What have you done?" she says, jabbing a crooked finger into my chest.

"Back off," I say. The other moms are politely ignoring us.

"You stole the spirit element! You enchanted the dwarves! You've brought shame to this family!" The words come spitting out of her.

"I didn't exactly have a choice, did I? I had to protect my kids, Aurora!" Now all eyes in the room are on us. I know we're making a scene, but I don't care anymore. *Think whatever you want about me, people! I just handed my mother over to an evil thug of a witch. Things can't get any worse.*

"What'cha done with them ashes?" Aurora shouts.

"They were mine to begin with. Jonathon and Jinathon stole them from me first," I shout back.

"You're a spoiled, selfish brat. Your mother would spit in the in-between if she seen what you've become. You've disgraced your family."

"You don't know what family is," I say, and Sophie looks up at me, her eyes wide. The other moms give me dirty looks.

The teacher at the doorway clears her throat. "Please use your indoor voices, parents."

"Outside. Now," I say to Aurora. I take Sophie by the hand, kiss her on the head, and push my way through the parents, out the door, and to the tot lot. Sophie runs to the monkey bars. She stops to inspect a scarecrow and suddenly I remember with some regret that I had promised to make her one. Another promise broken. Another hope swept under the rug. And a cold misery fills my heart.

"Jonathon and Jinathon *are* your family, and you've nearly destroyed them by what you done. They swore to protect Wilhemena's spirit. Nearly destroyed them, you have," Aurora says, waddling up behind me.

I turn to face her. "Why didn't anyone come and claim me after Wilhemena left?"

Her face is puzzled.

"I wish someone had told me that I had brothers and aunts a long time ago. I would have liked to know I wasn't completely alone in this world. It would have been nice to know that someone, anyone, loved me! You think *I'm* the selfish brat? *You* abandoned me. You all abandoned me? Do you know what that feels like? To be seven years old and alone?" My cheeks burn.

Aurora sighs. "I just assumed you knew we were looking out for you."

"No! I didn't. How would I know?"

Aurora is silent, but I'm not done flipping out. "I've lost everything! I've lost my husband, my best friend. My oldest daughter thinks everyone hates her because the coven hexed her to get to me!"

My body goes weak like a noodle. I slump to the curb and sit down in the freshly raked mulch. The world goes blurry as tears fill my eyes. "I know I betrayed my mother. I know I gave away her spirit. But I had no choice. I'm not magical, Aurora. You said yourself you're a C-minus, D-plus witch, well, I'm an F. An abject failure. I failed my family," I wipe the snot off my nose. "My magic has run away and hid and I can't find it."

Sophie runs up to me and hands me an acorn to keep safe for her. I press my face into my sleeve and pretend to sneeze so she won't see me like this.

"Gesundheit," she says sweetly and runs back onto the play structure. At least I can fool a three-year-old.

"That's your little one, hey?" Aurora says.

I nod.

"Sophie, right?" Aurora says.

I can't answer. There's nothing more I can say to her.

Aurora rubs her chin, pulls at a couple long whiskers. "It's not true what I said."

I look at her. The hard scrutiny in her eyes is gone, replaced with something resembling compassion. "I said your mother would spit in the in-between if she saw what you did. That ain't true. She'd be proud of you. You done what you did to protect your family. Just like she done what she did to protect hers."

I hiccup and the tears come in jolted breaths.

Aurora puts a hand on my shoulder. "I am sorry, niece. I reckon we were all trying so hard to protect you when you was a little thing, we didn't think what it must've been like for you."

"It was hard. I would have liked to know that my mother loved me so much that she had to give me up." I hiccup again.

"I can see that now."

Sophie waves to me from the top of the slide and I wave back. Suddenly, I know what I have to do. No more secrets. I turn to Aurora. "I need to tell my kids. They need to know their history. You can help me tell them. At least do that for me."

"Are you sure that's best?"

"They might have to face Freya themselves one day," I say, the harsh reality sinking in.

CHAPTER 31

No, no, my melodies will never die,
While nurses sing and babies cry.

Misery Shoal · *May 1984*

On the day of Allesone's seventh birthday, the sun rippled over the Atlantic, painting the waves a blinding white. Wind from the north swept across the dunes forcing Allesone to clutch her birthday crown of woven forsythia tightly to her head. She watched seagulls pick clams off the beach, ride the currents skyward, and then drop them against the rocks, their shells shattering, exposing the tender flesh inside.

Wilhemena had brewed a lovely tea of meadowsweet and mint, known to promote clairvoyance. She set up a long table and filled mason jars with bouquets of elder flowers, thistle, and brilliant white yarrow.

Millie was decorating the birthday cake with pansies and marigolds. Beatrice broke the buds off lavender and spread them in a sweet-smelling protective circle around the ridge. Jonathon and Jinathon took turns flying Allesone on their broomsticks over the long stretches of beach. For a present, they had given her a box of oddly shaped rocks—this one like a heart, that one a boomerang—as well as other curiosities like obsidian, fossils, quartz, petrified wood. Allesone thought that no one in the world could be happier than she.

When the sun began its slant west, Aurora arrived.

"You're late," Wilhemena said, taking Edmund by the leash and leading him over to a bowl of oats.

"Had to stop for my niece's present. Hard to find, you know."

"Present? For me?" Allesone clapped.

Aurora set down a glass bowl on the table next to the venison and plum pudding. It was filled with water, rocks and reeds poking above the surface. Allesone knelt on a chair inspecting it from all angles, imagining a palace for fairies in the green leafy columns.

"Look closely. There," Aurora said.

A greenish-blackish bug with six long legs, bulging eyes, and a rather prickly looking abdomen, clung to a reed.

"Wonderful," Wilhemena said. "Allesone, Aurora has given you a dragonfly nymph."

It sounded magical.

"It'll be a nymph for five years," Aurora explained. "Then, it'll walk up a reed, climb out of its skin, pump its wings, and fly off. One day becoming something else entirely."

"Like the caterpillars," Allesone said, thinking of creatures that reinvent themselves every season. It had been a year of proliferation for the woolly bear caterpillars, their dark orange stripes growing thicker than the black ones. This, everyone knew, was a sign that the maple trees would turn bright orange in the fall, rather than red or yellow.

"Does Sister Allesone want to play?" Jonathon said.

"Hide-and-seek?" Jinathon asked.

"Or seek-and-hide?"

"Not it!" Allesone declared and ran off down the doe path to the best hiding spot on the shoal, in between two granite boulders. Jonathon covered his eyes with both hands and began counting. Jinathon ran in the opposite direction down the ridge toward the mudflats.

". . . seventy-nine, eighty, eighty-one, eighty-two . . ."

Allesone peeked her head over the rock.

". . . ninety-seven, ninety-eight, ninety-nine, a hundred. Ready or not, here I come." Jonathon uncovered his eyes and made a great show of lifting tablecloths and looking under chairs.

Allesone giggled.

"Bet you're . . ." Jonathon jumped into a patch of saw grass. "Here!"

From where she crouched, Allesone could see Jonathon on the ridge, scratching his beard in bewilderment. Her heart raced, watching and waiting for her chance to run to home base. Jonathon wandered to the east side of the ridge to look in a thicket of gorse shrubs. *How silly,* she thought, *only a mouse could take cover in the low-lying gorse.*

She stepped out from behind the rock ready to make a run for it, anticipating the moment when she could yell, "Olly, olly, oxen free." But suddenly, Wilhemena appeared at the top of the path and signaled her to stay put. Her mother flashed her a look she'd never seen, and everything in her went numb.

Another woman appeared on the ridge next to her mother. She had flaming red hair and although Allesone didn't recognize her, she felt very special indeed to have so many witches and wizards in attendance at her party.

"You've no business here, Freya," Wilhemena said.

"Whose birthday is it?" the woman with the red hair said, picking up a forsythia crown from the table and tossing it on the ground.

"Never you mind," Aurora said.

Millie's high voice sounded from somewhere else on the ridge, "Please go."

"I'm here for Mama's ashes, sister," Freya said.

"No."

"We can share. Half for you, half for me."

"You can't have them."

"Join me, sister. I can show you what I've learned," Freya said.

Still hidden behind her rock, Allesone saw Jonathon walk by with his broomstick in hand.

Her mind went back to the game in all its sweet suspense. Waiting to be found, hoping not to be. *How fun it would be to play a trick on him,* she thought. She closed her eyes and imagined a fish. She envisioned the details—its dotted skin and scales, the lips turned in a perpetual frown. And when she opened her eyes, Jonathon was holding a huge, shimmering Atlantic salmon.

Jonathon yelped. He tossed the fish to the ground.

Allesone giggled so hard she had to cover her mouth, for fear of being discovered.

Freya walked to the fish and lifted it by the tail. "Who did this? Was it you?" she said, shaking the fish at Millie.

But Millie looked as shocked as everyone else.

"Or you?" Freya said, holding the fish up to Beatrice.

"Have you figured out transfiguration, sister? Hiding your skills all these years?" Freya dropped the fish at Wilhemena's feet.

Wilhemena glanced down at Allesone. For the first time she could remember, Allesone saw fear in her mother's eyes.

"Who then?" Freya yelled. "Which one of you is capable of this?" She kicked the fish so that it flew off the ridge and sailed over the edge to the two granite boulders where Allesone hid.

Allesone ran out from her hiding spot and stood behind Wilhemena's legs.

"Who . . . is . . . that . . . child?" Freya said.

"Leave us be," Wilhemena answered.

Freya spoke. "The eldest daughter of the eldest daughter." She was adrift in thought as the significance settled in. The eldest of the eldest is said to be that who stands at the threshold, the liminal state. It is the line between magic and witchcraft. One foot in this world, one in the spirit world. "And she knows transfiguration already."

Wilhemena reached behind her to shield her daughter, knocking the forsythia crown off Allesone's head.

"We don't want any trouble with you," Aurora said, stepping closer to Wilhemena and Allesone.

Freya ignored her. "Tell me, is the Daughter trained in the Old Ways?"

"We've never turned our backs on the Old Ways. Not like you."

"Does she know who I am?"

"She only knows about life on the shoal."

Freya walked over to Allesone and petted her hair. She twisted it into a knot and lifted the hair, revealing the back of Allesone's neck, and the pentacle birthmark.

"She bears the mark," Freya said, both admiration and anger in her voice.

"She's no threat to you, sister."

"No. Of course not." The heat rose in Freya's cheeks. "Not yet."

"She possesses no magic," Beatrice said.

"She can turn a broomstick into a fish without potions or spells. She's a talented child," Freya snapped. "An imaginative witch."

"Her imagination is a child's imagination," said Wilhemena.

"I could use someone with the power of imagination. Maybe I'll just come and snatch her while she's sleeping."

Allesone whimpered and held on to her mother's legs.

"Leave her alone. Or I'll spare you no mercy," Wilhemena said.

Freya laughed. "*You'll* spare *me*? I've been practicing all these years, you know. And what have you been doing—shucking clams and spinning wool and drying herbs?"

Beatrice snuck up behind Freya with her broomstick and took a swing. Freya turned around just in time. She ducked. The broom flew out of Beatrice's hands and sailed over the ridge. Freya picked up a rock and hurled it at Beatrice. It gashed her cheek. Blood oozed down her face as she fell to the ground. Millie moved toward Freya next, but Freya froze her with a paralysis spell.

"Stop this," Wilhemena said.

But Freya was beyond stopping. She murmured under her

breath and suddenly a garter snake slithered out of a hole toward Wilhemena and Allesone.

Allesone was accustomed to snakes and wasn't afraid, until the snake sped toward her, lifted its head, and stuck its tongue in and out, in and out. It lunged at her and bit the tender skin of her calf.

Allesone screamed. This was not the way snakes behaved.

Freya reached down and grabbed the snake. She held it out straight and its body coiled around her arm. She choked it until it fell limp. "Give me Mama's ashes," Freya said.

"They're not for Dark Magic."

Freya began muttering more words, spells that Wilhemena did not know. There was a rustling of grass. The snakes came, one by one, slithering toward them.

"Run, Allesone," Wilhemena yelled.

Allesone ran. Down the doe path, sand sliding downhill and into her shoes with each step. She ran to the bottom of the ridge and kept running, through the shallow estuary and into the mudflats. The snakes slithered behind her. They were joined by more snakes. Milk snakes, brown snakes, redbellies, garters, ringnecks, black rat snakes, and water snakes glided through the estuary after her.

As she ran, instinct took over. Her muscles were charged with adrenaline, her heart racing faster than a hummingbird's.

Snakes poured in around her. She ran in a zigzag, leaping over slithering bodies. She slowed down for just a second and a thick brown snake leaped up at her, setting its sharp teeth in her wrist. She didn't scream this time. She only ran. To the flats, to the marsh. The ground writhing with snakes until she was surrounded.

Allesone stopped, certain she would die.

From the sky, a hand grabbed underneath her arm and lifted her up. *This must be death,* she thought. As her body sailed into the air, she kicked a garter snake off her shoe.

She felt like she was rising about the earth now, Misery Shoal growing smaller and smaller beneath her, and she had the vague sense that her spirit was leaving her body, going to the in-between. Then she felt a tug at her arm and another pair of hands lifted her onto a broomstick. And suddenly she was sitting between Jonathon and Jinathon. Jinathon wrapped his arms around her while Jonathon flew her farther and farther away from the snakes.

She looked down and could see her house behind them. She could see the ridge, and her mother and the terrible lady who commanded the snakes.

There was a thunderous flash of green light, followed by a flash of white lightning. The white lightning was met with another explosion of green. Pops of light like firecrackers exploded on the ridge.

"Mommy," Allesone cried.

"Don't fear, Sister Allesone," Jinathon said, the wind rushing over them. He tried to comfort her with a story of the Old Ways. Even though most of his words were blown away by the wind, Allesone could hear the beginning: "Once there was and once there wasn't a fine witch named Wilhemena . . ."

CHAPTER 32

> Awake, arise, pull out your eyes,
> And hear what time of day;
> And when you have done, pull out your tongue,
> And see what you can say.

Telling Sophie and Henry I'm a witch and that their grandmother before them was a witch, and that the entire Ellylydan family tree is gnarled and knotted with witches is, actually, a piece of cake. They still believe in Santa Claus, after all.

"Every witch has a special skill set," Aurora tells them as we drink hot cocoa in the living room after school, Henry giving the cup with the most marshmallows to his sister. "Some commune with the animals, some can mind read, some got the gift to control water, some can levitate."

"What's 'levitate'?" Henry asks.

"It means you got the gift of flying."

"I want to fly."

"You will, my lad. Levitation runs deep in our lineage."

"What's 'lineage'?"

Aurora answers, "It's the people who knew you before you was born. Our people come from Scotland, from the bogs, so we come from there, too."

I didn't know we were Scottish. This is the kind of information that usually gets passed down through stories, or food, or heirlooms. I wonder if it would have shaped me differently knowing that I had ancestors from Scotland, or that I came from anyplace other than Charge of the Commonwealth of Massachusetts.

"Oh yes," Aurora says. "We are bog witches. Everything we

know comes from the bog. If we came from Australia, we'd probably have the power to jump around like kangaroos."

Sophie and Henry crack up at that.

Henry rubs his hands together in excitement. "What other powers do witches have?"

"Let's see, there's the ability to paralyze your attackers, remove curses, locate lost items. Some witches got the healing power—that's what your grandmother had. Me, I'm adept with tinctures and animals."

Henry is on overdrive. All this talk of battles, magic, powers. Good over evil. This is the stuff he lives for.

"They'll be a right fine witch and wizard one day," Aurora says, patting Henry and Sophie on the head.

"I was kind of hoping for doctor or lawyer."

"Then you'll be shit out of luck, I reckon," Aurora says.

I'm about to object to the swear words, but stop myself. Reality check: I'm telling my kids that everything they've ever heard about witches and magic is wrong. Magic is real. Maybe it's the only real thing in our terribly false world.

The door swings open and Gillian walks in. When she sees Aurora, who's dressed like a derelict bag lady, she freaks.

"Who's that?"

"I'm your auntie Aurora. Great-auntie, actually." Aurora sticks her hand out. Gillian looks at the frayed fingerless wool glove, the fingernails stained red with cranberry.

"My *what*? Mom, what is going on?"

"Sit down, we need to talk," I say.

"Where's Dad? Why's he away?"

"It's a long story and I need you to listen."

She cries. "Are you getting divorced?"

As kids get older, the questions get harder. God, death, where babies come from. I thought those were difficult to explain.

"Your dad just needs some time to himself right now."

Gillian collapses into the chair. "It's not fair. My family is so messed up. And none of my friends like me anymore. I didn't even get invited to Breanna's birthday party, and she invited every girl in the class. No boy will even look at me. Everyone thinks I'm a complete loser."

I put my arms around her and hold her the way I did when she was just a baby and I was her whole world. "We're different, Gillian. *You're* different."

She rolls her eyes.

"You're just going to tell me how special I am because that's what mothers always say."

"You *are* special. Your friends don't think you're a loser, Gillian. They're ignoring you because an evil witch has put a spell on them. I know this because I'm a witch, just like my mother was and just like your aunt Aurora here is. We are a family of witches. From now on, no more secrets."

She looks up at me, her face streaked and puffy. "Seriously?"

I raise a hand, a scout's honor. "Swear to god."

"We can levitate," Henry says, cheerfully.

Gillian's eyes dart around the room. She looks like she might bolt.

"Come on, now, lass, enough of all this talking. I'll show you what we can do," Aurora says.

We cross the backyard, slide through the apple trees, and walk into the cemetery.

Aurora stops at a tombstone so old it's cracked in half, the top portion lying in the overgrown grass. "Witchcraft works with imagination," Aurora says. She pulls a bottle out of her cavernous pocket and holds it up for us to see.

"Imagination is the ability to envision that what is not. It's the power to put yourself in someone else's place and understand what it's like to be them. Witches have fantastic imaginations. We understand another person inside and out better than they can understand themselves. Imagination helps you give people exactly what they want most in the world."

Gillian looks around, trying to figure out whether we've all gone crazy. I keep my arm around her as Aurora continues.

"Black magic uses imagination in the opposite way. Black magic imagines what someone fears and uses it against them. Black magic makes your fears real."

Aurora unscrews the cap of the bottle. "This here is the Endless Possibilities Potion. Very innocent little potion I happen to know how to cook up. Way it works is, you say a rhyme and then you try to imagine how the words would look if they were real."

"How?" Henry says, rubbing his hands together.

"Like this." Aurora pulls a bubble wand out of the bottle, blows into it, and sends a string of iridescent bubbles into the air. Then she closes her eyes and recites "Star Light, Star Bright."

Sophie sees the transformation first. "Stars!"

The bubbles have taken the shape of five-point stars. They shimmer in the sun. The wind carries the stars over the tombstones of the Revolutionary War soldiers, over the American flags and plastic flower bouquets, over the hydrangea trees, and up the hill. Sophie and Henry chase after them. When the bubbles fly away, the kids come running back, joy in their faces.

"Did you see that?" Henry says, jumping up and down.

"Children make the best witches in the world. Got to be creative to be a witch, and ain't no one more creative on this earth than a child." Aurora hands Gillian the bottle. "You try it."

Gillian, who's still skeptical, does exactly as Aurora did, but when she blows into the wand, all she gets are bubbles. Boring, round bubbles. Gillian blows into the wand again. Again, she fails.

"You must believe it to make it so. You got to be able to see your way into it," Aurora says.

Aurora hands Henry the bubble bottle. "Give it a try, lad."

He repeats the same procedure but he recites the words to "Humpty Dumpty." Instead of a string of round bubbles, when he blows into his wand, one gigantic egg-shaped bubble comes out. The egg has a face and legs and arms and a hat. The Humpty Dumpty egg twirls around, flailing its arms. It falls to the ground with a magnificent plop, splattering onto the grass in a soapy puddle.

"Fine job!" Aurora says. "Full of imagination, that one. Got plenty of pictures tumbling around in that brain of his."

"Me me me!" Sophie blows out a string of bubbles, then recites "Mary Had a Little Lamb." Her bubbles instantly turn into animated, effervescent lambs, bouncing across the sky.

Sophie keeps blowing, and out come more lambs.

Soon, lambs are all around the cemetery. Sophie closes her eyes and sings a song about a bunch of elephants who came out to play.

Suddenly the bubbles turn into elephants and Gillian and Henry chortle in delight. The wind shifts and the elephants change direction. The elephants ride an updraft and scatter away.

Aurora pats my back. "Just like you as a youngster. All's you got to do is remember how to imagine."

"MORE!" cries Henry.

Sophie closes her eyes again and sings a song about a dolphin, all those mommy-and-me music classes finally paying off. Now a pod of dolphins is diving and leaping and kicking their tails in the air. Sophie looks like she might burst with joy. Henry runs after dolphins. One of the dolphins veers from the pod and doubles back. It kisses Henry on the nose and pops in a splash of soap. Henry wipes his nose. He laughs like a maniac.

I'm about to thank Aurora, to tell her how much this means to me, but when I turn toward her, she's staring off into the distance, her face white as chalk.

Freya is walking our way from across the cemetery, her pink cape fluttering behind her. Her long string of pearls shimmers in the sun. Aurora and I walk over to meet her.

"You look . . . the same," Aurora says.

"You look old," Freya replies. She's young and beautiful again.

"I am old. So are you."

Freya grins, her eyes shielded by Chanels. "Training our niece in the Old Ways? Giving her Lessons, are you?" She turns to me. "My sisters were always more fond of Lessons than I was."

"The knowledge is her birthright," Aurora says.

Freya frowns. She looks beyond us at my children, who are occupied with making magical bubbles. "And I expect the next generation is learning, too. What a good imagination the little one has."

Shivers run down my spine. I search for my voice. "You agreed to leave us alone."

"Learning witchcraft was not part of the bargain." Freya lifts her glasses onto her head, revealing the malice in her eyes.

"Aurora's just showing us a children's game." I gesture to Aurora in her ragged sweaters and goat-chewed coat. "You're the one with all the spells and potions."

"Is that what you think this is? Child's play? Everything you see around you is my creation. This whole town is my creation. Do you think I'm going to let you come in and take that away from me? After all my hard work? I won't have the First Daughter of the First Daughter come along and ruin what I've built." Her voice cracks and I realize she's actually threatened by me.

"I'm not capable of taking anything from you even if I wanted to."

"Yes you are! You foolish girl. Tell her, Aurora."

"It's true," Aurora says. "You can transform. You have the gift. We all seen it. You just don't remember how to do it no more."

"And that's what Aurora is doing right now. She's helping you remember. She's training you in the Old Ways."

"She's got a right to her legacy," Aurora yells. "And Wilhemena wished it upon her."

"You always idolized our sister. Let me tell you something.

Wilhemena was just a stupid sentimental cow. She never saw the potential in who we are. She followed all the rules, all *their* rules, even when they torched our home. Even when they ridiculed and banished us. Allesone may be too simple to see past your plans, but I'm not." Heat is radiating off her. She turns to me. "She's teaching you magic so you can use it against me. But I won't stand by and watch it all taken from me again."

"Leave us alone, Freya," Aurora says.

Freya turns to face my children. My heart beats out of my chest. Gillian, Henry, and Sophie are blowing bubbles and chasing after their magical creations in the sky. Sophie stops and dips her bubble wand into the bottle. She blows out a long bubble in the shape of a dancing bear.

"Stick to your little healing balms. You're going to need them," Freya says. She focuses on the bubbles. Suddenly, the dancing bear melts away and the bubble lengthens into one long, slick cylinder. It grows and grows until it's ten feet long. Then it takes the shape of a massive snake. The snake coils itself in a ball, its head high, tongue flicking in and out. It slithers through the sky toward my children. Gillian screams. Henry runs. The snake gives chase.

In sheer panic, I run for my kids. Henry and Gillian are making their way back through the apple trees. But Sophie stands frozen in the grass, paralyzed with terror. The snake slithers toward her.

"Shut your eyes!" I scream as I race toward her. "Shut your eyes, Sophie!"

But it's too late. Sophie's imagination has taken over. Just as I get to her, the great bubble snake darts its head at my baby, and sinks its fangs into her arm.

It's only imaginary. It's not real. It can't hurt her.

I reach for Sophie and bat the snake away with an elbow. It pops and splashes to the ground.

Sophie falls into my arms. Her eyes roll into the back of her head.

I hold her, feeling the convulsions against my body. "Sophie! Sophie. It's okay. You're going to be okay. It wasn't real. It was only make-believe." I get on my knees to hold her steady, but I can feel her slipping away. "Call 911!" I scream.

My brain freezes, but my body springs into action. I lay her down and check her breathing. Nothing escapes her mouth. I check her pulse. Nothing.

I'm pinching her nose and blowing into her mouth. I do compressions to her heart, just below the sternum. I'm faintly aware of the sound of sirens getting closer. And then I'm in an ambulance, and they are holding a mask to Sophie's face. I'm being held back by one medic as another medic holds a defibrillator to her tiny chest, sending electrical impulses through her body.

The words coming out of the doctor's mouth don't make sense. "Acute muscular paralysis." "Respiratory failure." "Rapidly declining brain functioning." He is describing the chronology of chemical events that will take place over the next forty-eight hours, ending with cardiac arrest and death.

"But it wasn't real."

"We're analyzing the blood right now. Initial tox screening indicates it was a coral snake," the doctor says.

It's as though he's talking about someone else on a distant continent, or repeating a story he saw on the news. It cannot be Sophie he's referring to. It can't be Sophie lying in a hospital bed, comatose, with a ventilator breathing air into her lungs.

The floor in this room is beige and the walls are beige and the furniture is beige, and it is lit too brightly. There's an old man sitting in a chair reading a magazine. There's a woman in a wheelchair beside him with vacant eyes that stare straight ahead. There's a receptionist behind the glass partition tapping on a computer. She is working away, unaffected by the personal tragedies swirling around her. On her desk a bottle of

Glamour lime-basil hand lotion. I want to scream at her that my baby is dying, that my world is imploding, and how can she just sit there tap, tap, tapping away as if it were just another day at the office.

I try to focus on the doctor's words. He's tall and his fingers are slender and soft, so unlike Kevin's working hands. "Do you want a priest called in?"

Do I want a priest called in?

"It wasn't real."

"Mrs. Darling, unfortunately, the drug company that produced the antivenom stopped production in 2008. We're checking every poison control center in the United States to see if there's a stockpile anywhere. Coral snakes are incredibly poisonous. It must have been a pet someone released into the wild. We're going to make sure she doesn't suffer."

Aurora is on the couch with her arms around Henry and Gillian when I enter the waiting room.

"I don't understand. The snake wasn't real."

"The snake was and it wasn't," she says, just like Wilhemena's stories. "'Twas real in her mind. And that made it so. She'd be a powerful witch one day."

"There has to be something we can do."

She opens her mouth to speak, when Kevin bursts through the door. The sight of Kevin makes me snap. It is real. It isn't make-believe. Sophie is really dying. I fall over in pain. Gillian and Henry run up to him and hug him. He kisses their heads and holds them tightly. He walks over to me and kneels next to me and we hold on to each other. I sob into his chest. The ground below me has vanished and Kevin is the only thing holding me up from the abyss.

"Is she . . . ?" he asks, out of breath.

"They say there's no antivenom," I cry.

"How did this happen?" Kevin says.

I see the whole scene play over in my mind. Freya. The snake. The bite. And Freya's words: *Stick with your little healing balms. You're going to need them.* I grab Aurora by the shoulders. "You can heal her. Freya said so."

Aurora looks down. "I never was good with potions."

"You have to try. Please."

"Only one thing can counter the venom," she says, "and that's the spirit element of a healing witch. Wilhemena had the gift of healing even since we was wee youngsters. We'll need her ashes. But Freya ain't going to let 'em go without a fight. We don't even know where she's keeping them at."

"What the hell's going on? Who's she?" Kevin looks like he's going to punch something. Or someone.

"Name's Aurora. I'm Allesone's auntie," she says.

"What?"

"Handsome one you found yourself there, niece," Aurora says.

"Aunt Aurora is a witch, Daddy. She has superpowers," Henry says. "She's going to save Sophie. Mommy's a witch, too. And Sophie and I are already a witch and a wizard, and Gillian still needs to work on her skills."

"Allison, what's going on?"

CHAPTER 33

A shoemaker makes shoes without leather,
With all the four elements together,
Fire, Water, Earth, Air,
And every customer takes two pair.

Sophie's eyes are closed when we enter the room where she lies comatose, an IV dripping fluid into her tiny body. Thin blue lines cross her eyelids. Her hand hangs limp on the starched sheets. I stare at the spot on her forehead where I've planted a thousand kisses, wishing for the power to heal, wishing my mother were here now.

Kevin sits in the chair by her bed, eyes red-rimmed and bleary. I've explained everything to him as honestly as I could.

"So, all this stuff about spells and potions and witchcraft is real?"

"Yes."

"And the snake was imaginary, but the bite was real?"

"It was real in Sophie's mind, and that made it so. That's how the witchcraft works."

"And you believe in witchcraft and all that stuff. A hundred percent?"

I pause. "I've always known it's real. I chose to forget about it for a long time because it only brought me heartache. I'm sorry for everything, Kevin. I never meant to hurt you."

"You were under a spell?"

"Yes. I was. But it's my fault, too. I let myself get carried away with it. I didn't have to join the coven. I didn't have to take the bait. I risked losing my family, losing you, losing what makes our kids who they are. And now the worst thing I can imagine has happened." The tears gush in waves.

Kevin holds me. "And Astrid really is a witch, after all?"

"Yeah. The worst witch of all."

He rubs the stubble on his face. "I told you it was a cult."

I smirk. I lower my face to Sophie's and feel her warm butter breath on my cheek. Kevin strokes her hair.

"If Aurora's going to cure Sophie, she'll need my mother's ashes. It means I'm going to have to leave you and Sophie here so I can find them."

"Do whatever you have to do," Kevin says. "I'll keep Henry and Gillian with me."

"Actually, I need their help."

The clock is ticking. "Can you make a potion that makes someone reveal a secret?" I ask Aurora as we race home from the hospital.

"A good old Spill the Beans Potion is what you're looking for. Need some dried pintos and a few other things."

"Good. As soon as we get home, we need to get to work. Henry and Gillian, I want you to help Aunt Aurora in the kitchen. I need to get ready."

"Ready for what?" Aurora says.

"Shopping."

"Now?" Gillian says.

I turn around to face them in the backseat. They're drained of color, their eyes swollen from crying over Sophie. "I've got a plan."

"What?"

"I'm going to find out where Astrid is keeping the spirit element."

"How?" Aurora asks.

"By exploiting the coven's weakness."

"And what might that be?" Aurora snorts.

"Shoes," I answer.

One call to Geoffrey's Emporium is all I need to set my plan into action. Then I text Bethanny:

Me: Louboutins are in. Can't afford them. Yours if you want them

Bethanny: YES!!!!

Me: Meet me at Geoffrey's at 4:00

Bethanny: On my way

I have to hand it to Sissy Star. The shoes are to die for. Even me, in my twelve-year-old Uggs, cannot take my eyes off these shoes. They're so fantastic that all the saleswomen in the store have wandered over to gawk. A collective gasp goes up when the first one comes out of the box. They are open-toe platform pumps made of Javanese cobra skin with aurora-borealis Swarovski crystal-studded six-inch heels, Italian leather lining, and classic red soles signed and dated by Christian Louboutin himself.

"Is that them?" Bethanny walks up behind me.

"Do you want to try them on?" I say, trying to sound jaunty.

Bethanny takes the chair next to me and grabs the shoe out of my hand. "How much?"

"Sixty-five hundred."

"Ouch."

"I heard this kind of cobra is endangered," I tell her since only someone like Bethanny would consider that a plus.

She holds a shoe up to the light. While she's inspecting the crystals, I take the second one out of the box and sprinkle some of Aurora's Spill the Beans Powder into it. No one notices because they're all mesmerized by the bling.

Bethanny takes the second shoe from me and slips them both on. She walks around the store, modeling the shoes, checking herself out in every mirror. She cocks her head left and right, admiring herself shamelessly.

"Sixty-five hundred, huh?" Bethanny purses her lips together. "That's more than I expected."

I loop an arm through hers and walk her to the mirror again. "They're one of a kind," I say.

"I know, but even Chad would balk at the price and he *loves* Louboutin." Geoffrey, who's dressed in an impeccable trim-fitting suit, raises an eyebrow and purses his lips, and I return the look.

"They make your legs look amazing," I say.

"True." She balances on the balls of her feet, tightening her iron-toned calves.

Then I lay it on thick. "And holiday parties are right around the corner. You'll have plenty of opportunities to wear them. No one else will have anything like this."

"I don't know. They're so expensive."

A few more minutes are all I need. "All right," I say, dropping my head in disappointment. "I'll just call Kimberly and see if she wants them."

"Wait! I can put them on my credit card." She gives me a condescending look. "But you know I'm doing you a solid, right?"

"Thanks," I say, choking on my own vomit.

"Should I ring them up for you?" Geoffrey asks.

"My friend's had some financial strains lately," Bethanny says to him. Salt in the wound. "But I'm happy to help her out."

I swallow hard, force a smile on my face.

"Well, aren't you a thoughtful friend," Geoffrey says. "Let me box them up."

I grab Geoffrey by the arm. "No!"

Both Bethanny and Geoffrey look at me with surprise.

"They look so good on you. You should wear them home," I say.

Admiring herself in the mirror again, Bethanny agrees. "You're right, Allison, I will wear them home."

I've talked her into having a nonfat pumpkin spice cappuccino at Starbucks to celebrate her new purchase. She's happy to accommodate my request, and besides, it gives her a chance to show off her new shoes as well as her calves.

The foot potion should be settling in as we take a seat.

"I have the perfect dress to wear with these," she says, twirling her foot around so the crystals catch the light.

"How's work at Glamour?" I ask.

"You know I can't tell you anything about Glamour. Astrid says we're not allowed to talk to you anymore. I'm taking a big risk just being here."

I can't believe I ever wanted to be like her. "I'm just curious."

"It's fine. Work is fine." The light catches a crystal and flicks across the ceiling.

"I think I might have lost something there."

"Allison, I can't help you with your little problems."

She's rubbing the cobra skin with her palm, paying me no attention, so I use the spell Aurora gave me:

"Little Bo-Peep has lost her sheep,
 And can't tell where to find them;
 Leave them alone,
 And they'll come home,
 Wagging their tails behind them."

When I finish, Bethanny's eyes gloss over. She's under the spell.

"I need to know where Astrid is keeping the spirit element," I say.

She stares off into space.

"Hello. Bethanny. Are you there?"

A little drool comes out of her mouth. Maybe the potion was too strong.

I need to try another tactic. "Where can a shepherdess find her sheep?"

"In the clubhouse." Her voice is flat.

"What clubhouse?"

"Duh. The Salem Country Club Clubhouse."

"When?"

"Tomorrow night. The waxing crescent of the harvest moon. During the Halloween party. Six o'clock."

"Will the whole coven be there?" I ask.

"Yes."

"Will they be expecting me?"

"Totally." Even hypnotized by the spell, Bethanny manages to sound superficial. I think her IQ may have dropped a few dozen points when she put on the super sparkly shoes.

"What did Astrid say?"

"The harvest moon on Samhain comes but once every, like, three decades. Or something." Her voice is robotic.

"I mean about expecting me. What did she say about me?"

"We are to be ready for the outcast one."

"What did she say specifically?" I ask, my patience thin, the clock ticking.

Bethanny exhales sharply as her brain goes into high gear. "Hmmm . . ."

"Think hard. What did she say?"

"Oh . . . I remember . . . Two sentinels stand watch. Two at the threshold to guard. Two as shadows of night. And one, a herald, to sound the bell."

"Thanks." I leave Bethanny sitting in a stupor. I think about her driving home in her $6,500 shoes. She'll be disoriented when the spell wears off, but I'm sure she won't mention our little rendezvous to anyone else in the coven. After all, I'm a pariah now. And nobody wants to associate with pariahs.

I check my watch. 2:15 P.M. Sophie has forty-two hours. I break all speed limits getting home.

CHAPTER 34

This is the nicht o' Hallowe'en
When a' the witchie may be seen;
Some o' them black, some o' them green,
Some o' them like a turkey bean.

In the living room, Aurora yanks a plant out of its pot and shakes clumps of dirt loose on the rug.

She holds the plant up high and pinches her face in concentration. "Latin name, *Sansevieria trifasciata*. Description: Root plant featuring long, dark green leaves with light green bands. Uses: First aid for snake and scorpion bites. Potion: Steam leaves over river rocks. Pulverize with one part sage, two parts cornmeal. Mix with spirit element. Apply to wound."

"That's it? That's the antivenom?" I ask.

A look of doubt crosses her face. "As far as I can remember."

"Aurora, this has to work," I say.

"Don't fret. Have you gathered everything else?"

I nod. Fresh sage, cornmeal, river rocks. As a good house-witch, everything I needed was already here, culled from the cupboards, the garden, the forgotten beach pails crammed in the leaf-filled corners of the patio.

Everything except my mother's ashes.

"Is there any chance the potion could work without the spirit element?" I ask.

"Sophie was bit by an enchanted snake. A creature from a world that was and wasn't. The spirit element will coax her back to this world."

My thoughts flicker to my little girl who is lying in the hospital, inches from death, with Kevin by her side, and I'm gripped with despair. My eyes become so heavy they feel like they're made of metal. I start to cry, but catch myself. There is no time for weakness.

Our best shot of getting into the Salem Country Club tonight is to blend, so I send Gillian and Henry upstairs to rifle through closets for costumes. Don't worry if it's too small, or too big, or too outdated. Any old costume will have to do, I tell them. No time to worry about perfection. I find an old package of zombie makeup tucked in a drawer with stray Christmas lights and Easter chocolates, and smear green face paint across my cheeks, over my nose, forehead, and chin until I'm covered in green zombie paint. It smells faintly of Play-Doh. In the back of the coat closet, I uncover a pointy black hat and black cape, left over from a party of Halloweens past. How I labored over every detail of that party; the painstaking precision I took to make sure each cupcake was decorated with equal amounts of orange frosting and black licorice, the matching napkins and tablecloths I drove to three stores to find, the invitations I handcrafted out of vellum and felt, the goody bags I tied with perfectly curled ribbons. The world of a domestic divahood. Minutia. It all seems so insignificant now.

When I return to the kitchen, Aurora is pulverizing the snake plant with a rolling pin. Something catches my eye in the sliding glass door. I look again. Cleo is at the door, her tail swatting the air. I scream.

"Well, lookee there, Wilhemena's cat," Aurora says, rather nonchalantly considering we buried Cleo a week ago. She opens the door and lets her in.

Cleo nudges up against my leg, her fur matted in mud. She struts over to Aurora, meows, stretches, and runs into the living room.

"How can she be alive?" I ask, my mind spinning.

"Cats have nine lives. Surprised you don't know that."

"That's only a figure of speech! It's an expression."

"Words have meaning," Aurora says. "Surprised you don't

know that, too. It's just like all them Mother Goose spells we use."

"You mean Mother Goose rhymes?" I ask. "From children's books?"

Aurora pummels a leaf with the rolling pin. "They're spells. Created by witches. Passed down through the years."

"'Little Miss Muffet'? 'Itsy Bitsy Spider'? All of them?"

"Nah. Not all. But a lot of them are."

I think of all the mothers through the years who have sung these songs to their children, unaware that they were repeating spells. My mind leaps to Freya draped in her robe the night I gave her the urn. She was singing something as she went inside. What was it? It suddenly comes back. "Long live the witch on Samhain high."

Aurora drops the rolling pin. It falls to the floor. She turns toward me, slowly. "Where did you hear that?"

"From Freya. Is it a spell?"

Aurora gets jittery and paces the floor. Her hands go to her head.

"What is it?" I ask.

"'Long live the witch on Samhain high, Who brings to the cauldron Spirits nigh.' It's a spell for Long-Life. Never seen it done before. Oh Mother Shipton! Freya is trying to make herself immortal. 'Tis the darkest magic of all, my mother always said."

"Is that possible?" I think of the resurrected cat who just ran through my house. "I guess it is possible."

"Would take the spirit element of a mighty witch to give the potion its power. That's where dear Wilhemena is destined tonight." She wears her concern in the wrinkles of her brow. "Will be no easy thing to take those ashes from Freya, I'm afraid. Samhain high. A harvest moon on Samhain only comes once every thirty-one years. The veil between the worlds draws back. The line between the in-between and the not times will be the thinnest it can be. If she's planning on making a Long-Life

Potion, tonight is her only shot. She's been preparing her whole life and she will stop at nothing to pull off this glamour."

The last time I encountered Freya, my daughter ended up in convulsions on the ground, foaming at the mouth. "I will stop at nothing, too," I say.

The doorbell rings. Suddenly I remember the hundreds of trick-or-treaters who will be flooding the cobblestone streets of Monrovia tonight. I go to the living room, turn off the lights, and lock the door. But when I peek outside to see if the little ghosts, goblins, and fairy princesses have gotten the message, there's a brood of real witches and wizards.

Millie, Beatrice, Jinathon, and Jonathon stand with broomsticks in hand.

"Happy Samhain, Sister Allesone," Jonathon says.

"And honor to the spirits," says Jinathon.

"Don't you worry, Sister."

"We'll save yer wee one."

"Always take care of our own."

"We do."

"Else what's a coven for?"

After all I've done to them—deceiving them, stealing from them—they've shown up in my worst hour. Apologizing now seems insincere. I can't really speak, which is okay, because they seem to understand without a word passing from my lips.

Jonathon and Jinathon hug me.

"We forgive you."

"Live and learn."

"Forgive and forget."

"Water under the bridge."

Millie steps inside and peers at me. "And once we save your child, we'll take care of you." She stands on her tiptoes to whisper in my ear. "Not to worry. Happened to me once, too, my dear. A love potion gone all wrong. I thought kissing a frog would bring me a prince, but it only turned my face green. I know a tincture that can help."

I touch my face and see green makeup on my fingertips. "Ergh. Thanks."

Beatrice puffs on a cigar and blows the smoke in my face. "Here for your mother's sake only."

"Thanks for coming, Beatrice," I say.

She grunts and brushes between the dwarves, knocking them off balance with her massive bulk of a body. "We got a plan, or what?" she grumbles, stuffing her stogie into the empty plant pot.

Aurora comes in from the kitchen, unfazed by the arrival of our guests. Cleo trails behind her and nuzzles up to Millie's legs. "We're going to need to split up. Millie and I are gonna have to stay here to brew the potion. The rest of yous will have to go with Allesone to get the ashes from Freya."

I don't like the idea of splitting up, but she's right. Potions take time and patience.

"And what about them wannabe witches parked out front? What are we gonna do about them?" Beatrice says.

"Witches? Out front?" I peek out the window and see Heather's black Cadillac parked in the driveway with Erin riding shotgun. The two of them are waiting in the same spot where they picked me up in the limo a few short weeks ago for my initiation at the spa with all its bee venom face masks and talk of making Monrovia prosper. How quickly things have changed.

"Freya's sentinels," I say. Every move we make tonight will be under careful surveillance. "They're going to follow as soon as I get in the car. They'll warn Freya."

"Then we best not drive," Aurora says, hands on hips.

"You'll see, Allesone."

"It all comes back."

"Just like riding a bicycle."

"Or getting back on a hobbyhorse."

The dwarves are packing my gym bag with bottles of potions and elixirs I recognize from my mother's trunk at the funeral.

"Why are you so small?" Henry says, wearing an absurd witch costume that barely goes to his knees.

"Henry, that's not polite," I say.

"It's okay," Jonathon says.

"It's the way we were born."

"Aren't you going to get any bigger?" Henry asks.

"No bigger than three pumpkins, stacked end on end."

"Or a dozen ice cream cones, tip to tip."

Gillian rocks back and forth on her heels, tugging at the Little Red Riding Hood costume she's thrown on over black sweatpants.

"But we're giants to a grasshopper."

"Brutes to a bumblebee."

Henry laughs and Jonathon and Jinathon smile.

"These are your uncles," I say, to which Gillian responds, simply, "Cool."

"Can you fly, too?" Henry asks.

The dwarves nod enthusiastically. "And so can you, little one."

Henry jumps up and down.

"No," I say firmly. "It's too dangerous. Henry and Gillian are not flying."

They both protest. Beatrice tells me I'm being a wet blanket. Jonathon and Jinathon swear up and down that statistically it's safer than driving a car, which I point out is due to the fact that PEOPLE DON'T FLY BROOMSTICKS.

"Mom, I can do it," Gillian says.

"It's not safe."

"Sister Allesone, let the youngsters try it."

"Natural fliers, the wee ones."

I shake my head. "This isn't a game. It isn't like learning to ride a bike, or letting go of them in the pool for the first time. It's dangerous."

Aurora marches up with her broomstick in hand. "Ya haven't got time to spare, niece. Flying 'tis the quickest way."

"They can do it, sister."

"You did when you were but a bitty thing."

Henry pulls on my robe. "Mom, trust your feet, not your head."

I look down at him. "What?"

"That's what the Jedi say."

There's is a light in Henry's eyes that shoots straight to my heart.

"The Jedi aren't real, Henry."

"I know," Henry says. He looks at the dwarves, at Aurora. "But they're real."

He really believes he can do this. He's a Jedi knight, a superhero, and a wizard, all rolled into one. Who am I to stop him? I've spent too much of his life teaching him all the things that aren't possible, and ignoring all the things that are. Imaginary snakes can give fatal bites. Cats really do have nine lives. Little boys can be whatever they imagine. Families can be broken and put back together.

"Okay," I say. "Just be careful."

Aurora proceeds to demonstrate how to fly a broomstick. "Get a good running start, say the enchantment, and off you go. Use your body weight to steer." She closes her eyes for a moment, opens them, then runs across the grass shouting the words:

> "Hickory dickory dare,
>   I fly up in the air."

The broomstick rises in her hand. In one motion, she swings a leg over and straddles it. Just like that, she is cruising above the yard, over the garden, the fence, then high above the apple trees and maples, until she disappears into the darkening sky. A murder of crows caws and scatters out of the trees.

Henry and Gillian cheer and whistle, vibrating with excitement.

Aurora circles back around and lands in front of us.

"Your turn." She hands the broom to Gillian, and gives another one to Henry.

My palms are sweating as Gillian and Henry take turns running and jumping onto their broomsticks. I almost throw up when Gillian loses her balances forty feet in the air, but she recovers gracefully.

Jonathon and Jinathon take off next. Then Beatrice.

I give Aurora a thumbs-up, sling the gym bag over my shoulder, say the enchantment, run forward, and lurch into the air. I pull myself up and straddle the narrow stick, which feels less magical and more like a trip to the gynecologist ("Scooch down two more inches . . . a little farther . . . a little farther"). I adjust my weight by leaning forward and tucking my feet underneath me. After a while, I get the hang of it. I pull up, and the broomstick follows my touch. I level off over the cemetery, brittle heads of hydrangea swaying in my wake. I make a slow, wide turn and rise upward until I join the others.

I can hear Aurora from below: "Fare ye well. By Ursula's Broom."

Soon, we're flying over High Street, above the throngs of trick-or-treaters. They look tiny. My stomach does somersaults. I am giant to a grasshopper.

The sun sets and the moon rises, huge and orange, as we fly over the Route 1 Bridge, the skate park, the outskirts of Monrovia, and over the vast marshes of Essex County. I'm thankful to have my kids with me, along with my brothers, and the last of my mother's coven. Facing Freya is daunting enough and I'm glad for the reinforcements.

Gillian and Henry race each other through the sky, speeding up, slowing down, weaving and dodging. Henry does a duck dive beneath me and pops up right in front of Beatrice, who scowls at him. Gillian rumbles with laughter. It's been so long since I've heard her laugh, that it sends chills down my spine.

It takes us no time to get to Salem, and even in the fog, it's easy to spot the Salem Country Club with its fairways a chartreuse green.

We land on the eighteenth hole, right next to the clubhouse. The cavalcade of luxury cars and valets on the circular drive indicates this is another one of Freya's A-list parties. We stash our broomsticks under a pine tree and head around to the side of the clubhouse.

From a safe distance, behind a hedge of boxwoods, Gillian and Henry crouch behind me, the dwarves and Beatrice huddle close, and we all watch the entrance.

Dr. Yu gets out of his Lexus, dressed as Elvis, and I cringe at the thought of our kiss. Kimberly and Bethanny greet him at the door with double air kisses.

Two sentinels to stand watch. Two at the threshold to guard. Two as shadows of night. And one, a herald, to sound the bell.

"Kimberly and Bethanny are the threshold guardians," I whisper.

"Which is which?" Jonathon whispers.

"Who is who?" says Jinathon.

"Bethanny is in the skintight Catwoman outfit."

"'Tis tight indeed."

"Poor woman probably can't breathe," Beatrice says.

"And those heels are high as mountains."

"Must be quite uncomfortable," Jonathan says.

I watch Bethanny sway her hips and skim a hand down her Catwoman thighs, flirting with Dr. Yu. "Believe me. She's very comfortable," I say.

"Who's the other?"

"What's the other?"

Kimberly is wearing a bonnet, lace shawl, long skirt, and is waving the colonial flag. Of course. "Martha Washington. Only Kimberly would fantasize about being the first First Lady."

"They are strange costumes."

"A mockery of Samhain, if you ask me," Beatrice says.

"They'll never let us in," I whisper. "Freya will have threatened them with their lives. So we need a distraction."

"Fear not, sister."

"Count on us."

Jonathon and Jinathon scamper from the hedge to the front of the clubhouse. They are so small and stealthy, no one notices them.

They crouch behind a low-lying red maple in the front. Their lips move over a spell. One by one, the thirteen stars on Kimberly's flag disappear. It takes her a little while to notice, but when she does, she jumps to attention. The red stripes disappear next, followed by the blue square in the corner, then the pole on which it's hung.

"It's them," Kimberly says sharply. Bethanny shows Dr. Yu inside, then stands by Kimberly's side.

Jonathon and Jinathon turn their concealment magic on themselves. They don't disappear, exactly. They fade. They appear as fuzzy streaks, the impression of something moving in peripheral vision. They move from the maple to the front steps. One of them takes the now-white flag out of Kimberly's hand and runs into the driveway waving it. Kimberly chases them. They toss the flag back and forth in a game of keep-away, before they cut across the lawn to the golf course.

"Stay here," Kimberly says. She chases the blur of Jonathon and Jinathon down the eighteenth fairway.

"They did it," I say, but when I turn around, Gillian is gone. I look and see her walking toward Bethanny. "Gillian," I whisper. "Stop."

Gillian turns, gives me a wink, and walks up to Bethanny.

"You're Allison's girl," Bethanny smirks.

"That's right."

"Where's your mom?" Bethanny asks. Her voice has lost its Valley girl pitch.

"She's around."

Bethanny cranes her head left and right. Gillian takes a step closer.

"Stop right there." Bethanny puts up a hand. "You're, like, totally not welcome here."

"That's not very friendly. Didn't anyone teach you manners?"

Gillian holds up a vial she must have taken from my gym bag. She opens the cork and blows it in the air as she recites the rhyme:

> "Good night, sleep tight
> Don't let the bedbugs bite.
> If they do, take off your shoe
> And hit them 'til they're black and blue."

The powder lands on Bethanny's glossy Catwoman suit. She coughs and wipes it off her chest. "Gross. What is that?"

Gillian doesn't move.

"Get out of here, little girl," Bethanny says, scratching her arm, then her legs. Within seconds she's scratching her whole body. Bethanny takes off her shoe (the brand-new Christian Louboutins) and whacks it against the ground. "Shoo. Go away." She screeches and pounds at the imaginary bugs with her shoe again and again. Swarovski crystals go flying. Soon, Bethanny is overwhelmed by a swarm of imaginary bugs. She runs down the long driveway and into the night, itching and swatting.

With the threshold clear, the rest of us run into the clubhouse. I give Gillian a high-five as we pass each other.

"I'll stay here. Just in case," Gillian says.

After what I just saw, I think she can handle herself.

"Take this," I say, handing her my cell phone. "In case of emergency."

She gives me a Cheshire Cat smile.

Inside the clubhouse, Beatrice, Henry, and I are decidedly out of place. There are Elvises and Marilyns, James Bonds and Marie Antoinettes. There's a champagne fountain and a chocolate fountain, and a room full of kids with their nannies.

Lilith appears out of nowhere dressed in a vintage Hollywood Bride of Frankenstein costume, her wig streaked white and piled high on her head. *Two as shadows of the night.*

"Nice costumes," she says looking at us through condescending eyes. "Let me guess? Salvation Army?"

Bryson Proctor appears at his mother's side in a ninja costume, an antique sword and scabbard on his belt, along with an arsenal of knives, nunchucks, and grappling hooks.

"What are you supposed to be?" Bryson says to Henry. "A bed wetter?"

"I'm a wizard," Henry says.

"I was a wizard last year."

"I'm a real wizard."

"Whatever."

"It's true. I can fly."

"Baloney."

"I really can."

"Well . . . I'm a real ninja assassin."

"No, you're not."

"Am so."

"I don't believe you."

"I've killed twenty people," Bryson says puffing up his little chest.

Henry gets right up in front of him. "You shouldn't lie about that."

"It's the truth."

"Then you won't catch on fire."

"What are you talking about, you little bed wetter?"

"If you're telling the truth, the spell won't work."

"Whatever. You're a fat beetle-faced bug-eyed butt."

"I'm sorry, Bryson, but I warned you," Henry says. He pulls a vial of potion from his pocket and blows a handful of powder at Bryson.

"Liar, liar,
   Pants on fire."

Bryson flares his nostrils. He can smell the heat a split second before he sees it. When he realizes what's happening, he screams and Lilith screams and when he turns to run away, the flames lick the seat of his pants. He hops up and down, which only feeds the fire. I whip off my cape to douse the flames, but Henry stops me. "It's not real," he says. As Bryson's costume turns to cinder on his body, the magical flames leave his skin completely unharmed. The fire strips away the backside of his costume, then the front, then the weapon's belt, until he's standing in his underwear. Bryson runs toward the chocolate fountain. He pushes aside the younger kids who are dipping marshmallows. He must think he's still on fire because he jumps into the fountain. Lilith charges over to him, consoling him, and checking to see if his costume can be salvaged. He pounds his fists in the chocolate, splattering it across himself and his mother.

"Now's your chance, Mom," Henry says to me.

My brave little wizard. Strong on the inside.

With Lilith and Bryson coated in chocolate, I take my chance and run for the kitchen. Beatrice follows me. Surely, if Freya is making her potion tonight, she'll need a stove, a pot, and a few kitchen herbs.

As we near the swinging kitchen door, Miranda appears in front of us. *The second shadow.*

"Going somewhere?"

I'm about to speak, but Beatrice shoves me aside. "I got this skinny one," she says. She lifts the sides of her cape in front of Miranda, and I slip behind her through the doors just as I hear the words to "Jack and Jill went up the hill." I can't see how the spell manifests on Miranda as I run into the kitchen, but I have no doubt it will end with Miranda in a heap on the floor.

Inside, the kitchen is clamoring with the bustle of caterers. I look around the stoves, but there's no sign of Freya, or my mother's urn. I dash into the walk-in freezer, the pantry, every nook and cranny I can find. Nothing.

When I get to the plating area, I see Rosie adding parsley sprigs to the goblets of shrimp cocktail. *And one, a herald, to sound the bell.*

When she sees me, she drops the parsley and reaches for her mobile phone.

"Rosie, please," I beg.

She starts dialing.

"She's not who you think she is. She's a powerful evil witch named Freya."

Rosie lowers the phone. "She said you'd say that."

A take a step closer. "Did she say that Sophie is in the hospital right now? Freya put her there."

Rosie nods.

"She's going to die, Rosie. My baby is going to die. I can save her, but I need to find Freya. You know Sophie. You've watched her for me at the playground. It's my baby, Rosie." I search her eyes for empathy, some sign of the years of motherhood we've shared, of how we've both fretted over our kids since the day they were born, of the sheer weight of raising small children in this world. I look for a spark of recognition of the truth we both know: that it takes a village, and that we're in the village together. We've covered for each other countless times when one was too tired or unhinged to change yet another diaper. We've caught each other's kids when they've fallen, we've slipped them lollipops when they cried. We've felt joy for the other when things have gone right and we've lifted each other up out of the throes of self-doubt or tedium or anguish when things have gone wrong. We're more than just girlfriends who go out for a drink on a Friday night. We're momfriends.

Rosie looks me in the eye, puts her mouth to my ear, so that no one can see the words on her lips.

"Misery Shoal," she whispers. "Hurry."

While the others stay in the clubhouse to run interference, I dash outside to the eighteenth hole, grab my broomstick, and take off, alone in the night sky. I follow the shore north and east, until I'm directly over Salem. The sparkling lights of the city spread out like a jellyfish, its center brightly illuminated, its ever-less-populated tendrils faintly lit.

To get to Misery Shoal, I have to cross Salem Sound, but a fog bank has rolled in from sea. It swallows me whole. Land and water disappear and there's only gray. I squint, trying to make out shapes, but my eyes play tricks on me. One minute I see a dark patch, the next, it's gone.

I push the broomstick down, until I'm cruising a few feet above water. Suddenly a channel marker pops up in front of me, and I swerve to avoid it. One foot slips out from under me, and I scramble to get back in position.

I increase my altitude, rising through fog until the air clears and visibility is endless, and I feel like I could touch the stars. When I look down, there is nothing but fog. There are no lights to guide me or landmarks to point the way. I'll never find Misery Shoal. I think about landing somewhere, anywhere, stealing a car or hailing a cab, but it will take too long, and the road to the shoal could be underwater this time of day. I'll never find Freya. I'll never get the ashes in time.

I close my eyes, sick with dread. I think about Sophie. I think about my family, my coven. Then, my mother's voice comes into my head. It's sweet and gentle, like a song. She sings the first nursery rhyme I ever learned.

> "Luna, every woman's friend,
> To me thy goodness condescend,
> Let this night in visions see,
> Emblems of my destiny."

When I open my eyes, something below moves in the fog. A small patch of clouds starts spinning like a whirlpool. A hole forms in the center, and as it spins, it pulls away layers of fog, until there is a light in the impenetrable mass of gray. Through the hole, I can make out the moon-rippled water below, the sound of the ocean, and the unmistakable spit of land shaped like a talon. Misery Shoal.

"Thanks, Mom."

I push down the handle of my broomstick and bolt toward land. I'm going so fast that the strap of my gym bag gouges into my chest, the bag flapping behind me.

A fire blazes on the ridge, carrying in the smoke notes of juniper and rue, hawthorn, rowan, birch. The smells of my childhood. Torches of mullein and bushes of rosemary burn around the perimeter.

I pull up a second too late. My heels dig into the ground as I skid across the ridge. I lose my balance and tumble off the broomstick, gashing my arms and legs. I can feel warm blood where my skin has been scraped away.

I get to my feet as fast as I can, but Freya's ready for me.

A spray of salt hits my face. My skin stings, my eyes burn. I try to rub them, but I can't move my arms. Or my legs. At first I think I must have broken my back in the fall, severed my spinal cord, turned into a paraplegic. But I'm standing, so that can't be. My brain races to catch up with my body. *Some witches have the power to immobilize their attackers.*

"You're like a cat with ten lives," Freya says, her voice creak-ing with age. Her body is wizened, her face wrinkled, her hair white and gnarly.

My mother's urn gleams in the moonlight on a log next to the fire.

"Give me the ashes," I say, surprised that I still have my voice.

Freya lifts the urn, pulls off the top, and balances it precariously on the palm of her hand. "What? These?"

The urn wobbles.

"My daughter will die, Freya. Give them to me."

Freya laughs. "Your daughter. The Daughter of the First Daughter of the First Daughter. She should have enough magic to save herself. But then again, it didn't work out that way for you, did it?"

"I know what you're doing. You want to make yourself immortal."

She laughs. "I'm not a vampire, for god's sake. I can't be immortal. But I can buy an extra two hundred years, give or take. All I needed were the right ingredients. And a Samhain harvest moon, of course. The night when the crone goddess is reborn into a young woman. I will stay young and beautiful while everyone around me grows old and ugly."

"There's no shame in growing old."

"Wrong," she snaps. "Youth and beauty are commanding powers. People follow beauty. Obey it. Just look at our little town."

She steps toward me and the ground crunches underfoot. It's white with shards of broken shells. "Staying young is the greatest magic trick ever played. The ultimate glamour. I just needed you to get me my sister's ashes."

"So you did know who I was when you brought Kevin to work for you."

"Of course. Those dwarves put a strong enchantment on you, I'll say that for them. You were hidden from me for many years. But my stupid sister never embraced the modern world the way I did. Juvenile records, child welfare documents, place-ment agencies, medical records. There are ways of finding people."

"I was part of your plan all along."

"You," she says, "and this." She holds out a pearl that shim-mers in the moonlight.

"A pearl?"

"Not just a pearl. A rare pearl from a rare mussel that some believe can live five hundred years. That makes it the oldest liv-ing creature on earth. But unlike other long-living animals, the mussel itself lacks any symptoms of aging." She throws a bulb of bear's garlic in the cauldron that hangs on a spit over the fire, along with some yarrow, rue, vervain, mugwort, and thyme.

"In order to survive, a mussel larva must find a host, in its case, a salmon. It snaps shut onto the host's gills for nine months and travels hundreds of miles from home. Then it lets go, bur-rows in the sand, and grows. Every once in a great while, a grain of sand enters the shell and, decades later, voilà." Freya rolls the pearl between her thumb and finger.

"Today it starts a new life cycle. With a new host." She tosses the pearl in the cauldron. Then she lifts the urn.

"Please," I say. I struggle to move, but the spell that's hold-ing me tightens. "I'm begging you. Give me the ashes."

She smiles wickedly. Then she pours the ashes into the caul-dron. "Long live the witch on Samhain high, who brings to the cauldron spirits nigh."

I watch, helpless, as Sophie's only chance at life is thrown away. I can feel my lungs being squeezed. The sound of my blood pumping becomes a siren in my head. My eyes can't blink. All I can do is watch as Freya kills my baby.

She stirs the cauldron with a long wooden ladle.

"Daughter of Wilhemena. First Daughter of the First Daughter. Hah! You're as common as a titmouse. As common as your father. And grandfather."

I try to speak, but my voice fails me. She cackles again.

She's right. I am common. I am not magical. I am not special. I've worked my whole life to be as ordinary as possible. I intentionally distanced myself from all things Ellylydan. If I had learned to use my magic I could find a way out of this, but I've denied my past all my life. I was embarrassed by it as a child, and I denied it as an adult. Shame. That's been my legacy.

I wish I could turn back the clock, to the marsh, the night with the will-o'-the-wisps. *What you think, so it becomes.* That was my power. The ability to see that which is not. To perceive. To imagine. To transfigure.

I was Ellylydan once.

"I am still Ellylydan."

Freya doesn't hear. She leans over the cauldron, stirring her potion. I try, with all my might, to spin back time. I try to imagine Freya as a young girl on this shoal. I try to put her in Sophie's shoes—young, innocent, carefree. If only I could understand the moment she turned to Darkness, then maybe I could stop her.

I close my eyes and send my thoughts down the rabbit hole.

Suddenly I'm in the middle of the ocean on a squat dory, the shore a distant speck on the horizon. It smells of fish and diesel. The sun blazes against the high prow, casting a shadow on the flat bottom. A man stands in the stern, tying a metal jig on a long line. A little girl with flame-red hair stands at the gunwale, barely tall enough to see over the edge.

"The jig takes the hooks down to bottom where the cod and haddock are," the man says. He speaks with a Scottish brogue. "Now fetch the bait bucket and I'll teach you how to set bait."

The girl drags a bucket to the stern. She curls her nose up at the smell. A wave rocks the boat and she teeters over, her arm landing in the bucket of bait. The man laughs.

"Haven't got your sea legs yet, have you, Freya?"

Freya pouts. Her hands turn into fists and she glares at the man.

"Aw, don't be like that," the man says. "I'm only joking with you."

"Why can't you just use a potion, like Mama does?"

"Because we're real fishermen." He laughs.

"Mama could make a potion."

"Well, I'm not your mother." He grabs the bucket and starts baiting the hooks. Freya leans against the gunwale, turning her back on her father.

Once he sets the hand line, he takes a spot at the helm. He puts the engine into gear and idles forward, keeping a close watch on the bobber. "When the bobber goes under, we've got ourselves a fish," he says over the drone of the engine.

"Use your magic, Papa. Make the fish jump in the boat."

The man shakes his head. "I'm not a witch, Freya. I don't have magic."

"Why ain't you got any magic, Papa?" Freya stands next to him at the helm.

"Wasn't born with it."

"Why weren't ya?"

Freya's father stares straight ahead at the limitless sea.

"Mama's got magic. I got magic. Why ain't you got it?"

The man keeps a hand on the wheel and one on the throttle. "Being a witch doesn't make you any better than anyone else."

"But I can make potions."

"I know that."

"Well, then, I reckon I am better."

Anger fills the man's eyes, his temper as fiery as his daughter's. His tone is harsh. "Hush up, or you'll get a beating. And your magic won't save you from it."

This silences Freya only for a moment.

"Why'd Mama marry you if you're just a Commoner?"

"I'll have no more of that talk," he says. He looks at Freya and his face softens, his affection for her plain to see. "Your Mama and I loved each other. That's why we married. I knew she was a witch, and she knew I wasn't. But that didn't matter to us, did it? When you grow up, you'll see there are all types of people in this world. You can't change them, Freya. You've got to accept people for what they are. Being a witch doesn't make you any better than anyone else. Or any worse. Always remember that."

Freya scowls.

He wipes the sweat from his brow.

"Witches can heal. Commoners can't. That's better," Freya says.

"You can't heal everything. You can't cure a disease. You can't heal a dying man. Freya, you have magic, but you need to understand we all got our limits. Even your mama. Even you."

"Can so heal a dying man."

But her father has stopped paying attention. He drives ahead, focusing on the sea. When the bobber dips below the surface, he pulls the throttle into neutral. With great agility, he moves to the stern and pulls the hand line in, reeling it around a spool, a fisherman of a bygone era. It takes enormous strength to pull the line. His muscles are tensed, his face strained.

The fish appears like a goliath beneath the surface. "Hand me the gaff," he orders.

Freya steps to the bow and struggles to lift the heavy gaff stashed under the forward gunwale. It takes all her strength to carry it astern. She stops before she gets to her father, keeping the gaff just out of his reach.

"Give it here," he says.

The fish breaks the surface, its giant maw gulping air.

Freya stares.

"Freya, hand me the gaff. The fish is too big. It'll snap the line."

"Can so healing a dying man."

With all her strength, she lifts the gaff straight over her head, metal glinting in the sun.

Her father looks up just as the hook slices into the soft tissue of his neck, through artery, into bone. He lets go of the line and falls forward. He presses his hand against his neck as blood squirts from the wound.

Freya steps to his side, her father's eyes searching, trying to understand.

"Can so." Freya puts her tiny hand on her father's wound, closes her eyes, and recites a rhyme. She opens her eyes, but blood gushes out with every pulse of his heart. He moans in agony. Freya closes her eyes tighter, her lips moving in a silent spell. But it does nothing. Her face contorts. "Can so. Can so. Can so." She tries to heal the wound again with words as the color drains from her father's face. Soon, he succumbs to the bleeding. Freya cries out and lies across her father's chest.

The goliath beats its tail against the hull, then dives down into the cold depths.

When I open my eyes, Freya is stooped over the cauldron. Steam rises around her as she stirs and stirs.

Once again, my mother's voice comes to me in the dark: *What you think, so it becomes.*

As if she can hear it, too, Freya turns and looks at me. Our eyes lock. My birthmark throbs in blinding spasms.

I feel my thoughts as an electrical current running between us, connecting us. Sparks of light flash in the fog. Her eyes widen.

Everything I've just seen in my mind, she now sees. The memory races back in excruciating detail. She can see the shadow of the boat's high prow, smell the fish and diesel. She can hear her father's moans. Deep in her veins, she can feel his love for her and relive her failure to save him.

She presses her hands over her ears. "Make it stop."

Then she doubles over in pain. She sits on the sharp carpet of shells and crawls into a fetal position.

As Freya rocks back and forth like a child, I can feel the

pressure lift from my chest. My arms break free from their invisible chains, then my legs, until I'm mobile again.

I shake out my legs and walk to her, huddled on the ground. I may not have control of my power, but now I understand it better. Transfiguring isn't just about turning an apple into an onion, or a broomstick into a fish. It's about giving my thoughts an escape. It can turn a buried memory into reality, if that's what the memory needs.

Suddenly, I turn my attention to the urn, hoping a few ashes still remain. But it's empty. Used up in Freya's vain potion. My mother's ashes can't save Sophie's life now.

Or can they?

I burn my hands lifting the cauldron off the spit. It's too heavy to carry on my broomstick, so I search frantically for something lighter. Ten yards away, perched on the edge of the ridge, I spot my gym bag, which must have fallen off in my crash landing. I rifle through: a pair of socks, a bag of Goldfish. A sippy cup. *Bingo.*

I dump out whatever old juice it held and scoop up a sippy cupful of Long-Life Potion.

As I take off into the night sky, I can see Freya, crumpled into a ball, the old hag who will never pass into the young goddess.

The harvest moon lights my way back to Monrovia.

CHAPTER 35

At the hospital, Kevin's hand is like a vise on mine as Aurora pours the Long-Life Potion into her salve of cornmeal, spider plant, and sage. The doctor and nurses have left us alone, encouraging us to say our final farewells. They eyed me suspiciously when I entered the room, bruised and bloodied in my witch costume, but I didn't explain myself. I thanked them for their efforts and closed the door behind them so we could get to work.

Gently, I pull the dressing off Sophie's wound, and Kevin brushes her hair out of the way. Aurora applies the salve over Sophie's neck.

Sophie's face is ghostly white and streaked with blue veins. No one breathes. We watch. And hope. Within a minute, the pink returns to her cheeks. After another minute, her eyes open. By the third minute, she's sitting up and chatting away as though nothing ever happened.

"I made elephants!" she says, her voice hoarse. "Big bubble elephants, and lambs, and dolphins."

"You sure did, love," I say.

Kevin and I take turns kissing and hugging and holding her.

Doctors and nurses rush back into the room. They check her fluids and her vitals, shock on their faces.

"How did this happen?" one of them asks.

"Mommy's a witch," Sophie says.

"The things kids say," Kevin says.

While the nurses tend to Sophie, I ask Aurora to step out in the hall to grab a cup of coffee with me. As soon as we're alone, I press her for answers. "Does this mean the Long-Life Potion will affect Sophie?"

Aurora looks concerned. "Not sure. I ain't never seen anything like this done before."

"So, do you think Sophie's going to live another two hundred years?" I ask.

"I reckon that's how it works."

I let out a deep sigh and run a hand through my gnarled hair. "Will she age? Or is she going to be three years old for the rest of her life?"

Aurora's face contorts into her thinking look. "The potion will slow the aging process quite a bit." She throws up her hands. "Ah well, might be fun for her to have the smarts of an adult in the body of a wee one."

I slug back my coffee and consider the ramifications. Inadvertently, Sophie has become the most powerful witch of us all. She will outlive every one of us. She will outlive her children, and her grandchildren. It's a gift and a burden, and it will be hers to figure out on her own.

Kevin walks down the hall, holding up his phone. "Why are you texting me?"

"I'm not." I reach for my phone, but remember that I gave it to Gillian.

"Let me see that," I say, reaching for his phone.

There's a message from my phone:
Where R U?
I type back: Gillian? Is that you?
Gillian: Yeah.
Me: At hospital. Where are you?
Gillian: On way home. Did u get the ashes?
Me: Yes. Sophie is alive & well.
Gillian: :)
Me: Call me
Gillian: Too windy up here
Me: Stop texting & flying!

CHAPTER 36

I reach for a few sprigs of rosemary from the bountiful pots that now line my kitchen windowsill, so thick and tall, they nearly block the view of Kevin and Henry tossing the football in the backyard. Rosemary. Scientific name: *Rosmarinus officinalis*. Uses: Restores memories and mends broken hearts. Potion . . .

Today I skip the potion and stuff the rosemary into the turkey, along with some black trumpets, thyme, and a few other herbs Aurora has dumped from her rucksack onto the kitchen counter, her contribution to the Thanksgiving meal. And most people just bring a bottle of wine.

"Heads up," Kevin says, charging into the kitchen with Henry. A football arcs toward me, knocking me out of my reverie.

I catch it with one hand.

"Goal!" Henry yells, cheeks flushed red.

"Goal," Kevin repeats, untroubled with his son's mixed sports jargon. He gives me a kiss and swipes a handful of peas from a bowl on the counter.

Gillian bounds down the stairs in torn jeans and a short-sleeve shirt.

"It's November," I say. "You need socks and a hat."

"Can't I just use a warming spell?"

"No spells in public. That goes for everyone."

Sophie pouts. "Please, please, please." She's been absolutely, positively dying to try out some new nursery rhymes she's learned in school to see what will happen. As impatient as a three-year-old can be.

I kiss her forehead. "Don't rush. You have all the time in the world."

There is no hiding from our witchcraft anymore. Even Kevin's gotten into potion making with the kids, looking online through some Wicca Web sites to get ideas, though he'll never have the magic to make them work. But being magical doesn't matter to him. He's just happy to be together.

The phone rings and I go to answer it. "Why the hell does my cranberry sauce look like cow brains?" Judy says on the other end.

"How does it taste?" I ask.

There's a pause.

"Leonard says it tastes like piss and vinegar. Only more bitter."

I laugh. "Maybe you need to add more sugar."

"Yeah, all right. We'll get it straightened out before we come over. Are you sure I can't bring anything else?"

"I'm sure." I rub the back of my neck, feeling the raised skin of my birthmark. "Thanks, Judy."

"Why you thanking me? You're the one doing all the cooking," she says.

"No, I mean . . ." I search for the words. "Thanks for letting everything go. I know I did some awful things to you. I wasn't sure you'd ever speak to me again. You're a true friend."

"Well," she says, "just promise me we can burn that stupid pink cape later today. We'll fire up the hibachi."

I laugh. "But it's *cashmere*," I whine.

"I'll bring the charcoal."

"See you later."

"Later."

Later this morning Kevin will take the kids to the annual Monrovia Turkey Parade followed by the high school football game and then we will have a great feast with family and friends.

But first, Aurora and I have a little outing planned. We are going to the marsh to say our good-byes.

It's a crystal clear day, the smell of snow looming. The gray crystal clear skeletons of maples and oaks line High Street. As we head farther away from Monrovia, I suddenly remember that the turkey needs to be basted, the sliced apples for the pie are browning, and that I forgot to pick up cream cheese for the mashed potatoes. But I let it all slide.

When we get to the edge of the great marsh that seeps through the coastal land of Essex County, carrying on its tides the soil of my ancestors, I park the car. Aurora and I cut through a hay field and through a small wooded area to a fen that rises above the meandering streams and low-lying marsh.

"Here?" I say.

"Good a place as any."

I close my eyes, let go of my thoughts, and let my imagination carry me back through time. There is magic in the marsh—the smell of salt and clay, the sweet songs of kingfishers, of bullfrogs, the cry of geese, the rustling of the reeds and cattails, the green light of the will-o'-the-wisps waiting 'til dark to come out, the sun in my hair.

When I open my eyes, I am in the in-between, my mother beside me. My tiny hand in hers. My heart filled with the strength of a child's conviction, that family is all that matters in this world. My mother sings a lullaby:

> "Silver moon on rippled sea,
>   Land of rosemary, rowan, and reed.
>   Will-o'-the-wisps dance in-between
>   To guide us home
>   Where again we'll meet."

And since I know that this is our good-bye, I turn to her and say the words that ran away and hid for such a long time, the words that have finally found their way back to me: "I love you, Mom."